BLOOD SUGAR

KAT TURNER

CITY OWL
PRESS

BLOOD SUGAR
Coven Daughters, Book 2

CITY OWL PRESS
www.cityowlpress.com

Cover Design by MiblArt. All stock photos licensed appropriately.

Edited by Tee Tate.

For information on subsidiary rights, please contact the publisher at info@cityowlpress.com.

Print Edition ISBN: 978-1-64898-091-6

Digital Edition ISBN: 978-1-64898-090-9

Printed in the United States of America

PRAISE FOR KAT TURNER

"A fledgling witch finds love with a mature rock star in the midst of occult danger in Turner's magic-heavy debut and series launch. Turner sets up a promising world that readers will be pleased to return to in subsequent installments. Paranormal fans should check this out."

– Publisher's Weekly

"*Hex, Love, and Rock & Roll* is clever, witty, and captivating from chapter one. Helen and Brian pull you into their world and refuse to let you go. It is utterly a bewitching love story that has it all: chemistry, mystery, *love*, but most of all– rock and roll."

– Jaqueline Snowe, Contemporary Romance Author

"Fantastic, vivid writing and great characters make for a fun, sexy, emotional paranormal riff! Get *Hex, Love, and Rock & Roll* as soon as you can!"

– Celia Juliano, Sexy, Heartfelt Romance Author

"One of Turner's hallmarks is powerful heroes who are tempered with rich emotional intelligence. In *Blood Sugar* Readers can expect Turner's trademark snark mixed with magical and metaphysical mysteries, a well paced plot full of unexpected twists, and two layered and complex characters winning their happily ever after."

– Janet Walden-West, Award-Winning Author

"A spellbinding debut, Hex is a witchy love story that you won't want to miss. There's a paranormal plot with villains, hexes, and demons, but the real centerstage act is the magical happily ever after."

– Luna Joya, Author of the Legacy Series

"In her debut novel, Kat Turner's descriptions are exceptional and the spit-fire voice in this work is vibrant and fresh. The character's are so real, you step into the page."

– Poppy Minnix, RomCom and Paranormal Romance Author

To my guardian angel (you know who you are!).

ONE

Before Eve knew of her clairsentience, mortuary science seemed like the perfect career choice. She'd gravitated to the profession for the quiet and lack of drama, only to find out that dead people never shut up. Irony was one evil clown.

She locked the front door of the funeral home and extended her umbrella, stepping into the night after a draining day of consoling the panicky deceased. Fat raindrops drummed a litany of heartbeats. Reflections of red and green streetlights turned puddles into glimmering pools.

A breeze batted a few loose curls into her face and made her shiver, but the air's aroma of autumn leaves lifted her mood.

One backwards glance at the bronze plaque above the doorbell sneaked a smile onto her lips. *Evelyn Conley-Adyemi, Funeral Home Director*. She was a damn good mortician and adept shepherd to those who departed with unresolved issues and needed her help to pass on to the afterlife. Reminding herself of the contributions she made helped to ease the stress of difficult days.

Tucked in the back pocket of her pants, Travis Williams's spirit warmed her butt cheek. He'd stay put for a little while, attracted to her life force. Time to hurry home and process him before he faded away. Or worse.

Eve hustled through her Old Louisville neighborhood, rubber boots splashing against the sidewalk. Rain struck its rhythm against her umbrella. Vintage gas-lamp porch lights lit her path. From someone's stoop, the yellow glow of jack-o'-lantern mouths and eyes warded off sinister spirits.

She tipped a nod at a grinning pumpkin. Malevolent forces were not to be trifled with. A chill shot up her back, but she pushed aside memories of her past blunder and focused on the voice of Travis inside her head.

"And that's when I decided to take a more aggressive approach to my stock market portfolio. Stupid me, never listening to that financial adviser." Travis droned on about his life story for several blocks. The tale of Travis was remarkably average and semi-charming at best, but she didn't mind being a sounding board for the dead. They provided decent company in her three-thousand-square-foot house, lounging in the containers she'd blessed for them until she got the signal that they were ready to pass, like Travis was. Every spirit followed a distinct process as unique as their individual personalities.

The Victorian mansion she'd inherited from Grandpa Barney would soon welcome the elements of Travis's spirit still clinging to the earthly plane. After she did her ritual, the noblest parts of him would cross over with grace. His body, well, that was worm food.

Death was a complex process with a lot of moving parts, but most people didn't want the details. Eve told the dead man's young widow and their daughter that God had transported Daddy to heaven. A simple, safe, half truth.

The intersection stoplight turned red. Eve paused at the end of the sidewalk and peeked inside the popular neighborhood Italian restaurant to her right. Happy couples enjoying each other's company over wine and pasta packed the quaint place at the end of the block. The sight pricked her heart.

Her unsmiling reflection, a faint apparition in water-splattered glass, stared back at her. Eve looked younger than her thirty-five years—the tawny skin on her freckled face lacked one single crack—but nonetheless it was time to give up on dating. Men couldn't get past the mortician thing. Besides, if her shit-ass ex taught her anything, it was that love stinks worse than a lifelong alcoholic dead on the slab.

An emotion born of equal parts envy and self-righteousness curdled near her navel as she people-watched from the outside. She didn't need romance. She had a calling in life. A spiritual purpose, one she could not afford to stray from again. Not since she'd made an unforgivable mistake last year.

"Walk," the crossing sign instructed in its electronic voice, interrupting her thoughts before they took a dark turn. A white stick figure, pixelated legs swinging, flashed on the signal box. While Travis reminisced about his favorite beach vacation, Eve resumed movement.

Soon she came to her wrought iron front gate and fumbled with the slick latch until it opened. Keys jingled as she fished them from her purse while taking careful steps down the slippery cobblestone pathway to her door. Her own Halloween pumpkin, carved in the pattern of an arched cat, bathed the front steps in festive tones. The flame of the candle inside of it flickered as if amused. The neighborhood decorations committee did an amazing job keeping up with the details, lighting her jack-o'-lantern while she was at work.

Under the brick canopy shielding her concrete stoop from the downpour, she closed her umbrella.

"Excuse me. I need your help." A man spoke in a posh English voice quickened with distress. The worry in his tone prevented an onset of terror, but she clutched the pepper spray canister on her keychain all the same.

She reluctantly turned to face him. A sense of uncanniness froze her mind at the first sight of the angular, familiar face looking down at her. Though he stood in the shadows, she recognized the distinctive cut of his aquiline nose.

Could he have some connection to her past? Might he be a cousin or friend of the dead woman she'd wronged? "Help with what? Who are you?"

Eve scanned him, searching her memory. He was white, or perhaps multiracial like her, with ear-length dark hair secured in a blue bandana and a few days of stubble crawling over a jawline as defined as the rest of his elven facial features. Large hands disappeared into the pockets of black jeans painted onto stilt-like legs. Lean arms went on for days. Palpable sadness offset his striking looks, all of it adding up to a compelling impression prompting her to forgo telling him to get lost.

"I need to talk to you. Please. I mean you no harm whatsoever. I realize I should have rung first, but I wanted to explain my outlandish predicament in person. I was afraid if I phoned you and launched into the entire story, you'd figure me for a prankster and hang up straight away."

He pressed his lips into a line. The pleading manner of his speech left her no lingering doubt of his honesty, and the way his head hung and his broad shoulders drooped triggered an ache beneath her breastbone. What remained of her initial spark of fear died. Nothing about this man was threatening or sketchy. Rivulets of rain sluiced down his sleek leather jacket, enhancing the tragic energy around him. Poor guy walked over without an umbrella. Eve relaxed her grip on the pepper spray.

"Okay, I'm listening. But I'm sorry, you look so familiar and I can't help but be distracted by this sense that we've met before. Have we?" Who *was* this person? Someone from mortuary school, a long-forgotten high school acquaintance? No, she'd never known any Brits.

A half-smile curved his mouth as he stepped out of the shadows. Though darkness obscured the color of his irises, night couldn't hide the playful glimmer in his gaze. "Bet you've seen me on the telly."

"You're on television?" A screeching gust of wet wind blew his scent in her direction, and she caught whiffs of wet leather, cigarette smoke, and spicy aftershave mixed with male pheromones. A tingle chased through her, an effect of the intrigue. And *maybe* Mr. Mystery's sexy aroma. Eve's ex smelled like beer and lazy hygiene, a contrast heightening her sensory enjoyment of the man in front of her.

Mr. Mystery withdrew his hands from his pockets and rotated a ring around the longest, shapeliest finger she had ever seen. He wore a couple of additional rings, none of them wedding bands. Ridiculous that she noticed that in the first place, worse that she got a minor head rush when she did.

Still playing with his hands, Mr. Mystery looked Eve in the eye. Maybe what interested her most about this man was how large he loomed despite his nameless, anonymous status. Like some old-world deity walking amongst mere mortals. "All over it. Music videos, interviews, documentaries and whatnot."

"Are you famous?" If so, what the hell was a famous person doing at her place, soaked to the bone and in trouble?

"Yeah." The smug yet shy way he spoke the word, and the hint of a cocky smirk that accompanied it, sent warmth spreading through her core. Dude had a presence. One of those people whose personality expanded to fit the room, who strutted through life like sidewalks were catwalks. Even drenched and under duress, he projected panache down to his toes. Wild ankle boots, fuzzy and printed to look like a spotted cow's foot, adorned the toes in question.

But she would not become a star-struck mess. Protecting Travis came first, and the window of time to do so closed by the minute.

"I need that explanation now, the whole part where you tell me who you are and why you walked through the rain after dark to come to my house. Because I'm in a hurry." She propped the umbrella against a wall and folded her arms over her chest, forcing herself to stop thinking about his gorgeous face and trim body, his killer style. It didn't matter.

Besides, she looked like crap. Damp conditions made a frizzy disaster of her ponytail of black curls. The acrid odor of embalming fluid hung around her like always, and Travis's bereaved widow had snuffled tears and snot all over the shoulder of Eve's cute new blazer.

"You know the name Jonnie Tollens?" He spoke his name with crisp pride as he squared his shoulders and straightened his spine, gestures indicating she should know of him. With his posture corrected, Jonnie towered above her five-six frame.

"I don't." She'd have to stand on her tiptoes to kiss his lush mouth, not that she was entertaining such a notion. Nope. She was not.

He waved a hand in the air. "Look, it doesn't matter who I am. I need your help. I've heard what you can do with spirits."

Her stomach dropped, taking the stirrings of attraction with it. Word about her ability had gotten around. Since last year's *incident* involving a dead cult member, she had no desire to be famous or infamous. She should tell him to take a hike. But the broody Brit appealed to her empathy, so she afforded him another opportunity to explain himself. "Heard how? From whom?"

"Overheard someone backstage talking about your work. They had a business card."

Travis talked about the final chapters of his story, his chemo treatments, meaning she needed to get inside and deal with him. "If you know who I am, you know I have a very specific ability. Ensuring the souls of the troubled dead pass safely into the afterlife." *Except the one you failed.*

Eve swallowed. She stuck the front door key in the lock. One time, one person, one failure. One person whose tortured screams still haunted her nightmares on those nights she managed to steal sleep from the sadistic claws of insomnia. One person whose family's letters threatening to kidnap her and burn her at the stake made checking the mail a dreadful task.

"I know." His tone came out curt and more than a little droll.

At this point, Jonnie was wasting her time and thereby putting Travis at risk. Hadn't he registered the whole part about who she could and could not help? What did he want from her?

Eve turned around to face him, pulling out her key ring as she did. "Do you see the problem here? I help dead people."

And speaking of dead people, she had about five minutes to send Travis on his way. Another fuckup would not happen on her watch, and Mr. Mystery amounted to a big roadblock standing in the way of her goal.

"I realize that."

She indulged an exasperated sigh. "You keep repeating that concept, but allow me to restate the chief issue. I help dead people. You, by contrast, are alive."

"I'm just going to blurt it all out."

A confused chortle popped from her throat. "Fine. Make it quick."

"I underwent a medical procedure that caused some alarming side effects. My blood is toxic, and I need these under-the-table transfusions to prevent lapsing into a coma. I don't want to use the V word quite yet, but there are other symptoms that make me think it applies in this case. Changes to my body, new things happening every day. Fangs. Cravings.

You see, I think I am dead. Or undead, rather. So perhaps you can help me pass over."

Undead? Fangs? The V word, as in vampire? This guy was delusional. Vampires came up now and again in the pages of the trusty encyclopedia of magic she'd scored while thrifting with her mom, sure, but Eve figured the mentions were allegorical. Monsters didn't roam the streets of downtown Louisville or fly into bedroom windows at night. Heck, she'd never even met another person with gifts like hers.

"Sounds like you need a malpractice lawyer, not a spiritual guide to the afterlife."

"Fine. I'll show you proof, if that's what it'll take to convince you." Jonnie took a step closer and pinned Eve with his stare. The whites of his eyes darkened. His pupils stretched to vertical slits. Her pulse accelerated, then dropped low, lower.

Her mind grew foggy and fuzzy. Then it blanked. The air left. Her jaw fell as she stared into his eyes. She could only gawk. Nothing more than his eyes existed in the word. His eyes were all that had ever been or would be.

Keys fell from her hand and clattered on the ground.

"Do you believe me now?" His voice spoke inside her mind.

She felt her head bob up and down like a manipulated marionette.

"I swear to you I'm not alive anymore, not in the normal sense," he whispered out loud, enunciating his syllables like each one dropped a bombshell revelation.

The spell broke. Eve sucked down air, desperate for breath. Her heart did fluttery things, like its beats were catching up after hanging in stasis.

Spacey and shaking like her blood sugar had plummeted, she pulled it together enough to gather up her keys. Too amazed to be terrified, she scrambled to make sense of what happened. Was he a super powerful psychic? Had he hypnotized her? "What the fuck was that all about?"

"I'm sorry. I don't know." His voice trembled, and he backed away with a palm over his mouth. Raindrops glistened on his lashes like dew on blades of grass. "But I don't like it. It's a new development, and it's driving me barking mad. There's more. It's a lot. Help me, Evelyn, you're my last hope."

He knew her given name, meaning he'd done his research.

"I don't think I can. And you need to let me help those I'm able to assist. Speaking of which, I have a soul in my pocket who needs to pass over." Whatever troubled Jonnie, she couldn't even begin to think about how to alleviate it.

"Please give it a try, Eve."

"I apologize, but the answer is a firm no. Goodnight." She turned to her front door and resumed unlocking it. Seconds passed without a reply from Jonnie.

She'd rejected him in his time of desperation. But what could she have done? Without more information, nothing. But damn, failing people in need tore her apart.

"Jonnie?" Eve turned, but where he'd stood, an empty spot remained. He was nowhere to be seen amidst the darkness shrouding her tree-lined historic neighborhood.

Well, she tried. Eve let herself inside, kicked off her wellies, and dropped the umbrella in its stand.

No time to waste, no time to wallow or brood. Clearing her head of the encounter with Jonnie, Eve bolted up the creaky spiral staircase leading to her second floor, then coiled her way around the tighter one that twisted upward to the third level. She dashed down the carpeted hallway and turned the crystal doorknob leading to her sanctuary.

"Okay, T-Bone, let's get you home." In her pocket, his soul pulsed happily at her utterance of his frat-house nickname.

Jars holding ghosts crowded the surface of her oak vanity. Celtic knots and crosses patterned pewter and ceramic containers in various shapes and sizes. Mom theorized that Eve's powers came from her Irish heritage, and thus kept her stocked up with sacred Irish artifacts, in other words stuff she found at yard sales.

A quick check confirmed that the golden lights of other ghosts filled her Irish jars with warm and cozy reminders of life.

Smiling despite the urgency of her situation, Eve hustled to her other antique dresser, the one covered in allegedly sacred Nigerian artifacts (stuff Dad scored off online shopping websites). Her supernatural abilities bred loving competition between her weird, wonderful, accepting parents. She bet the ghosts would hang out in old sour cream containers without complaint, but this way her family had a quirky tradition.

Finding one of the woven jewelry baskets empty, she scooped Travis's spirit from her pocket, a wad of pale golden light about the size of a glass eye swarming around her fingers. Quickly, she shucked his clingy essence into the box and closed the lid.

Now came part two.

Eve sat in the middle of the floor and closed her eyes. A few deep breaths lowered her brain waves to the proper state to access the spirit world. Soon, voices filled her head. So many voices, all speaking at once, blurred together into gibberish. She needed to keep breathing, or according to her big reference book of magical and esoteric things, she could have a brain aneurism.

A low hum, similar to the "om" chant her yoga teacher used, sounded in her ears.

"Your name is Travis Williams, and I give you permission to let go."

"Are there people where I'm going?" Travis whispered with the typical blend of amazement and fear.

It touched her how vulnerable folks were as they prepared to pass over. At the end of the day, humans wanted to be with others. Wanted to be loved. And she was grateful, because among her family and friends, she had plenty of love in her life. Plenty.

"Yes." She meditated, focusing her attention on making a blue light spark in the void. The light would lead Travis into the afterlife, a place rich with the companionship and affection the dead sought. Eve knew this in her heart.

A plume of blue fire, the hue so saturated it surpassed the flame on her gas stove, burst into being. "Do you see it?" she asked.

"I see it."

"Follow my voice, Travis. Into the deep."

He did, and his essence drifted away from her mind until the fire flared and blinked into nothing.

She concentrated on her breath until the trance lifted. Her lids wanted to stay down, but she urged them open. A little groggy but otherwise fine, Eve rose, yawned, and strolled out of the sanctuary.

Blowing out a breath, she wiped away the cool sweat beading on her brow.

The threat of the flame changing to red haunted her during ceremonies. It was anyone's guess what type of mishandling allowed the red flame to ruin a transitioning ceremony. Her reference book called it The Thief, and according to her reading she'd sent poor Lacey to a place of grief and suffering. Extensive research into demonology and door opening hadn't yielded any answers on how to save the girl. Eve frowned, a sour slosh roiling her insides.

Entering her living room, she forced the sight of mahogany bookcases, overstuffed furniture, and low lighting to relax her. She hadn't banished the young woman on purpose. Likely, the girl carried some residual negative energy from the creepy Hollywood cult her parents saved her from before she'd killed herself. These facts, though horrible, tempered Eve's guilt.

Nope. Still your fault. Before she could fall down the rabbit hole of obsessing, she curled up on her paisley couch, picked up her vintage rotary phone's receiver, and dialed her best friend Meg's number. Her emotional state improved as the dial spun through digits. The heaviness and smooth feel of the inherited retro artifact made for a comforting reminder of her favorite grandfather.

After one ring, a click came through the line. "Are you calling because you're finally ready to try speed dating with me?" Meg teased in a Kentucky twang muted by living in metropolitan Louisville.

Rolling her eyes, Eve twirled the chunky curlicue cord around her fingers. "I think I have plans that night. Like staying in and pulling out my own fingernails with rusty pliers."

Meg huffed. The self-styled matchmaker extraordinaire had been trying to find the perfect guy for Eve since their days at Manual High School. An exercise in futility, but Meg's stubbornness didn't let her see that. "I didn't even tell you which day."

"My point exactly." Eve tapped her temple like Meg could see the gesture. Sparring was part of her and Meg's love language, and neither would have it any other way.

"So, what's up?" In the background, one of Meg's cats meowed.

"I had kind of a weird night." Would Jonnie come back? How would she feel if he did?

"With a ghost?"

Eve laughed. What a blessing to have friends and family who supported her gift and didn't judge.

Jonnie's scent lingered in her nostrils, and the way his dark eyes blazed nagged at her. There was something big about their encounter, something important. Though on most days her mind worked like a bear trap, irksome memory loss bothered her. She'd forgotten a significant detail about their meeting. "No. Before that. I met a famous person."

On Meg's end, a metallic object clattered to the ground. "What? Who?" Surprise raised her voice.

"You know who Jonnie Tollens is?" Flush crept over Eve's cheeks. Jeez, listen to her acting like a teenager, gossiping on the phone about hot celebrities.

A big gasp. "Shut up."

"I take it that's a yes."

"You really need to start listening to more than Bach and Beethoven. He's in that Chariotz of Fyre band, the one with all the pyrotechnics and stuff. They're playing downtown tonight."

Eve sat bolt upright on her comfy sofa. Maybe she could reconnect with Jonnie and apologize for driving him away. "What time?"

Meg barked out a laugh. "Like, right now. You're acting weird. What's going on? Wait. Shut the front door. Is there something you aren't telling me? Did you hook up with him?"

The suggestion planted a half-formed fantasy in Eve's mind. What would his slim figure look like naked? Did he have tattoos, piercings? She squeezed her legs together, attempting to halt a tingling pressure between them. "Of course not. He came by unannounced, asking me about my work with the ghosts."

"Whoa. That's random. What was he like?"

Eve flinched. What a jerk move she'd made, dismissing him. "He was acting off. Desperate. He'd walked over without an umbrella. It seemed like an urgent situation."

Dull pain gathered below her ribs. She had let Jonnie down royally.

"Weird. Was he strung out on drugs, you think?"

Snaking the black plastic coil up her forearm, she considered Meg's question. "I don't think that was it."

"Well, I'm so curious it isn't even funny. You wanna go loiter by the arena and see if we can catch him after the show gets out?"

A long shot, but she'd take it if it meant giving Jonnie another chance. Her calling obliged her to use her unique power in service of others. Perhaps he had a dying loved one who needed her assistance. Déjà vu rippled through her mind. He'd said something about someone being not alive. "You're sure you don't mind?"

"You kidding? This is the most interesting thing that's happened to me all week."

Eve would get to the bottom of her beguiling celebrity encounter. "Let's do it."

"Be right there."

She set her receiver in its cradle and reclined on her couch. What had he said, done, that was so odd? Drawing a blank, she stood. With any luck, she'd link up with him later. Belly buzzing in anticipation, Eve ran to her bedroom and hurried into a dress.

TWO

Jonnie wove through the post-show backstage crowd, avoiding sweaty bodies packing wide arena hallways as he made a beeline for the rendezvous point. A ponytail whipped his cheek. The air hung heavy, sharp sweat and woodsy bath products mingling with the chemical odor of electronic smoke. Men and women laughed and chatted, some yelling his name over the recorded music of his band blasting through speakers. Roadies slapped his arms while hauling out equipment, everyone clamoring for attention.

But he couldn't be bothered with the after-party. The symptoms had started while Fyre played their last song of the night. According to his personal physician, Jonnie would be paralyzed in an hour, meaning he needed to connect with the doctor and endure a procedure. If the shady fellow was telling the truth, forgoing treatments could cause Jonnie to lapse into a coma.

If that happened, Jonnie could neither earn money for Cara's medical care nor die and leave his niece his inheritance. He'd be a useless lump on a hospital bed for God knew how long, losing precious time. Before Cara got sick, Jonnie's sister and her family moved to Iowa for her American husband's job. They'd emigrated to a far inferior health care system, and now there was never enough money. But Jonnie could help. And if he got out from under his own burden, he could help even more.

He shoved open the stadium's back door and burst into the same wet, windy Louisville night he'd run through in his misguided quest to find solace in Eve. Eve Conley-Adyemi, whisperer to the dead, one of the local crew had referred to her before Jonnie accosted the young lad and grilled him for information.

At the edge of a parking lot, the Ohio River flowed a couple dozen feet beyond the concrete alcove where he stood. Two of the crew's tour buses idled at his left.

Jonnie paced. Sensation drained from his toes. He fixed his gaze on the street leading to the loading zone. Numbness in the extremities ought to cause alarm, according to the doctor. He scanned the road for a glimpse of the black sedan he'd come to know far too well. *Hurry up, you bloody ghoul.*

He never should have agreed to that sodding treatment. Youth forever, they'd said. Sounded like a good idea at the time. Endless years to possess the love of his adoring fans. Years to be somebody special for those fans and his band family. Rock stars were supposed to stay young. Shrewd salespeople, heaps more persuasive and charming than the snake he was now stuck with, dangled the promise of basking in the eternal flame of celebrity. But they glossed over the side effects.

Cars whooshed across the interstate overpass looming above his head. His mobile buzzed in his jacket pocket, the vibration flipping his stomach. Any call could be The Call. He whipped it out, sighing in relief when he saw the picture ID. Some industry person. Not the photo of Cara, smiling despite the medical tubes snaking from her seventeen-year-old body. His brave niece believed she was kicking stage-four cancer's arse, terminal prognosis be damned.

But her time hadn't run out yet, meaning he had time to earn money for her chemo, radiation, and surgeries. Provided Murray Connors showed up.

A car rolled over a slight hill and slowed to a halt, blacked-out windows giving away its identity.

"Finally." Jonnie jogged to the door and fumbled numb fingers against the handle. After a couple of tries, he got it open and climbed in the backseat beside Connors, who wore a cheesy smile on his tanning-bed-baked face.

"Time for an emergency refresher?" Connors's meaty hand squeezed Jonnie's thigh as the driver took off. A ruby jewel on the physician's tacky class ring resembled a drop of blood. Another round of rain pelted the windshield, a nearby traffic light tinting the clear fluid red.

His mouth watered. Fuck, he hungered to bite. To suck.

"Don't bloody touch me." Jonnie swatted off the man's sausage fingers. Though desperate, he'd go comatose before he put his mouth on this sleaze.

"Relax, man. There is no shame in what we do. I could use a few procedures myself. A little nip, a little tuck. Botox." Connors took out his phone and used the screen like a mirror, picking at porcelain veneers and fussing with his crown of bright blond hair.

Nausea clenched Jonnie's stomach. What had he become? No better than some addict.

"There is no we." Jonnie glared out the window and scooted an inch farther away from Connors. Water ran down the glass like tears. "And you already look like a knockoff Ken doll. So I say mission accomplished."

"Aw, Mr. Rock Star gets cranky if he doesn't have his meds, huh?" Connors chortled at his own joke.

He ought to power through his revulsion, push down his fangs, and use them to slice open the wanker's jugular. Then laugh while Connors bled out and clutched his ripped throat. Jonnie was an evil fiend of the night now, after all. But acting out wouldn't accomplish anything. Wouldn't save Cara, wouldn't kill him. Instead, he tapped his leaden foot, counting off seconds as the sedan pulled into a secluded corner of the parking lot under the highway bridge.

Jonnie pressed his temple into cool glass while Connors unzipped his supply kit. Some comedy news program played on the car radio, carefree people laughing at dumb gags. A protective seal snapped as Connors prepared materials. Jonnie couldn't look. Couldn't look at the physical signifiers of his monstrosity. Instead, he watched waves lap against the hull of a steamboat that sat docked by the shore.

Connors whistled, a tube popping into place. Plastic clicked, and soon the transfusion machine's low hum filled the car. Jonnie swallowed a lump in this throat, forcing desensitized hands to yank off his jacket while he stared at the boat. Golden words painted onto the side announced its name as Belle of Louisville.

Belle. Ironic, how he read a word that meant beauty.

Jonnie hatefully stuck out his arm. The needle pinched like a bee sting. Needing to put something beautiful into his blackened mind, he brought up an image of Eve's face. Now there was a beauty. A real belle. Plump lips, big cat eyes, riot of tight dark curls he'd love to tangle in his hands. But subtler elements also attracted him to her. He had a feeling, perhaps nothing more than a fantasy his lonely heart created, that she too was a wounded soul in need of healing.

The pain he heard behind her sweet southern drawl made him crave the sight of pleasure and happiness lighting up her eyes. Perhaps some inexplicable, unquantifiable magnetism drew him in. He met thousands of women on the road. Some were more real to him, plain and simple.

Connors hummed an inane tune as the device removed Jonnie's toxic blood and replaced it with fresh, clean donor fluids.

"What did you people do to me?" The needle left his arm with a minor nip. Dark river waters churned. Downstream, an illuminated bridge cycled through a variety of primary colors.

His surroundings didn't make him feel much. Grim yet essential moments like the one he'd tolerated sucked out his joy right along with the dirty blood running through his veins. Reminded him that his entire essence was poisonous, sick.

"Hemotoxic venom," Connors chirped, packing up paraphernalia with soft clacks and the metal-on-metal noise of a zipper closing. He laid a circular adhesive bandage over Jonnie's needle stick.

"Excuse me?" He slashed his eyes to the plastic surgeon, finding him texting. Why did he even ask? Every time he pressed for more clarification on what he'd undergone, the resulting details disturbed him while offering him nothing useful on how to stop his dependence on Connors and the transfusions.

"The vampire treatment entails replacing the customer's blood with a synthetic formula that mimics the effects of hemotoxic venom. What vipers use to immobilize their prey. The formula staves off the aging process by halting cell degradation, but after a few years in the patient's system, it turns on the body. Hence the need for refills. Think of it like changing the oil in your vehicle. But hey, you'll be driving a shiny new sports car forever, so that's a positive."

Connors flashed a wink and toothy grin combo fit for a used car salesman. How apropos. At least the man harbored a modicum of self-awareness.

The sales pitch for the Vampivax treatment sounded too good to be true, and he'd assumed the brand name was an exercise in cheeky irony to match the product's campy packaging.

He should have seen through it all. But he'd been thirty, drunk on fame yet old enough in rock star years to feel the impending terror of age snatching that fame away. Took ten years for the first symptoms to show up, and another ten for them to require regular management. For twenty years, he'd kept his condition secret from his band. They bought the lie that he had good genes and used top-quality moisturizer.

He might have been stupid to sign up for the serum, but he wasn't dumb enough to out himself as a freak in front of his mates, his second family. "What if someone drives a stake through my heart? Will that end my miserable existence?"

Connors snorted. "Nope. That's a myth, pal. Your Vampivax will rally around any intruding agent and push it out. In more good news, you can eat garlic all you want. Speaking of, a boutique Italian eatery just opened over on Fourth. The red sauce is to die for." Connors kissed his fingertips like a European chef.

"What about the fangs?" Those lovely little pointy things made their first unscheduled appearance a year ago. His fiancée had thrown the ring in his face and run off screaming.

"They show up when the reptile DNA booster in your Vampivax mutates. Happens after fifteen to twenty years. Natural part of your progression."

"What else can I expect as a natural part of my progression?" He stroked the undersides of his pale arms, pushing on one of many small bruises. The sting of self-inflicted pain overrode his emotional hurt.

"Keep seeing me and you won't have to worry about it. Ready to settle up?"

Jonnie took his wallet out of a coat pocket and thrust a credit card at the doctor. Connors swiped it through the white plastic square topping his mobile, smiling at the screen. The scumbag was right about one thing. Jonnie didn't want to know what new, horrific surprise lay in store for him next. "Drop me back at the arena."

The driver obeyed, hanging a tight U-turn in the parking lot and exiting back onto the street. He pulled into the loading dock, where Jonnie got out without a word. At least the rain had stopped. Its residual wetness made slick car roofs glimmer, and errant drips struck the pavement in a musical rhythm. He inhaled the mineral odor of wet rock mixed with funky fishiness from the nearby river, enjoying feeling normal as he resigned himself to another week or so of healthy living.

Between the two tour buses, Fyre's bassist, Thom, thick waves of hair cascading over his beefy shoulders, puffed a cigarette. He blew two rails of gray smoke out of his nostrils like a fire-breathing dragon. Thom's bass tech, Dusty, leaned against one of the buses, smoking and talking.

Playing with phones, two groupies with mussed hair stood next to the boys.

The bassist nodded once at Jonnie. The pungent, woody aroma of tobacco smelled familiar and grounding. Smelled like his band, the blokes he'd known for decades.

"Where did you skip off to?" Thom asked in his deep, husky voice.

A security lamp offered enough yellow light for Jonnie to catch suspicion in the man's brown eyes. Thom had been onto him and his disappearances for a while. On the selective occasions when Jonnie met a woman after a show, he tended to vanish until after breakfast the following morning.

"Running an errand." Well, that sounded preposterous.

Thom narrowed his eyes, shaking his head as he drew down another drag of smoke, the cigarette's flaming cherry tip crackling bright in the night. "Sneaking about isn't a good look on you, mate. Makes you come across like a naughty schoolboy."

For all of Thom's questionable qualities, the lad spoke his mind and didn't mince words.

Dusty wrapped a spaghetti-thin, tattooed arm around each of the women, a redhead in denim shorts as tiny as panties and a blonde with bloodshot eyes. "We're rock stars, bro. We don't run errands. That's what lovely ladies like these are for. Now one of you girls go get us some beers."

Roadies and crew made up a changing cast of characters, lifetime temp workers who drifted in to and out of the touring scene. Some, Jonnie treasured. Others, not so much. Dusty belonged to the "others" group.

"Thom and I are rock stars. You're a roadie." Jonnie didn't wish to come off as a snob or an elitist, but he'd had his fill of creeps herding him into a "we" he had no desire to join. He might be an abomination with fangs and venomous blood, but he still had some principles. Like treating women with respect.

"You need something, hon?" the blonde asked, training her gaze on Jonnie.

Dusty pulled his hand to his mouth, forearm circling around the blonde's neck as he made the blowjob gesture, pumping a fist at his face and poking his tongue into his cheek. For added emphasis, he threw in a suggestive wiggle of his eyebrows.

"I got the innuendo without the pantomime, you arse," Jonnie grumbled. Not like it was some mystery what the girls wanted to do. Many of them figured, for whatever sad reason, that sexual favors were all they had to offer another person. The emptiness in their stares gave it away.

The blonde giggled, struggling against Dusty's hold. "For real. You want your cock sucked, Jonnie?" She squirmed free and rubbed her neck.

"No thanks. I'm good." Though he was no monk and succumbed to the temptations of eager fans now and again, he at least picked lovers with whom he shared some chemistry.

Unbidden, Eve's face popped into Jonnie's mind. He wondered what she was up to this evening. Now there was a woman he'd like to get close to. She'd had no clue who he was and wasn't impressed by him. Meaning that he'd, in theory, have to work to impress her. What a novel and electric concept.

"The blokes from Drops of Time are backstage. Thought we could connect and jam in the suite for a bit." Thom stubbed out his smoke and fired off a text, unkempt hair falling in his face.

For the first time in a while, Jonnie smiled. Collaborating and making music, nurturing his creativity while spending time with his band brothers and other musicians, fed his soul. Reminded him he still had a soul. "Yeah. Sounds good. I think I'll take a walk for a bit first. Clear my head. But I'll be by the hotel later."

"You alright, mate? What do you need to clear you head of?" Thom's inquisitive eyes, betraying genuine concern, locked Jonnie's.

"I'm fine. Just in a pensive mood, I suppose." He could tell his bandmates, sure. But why, and to what end? He fit in with his musician friends. His families of origin were scattered across the United States, Britain, and New Delhi, and the stress of Cara's diagnosis, combined with his recording and touring schedule, put strain on those relationships.

Why confess something that could set him apart from his closest people? Music offered solace. Musicians were his compatriots. They accepted him, and he wasn't about to sabotage that.

"Are we invited to the party?" the redhead wheedled in a baby voice.

"No." Dusty laughed as he removed his arm from the groupie. "But your technique was solid, Red. You suck like a Hoover." He made a slurping noise, stuck a hand in the back pocket of his ripped jeans, and pulled out a laminate pass to some upcoming show.

Dusty's reply was repugnant, but for the best. One fewer event where these two women would be treated as sex toys.

"Can we fire him?" Jonnie asked Thom. The bassist enabled some roadies' gross, exploitative behavior by partying with them.

Thom shrugged. "He's strong and he shows up on time, sober, and ready to work. Keeps the rest of the crew in line."

Dusty beamed like a star student with a trophy. Which Jonnie suspected he'd never been.

The groupies lost interest and drifted off, name-dropping various other musicians.

"Get my equipment to the suite, would you mate?" Thom used his authoritative, bossy voice on Dusty.

"You got it." The lanky roadie sprinted into the underground parking garage, stringy hair swishing goodbye.

With the others dispatched, Thom stepped closer to Jonnie, close enough he could smell the groupies' flowery perfumes emanating off his bandmate. At this proximity, the halogen glow of the streetlamp would expose dilated pupils or red squiggles.

"What's going on, Jon? Tell me you aren't using." The bassist's stare dug deep.

Jonnie didn't blame the man for his concern. Though hard drugs had never touched the band itself, heroin tore through the crew a couple of years ago, nearly destroying a summer tour.

"Of course not. You know me. Just got a lot on my mind, with Cara and all."

"Did something happen?" Thom didn't sound convinced. Though a shameless libertine, the man's mind was as sharp as the points of Jonnie's sheathed fangs.

"It's stage-four cancer. Something could any day."

Thom backed off and stayed silent for a beat. He opened his mouth, then clamped it shut as if to swallow more nosy questions. "Sorry to pry. See you soon."

"You will." He hugged the bassist and rounded the corner, coming to face a hill flanking the side of the building. Inlaid stone steps led to the front of the arena and a downtown street, and he hiked up stairs until the city emerged in a carnival of honking horns and chattering people. A horse-drawn carriage sat idle on the curb, and the animal snorted and stomped a hoof. Odors of fried food, exhaust, and beer mixed with post-rain wetness.

Strolling at a fast clip down the sidewalk, he kept moving before anyone in the smattering of remaining fans lingering outside the venue spotted him. He didn't mind chatting with the folks who paid his bills, but tonight, solitude called. Tonight, darkness sang its siren's song.

He walked down Main Street, dodging small rainwater pools as he looked up at buildings jutting toward obsidian skies. Cabs idled by the curb, the hot breath of their engines like puffs of hellfire in the crisp climate. A large, drunk group in matching tee shirts clomped by him as they stumbled to their next bar.

Jonnie sauntered, slipping into the night like a pair of custom-made trousers. He'd felt more and more like a loner lately, more drawn to the evening's black cloak and its heady, teeming vibrations. The cosmic blanket and cool atmosphere slid over his sensitive skin in sensual caresses. Fast clouds blew past like cigarette smoke, revealing peeps of stars amidst light twinkling in windows.

The heightened emotions that people expressed when free of the sun's judgmental glare made for a devil's playground. Night stoked desires. Bred intrigue. Fed the id's mischief. Night was *noir*, in the richest and most luscious sense of the word.

Shite, he was starting to enjoy this vampire thing, an unsettlingly liberating realization. Didn't he want to die?

Jonnie's ruminations ceased as he spotted Eve a few feet in front of him on the sidewalk, strolling with a friend. For the first time in ages, fate had winked at him. Delivered the enigmatic, melancholy beauty who'd woven her way into the wrinkles of his brain.

And damn, what a knockout. A simple black dress hugged her round, proportional hips and breasts. Straightened sheets of black silk rested on her shoulders. Sexy heels showed off toned legs. White car headlights and ambient light from restaurants cast her skin in shadowing fit for a femme fatale.

At first, Eve said nothing, she just stopped in her tracks and looked up at him with a keen stare. He still didn't know her eye color. A travesty.

"Looks like we're destined to find each other." With a decisive step, Jonnie closed some space between them, catching a hint of a scent befitting her name. Like honeyed apples, the aroma of Eden's forbidden fruit. God, to bury his face in her long neck and breathe. Breathe in sweetness and femininity and escape. Then sink his teeth into her and drink her essence like ambrosia.

His cock twitched against the prison of his tight leather pants. If she would have him, he could escape his walking death sentence for a bit by sliding inside of her and affirming life in the most primitive of ways.

Her gaze drifted to the side, mouth curving into a crooked smile. Despite the shy deflection, her posture, comported as a debutante's, didn't slouch. She moved so fluidly, demure though decisive. He fought the urge to adjust his fly. Could she see his rising excitement?

"Looks like it. Sorry about earlier, but you confused the hell out of me. Has anyone told you it's shady to lie in wait on the doorsteps of women you don't know?"

Eve's friend gasped and waved her hands in the air. "Oh my God, oh my God. Jonnie Tollens. Chariotz of Fyre. Fangirling so hard right now."

The behavior didn't faze him. People acted all sorts of goofy in the presence of celebrities. He'd been a stammering fool when he met his guitar idols.

"Hello, love." He signed his name on a scrap of paper the friend handed him before turning to Eve.

His fingers itched to brush an errant strand of hair from Eve's cheek. Would her skin feel as soft as velvet? How would she react if he gave in to his desire? "Can we go somewhere and talk?"

Passersby whispered as they strode past the trio. A woman jerked her head over her shoulder. "I'm positive he's somebody," she told her date in a loud hiss.

The person's conspicuous act drew the attention of a group of teenagers leaning against a mailbox. One snapped a picture on his phone, intensifying Jonnie's urge to keep moving.

Eve touched her friend's elbow. "I think I'm gonna hang out. You okay with that?"

The friend whipped out her phone and pushed buttons, a smirk bending her lips. "Are you kidding? That was my whole...what I meant to say was of course. Call me the second you're in a car, okay?"

"Sure thing. Thanks, hon." Eve slid off her heels and took soft, rolled up flats from her purse. As she slid them on, he licked his lips at the sight of her dainty feet. Princess feet.

He'd kiss and suck every one of those petite toes, then cover them with massage oil and rub his stiff dick between her soles until he shot his seed on her sculpted ankles. Huh. He'd never had a foot fetish before. The thrill of novelty blazed through his veins.

Intoxicating, to feel something besides the usual cynicism and ennui. To feel lusty, animal. To *want*.

"Thank me with seven-layer dip," Meg called while pouring herself into a hatchback with a pink ride-service logo sticker on its back window.

Jonnie walked down the hill, guiding Eve by placing his hand on the warm, swan's neck curvature of her spine. Touching her filled him with a glow. For a sweet second, he pretended they were a couple.

He caught a change in her breathing, a hitch, and she moved a bit closer to him. Realizing that she responded to his touch delivered a hit of heady pleasure as they took careful steps down the wet sidewalk. It shone silver, like night magic kissed the spaces between pulverized rocks in the concrete.

"Let's take it from the top. What happened to you, again?" Eve asked with interest as they passed a bar with an outdoor patio. Pop music streamed from the pub, patrons on the terrace chatting and drinking pints of brew. A fire hydrant sprayed water onto the road, adding to the urban liveliness.

"Skip the pleasantries, eh?" Jonnie withdrew his hand from her back and played with one of his rings. He'd hoped that they could get to know each other a bit before getting down to business, engage in social conversation befitting the vibrant city nightlife.

"I think we're past pleasantries." Her voice carried a brusque inflection, tempered by kindness. And she had a point. He'd darkened her doorstep, begging for her services, and no doubt come off like a barking mad lunatic. He'd even put her under his weird new spell for dramatic effect, for Christ's sakes. They were light years beyond idle talk about favorite sports teams and what they studied at university.

They approached a long stretch of green space flanking the river. Trees and playground equipment dotted a park. A couple walking three fluffy lap dogs watched the water from an overlook, and a lone teenager swung on one of the bench swings, none of them appearing particularly concerned with the activities of others. Jonnie gathered his thoughts as he and Eve turned onto a walkway parallel to the rushing water. The illuminated bridge cycled through its light show, and now he was actually in the right frame of mind to appreciate the spectacle.

Parallel rows of black poles fashioned to look like Victorian gaslights lined the walkway, their gentle light blending with the cool glow from a fang of a moon peeking out from fast-moving, gauzy clouds. Jonnie inhaled the river's rich aroma, a sense memory of smelling the Thames as a boy bubbling up in his mind. Felt almost like a part of him had been transported back to the nineteenth century, into some mythological corner of the past where an immortalized Jack the Ripper could slink out from behind a tree.

Yeah. The vampire in him was taking over. What did that mean? Could he expect more changes to his mind and thought process? As if in response to his ruminations, his heart jumped. Was he feeling anticipation? Did he have a desire to stick around and find out all that vampire life entailed? Bollocks. He shut off the chatter in his head. "I was hoping you could help me with my condition."

"I'm a mortician, not a medical doctor. Is there a spiritual component to it?" Her lightning-quick reply coming out both wary and curt, Eve proffered him a narrow-eyed look. She had her guard erected. Fair enough.

"Yes. I need you to save my soul. You can save souls, right?"

Eve waited a beat. Faint traces of downtown revelry provided background noise to the quiet park. "In a sense."

"So you can help me."

"How?" Her voice approached a whisper and came with plenty of confusion.

The request he prepared in his mind no longer issued from a completely authentic place, and she would be able to tell. With any luck, she'd dig deeper and uncover the truths that eluded his conscious awareness.

A light breeze blew, though the air grew heavy, weighty. Sounds filled his ears. A dog's yappy bark. A rhythmic thunk of the boat hull against the dock, an errant whoop.

Had his hearing always been ultrasensitive, or did the heightening come from the vampirism progressing? Or did paranoia about the vampirism progressing prompt him to notice what had always been there and ascribe a state of change to what was, in fact, a constant state?

Why in bloody hell did it make his insides teem with excitement?

These days, he often felt like he'd fallen through a portal in his own head and landed in a twisted funhouse. Worry knotted his heart. Was he going mad? Wasn't that a thing, vampires turning into madmen?

Seeking some semblance of grounding, he looked at his hands while wringing them. She wasn't going to like his answer to her question on how she could help, but no better time than the present to spit the fuck out how he was worth more dead than alive. "By killing me."

Each syllable stretched, the pauses between them infinite, before finally scattering through the night air as ashes. Her soft feet padded on concrete as they walked. He shouldn't be able to hear such soft footfalls, right?

Why wasn't she saying anything? His ash-particle words hardened into lead and dropped into the swirling river like coins into a wishing well. A frightening, tantalizing influx of curiosity about how Eve would react kept him on the hook.

"I don't do assisted suicide." Her voice was too crisp, though, too automatic. The sound of denial. Some wall of hers vaulted up higher, a wall he longed to smash without knowing why.

Toeing wet leaves out of his path, he forged ahead. "I'm already dead. You'd be exterminating my body and seeing that my soul, if I have one, passes on to what's next. There is more than this, right?" He waved a hand in the air.

Perhaps, in a sense, he sought Eve out for reassurance that more existed beyond the physical world in all its ugliness. Greed. Abuse. Heinous diseases killing innocent girls. Could she show him a corner of beauty deep within the recesses of his dark heart?

"There is an afterlife." Eve's confident posture underscored the conviction in her speech. "And I have a feeling you're going to circle back to your vampire theory, aren't you?"

Jonnie smiled at the sight of Eve's profile, her button nose and the smattering of black freckles dusting her cheeks. But more so, he smiled at her dry, irreverent tone. In his bones, he knew that he wouldn't scare her off. Besides, he wished to commission her services, not woo her into a romantic relationship. Full and unfettered honesty could flow in a current between them. "Yes. I'm a vampire, like I stopped short of saying at your house. I wasn't kidding."

"For real?" She didn't miss a beat in delivering her earnest question.

His smile grew alongside his respect. She was brave and calm, open-minded yet logical. It seemed stupid to attribute these qualities to her like he knew her, but he did it anyway. Eve yanked him out of his own head the same as music did. Made him aware of the present moment and able to lose himself in pleasure. That such a feeling had an expiration date gave it a bittersweet quality. A quality akin to the power of love, which was powerful due to the threat of grief snatching one's beloved away. Considering Cara's ordeal, he classified grief as a shadowy cousin to love.

"For real." He didn't allow himself to touch her lower back again, because romance or seduction didn't factor into the plan.

They walked in silence for a couple of minutes, the river gurgling to their left. Birds, bats, and bugs—he could now discern each species' unique vocalization—supplied a harmonious chorus. His hearing sharpened by the second.

"I don't know how to deal with undead. It's outside of my area of expertise. Until today I didn't believe they existed." She delivered her statement in a bone-dry deadpan. Damn, this woman interested him. Did she appreciate the macabre? Seemed to suit her, with her mordant manner, her magnetic blend of tempered affect and empathetic responsiveness. What a fine combo of personality traits.

He could kiss her now. Stop this walk along the river her and claim her lips. Because she was so goddamn cute and professional and smart and...*something* that he burned for her. Eve had the X factor, magic difficult to quantify. "Surely you could learn."

"Well maybe, in theory, but I have no idea how long it would take. I'd have to do a ton of research. Don't you leave soon? For your next tour stop?"

He stopped walking and touched her elbow, stilling her. She didn't pull away, so he spoke from his heart before he could overthink. Before he could change his mind. "Yes. We leave in the morning. Come on tour with me until you figure it out. You could catch up with me on the next stop if you need some time, but I need your help, Eve. My niece is sick. This vampire condition is getting worse and sucking up all my money. I need to stop paying medical people. The money could go to my niece. If I pass on, I free up my inheritance. Name your price, of course."

She looked up at him with her deep pools of eyes. Gentle wind caused goosebumps to bloom on his neck and made her hair dance. The charms of evening swept Jonnie into their spell, singing invisible, imperceptible songs of allure and danger. The river blew a breath of wet earth touched by decay into his nose.

Stepping closer to Eve, Jonnie parted his lips. He could hear her heartbeat. See it, even, as if her skin were translucent. Her fragrance overwhelmed him. He could take her up against a tree. Her blood would taste as sweet as sugar, and he'd drink himself stupid on it while his cock plunged into her.

The hypnosis bolted up his spine in an electric jolt, and he looked away before he stole her mind. This was madness. Madness he needed to end before he became a live wire of lust and depravity. He couldn't look into her eyes, couldn't risk doing something that would make her pliable, malleable, his. Like he owned her. His balls tingled, and he hated it. This was all twisted and sick, perverse. Not right, not him, and he needed it to end.

No more getting off on thoughts of vampire debauchery or fantasizing about Eve saving him from himself. He needed peace, solace, escape. Eternal rest. Death. "Please, Evelyn."

"Alright," she said. He couldn't see her face with his gaze fixed on some crack in the sidewalk, but her voice, the voice of an angel about to spare what remained of his undead soul, smoothed ointment on his wound.

"Bless you." He'd never uttered that phrase before in his life. And he needed to keep his filthy vampire hands off this goddess before the monster overtook more of him than it already had. Because who knew what it was capable of if given free reign and full expression. But Jonnie wasn't about to find out.

THREE

"You've got to be kidding me." Meg pushed out a loud, dramatic whisper, her hazel eyes going bulbous. In one swift pull, she dragged Eve by the forearm, leading the women through a room of folks saying final goodbyes to Travis.

Eve trailed behind, bracing for proverbial impact. Perhaps she should have eased her best friend into the news that she would be joining the last leg of Jonnie's tour as his spiritual counselor, but she didn't care to fancy-pants around things.

Meg stopped the pair in a corner by the bathroom and ushered them behind the funeral home's potted tree, its plastic leaves offering cover from the crowd.

"I've retained clients for ongoing projects before," Eve lied, fanning her overheated face with a program of Travis's funeral services. Air conditioning blasted through the parlor room, and a powder-scented candle added to its soothing atmosphere. Still, Eve's favorite dress for services, a tea-length pewter number with a flared skirt, itched against her skin. At least she'd secured her hair into a French braid and didn't have to worry about sweaty strands irritating her neck. "And I can't believe you crashed a guy's funeral to hassle me about how I render my professional services."

Yes, Eve was acting impulsive. Brash, even. Who runs from her adult responsibilities to go on tour with a rock band? But she couldn't reject Jonnie a second time.

She didn't totally buy the vampire thing. But as she'd stood with him on the bank of the ripe Ohio River under a moonlit sky, she'd ridden the wavelength of his sincerity. She could help him, knowing deep in her bones that she could bring his anxious mind peace. Plus, Eve refused to allow another soul to experience torture on her watch.

Didn't mean she had a damn clue on what to do, but it wouldn't stop her from trying.

After all, she'd been flying by the seat of her pants since that first mortuary school cadaver had shared a sad life story. Liz from Montana, single mom, Iraq war veteran. An IED had detonated their Hummer. Shrapnel blasts turned Liz's insides to hamburger and her once-pretty face into a horror movie mask. She'd suffered an excruciating death amidst the hell of war. The poor woman had begged for a closed casket service, as if there was any doubt.

Easing an angsty rock star's spiritual malaise? Child's play compared to calming the tormented souls Eve had guided to peace.

"Don't lie and don't change the subject. You're going on tour with him? To do what exactly? And who will take over here?" Meg grabbed a complementary funeral cookie from a nearby snack table and nibbled, forehead scrunching into a frown.

A gaggle of tittering, gray-haired ladies, five stooped ravens in feathered fasteners with birdcage veils shielding faces, shuffled past. In the south, funerals were as much of an excuse to showcase one's fanciest hat as they were a time to pay final respects.

One crone eyed a young mother across the room. "Brenda's been working on her body. She looks fabulous." After delivering her hushed morsel of gossip, the granny in a wide-brimmed, ebony masterpiece exploding with lace and fake flowers caught sight of Eve and pulled a somber countenance. "What a tragedy. Travis, gone too soon. But you've put together an absolutely grand affair, Ms. Adyemi."

Schooling her mouth into a thin-lipped smile, Eve soaked up the brief moment of reprieve the biddies offered from Meg's onslaught. She fingered a seam on the petal-pink chaise to the right of the plant. "Thank you. He led a life worth celebrating. How did you know him?"

"Will you ladies excuse us, please? I'm in mourning." Meg oozed her sweetest southern charm, resting a hand over the strand of pearls overlaying a silk blouse the color of coal. Once the old women joined the other guests, Meg turned her attention back to Eve. "Are you in love with this guy, or what?"

Of course not, yet Meg's words sent a rush of effervescent energy through Eve. Biting off a girlish giggle, she managed to roll her eyes. "That's ridiculous. But if I can help him in any way, I damn sure will."

Next step: figure out what to put in that "any way" blank.

Meg quirked a brow as she chewed and swallowed. Ugh, Meg had unleashed her psychologist's eyebrow. "You want to absolve yourself of the guilt from hell-dimension girl."

Eve's stomach sank. She hated that subject. Fucking hated it. "Her name was Lacey. And no."

Maybe, but no. Jonnie was a special case. She wouldn't tread into the dark waters of euthanasia if he pressed the matter, but she bet he would not. The man needed counseling. Comfort. She could comfort his lost, maybe vampiric but probably not, soul. Like a life coach, almost. Yeah.

Meg tilted her head, messy brunette bun wobbling. "I can see it in your face. You're reenacting the Lacey situation with a different player and a different setting."

"Don't analyze me." Eve crossed her arms over her chest like the defensive gesture would stop Meg's insight from invading her thoughts. Damn shrinks, always messing around in the mind, turning over rocks. Never leaving things alone.

With a sigh, Meg put up her hands. "Okay, sorry, the whole thing is just so weirdly impulsive for you."

Tingles lit up Eve's nerves, her senses heightening. A whiff of spicy-sweet lilacs and roses from Travis's floral spray delighted her nose. Someone laughed at a Travis story. People hugged. At their best, funerals did celebrate life. And Eve loved that life-affirming element of her profession. In the same way, she treasured her work with the souls, cherished sending them to a better place.

There was more to life than ashes to ashes, dust to dust. A precious, mysterious reality existed in a playful dance of energy, a flow. Every now and again, time froze into something sublime, but the second one tries to name or catch the moment, it flits away like a fickle butterfly.

She lived for those fleeting glimpses, eternities she sometimes caught out of the corner of her eye. And with Jonnie, she had a feeling that those moments would unfold more often, like shy night blossoms. Maybe she could even plant a few flowers in Jonnie's jaded heart. Show him their reality and beauty.

Her goal emerged into clear focus. The Jonnie project would rekindle the sense of wonderment that working with cadavers and death diminished. "Maybe I want more impulsivity in my life."

"Who will take over here?" Meg pressed, leaning forward. Her jaw locked as her nostrils flared, giving her the look and vibe of a piqued pit bull.

"Fred." Eve's embalming apprentice had mastered his assignments. The serious, studious young man lived for his work. He would welcome added responsibility.

"Can Fred help the ghosts?" Meg concluded the pointed, non-earnest question with a smirk. All she needed to do was shout "gotcha."

True, she couldn't teach the ghostly aspect of her duties to Fred. Nobody besides her, that she knew of, possessed her gift. "The tour's only one more week. I'll fly back here if I need to process anyone before their funeral or if anyone at home needs to cross over." Some reached out to her, some didn't, and some started the process but never asked to pass fully to the afterlife. The entire thing amounted to a crapshoot that was likely determined by the deceased's faith and relationship with spirituality.

Odds were a few would crop up, but one never knew, with the notoriously unpredictable death industry. She'd just have to wait and see. She needed a break, dang it, something in her life besides the funeral home and a cavernous mansion inhabited by ghosts. Hell, she felt like a ghost there, too. Floating around, lonely and alone, another forgotten anachronism amidst her inherited antiques and vintage furniture.

"That'll get expensive." Always the pragmatist, Meg plucked a single white cat hair off of her pants.

"I have a ridiculous amount of frequent flier miles." No lies there.

The last vacation she'd taken had been years ago with her parents. Technically, she'd been tagging along for their anniversary trip. God, how lame. Time to shake up her routine.

Meg ate the rest of her cookie, staring with a combination of disbelief and amusement. "You've got it bad for this Jonnie guy. I mean, he's hot, sure. And a mega-famous rock star, which I'll grant you has serious appeal. But still."

Her friend's scalpel stare attempted to cut to the heart of the matter. But Meg was *wrong*. Eve had a mission. She wasn't mooning, weak and boneless over a famous person.

"If by 'got it bad' you mean I've got a sense of duty. An ethical obligation." Not that she'd admit it to Meg, but maybe she had a teensy little crush on handsome, thoughtful, and talented Jonnie.

Eve was no fool. Jonnie had looked at her with the glassy male gleam in his eye that meant one damn thing. His breathing changed in her presence. This all, admittedly, thrilled her.

So sue her, she craved a thrill in her life. Not like she'd act on it. She'd fulfil her obligations from an emotional and physical distance. Perhaps indulge a fantasy or two while self-servicing her sexual urges. Nothing more.

Meg snorted. "Yeah, right. Speaking of men, I think I'll go commiserate with him." She tipped her chin at an attractive guy in a sleek pinstripe suit. "Call me before you leave town, okay?"

Eve battled a grin as Meg sauntered off, short heels of her sensible pumps tapping against hardwood flooring. Sparkling with anticipation, Eve worked the crowd. She consoled Travis's crying widow and listened to stories. Mind wandering to half-formed thoughts of the tour, she circled and chatted, complimented outfits, and stooped to entertain ignored children.

As the services ended, guests trickled out. Mourners exchanged hugs. Eve fielded praise and offered condolences.

When all was said and done, she turned off lights and locked up, the familiar routine bringing drudgery more than comfort. A procession of cars led by a hearse, engines humming, snaked through the building's roundabout.

Pallbearers loaded Travis's casket, and Eve climbed into the passenger seat. Emerging from the hearse offered a certain flair, a presentation, and besides she didn't feel like driving.

Odors of leather, berry air freshener, and citrus wood polish from the coffin swirled through the vehicle interior, scents of everyday life symbolizing a routine facing disruption.

After getting through this burial, she'd go home, buy a ticket, and pack. Then, if luck took her side, sleep. Then wake up, call Jonnie, and ship out. Jesus, it was happening. It was real.

And she better get busy figuring out how to even begin thinking about assisting him with his problem. She pulled on the hem of her skirt, losing herself in thought.

"You alright? You seem distracted." Gil, the driver, was a mild, unassuming man in his thirties with sloped shoulders and a receding hairline. One of those people with a knack for blending into the background, Gil cleaned the funeral home on Saturdays and did odd maintenance jobs as they arose. The sleeves of his too-baggy, rented suit hid his knuckles, giving him a childlike appearance.

"Yeah, I, uh...never mind." Not like she could tell Gil the truth or make up an excuse. Everyone familiar with the predictable, lock-step nature of Eve's life would see through lies.

Gil fired up the ignition and took off, leading the line of cars. "There's something in the air." He tilted up his head like a hungry baby bird and flared his nostrils, hanging a left on a residential avenue leading to the cemetery.

Sweat glued the backs of her knees to smooth upholstery as the car crawled down a road flanked by parallel-parked vehicles. She squirmed in her seat, the movement releasing a musty mothball smell from the old cushion. Why did she suddenly feel ill at ease? A wet trickle slipped between her shoulder blades.

"I don't know about that." Upswing turned her statement into a question, neutralizing any attempt to convey authority. Epic fail for the boss lady.

"It's true. Human energies are attuned, like cycles. Living and dead. So our moods, as a species, rise and fall together. Collective consciousness. Hauntings and possessions are most prevalent at these times. Dips in the frequency, intervals of negativity, cause them. Some spirits are opportunists, taking advantage of the low points in the energetic emotion cycles."

Lacey's wholesome face flashed in Eve's mind. Worry ricocheted through her, a dense racquetball threatening to explode into full-on fear. By the time Gil stopped in front of the cemetery, a chemical-green plot spotted with weather-beaten headstones and plastic flowers stuck in bronze cups, she was unsettled without a distinct reason why.

"Someone's been going to Paranormal Society meetings." She forced the words out through tight lungs, unsure if she intended her statement as a ribbing, a simple acknowledgment of fact, or a question. Disorienting fog clouded her mind. An ominous feeling hung over her head like ectoplasm, spreading outward.

He killed the ignition, turning to her. "You feel it, don't you? Negative mojo? The feeling that something is coming, and it isn't good?"

Silent beats played. His twinkling, bottomless blue eyes looked at her. Into her. He *saw* her. Saw dark shit she kept to herself. Gil reached into the backseat, grabbed an umbrella, and handed it to Eve.

Eve eyed Gil's offering. "The forecast didn't mention rain."

"Like I said, something is coming."

Whatever. Needing to be done with this guy, she snatched the umbrella in a clammy palm, jumped out of the hearse, and slammed the door.

A splash of dishwater clouds dulled the sky, and several gray squirrels skittered down trees and across grass. The bland temperature rounded out a mild, unmemorable afternoon. Still, Eve twitched. Her eyes darted, like a hand could erupt from a grave at any second.

Heels she'd forgotten to change in favor of more suitable shoes sank into soft sod while she hiked through the manicured cemetery lawn. Tombstones gave off spookier-than-usual vibes, many toppled and bleached from age and weather. A foil pinwheel stabbed in the ground near a grave spun in the absence of wind, reflecting bits of sunlight. Eve's heartbeat kicked up, and she clenched a death grip around the object in her hand.

Sighing out her dumb jitters, she continued her awkward slog to the burial site. She told herself she felt off-kilter and self-conscious because she hadn't worn proper footwear, a conclusion incapable of bringing peace. In an absent gesture, she poked at soil with the metal tip of her umbrella, an unfocused and queasy sensation junking up her thoughts.

One white tent protected a dozen relatives and a well-dressed pastor, Bible in hand, standing around the grave. The hole marking Travis's final resting place was a six-foot-deep depression identical to the ones that had marked so many others' final resting places. Eve scoffed for her own benefit. There was nothing *in the air.*

Heeding protocol, she stood amidst the mourners.

With an involuntary twitch, she shifted on her feet, driving the damn shoe spikes farther into the ground. The pastor licked a finger and turned pages in his Bible.

Stoic people stood as still and ramrod straight as chess pieces. Could the officiant fucking start already? Get this over with? Eve bit a curlicue hangnail, abusing the hard sliver until she drew blood. *What's wrong with you?*

The Jonnie situation, an impending upheaval to her boring life, had agitated her on a mundane day. Finally, the pastor began reading from a King James Bible, voice deep and assuring. Eve exhaled as her elevated pulse tapered to a normal resting state and the cacophony in her head ceased.

Pulleys lowered Travis. A woman in a gray suit threw yellow roses onto the top of the casket. Tears burst. Someone lit a pungent cigar. Eve found the smelly indulgence inconsiderate but forced herself not to plug her nose so she didn't look like a diva.

A bowling pin crack of thunder shattered the din of soft crying and sentimental chatter. Umbrellas burst open in a choreographed snap of rainbow domes. Eve popped hers as cold pitter-patter turned to splats.

While rain went rat-tat-tat on her shield, a flash of white across the graveyard caught her eye. The size of a cucumber, it slunk out from behind an upright headstone and moved closer. Streams dribbled down plastic, muddling her view through translucent lavender as some creature made a beeline for her.

She squinted as the animal approached. Didn't they typically seek shelter from storms? Chilly drops kissed her legs through pantyhose, making her shudder.

An albino squirrel ambled to the gathering. The pastor continued preaching as the rodent encroached, steps decisive, so close now she could see its beady red eyes.

Red patches marred its haunches, its back. Mange riddled the poor thing. Her mouth dried. The inexplicable unease she'd felt earlier crept back over her. A slow, understated terror, like something was, indeed, in the air.

"I just wanted to thank you again for everything. For handling the services in such a classy, humane manner." This from Mrs. Williams, rheumy-eyed and sniffling into a tissue. Smiling poop emojis patterned the widow's umbrella, an absurd detail that should have tempered Eve's distress with its silliness.

"Why did God put Daddy in the bye-bye box?" a child whined, pulling at the widow's coat.

"Hush," Mrs. Williams scolded.

Eve slid her gaze from Mrs. Williams to that damn squirrel. Closer, closer it came.

"Of course. Is there anything else I can do for you?"

In reply, Mrs. Williams launched herself into Eve's arms and wailed. Eve hugged the woman with one arm, the other precariously angling her own umbrella while blocking the widow's from stabbing her in the face. The squirrel was around five feet away. Eve's body temperature dropped. The edges of her perceptual field blurred.

"American health care is a joke," Mrs. Williams murmured into Eve shoulder. "Here, have some more chemo. Poison not working? Here, have this radiation. Slash and burn, their primitive fucking methods made him sicker. And now he's gone."

Inhaling cloying perfume, Eve averted her stare from the animal as she turned her thoughts and attention to the grieving customer. People handled male morticians with a certain detachment, treating them like somber, serious undertakers best left to do their grim tasks in peace. They expected Eve, though, to play the role of counselor. Emotional labor made up a large part of her job. This was fine, and she had to focus on providing her services at the moment. "Your anger is completely natural and normal."

The fucking squirrel, though, was not natural, normal, or fine. It advanced, a ratty thing. Red blotches like huge zits ruined its alabaster pelt. Why was this animal acting so weird? It approached her like it carried out a mission. Like it had intention. Purpose. Self-awareness.

"Thank you. I am angry. I'm fucking furious. I want to scream." And scream, she did. The widow's shriek pierced Eve's eardrums with bright, stabbing pain, but the squirrel bothered her more.

It stopped at the edge of her toe. Eve stroked the wailing widow's back.

Her perception quivered in abject horror, so acute it eclipsed a physical response numbing her. The white caging of its little ribs peeked out beneath ripped skin. Red meat ribbons hung from bone. Its once-fluffy tail was a knobby skeleton's finger. A gleaming, striated facial muscle, obscenely red and visible where fur should have been, twitched in its jaw. Brown dirt clumps and slivers of Kelly green grass stuck to what remained of its coat. The squirrel was rotting. Had the thing crawled out of the ground? Was it an actual zombie?

Eve jerked her head back and forth, parched lips trembling. Did anyone else see this monstrosity? But the guests carried on like normal, making idle chit chat. The pastor milled about. Should she alert the widow glommed onto her torso? Would that accomplish anything?

"Fucking bitch." The monster spoke in a grainy, snarling male voice, mouth moving to enunciate syllables and reveal yellowed hooks of rabbity teeth.

Neither widow nor daughter seemed to hear the small fiend talking.

With the woman and her child distracted, Eve wound up her leg and kicked as hard as she could at the squirrel. But she missed, swinging at air as the monster leapt backward in a single, fluid motion. Eve swore that she saw mockery in its hollow, bloodied eyes, and surfed a raging tide of humiliated frustration. This creepy thing had the upper hand already.

Safe from a punt, it looked up at her, skinned face and body like something out of a PETA shock advertisement and especially grotesque in the light of day. The eyes were by far the worst, though. They registered her. They hated her. "Can't catch me, fucking witch bitch. Lacey knows your dark arts. Black magic. Witch," the beast hissed through its skull of a snout.

The mention of Lacey ushered in a fresh wave of dread. The Lacey problem wasn't going away. Correction: The Lacey problem was getting worse and was somehow now connected to this albino rodent zombie.

Lacey's former cult had gotten up to a lot of insane, far-flung shit. Conjuring demons for personal gain. Mind control. Had her parents somehow backslid into that nightmare themselves? Stuck this demonic little entity onto her, and if so, to what end?

A crisp gust blew the squirrel's smell, a predictable odor of wet dirt and dead flesh, in her direction. Bile rose in her throat as she waited.

"We want more." The squirrel's voice fell to a greedy, throaty whisper. "You will join her. Burn the witch and make it dead. Burn the witch and cut off its head."

After delivering its heart-shriveling, evil sing-song rhyme, the squirrel bolted. Eve fixed a hard stare on it as it scampered up a tree trunk. Sunlight flickering through the leaves blinded her, causing her to lose sight of the zombie.

Frozen, Eve rode a sizzle of adrenaline. Mrs. Williams broke free with a gasp. "You're an angel. Thank you. God, my sister was right about the benefits of practicing scream therapy."

"My pleasure," Eve managed, now aware of ringing in her ears. Between scream therapy and the squirrel, she needed a nap and maybe an exorcism.

Things wrapped up without further incident. A short walk landed Eve back at work, where she gathered her things, changed shoes, and sped home. She dashed upstairs and packed, mind racing. Time to get the hell out of Dodge. She couldn't do a damn thing about Lacey or that screwed up critter, but she could help Jonnie.

On some level, she knew running was the coward's way. Running to another person, another problem, another city. But fuck it. She'd made up her mind and made her choice. Perhaps Gil was right, and something evil corrupted the air. Could good works on Jonnie's behalf neutralize whatever sinister forces blew through the atmosphere? One way to find out. She sat on the floor and texted him.

E: *I'll meet you in New Orleans tonight.*

Seconds later, her phone blooped. J: *Perfect. Thank you.*

E: *Of course. Going online now for ticket.*

Eve leaned against a wall and pressed the phone to her chest.

Pressure gathered in her midsection as she stared at the walls, cataloging nicks in the wallpaper and other trivial details. Walls seemed to come forward, advancing as they closed in on her. When she shut her eyes and attempted to meditate, an afterimage of the awfulness from the burial site seared onto the backs of her lids.

In a torrent of spontaneity, a primal scream tore from Eve's mouth. Blinking open her lids, she snorted out a laugh as tension ebbed. The widow had the right idea with scream therapy.

Catharsis achieved, she logged onto her frequent flier account and cashed in her miles for a red-eye flight.

Maybe if she ran, she could hide.

FOUR

Hot night wind breezed through the open window of Jonnie's New Orleans flat, animating his flimsy drapes. Inhaling the tangy aroma of his mum's masaman curry simmering on the stove, he plucked out a few chords on his yellow Fender. He used this guitar when tense, wound. Pressing callused fingers into brass string as he sank deeper into his overstuffed easy chair, Jonnie strummed. The melody overcame him, its sound taut and craving release, until he teemed with energy.

The sounds and smells of funky old New Orleans, inebriated yells and brass horns trumpeting and briny, creamy jambalaya cooking in the restaurant below his condo penthouse, created a rich backdrop. When musically sated, he took off his guitar and propped it in the floor stand next to several others.

He padded to the kitchen, scuffed hardwood floors creaking beneath his bare feet, and turned off the stove. With a swipe of sponge, he wiped an errant bit off sauce off the chrome surface. A bit of remodeling had spruced up the vintage, open floor plan condo he enjoyed when Fyre came though and during those non-summer months when they took time off from touring.

Those months would become more frequent now that Brian and his wife were trying to have a baby. His chest ached as his mind wandered.

Jonnie's death would break Brian's heart. Would the man recover from his grief? Could Jonnie inflict such suffering upon his best mate? If he went through with his plan, would Fyre move on and replace him? How soon?

Jonnie ducked into the little nook behind the wooden partition demarcating his study, routing his thoughts back to the logistics of his problem as he awaited Eve's arrival. Charts covered the walls, collages of gritty black and white photos, newspaper clippings, and stories printed from websites.

Green marker lines connected Murray Connors to his bosses at the pharmaceutical company that manufactured and sold Vampivax. Red lines connected those individuals to the scientists responsible for creating the "miracle" drug, and more webbed out and landed on the universities that supported the scientists.

Black streaks linked the universities to a company called Scarab, currently standing trial for war crimes in the international tribunal. According to a famous whistleblower website, this company had run secret prisons where they conducted top-secret medical experiments on people, individuals now tucked away in witness protection.

His research project started with the goal of finding antidotes for Vampivax and led him down a dizzying array of blind alleys, twists and turns into more and more shadowy involvement. Did Scarab test Vampivax on unwilling captives, making them into monsters like him? Did they have labs somewhere, stocked with cures?

He'd dug and dug, clinging to shreds of hope as information on Scarab became scarcer and scarcer until it faded into nothing but maddening question marks. If a cure existed, he'd failed to chase it down. Which meant it was time to give up and, with Eve's help, say goodbye to his state of living deadness.

Jonnie puttered around to kill time, using a feather duster to brush specks off flat surfaces. While he straightened the jars of oils and loops of brass string covering the long surface of his guitar repair bench, the doorbell rang.

As of now, lacking a firm grasp on what the extent of Eve's abilities involved, he had no sense of what all she could do. But at the very least, it was bloody unburdening to finally confess his nightmare to someone.

Someone who, perhaps, cared about him despite what he was. If anyone could assist, this death angel could.

Before he could go all sloppy and sentimental, Jonnie yanked open the door. Eve stood before him, an exquisite vision in jeans and a red tee shirt from some bike race.

"Come in." He motioned for her to enter with an outstretched arm, mentally kicking himself for not having a cool, suave line to deliver.

Not that he used cheap lines on women. Not that he had any right to think about her like a woman, though her eyes and lips and the way a drawing of racing bicycles stretching across her round breasts made avoiding such thoughts damn difficult.

Wheeled suitcase squeaking against wood flooring as it trailed her, she graced his threshold. "Gorgeous place."

He surveyed his flat. A built-in bookcase of records dominated an entire wall. Vintage furniture and crocodile-colored wallpaper pattered with the fleur-de-lis symbol completed a retro aesthetic.

"I always work better here, it seems." He stroked his chin, unusual warmth lightening and calming him.

"They say this city's food for the muse." She spoke the truth. He connected to his music on a deeper level in New Orleans.

Eve rested her bag against a wall and strolled to an open window. Saying nothing, she looked out on the city. A breeze lifted her hair, making it flutter. In the absence of their speech, horn music and tourist laughter filled the silence.

Compelled, Jonnie walked over and stood behind her. He touched a coil of her silken hair, stroking the curl so gently that she couldn't feel it. Because she wasn't supposed to take notice of his touch. She shouldn't register him as much of anything other than a problem to solve. He wasn't a person. He was an other.

Eve turned around. In the soft light of his shaded lamps, he could finally make out the color of her eyes. Slate gray, a brewing storm cloud passing over placid ocean. Did the hue of her irises reflect her essence, still waters running deep?

"How long have you lived with it?" Her lips parted. On purpose? Why did it matter either way?

"Been twenty years now." Jonnie scratched his neck. No pleasantries, right. He needed to give her information.

"Have a seat?" He gestured with an open palm to one of two plush easy chairs resting against the wall opposite his record collection. She chose the cobalt fabric one, sat, and crossed her legs.

Jonnie joined her, sinking into his russet leather recliner. In between them sat the circular, white marble table with its claw-footed stand. He fingered its glass-smooth rim.

Eve waited, looking into his eyes like she was searching behind them for something. It made his heart hurt, and he didn't want to think too much about it.

"How about we chat over a drink?" he said.

Her posture relaxed, legs uncrossing as shoulders loosened. He couldn't get over the feline fluidity of her movements. She came off so self-assured, so at ease. A person who didn't fear him. Wasn't repulsed by him. "Sounds great."

"Sazerac alright?" He sprung to his feet, chancing her a glance of affirmation over his shoulder. She blushed and looked away, lower lip sliding between her teeth. Hold on. Had she been checking him out?

"Perfect." Eve cleared her throat, the sound cute in its awkwardness. He couldn't deny she excited him. The entire situation excited him. The danger of it. The risk.

He strutted to the kitchen, took down two lowball glasses and several bottles, and mixed up fragrant drinks with rye whiskey, absinthe, bitters, and a touch of sugar. After swirling the contents with a long silver spoon, he peeled off a sliver of lemon and dropped it into each pool of amber liquid. Nodding to himself, he gathered up the drinks.

When was the last time he'd felt so content around a woman? Probably never. The calm in his chest had him feeling fine about this meeting, about who he was, right down to his vampire self. Not proud, but not humiliated either. Unrepentant. An emotion that was downright sexual, positively kinky.

"Thank you." Eve took the drink from his hand. "Floral. I can smell the licorice."

"Cheers." He offered his glass, and they clinked.

"Hold up now." She wrapped those lush lips around her glass, a twinkle sparkling in her stormy eyes. "I thought you were a vampire. Aren't you only supposed to feed on blood and the terror of your hapless victims?"

Laughter charged up his throat, and he had to press a fist to his mouth to avoid spitting out his beverage. Eve's irreverence swept away his gloom like a broom to cobwebs. "I was brought up to believe it was déclassé to serve bodily fluids to guests." A sip of the heady, sweet and bitter concoction warmed his throat and loosened his muscles.

"At least not on the first date." With a wink that tickled his balls, she took a big sip and set her glass down on the table. The ensuing soft clack was an invitation to banter, a shot fired.

"This a date?" The question popped right out, packaged in a flirty tone he didn't intend. A smirk stole its way onto his mouth. On their own volition, his long legs widened. He knew he had great legs, but tantalizing Eve with them hadn't been part of tonight's plan. But if the hot, thick energy between him and her was any indication, plans might be begging to be led astray.

"It's a consultation." Her tone smoothed over, growing tart as her body returned to its prim comportment. She finished her Sazerac.

"Right. Fancy another?" He knocked his down the hatch and set his empty beside hers, enjoying the sight of their side-by-side glasses in some off-limits way. Like they were matched pieces of a set.

"I better not." Ah. Okay. Eve would act as the brake. Just as well.

"So shall I take it from the top?" He glanced left to his study, his project, where papers plastered where wallpaper once showed. Wallpaper he'd smothered to make room for his obsession.

"The more facts I have, the more accurately I'll be able to assess whether or not I can help." With her index finger, she stroked a side of her empty glass. Jonnie imagined that finger tracing the seam of his lips. He forced his eyes to his wall of records, their slim spines pressed together, sections delineated with a label maker.

"It started with a fringe medical procedure." He launched into the entire asinine spiel that would no doubt make him appear vain, impulsive, and irrational. Appearance obsessed, uncritical, deserving of what he'd gotten. Let the buyer beware and all.

Nevertheless, he confessed it all to Eve. The youth treatment that

Fyre's then-manager Joe pushed him to get. The onset of the first symptoms, their progression. Murray Connors. Cara. The bizarre labyrinth his research led him into. Fading hopes for an antidote. Brighter ones that she could end him.

"So, the gist of it is that I'm a huge sodding fool. And I'm not telling you any of this to tug at your heartstrings. I don't want your pity, but I could use your help." He blew out a puff of air, freeing about ten pounds of stress.

Time passed, seconds. He avoided looking at her, into the mask of her judgment. Instead, he counted his records. Counted the row across the top. Then the column stretching from floor to vaulted ceiling. He mentally multiplied them. A lot of records. Wait, since when had he been into counting?

"I'm sorry, Jonnie," she finally said, her voice a slow, quavering whisper.

He glanced at her, a gust of warm air from the window caressing his skin. Her eyes were misty, her features soft with lips parted and head bent at a slight tilt. He itched to hold her, to touch her. Take her to his bed, lose himself to her body and the street sounds of this enchanted, haunted city. "Don't be. It's my fault."

"No. You were misled. Ill-informed. It's unconscionable how they withheld information from you. Does this company have a medical license? Because if they do, it should be revoked, and you should sue them for malpractice."

Her storm-cloud eyes grew turbulent, a sheen upon her light brown skin catching the light. A corner of his mouth twitched, and along with it a twinge plucked below his navel. "I don't think they're exactly on the up and up."

"So what do you know?"

He stood, beckoned with one hand, and led her to his study. Boards creaked behind him as she followed.

"Have you heard of any of this?" He pointed at poster boards, news clippings, and highlighted paper he'd printed out. In front of anyone else he'd fret about looking like some conspiracy nutjob, but Eve he trusted.

Sure, he barely knew her, but Jonnie respected his instincts. His gut. The same force told him to pursue a music career in the face of impossible odds, to stick with Fyre even when things had gotten shaky. It had only failed him once, the time he'd told it to shut up and go along with the Vampivax procedure.

She settled beside him, close enough he could feel her body heat, smell her scent. Was the woman just plain comfortable with proximity and touch, or did she want to be close to him in particular? His brain hoped for the former, while his heart and body longed for the latter.

A weighty exhale left her. "Yeah. I have. I saw something about the trial online, then tooled around social media reading about it. It's a weird story, this Scarab thing. But I figured the trial in The Hague ended their mischief."

A hodgepodge of thumbnail pictures and strings of colored yarn and printed websites stared back at him like a chaotic jigsaw puzzle. "From what I can tell they just went deeper underground. Changed names, locations, moved operations into subsidiary companies. For awhile I hoped I could track down a cure." He touched his jawbone, remembering how he'd shaved for her visit and worn a long-sleeved Henley tee to hide the bruises on his arms.

She touched his wrist, prompting him to make eye contact with her. Something stern and serious, no-nonsense, hardened her gentle features. "Forgive me if I'm being presumptuous, but when you talk about all of this you don't sound certain."

"Of what?" His heart rate quickened as he played dumb. She saw right through him.

Eve shrugged, scanned the wall of evidence, looked back at him. "That being through with this vampire thing is what you want."

Though the changes scared him, he could no longer deny they fascinated him as well. To an extent, he liked his new self. "I hate the procedures. Spending money on them." He flicked a dismissive wrist at a headshot of the corrupt "doctor" Connors he'd clipped from some magazine. "I hate dealing with him."

"What if there was another way to sustain yourself."

His heart jumped, an illicit feeling brought about by a forbidden suggestion. "I know what you're getting at." He could never bite people, though. Not against their will, at least.

"Don't you think you're more help to your family alive than dead?"

A stiffening sensation, like an exoskeleton forming over his skin, hardened Jonnie. He needed to quit with his fantasies and flights of fancy. All signs indicated she was spooked and trying to extricate herself from the project. He should have known.

"You know what? Forget it." He brushed past her and out of the study, aimlessly making his way into the kitchen. Beyond the window with the deep crack, a drunk, screeching bachelorette party stumbled down a busy sidewalk. Their blood smelled of ethanol, and he wrinkled his nose while moving the pot of food to the side. What a dolt he'd been, to cook her dinner.

"Just hear me out." She emerged in the kitchen beside him. "Something smells amazing. Wow, did you make this?" Peering into the bubbling Dutch oven, Eve licked her lips.

"Mum's recipe. Threw it together in case you were hungry."

"Actually, yeah, I'm starving."

Jonnie marshalled his rational faculties. He could stand to be less defensive and hear what she had to say. "Good. Let's talk, then." He got down a pair of simple white ceramic plates.

"You like wine?" Tilting his chin at the full, six-bottle iron rack sitting on the counter, he grabbed a ladle from a drawer and scooped two portions of food onto the dishes.

"I do. And I think this conversation calls for more libations." Brushing up against him, she took the liberty of opening the glass-front cupboards and taking down two stemless glasses.

He laughed lightly, like he found himself doing sometimes in her presence. "Without further ado." With a wry look in her direction, he snagged a bottle of red and a corkscrew and popped the cork, indulging a daydream about the taste of her as he poured two measures.

"To thinking outside the box." With her usual poise, Eve raised her glass and clinked it into his, a tiny gesture that shored up the early stages of a budding partnership.

"I'll drink to that." Jonnie managed to escape his malaise as they sipped in unison, an action charged with layered, subtle eroticism he didn't allow himself to get too caught up in.

In the dining room section of his place, his rustic, dark wood dining table awaited like an old friend. Sure, he'd had dates over for dinner before, but none had felt as natural and seamless as this.

She settled into her high-backed chair, glancing up at the ceiling with its exposed pipes and sleek, minimalist chandelier. Her gaze drifted to the slotted wooden partition marking the boundary between the dining room and his bedroom. He swore her eyes lingered on his low bed, its dark blue sheets. He'd always found it sexy, how the bed was undeniably visible in his flat.

Impossible to ignore, its presence daring the mind not to entertain suggestive thoughts.

Nuanced seduction via home design. Rather brilliant if he did say so himself.

Jonnie straightened the leather belt cinching his snug black jeans, drawing a breath of warm air spiced with the fragrant Indian dish. "What was it you wanted to say?"

He pushed food around his plate, sneaking glances of her plump, pursed lips blowing steam off her fork. A brush of tint reddened her pout, a gleam of gloss catching the light.

"I know I'm probably stepping out of my lane here, but it seems to me like the piece of this that really bothers you is the treatments, not what they made you into."

He considered the point, savoring a bite as he tore his focus from her lush lips and to his predicament. "There's a truth there, I suppose."

"Have you told anyone but me?" As she ate, her eyes widened. "This is fantastic."

It had been a while since he cooked for a woman, and the pride he took in her enjoyment of his traditional fare lifted his spirits and made him sit up taller. "Thank you. And no, I haven't."

"May I ask why?" Eyes flicking between her food and him, she took a bite and chased it with wine.

"I suppose there is some shame and embarrassment that I went through with the stupid procedure in the first place." Jonnie ate a big forkful, in part to stop himself from talking any more. What was it about Eve that put him so greatly at ease? Christ, a part of him wanted to curl up in her lap and tell her his life story.

"You know, the thing is, it's been quite awhile. I really doubt that your bandmates would turn their backs on you now. After all of these years."

"Fair." Considering her point, he used his knife to scoot a few saucy peas onto his fork.

"And as crass as it is to talk about things in strictly monetary terms, there are the numbers to think about, too. If you die, Cara gets an inheritance. Sure. But these things take time to process. I won't pry into your finances, but I'm guessing among the tours and record sale royalties and all the rest, you pull in a pretty good salary. It stands to reason that your better bet is to continue to do what you're doing and get her money for the treatment that way."

A flush heated his cheeks, and he stuffed a silly, boyish grin as he pushed food around. "If I didn't know any better, I'd say you liked having me around."

Another big mouthful of curry shut him up before he spilled his guts. He hadn't felt this way around another person—an intoxicating combination of shyness and boldness—since he'd been the outsider at secondary school.

Jonnie had found solace in the music room and auditorium, freedom from the bullies who tormented him for being skinny and sensitive and smelling of ethnic food. In those sacred spaces, Brian, Thom, and Jonas accepted him into their ragtag band of misfits. With Jonas being the only other non-white kid in the secondary school, and Brian and Thom having train wrecks of home lives, the other three blokes who would one day become Fyre felt Jonnie's outsider pain.

Eve pulled the fork out of her mouth slowly. He caught a flash of her tongue but couldn't tell if she was flirting or not. This woman was guarded, careful, difficult to read. Traits which drove him wild, made him want to reduce her to a moaning mess of lust.

"Yeah, you seem like an alright guy. But I need to tell you something." She clanked her fork against the plate as the words landed heavily, her stare falling to the table. "I don't think I can help with the spiritual piece of this. I, um, I don't think I'm qualified anymore. I made a mistake by coming here."

Her reversal of position made his heart tumble, shrinking to a chilly lump as he watched her fidget with her utensil and avoid eye contact. "Why not?"

A band of silence tightened the air. Metal clinked against ceramic in a three-quarter beat. With the night wearing on, the intensity of sounds from the street below picked up. Smells of fried food from the restaurant mingled with Jonnie's cooking. He fought the urge to tap his foot.

Finally, she looked up, though she didn't meet his eyes. Instead, she cranked her neck to the ceiling like the answers she needed floated up there. "This is going to sound nuts."

"I'm the one who told you I'm a vampire. I'd say we've long since left the territory of the mundane."

A quick chortle, and she moved her face to level with his, fingering a spot above her cheek when their eyes met. "Touché. Okay, here we go. A while back I was transitioning a soul who was a special case. Not the garden variety dead person with your standard unresolved problems. She had some heavy spiritual issues, and I didn't manage them right. I'm reluctant to take on another case out of my comfort zone, to work with someone whose soul is in a space that I don't one hundred percent understand."

Jonnie licked spicy sauce off of his lips, his appetite vanishing. He knew it—she did find him to be a freak. Not like he could blame her. He laid his napkin over his half-eaten plate and pushed it toward the center of the table. "What happened?"

"This girl, she moved out to Los Angeles to pursue acting and singing, and along the way she got mixed up in some cult. Hollywood occult nonsense, wannabe Illuminati. At least I assumed it was wannabe. Anyway, her parents told me all of this when they commissioned me. They flew out to Los Angeles to rescue her and bring her back to Louisville, our hometown. By the time they got there she was sick. Physically, but also mentally. Babbling about demons and mind control. She, well, she killed herself the first night back home, and the parents found me and begged me to help. But I messed up."

Coldness settled in Jonnie's stomach and spread outward. Hollywood cult? No way was this connected to the Hollywood cult his deceased manager Joe had been embroiled in. Jonnie didn't know the entire story there, but he knew that Joe's involvement with the lunatic group had somehow gotten him killed. A group of occultists were also tied to Scarab, as far as he could surmise. His skin crawled as he processed the too-perfect coincidence. "Messed up how?"

"I couldn't..." Eve's voice shook as she struggled to finish her point.

"It's okay. Never mind." He touched the top of her smooth hand.

"I'm fine. I couldn't save her soul from whatever they'd done to her, and I sent her somewhere awful. I was honest with her family about what happened, and they blamed me. They've threatened me, and now, I can't explain it, but it's like she's haunting me."

"Haunting you." Jonnie traced a prominent vein below Eve's knuckle, wishing he had something more comforting to offer than repeating her own words back to her.

She nodded, shoving her plate away. "Yeah. Look, Jonnie, I'm sorry. For wasting your time. I can leave tonight." Eve pushed back in her chair, wood grinding against wood.

"Don't go." He tightened his grip on her hand, bending his head toward the study. "Perhaps we can help each other."

"How?"

"The company that made me into a vampire is affiliated with occultists, and they have Hollywood connections. It may be the same people, meaning you might be able to find solutions to your haunting. And help get this girl where she needs to go."

With apprehension in her gray eyes, she looked at his wall of paper. "So you're saying that all roads might lead to Rome." Eve pivoted her attention to Jonnie, the weight in her stare as stalwart as steel beams. In that moment, he knew. They were in this together and could pursue their respective goals as a team. And Jonnie thrived in teams.

"We can start researching tomorrow." Jonnie cleared dishes as his mind raced with optimism, with possibilities. "I have to get to the arena by six, but that affords us an entire day to work. Why don't you stay here? You can take my bed, and I'll sleep on the couch." Wincing, he washed and dried the plates. His tone came out overly casual, like he was trying too hard to keep her.

"Sounds good, Jonnie. Thank you." Eve rose from her chair and joined him at the sink, leaning against it with a gleam in her eye as she watched him clean. Half of her mouth curved into a luscious, bewitching smile.

"My pleasure." He put everything away before stopping his chore to smile back at her. His grin was stupid, all gums and teeth and plenty inappropriate given the dark situation. Yet another burst of kerosene energy ran from core to fingertips. This project was bound to be interesting, and more than a bit of a challenge.

FIVE

Lying alone in Jonnie's low, wide bed on a mattress firmer than her own, Eve stared at the hardworking ceiling fan above her head. Warm darkness surrounded her with a broken promise of rest. She couldn't look at the digital clock's hell-red numbers anymore, as the sight of the time would bring only despair.

Her senses, warring factions within her body, had reached their familiar heightened state brought about by too much time awake.

The scents of him, smoke and leather, aftershave, and male musk, perfumed the sheets and quickened her heartbeat.

Unfamiliar textures of high thread count cotton twisting around her limbs stimulated her sweaty skin.

Red wine and the flavorful dish he'd cooked lingered beneath toothpaste on her taste buds.

A wall clock ticked off seconds. In the still of the night, the volume of the second hand striking landed like thunder.

Red and blue lights skittered across the ceiling as a police car screeched down the street below.

On the couch, Jonnie slept silently. Beneath them, New Orleans partied on. Honking horns, music, and all manner of whoop and scream penetrated the walls.

Sleep would elude her. Soon that first blush of watery bluish dawn, the light that made her heart harden every damn time she saw it, would bruise the sky. Eve swung her legs over the bed and scrubbed a hand over her face, sitting up to look out the big, cloudy window embedded in the brick wall.

Fuck insomnia. She'd even taken an Ambien. Maybe she needed to talk to her doctor about upping the dosage. Her thoughts raced, her pulse raced, all of it exacerbated by the situation. The strange location. The strange, enticing new man sleeping in the other room.

Keyed up and bored, she padded to the bathroom. The cute, retro space housed a claw-foot tub and a white floor made up of a jigsaw puzzle of ceramic teeth. She absently opened a cabinet drawer, finding a stash of boxed toothbrushes, a few tubes of ladies' travel-sized deodorant, and around ten packages of makeup wipes. A kick of hurt landed in the center of her chest.

Rolling her eyes, she shut the drawer. So what? He slept with women. Eve had no right to be mad or jealous. At least he was considerate to those overnight guests who forgot their essentials.

Eve examined her tired face in the mirror above the bathroom sink and sighed. She opened the door to the medicine cabinet, feeling marginally guilty for snooping but mostly just fidgety as she surveyed the contents. Two loose, unused cotton swabs. Plastic jar of generic ibuprofen, unopened bar of mid-range soap. Small bottle of expensive-looking aftershave that she sniffed. She closed her eyes, nostrils flaring as she imagined kissing Jonnie's throat, chin, lips.

Kissing his hard prick. *Quit being weird.* Eve replaced his bath product and shut the slim door, coming face to face with her reflection again.

She wandered the loft for a bit, running her fingers over the thin, hard spines of his impressive record collection. Inhaling oily polish and brassy metal scents from his guitar stand, she read the titles of books filling his stately, built-in bookshelves. Lots of music biographies: Hendrix, Joplin, Clapton, Ronstadt. Also ones about someone from KISS and someone from Def Leppard.

In the fiction department, Jonnie owned the *Song of Ice and Fire* series, in hardcover, and a couple of Sookie Stackhouse paperbacks. Some history titles and assorted scientific nonfiction rounded out his book collection.

Endeared, she smiled. "So this is what a famous rock star's second home looks like." Her soft syllables danced through the airy loft like sprites.

She'd expected more of a mess. More beer cans and fewer books. Clothes on the floor, porn and cigarette butts, et cetera. But Jonnie was a well-read and down-to-earth man, not some stereotypical hard-partying druggie or crass horn dog. Intrigue sparkled in her veins. Steps bouncy and light, she pulled out a book on haunted New Orleans, opened it, and smelled the pages. She smiled with her eyes shut, smelling him.

A flutter of movement and a wink of light appeared in her peripheral vision and prompted her to turn her head. It came from the kitchen, where gauzy red curtains, mirroring the currant hue of the curry they'd enjoyed, flapped in the night breeze.

She replaced the book and ambled over, enchanted by the buzz of southern witching hour mystery circulating through humid air. Eve threw open the shutters and leaned half of her body out of the window, soft and fluttery feel of her cotton tee and boxers sensual against her skin. On the brick street, a couple stumbled by, arm in arm. Jazz music floated through wrought iron trellises and in between pink and yellow French Quarter buildings. When Eve had her fill of New Orleans vibes, she turned around and prepared to go lie back down.

Jonnie stood before her, watching in silence. He wore the holey Sex Pistols tee and baggy black sweatpants he'd put on to crash on the couch. Brown eyes vacant, he looked a million miles away. He glanced side to side, his movements too slow, too robotic.

A chill bolted up her spine as she gawked, frozen.

Well, obviously he was sleepwalking. Eve laid a hand on her heart and calmed herself with three long inhales and exhales. She was piqued and jumpy from lack of sleep was all.

Best to let it play out and not wake him—at least that's what she remembered hearing on television. Leave sleepwalkers alone.

He cocked his head as if regarding her, though his stare showed no life. A small, disturbing smile curved his lips, and he turned on a bare heel and marched back to the couch with slow, awful, automated steps. Fear dulling to morbid fascination, Eve followed him.

Still smiling like a dog who'd trapped a pet bird in his mouth, he lay back down on his long golden couch and pulled a thin white sheet over his body.

She stood over him. The clock ticked down seconds.

Jonnie opened his lips and hissed. She sucked in a thin gasp, a needle of adrenaline stabbing her chest.

Two fangs, long as fish hooks and ivory white, protruded from his gums and twinkled in the ambient streetlight.

His face changed. Subtle at first, so subtle she told herself she was imagining things. But no. Chin and nose grew longer, bonier, spikier. Eyebrows rose to sloped peaks. Everything shifted around, like his flesh was a clay head in the hands of a sculptor.

Jonnie's eyes, their shape stretched feline and oval, snapped open. His irises gleamed emerald. The pupils weren't normal. They were vertical.

Eve blinked, her throat seizing. He looked unholy, demonic, abhorrent. Like a monstrous cross between a person and a snake. A nocturnal lizard-being, all heavy viper brow line, pointy features on a lance-shaped face, and lithesome, serpentine body.

Perverse interest, like a twisted cousin of sexual arousal, shimmied up her midsection while she beheld the creature before her. He gave off a subtle light, a glow as cold as the moonlight streaking the panels of his hardwood floor. A light that didn't warm.

Transfixed, she slunk closer to him. The fiendish face made her hot, made her pussy clench. Acting on wild impulse so new to her, she mounted him on the couch, feeling his tense muscles and hard cock beneath her. He slid a hand up her shirt, slowly, staring at her with those evil eyes.

His touch was ice, yet it seared with the heat of Hades.

Eve woke up in bed, limbs leaden and slow, like she was trying to swim through a river of molasses. Eyelids were iron curtains she struggled to lift. Her world hung suspended, upside down, in a state of utter disorientation.

After a few seconds, her blurry vision focused on a white blob perched between her breasts. Twin laser pointers of red eyes peered down at her. The zombie squirrel. Terror shot through her veins like lighter fluid as her vision adjusted to the darkness.

The hideous little thing's state of decay had progressed. The face was barely more than a bloody skull with a few rancid meat strips clinging to bone.

"Burn the witch and make it dead. Burn the witch and cut off its head." Miasma, the acrid odor of decomposition, flowed from its moving lips and flooded her lungs. The funk of a thousand graves stole her breath and left her wheezing.

A lone tendril of translucent red smoke curled out of her mouth and into the squirrel's open jaw.

Eve fell out of bed, clutching her chest, gasping. A heavy, heavy weight had been there, pressing into her lungs until they had stopped working. She'd been dead for a little bit. She knew this for a fact. Finally, her heart resumed its beats. She knelt on the hardwood floor, sucking wind, fists balled at her sternum. Dreaming, or awake? She floated in some in-between, her bearings gone.

"I'm alive," she assured herself as she came back to full consciousness. "I'm breathing again."

On her knees, she mentally catalogued her symptoms and chalked them up to an adverse reaction to the Ambien. Still kneeling, hands clasped over her heart like some supplicant prostrate before a dark chaos god, Eve composed herself.

"Eve? Sounded like you took quite a fall there, you alright?" Jonnie's sleepy voice startled her; his gentle hand on her shoulder made her yelp. She rested her hand on his, finding his skin warm. She looked up at him, at his concerned face and messy hair.

Some twisted part of her was a little disappointed he wasn't the deathly frigid monster-man of her dream. She crammed that dirty little piece of candy into a junk drawer in her brain before it could entice her anymore.

"I'm fine." She rose on rubbery legs, Jonnie's firm grip on her upper arm offering assistance. With a graceless tumble, she fell into bed. Eve felt her forehead, halfheartedly feigning illness in some lame attempt to cover her embarrassment and save face. "I might be coming down with something." *Ugh. Did you really need to add that?*

Jonnie sat on the edge of the bed, his posture straight, watching her in silence for a beat. Sensual talons of guitarist's fingers fanned over his defined kneecaps. Black hair hung in his face, shielding his eyes while emphasizing his jawline and his high cheekbones. The aroma of that aftershave she adored drifted to her nostrils.

"You have a nightmare, love?" A gravely note in his voice, husky and thick, rekindled the residual sexual arousal from her dream. It ignited a dark fire deep in her body, deep in her subconscious.

She snapped her gaze to his. The moment their stares locked, the atmosphere changed. Air grew dense with realizations of desire, unspoken yet mutual. Inevitability danced in the space between them like a charmed, sensuous cobra. "Are you here to make me feel better?"

"Come here." His words were a tender order, a sumptuous drink of wine with notes of macho arrogance, sweet surrender, and humble request.

Time stretched to infinity as communion flowed between them. They rode one wavelength, in sync.

Beside herself, caught up in the vapor swirling around the loft, strangeness heightened by the ebony shroud of the small hours, Eve sat up and pulled on Jonnie's shoulder. In a single, silky motion, he slid a hand up her cheek and brushed his nose against hers. At the feel of skin on skin, she tightened her grip on him.

Emboldened, she allowed her touch to make initial explorations of his body. She rubbed his collarbone, then his long neck, with the pad of her thumb. He arched his back and moaned. His sound of pleasure made her pussy dampen. Newly siren-like for this man, she permitted her lips to hover a millimeter from his, taunting him. His breathing changed, sped, the sound filling her with a head rush of female sexual power.

Jonnie moved forward, and she inched back before he caught her lips. Teasing him, keeping him on his toes, stoked her desire. What would he do, how would he respond? A dark glimmer crossed his narrowed eyes. Not quite the monster face, but sharply sexual, a mask of arousal finished with a touch of danger. Seeing him like this made her hot and swampy, a bayou at midnight under the spell of sex magic.

"You gonna let me kiss you?" he murmured, tilting his head. Jonnie touched her bottom lip, pulling it down with one finger to expose the wet part.

In reply, she moved in for the kill. Their lips met in a crash. Animalistic hunger fit for the pre-dawn darkness, Dionysian vibes teeming in gravid, southern air, swept her away. His mouth was hot and dry, then wet as he invaded her with his tongue. Her sex slick with arousal, she pushed her own tongue in, stroking his, her hand sliding down his back to feel his slopes of shoulder blades.

Eve's sexual aggression was alien to her, as forbidden and unknown as voodoo. She traced his spine, claiming the very backbone of him.

Heartbeats murmured in the minimal space between them as he slipped a hand up her shirt, caressing her side with his warm, callused fingers.

"Yes," she managed to murmur against his plush yet masculine lips, drunk on his scent. He explored her ribs with an assured touch before slipping his hand upward to graze the bottom of her breast. Her nipples tightened; her thoughts turned to mush.

"Yes." More sophisticated words and phrases had long since abandoned her.

Mouths molded, sucking and probing. His weight pressed into her, firm sinew and bone on female softness. Two bodies dancing in the dark, they moved as one and lowered onto the bed. He moaned again then, into her lips, and she spread her legs.

Eve made a study of his thin hips, points and angles filling her palms. She'd never imagined slender could be so sexy, so different, so cool. But she wanted to feel every centimeter of this slim rocker's taut, lean, gymnast's body. She pulled at his shirt, yanking the hem over his navel.

He took her cue and tugged it above his head, flinging it to the ground with wild, dangerous determination apropos to the situation. Now he was kneeling between her widened legs, looking down at her. She propped herself on her elbows and ran two hands over his olive skin, learning his form. Slight show of ribs, suggestions of hard bars against smooth flesh. Hairless torso, twin silver hoops impaling each small nipple.

In an outrageous moment of wanton impulse, she tugged one metal loop. "That feel good?"

He growled a little and lowered on top of her, brushing his lips against her neck. "Makes my balls ache, love." Hot, fast breath breath tickled her throat as he nuzzled a patch of skin just above her clavicle.

Eve arched into Jonnie's featherlight kisses, rubbing the spots where his legs met his midsection. His erection, stiff as a poker under bunched, thick cotton, rubbed the swollen target between her legs. She bucked into him, matching his thrusts so they moved in tandem.

He growled, the sound from the dream, and slid a tongue as rigid as his dick up her neck. He lapped, licked, striking some tingly pressure point behind her jaw. Sex noises, sounds of desperation and craving, flowed from her mouth. Her clit throbbed. Every nerve ending came alive, became electric. Her own drumming pulse thumped in her ears.

"Do you want to bite me?" she whispered like they shared a secret. Which, in a sense, they did.

"Of fucking course I do." Pelvic thrusts quickened the pace of his erection, dry humping her barely clothed, wet and ready sex. Teeth brushed her skin, points nicking oh so slightly...*the fangs?* Her core squeezed at the thought, and fresh wetness flowed from her.

She grabbed his firm ass in two handfuls, pushing him into her needy female flesh. His rock-hard cheeks clenched in her squeezing palms. "Do it while you fuck me."

Such behavior was so unlike Eve she legitimately wondered, for a second, if she'd fallen under an actual magic spell. Sex for her was typically undertaken as a prim, practical affair, a polite rite of passage dealt with after third dates that went well enough and obligatory, awkward conversations about STIs and birth control.

When it happened for her at all, Eve had intercourse. Sometimes she climaxed and sometimes she didn't, but she sure as hell didn't fuck. And hot damn, had she been missing out.

But Jonnie didn't answer her plea at first, neither with a change in his body language nor with words. After too much time had passed, she clenched her teeth and berated herself for blowing it. He kissed her neck for a bit, the feel of his lips transitioning from passionate to sweet.

She fought an exasperated sigh as he moved those kisses to her cheek. He dropped two chaste ones on her lips while playing with her hair. Then, in one deliberate motion that made her grimace, he pulled back from her. The rigid length between his legs no longer tantalized her with its promises.

"What's wrong?" Voice clipped and annoyingly squeaky, she managed her dumb question while he gazed into her eyes. What she could make out in his dark stare was distant, perhaps sad, maybe even maudlin.

He inhaled audibly. Swallowed, Adam's apple bobbing. His jaw twitched. "It's not a good idea for us to fool around. We both know that."

"Why not?" She played with the elastic band of his pants, spying black ink tattoos that began below his navel and disappeared into regions one could only see if he was fully naked. Two sets of vertical lines, like claw scratches.

Her chest tightened. Other women, the ones who had helped themselves to toothbrushes and wee tubes of deodorant, had seen those cool tats. In the moment she envied those women, greatly and with startling bitterness. For Eve had been rejected where they had not.

He rolled off her and flopped on his back, fixing his stare on the whirling fan. She shifted to her side, waiting for her answer. A flash of headlight briefly illuminated the sharp edges of her almost-lover's cut-crystal profile.

"You had a dream about me, didn't you?" he asked at last.

"How did you know?" She watched him watch the fan, the frustration borne of unmet sexual need drizzling away. Low-grade dread took its place. Weird shit was happening, escalating, and she'd be remiss to forget it.

"I walked like a somnambulist. Lay on the couch and transitioned while you stood over me and got on top of me." He spoke in monotone, like reporting the occurrences in a "just the facts, ma'am" manner would make them less insane.

"So we met in some third place." She'd read about and heard of such realms. Astral planes, other dimensions. What they were was anyone's guess. In the domain of the esoteric, there were more questions than answers.

"Right. Eve..." He flipped, moving to face her. Threaded a lock of her mussed hair around his index finger. "What I know is, things are changing. Getting worse. I feel it, speeding up. And I don't know what I'm capable of. I don't know how I'm changing, you know? Seems there's a new, terrible surprise every day now. I don't want to hurt you."

"What if the surprises aren't all terrible? You won't hurt me. I can tell." She stroked his arm like he was a lifeline. Like if they held each other they would be safe, ensconced in the escape of passion.

His brows drew together as he searched her face. "What if you're wrong?" He lowered his voice, playing the pause after he spoke. Possibly trying to scare her, push her away.

"I'm not afraid."

"You should be." He looked to the side, his jaw firming like he ground his molars. Jonnie scooted a couple of inches away from her, a physical retreat to mirror the emotional one.

She crossed her arms over her chest, a stew of embarrassment and aggravation eating at her stomach lining. Didn't he realize they would fare better as a united front, in agreement on how to move forward? "Well, the fact remains that we're seeing the same crazy stuff now. And I need answers on this mess with Lacey, because whatever is going on, I don't know if her stalker parents are summoning demons, or screwing around with the occult, or what, but you're the only person who seems to have broken any ground on this whatsoever."

Eve bent her thumb in the direction of the room with the clippings. Normally upon spotting those she would have dismissed Jonnie as a crackpot, called herself a car, and beat cheeks out of there. But he obviously had some leads. Making him the only lead she had to resolve the Lacey situation, annoying lust or no. And as much as her neglected sexuality tried to convince her otherwise, they needed to keep the extent of their involvement guarded and on task.

Because although the rejection hurt, he was right. The man was a vampire, undergoing some alteration process, and who knew where that would lead. But any fool could deduce that tempting fate was a bad idea.

The bed creaked as he sat, positioning himself to face away from her. He clenched the edge of the mattress, his straight, bare back moving with his breathing. "I need a cure, you need closure. I might have the means to lead us to both."

"We're working together because our goals align, and we can help each other. Simple as that." She pitched her statement in an overly declarative and formal way in a desperate effort to will it into existence and crush her desire for him in the process.

"Simple as that." Jonnie hung his head for a second, heaved a sigh, and got out of bed. An ugly dawn had broken quickly, morning light garish on the unmade bed. "Try to catch a nap. I have an interview and some business before sound check at five, but we should try to squeeze in some research. I'll run out and get us a bit of sustenance for when you wake up." He chanced her a wary glance. "You want to come see the show, yes?" A note of optimism brightened his voice.

The shy beginnings of a smile crept onto Eve's lips. It wasn't smart to get physically intimate with Jonnie, but they could enjoy each other's company as much as the situation would allow. "Sounds fun."

"We always hope so." After proffering her a subdued smirk, Jonnie walked off. A door opened and shut with a squeak, then water sloshed. Floorboards creaked, and the heavy front door opened and closed.

Once he was gone, Eve buried herself in sticky sheets and screwed her eyes shut. Jonnie was one hundred percent correct. With the situation growing both more frightening and less clear, they needed to buckle down and find some solutions, pronto.

Because, as he'd said, who knew what terrible surprise lay in store for them next?

SIX

IN THE SMALL, WINDOWLESS ARENA DRESSING ROOM, WITH ITS FOUR white walls and wheeled rack of clothing, Jonnie breathed stale air. Smells of sweat and men's bath products blended with a residual odor of drying latex paint to knot his already upset stomach.

Brian's singing voice, though harmonious and in key like always, stabbed icepicks into Jonnie's ears. So loud, so close.

Heart fluttery, he crouched, opened the mini fridge, and pulled out a third bottle of water. Sighing in relief as he pressed the wet, chilly plastic to his hot forehead, he told himself that it was just nerves. He still got stage fright now and again, especially before playing huge venues like this one. Too bad Eve hadn't come, but he understood why she'd changed her mind and decided to hang back at his place instead of seeing the show. She wasn't in the mood for a concert and felt it more pressing to focus on research. Made total sense. Eve was a pragmatist, through and through. Still, he missed her.

Brian stopped the vocal warmup exercises he'd been doing and cleared his throat. "You don't look so good, mate."

"I'm fine, just a little overheated." Understatement of the century. Jonnie cracked the bottle and chugged its divine offering of refreshment.

He drained the water in a few gulps, but unfortunately, as soon as it was gone his throat resumed burning like he'd attempted to eat a hot coal.

"You have a rash—Christ, those spots are the size of quarters. I could text one of the nurses." Concern thick in his voice, Brian reached for a mobile on the top of the stout refrigerator.

Jonnie strangled a bitter snort in his throat. He doubted any of the temporary medical crew on the tour would be able to help.

Only one man could step in to pinch hit. An overwhelming mixture of anger, fear, and dread flooded Jonnie's veins. Connors, Vampivax, Scarab and demons, and the weird dreams he shared with Eve spun a funhouse in his brain. Unknowns whose mysteries rendered them horrifying.

"I'm fine. It's about a hundred and twenty degrees outside is all. Christ, are they even running the air conditioner in here?" He stuck his head out of the oppressive, crowded room's doorway, glancing up and down a cavernous cinderblock hallway where crew bustled about.

Jonnie waved at a young woman wearing an all-access laminate pass. "Have someone crank the cold air in here, will you, love?"

The baby-faced brunette scrunched up her eyebrows and bit her lip. "You want, um, an ibuprofen or something?"

"No, just tell the people who run this place to stop scrimping on the utilities. It's a bloody sauna." He fanned the air for emphasis as sweat dampened his underarms, melted his gelled spikes of hair into limp noodles.

She hustled off. He ducked back inside and collapsed on a loveseat, crunching the empty plastic bottle in his fist. The minor act of aggression did nothing to relieve his stress, and he threw the garbage in a recycling bin before looking at his arms. Brian was right. They were mottled, splotchy like he'd broken out in hives. His guts churned. This wasn't okay, wasn't normal or right. He was a disaster, falling apart.

Jonnie continued to stare at the blotches. Were they getting worse by the second? Was his face getting hotter? He'd felt fine when he'd stepped outside to sign autographs. No more than thirty minutes in the sun, how in bloody hell had the heat managed to affect him so profoundly?

Next to Jonnie, the seat dropped as Brian sat. A few moments of miserable silence followed. Perspiration leaked down Jonnie's temples.

His skin flared, ached, pulsed—as oppressive and tight as a straightjacket. A wave of dizziness, like his blood sugar had crashed, washed over him.

Brian's worried blue eyes swept Jonnie's body.

Crabby and ashamed, Jonnie tucked his shaking hands under his thighs.

Beyond the small room, voices clamored as roadies completed last-minute prep. From the show floor, indistinguishable chatter and streamed Fyre music flowed.

"Do you have HIV? Because if you do, we'd stand by you and support you. I hope you know that." Brian reached for Jonnie's arm.

"Don't be daft." Lightheaded, he summoned the strength to brush Brian's touch away with a sweep of his arm. How would his first-ever best friend, the man who'd become the brother Jonnie had dreamed of as a middle child between two sisters, react if he knew the truth?

A truth worse than any disease or condition one could imagine.

"Well, you're keeping secrets and telling lies. We aren't stupid, Jon, everyone has noticed the changes." Brian raked a hand through his short, salt and pepper hair. Planted his elbows on his knees and leaned forward. "If you don't tell us the truth, we can't help you."

"Got a bit of a sunburn. Jesus. You my mum now?" Woozy, he forced himself up off the couch and stalked to the doorway, fleeing the claustrophobic box and Brian's inquisition but unable to flee the truth Brian sought.

As he marched down the long tunnel, greeting roadies for something to do besides deal with Brian, a firm hand caught his wrist. "Does it have to do with Cara? Because—"

Jonnie broke out of the hold and whipped around, looking at Brian's brow line to avoid his eyes. The man got to be normal, go on as usual, with his rolled up sleeves and worn jeans, the same costume he'd played in since they convinced the label to let them ditch the school uniforms.

The front man got to go home to his wife and a healthy daughter the same age as dying Cara. He got to go home to his own health. "Drop it, Brian. Okay?"

Instead, Brian stepped closer, invading Jonnie's personal space bubble. His blue-green gaze hardened to signal the curdling of worry into annoyance. The man was a control freak and hated more than anything to be thwarted. "We've come this far. Whatever's happening, whatever you're *hiding*, I don't want to see it ruin you. Ruin us."

"Don't you worry, mate." Jonnie delivered two condescending slaps to Brian's upper arm. "I'll keep right on playing and strutting around up there. The cash flow isn't going to be drying up anytime soon." His moronic deflection, some half-arsed attempt to alienate Brian by accusing him of craven motives and lack of integrity, made Jonnie feel even worse.

"What the hell is wrong with you?" Brian shook his head. Of course he saw right through the stupid effort to piss him off and push him away.

"Nothing." He could barely eject the word.

"Suffer alone then, I suppose." Brian spun on his black heel and stomped down the hall, fists balled and shoulders bunched.

Catching his now-ragged breath, Jonnie pressed his blazing forehead against the wall's cool hardness, stealing another nip of minimal relief. He swallowed into a swollen throat, wincing against the pain inside. He could ring Connors for a blood change, but surely he didn't need one already. It had only been two days since Louisville, and the treatments were supposed to last a week.

This so-called progression was occurring in his mind only. Yeah. The show had to go on. He was out of sorts about Eve was all, and the stress had walloped his immune system.

Surely. Of course. He needed to focus now, needed to get in the zone.

Jonnie peeled his face away from the wall and dragged himself down the corridor. He had to concentrate on each step and force himself to keep going. Avoiding staring eyes and whispers, he passed crew and assorted backstage guests.

Enduring another excruciating gulp of thick saliva, he made his way to the heavy black curtain shielding the stage from the seats. At least he didn't have to sing.

Fans whooped and cheered as the recorded music stopped. *There is nothing wrong with you.* He mentally repeated the mantra over and over, as if lying about something could make it true.

A burly guitar tech waited in the wings, holding Jonnie's mint-colored

Stratocaster by the neck. The roadie's lips parted and he shifted on his feet when the men's gazes met, but he didn't say anything.

Jonnie nodded once, snatching the instrument from the bloke's meaty hand. Making a show of defiance as he struggled to prevent the prized item from slipping through his weak, slippery grip, Jonnie slung the strap over his back. The guitar would be his armor tonight. His battle axe.

As he lurched to the white X of masking tape marking his placement on stage, he became aware of the burning sensation in his eyeballs. It was a scabby and chemical burn, like he'd washed his face with acid.

His throat inflamed. For a second, he swore he tasted bleach on his tongue. *I'm losing my sodding mind.*

Clutching the neck of his guitar like he wanted to strangle it, he stomped to the X and stood in his spot. His feet felt so goddamn heavy, bricks in his shoes dragging him down.

Thom and Brian exchanged cringing glances as Jonnie entered their field of vision. He couldn't see Jonas behind his drum kit at the back of the stage, but he probably pulled a face, too.

Well, screw them. He could fight this alone, take it on alone. Being different suited him. Besides, Eve would not want to see him this way. She would balk. She would run.

He didn't deserve someone as kind as her, didn't get to have a mate. Not with symptoms like this. He was the puzzle piece left over after the picture has been completed.

The rock in the shoe. An aberration without a place in the nice, tidy system.

He would march to the beat of his own drum from now on. Take on the world alone. Pretty fucking rock star. An iron spike of a cramp bit into his midsection, but he sneered like a badass all the same. Nobody had to know his dirty secret.

"Ladies and gentleman!" The PA's booming, godlike voice blasted over the sound system. Blocked by the curtain, the crowd went wild. Screams and cheers pierced hooks into his eardrums. Jonnie stumbled, an oil slick of nausea spreading through him. Sweat stung his eyes. His entire body was a burn, scorching, hurting. So goddamn hot.

A few feet in front of Jonnie, Brian struck opening chords to "Mercy of the Gods," a beloved early hit.

"Give your best New Orleans welcome to the one, the only..."

Fans yelled even louder, beside themselves, crazed. Had they always been this fucking loud? His scalp sizzled. He swatted at his face as the room started spinning. Slurping thin, unsatisfyingly shallow breaths into collapsing lungs, he looked up in some frantic effort to ground himself.

Mistake.

Above him, the band's monstrous set piece, two mythical horses pulled by a black carriage, loomed large. All vacant, crazy eyes and toothy mouths, the maniacal stallions, one fiery orange and red, and the other silvery white, glared down at him. No, no, no. Around and around they went, evil as they circled him like members of some twisted carousel.

Up in the rafters, rows of lights blazed to life, turning the stage into an inferno. Jonnie blinked. His mouth went to sand. His head broke off and floated into outer space, where it orbited Earth as a lonely satellite.

"Chariotz of Fyre!" No, no, no. Dread cratered his spirit. He wouldn't be able to hack it.

Jonnie fumbled at his guitar strings in a feeble effort to complement Brian's playing, bumbling out a few sour notes before his sweaty hand slipped. Somehow, a sharp edge on the instrument caught his finger pad, slicing it. Pain reunited him with his body. Blood dripped onto the fretboard, and his head spun along with the room.

The curtain fell, pooling on the floor like a lady's evening gown. At the first sight of the crowd, Jonnie's vision darkened. His heart clenched in a painful spasm. He was used to facing big crowds of all ages and walks of life packing arenas.

But people didn't fill the stadium. Each seat held a white squirrel like the one that tried to steal Eve's breath in their shared dream. Some of them were normal, others flayed and bloody ruins, still others mangy and decomposing.

"Burn the witch," the demon-rodents chanted in unison. "Burn the witch and make it dead. Burn the witch and cut off its head."

That's it.

First, Jonnie's legs gave out. He fell to his knees. Next, his head dropped like a bowling ball as he slumped forward. To the sound of screams and shouts, his cheek hit hard ground, and he blacked out.

* * *

"UGH." JONNIE CAME TO IN A COLD, DIMLY LIT ROOM. HE ACHED ALL over. Too weak to move, he processed his surroundings. Quiet beeps, occurring in two second intervals, hit his ears.

Blurry eyes focusing on some impressionist-style art print of a pastel field, Jonnie realized he lay in a hospital bed.

He forced his boulder of a skull to the side. At his bedside, a redhead nurse in magenta scrubs fiddled with a chirpy machine. Attached to it were tubes connected to a plastic bag that fed cooling liquid into his system.

"How long was I out?" His voice croaked, throat raging like Satan had ripped out his esophagus.

She gasped, jumped, smacked a hand to her chest. "You scared me." The nurse looked at her watch. "You were unconscious when you arrived, so two hours."

Queasiness sloshed his stomach. This had to be the beginnings of deterioration. Meaning only one thing would solve the problem, and it wouldn't be the temporary fix dripping saline into his body. "Give me my phone. I need to call my personal physician."

She shook her head, jiggling the bag of solution they fed him. "What you need to do is sit tight until we finish running some tests. Don't worry, we'll take good care of you here."

No time. He'd have to hypnotize her. Marshalling every bit of his remaining strength, Jonnie circled a hand around the woman's wrist and urged the glamour up his spine and into his eyeballs. It sizzled his optic nerves like oil on a hot pan.

He locked her brown eyes with his inky, magic-filled ones, and barreled in. "Bring me my things."

She got that glassy, faraway look in her stare that let him know it worked. The muscles in her arm slackened, and he dropped her wrist. Guilt for messing with someone's mind prompted him to turn his head as she scurried off, white soles squeaking against linoleum flooring.

Beyond his window sat a parking lot, empty except for a couple of run-down cars. A security light swarmed by enchanted moths bathed the space in an ominous, orange glow. What were his bandmates doing? Sitting in the waiting room talking about him, staging an intervention?

Before he could go down the rabbit hole of obsession, the nurse's noisy rubber shoes signaled her return. The sounds ceased as she approached, zoned out and holding his possessions.

Jonnie collected his wallet and mobile phone from the poor, dazed woman. Someone must have had a roadie bring the items over in case the medical personnel needed his ID or contact numbers off his phone. He pulled tubes from his arms, setting off a wicked series of beeps. Fuck. Alerted, more staff would arrive soon, meaning he needed to move. All he could do was hope that the stuff they'd shot into his veins would buy him adequate time before he started boiling again.

He walked the nurse to a vinyl chair and sat her down. "Close your eyes. Stay here and don't budge."

She nodded, compliant.

The brainwashing would wear off in an hour or so, and her colleagues would assume that she fell asleep at her station. Shite. The assumption in question could get her fired. He plucked a business card from his billfold and wrote, in his distinctive handwriting, "not her fault" on the back. Jonnie laid the paper rectangle on her lap.

He changed into his sweaty, stinky clothes from the concert, pocketed his mobile, and slipped into the hallway. Fortunately, there was no activity at this hour, and he carried his shoes as he strode down the corridor and breezed out an exit.

A hot and humid night, unusually windy, raised his temperature a few worrisome degrees. Palm trees fluttered in the gusts, and Jonnie slunk into a corner behind a ripe dumpster, hurried into his shoes, and texted Connors.

The black car rolled into the lot. Jonnie hailed the driver to where he stood and climbed in for the familiar, loathsome ritual. "Since you follow the tour, I suppose that means I'm your only client."

Jonnie watched the cluster of crazed bugs bang at the light, frantic wings flapping, while Connors prepped. Jonnie was no better than those dumb moths, stupid for their fix. A moth to flame, seduced by the lure of youth.

Clicks and clacks ensued. "I've actually been meaning to talk to you about that." Nerves tightened the doctor's voice as he swabbed the injection site with alcohol.

"How so?"

"The higher ups have relocated me. So I won't be on call, or available much at all actually, after this evening." Connors whistled nervously, sticking the needle in and firing up the machine.

Jonnie's abdominal muscles tensed. Horror crashed through him in a series of thunderous peals. His lifeline was retreating. "The progression is speeding up."

"Yup. It'll do that. What landed you in the hospital?"

Jonnie gave Connors the gist.

"Sunlight aversion kicked in early. Congratulations, my friend. You are officially a creature of the night."

"So if I avoid the sun, how much time do I have before the coma?"

Connors yawned. He finished the procedure and tucked away his supplies. "A week, maybe more."

A week was nothing. "Can you give me a referral?"

"Nope. Sorry. And you don't know me, and we've never met. You're loaded, though. I'm sure you'll figure out some way to get those treatments."

Jonnie paid Connors in cash, the final transaction bringing a combination of dread and relief more sweet than bitter. Though having the rug pulled out from under him didn't feel good in the slightest, it also meant this abominable aspect of his life was over and done. The uncertainty remaining in its wake frightened him a bit, but he managed to hang on to grounding perspective. He knew what he needed to do going forward. "Right."

"Good luck, man. Pleasure doing business with you."

He denied Connors the validation of a nicety, exited the car, and called Eve. The plan to track down a cure had hastened.

SEVEN

Seated on a cushy throw rug covering Jonnie's wooden floor and surrounded by a white fan of papers and clippings, Eve picked up a printout from the Internet. Abiding Jonnie's color-coding system, she highlighted a paragraph in green and reread it. "I can't tell if this is legitimate or not, but it's the best lead we have so far."

During the disastrous concert and trip to the hospital he'd told her about, she'd hung back and read everything she could get her hands on, from his research and a general Internet search, on Vampivax and vampires and this company that created them through its youth treatment. Though his story of the collapse filled her with worry, her practical brain managed to stay focused on finding a solution.

Anything could lead to information about an antidote or cure, natural and medical methods to halt, slow, or reverse the condition. And maybe along the way she'd stumble across some paranormal tidbit she could use to help her with the Lacey situation and its apparent, attendant squirrel haunting.

She'd run down several blind alleys and encountered numerous redacted PDF files and other black boxes of non-information, but her work had turned up a single, strong lead.

Apparently, a community of shifters and other supernatural people thrived in the Peruvian jungle, and vampires lived among them. The vegetarian ones used, and sold, some homemade herbal blood substitute.

Jonnie paced. Behind him, rain drummed against his floor-to-ceiling window, streaking the glass. "I'm inclined to believe it because of the connection to Scarab. I'd bet that the people broken out of their prison ended up down there. It's like a sanctuary."

Eve paused from arranging the documents into color-coded stacks. Jonnie didn't look well. Dark circles ringed his eyes, and spotty pink blotches crawled over his neck. Though he complained of feeling overheated, he also shivered.

"What's going on with your bandmates?" She folded the corners of some fringe newspaper clipping, the article a lurid and conspiratorial exposé on a top-secret program involving training supernaturals in underground bunkers for use by private military contractors.

Her heart beat in time with the rain. Was all this real? It was tough to draw the line between truth and falsehood when it came to far-out stuff, but if even a fraction of it was authentic, the implications were profound.

Right now the priority was getting Jonnie well. If she could heal Lacey's soul and exorcise the rodent-demon attached to it, win-win. At that point, she'd need to figure out if Lacey's parents were behind the haunting, but she couldn't risk getting ahead of herself or scattering her focus.

He rubbed his arms. "I'm sure they're in the waiting room, waiting for an update from the doctors. The nurse will wake up in thirty minutes or so, and at that point it's just a matter of time before they know I escaped."

"The nurse will wake up? Why is she asleep?"

A rueful half-smile from Jonnie. "Long story. Vampire skills."

Despite the insane situation, despite herself, Eve smiled back at him. He stopped his pacing for a moment while they stared at each other, two screwed up and haunted people. In a shadowy loft near the banks of the Mississippi river delta, they pushed against flood waters of madness threatening to breach their psychic levees.

"Wanna light some candles? I feel like we need some mood lighting. Maximize the whole broody atmosphere." Her utterance of the words "mood lighting" made her cheeks flame and her thighs squeeze together. Now wasn't the time for desire, of course, but her attraction hadn't gotten the memo. Hadn't tempered. It had strengthened, in fact, as her concern for Jonnie's health added a layer of depth to her feelings for him.

He took a seat on the floor next to her, folding his legs to the side. The gray athletic shorts and white tee shirt he'd changed into after showering emphasized his lean muscles and long limbs. His body reminded her of a male ballet teacher whose classes she'd once taken.

"I'll play some classical music, too. The most depressing violin concerto I can find." As he reached for a paper, he brushed his thumb against one of her fingers.

His gentle touch made its way to her cuticle bed, a tiny gesture of intimacy that delivered an emotional payload larger than it should have.

"Are they worried about you? The Fyre guys?" Her words came out low and husky, suited to the darkness and their shared vulnerability, befitting their common fear and confusion.

"Yeah. As soon as someone tells them I ran out of the hospital they'll start calling or come over here." Eyes downcast, Jonnie stroked Eve's knuckles. He traced a vein on the top of her hand, following the raised line. As she watched him touch her, she thought of the Amazon river. Of the two of them riding down it in a boat, searching for hope and answers in the depths of the jungle. Together.

"Why can't you tell them? You told me." She allowed her hand to relax, fingers uncurling. Eve tapped one of Jonnie's rings, a smooth disc of silver where a stone would normally be. She walked her fingers over his knuckles and picked at chipped black polish on his pinky nail. He could use a touch up.

He scooted a little closer to her without taking his wandering fingers away. The aroma of soap on his clean skin made her breath quicken.

"Because you live these things, these far out supernatural experiences. You know. You endure it. They, I mean, they wouldn't get it. Brian's wife is a witch, so perhaps in theory he wouldn't balk and call me barking mad, but it's still a big leap. Practicing magic is one thing, but this is a whole other level. To think they'd accept me without judgment is, well, optimistic at best. And if I noticed things changing, like them growing more distant day after day..." His shoulders slumped, and his grip on her hand tightened.

Her heart kicked into her mouth. Darkness hung heavy, a measly glow from a shaded lamp doing nothing to brighten it. She suddenly and irrationally wanted to jump up and turn on every light in the suite. And, at the same time, her intuition urged her to pull Jonnie close to her and hold him tight.

"You know a witch?" In her minds eye, an image of the squirrel's mangled death mask of a face superimposed over Jonnie's profile. *Burn the witch and make it dead.* The sick, sneering little voice bounced off the walls of her mind.

"Yeah, I mean, she's not too active from what I understand. Mostly she does these deep meditations and trance workshops at her yoga studio. Why?" His eyes cut to Eve's, the low light emphasizing their narrowed, quizzical cast.

Eve fidgeted with the papers, rearranging them for something to do besides look at Jonnie. She hated to talk about it. Hated her uselessness to help, her complete and total ineffectuality. Hated how the creature reminded her of the deadly error. "I have recurring visions and dreams of this little squirrel zombie thing. It calls me a witch. There's a story there, a long story."

Lively noise of New Orleans nightlife filled the silence that followed, eighties rock music blasting from a strip joint or club on Bourbon Street. The effect was an incongruous one, like she and Jonnie existed in a glass bubble, their own weird world, separate and distinct from the city.

"I've seen it too." His voice, burdened with emotions that she couldn't quite pinpoint and spoken in a low volume, shook.

Eve drew inward as her body tightened. A ball of iron settled in her stomach. Suddenly, the papers around them looked sinister, ominous. She fought the urge to jerk her head over her shoulder, swept up in some irrational fear that if they continued speaking of the little devil, it would appear. "Where?"

Above their heads, a ceiling fan hummed. Its monotone sound was a small measure of comfort in the eerie silence, but not enough. Energy hung in the space between their bodies, vibrating in a high-voltage electric current. A secret, frightening and alien, bound them together.

"In the shared dream, or visit to the third place, or wherever it was. I saw it. Sitting on your chest."

Dread both dragged her down and amped her up. Her pulse banged in her ears, and a shiver slithered over her skin. She glanced at his sharp profile, his strong bone structure rendered foreboding in the minimal lighting and disturbing context. "What do you think it means?"

He shook his head, glancing at a grandfather clock, his gesture seeming to make its ticks strike louder. "We should go."

"Go where?"

"To Peru." Jonnie grabbed both of her hands and stood, urging her to rise along with him.

She did, a wild and volatile cocktail of emotions brewing in her chest and stomach. Her breathing quickened, making her breasts heave with each inhale. He towered above her as a god of the night. She could flee or could fall into his arms. A force deep in her bones longed to scream a crazed and primordial howl, to release the id.

Before she could formulate a thought, let alone answer, he dropped his hold and sprinted off. Jonnie returned with a duffel bag, which he filled with the papers. While she watched, excited and scared and fucking crackling with sparks from head to toe, he zipped up the bag. Jonnie dropped the sack and texted.

"A guy will be here in fifteen." A fast, breathy timbre in his tone made heat bloom between her legs. He'd sounded the same way when they'd kissed, smashed their bodies together in a fervor of forbidden pre-dawn lust.

She knew the sound of his excitement. Knew an intimate detail of him and craved more.

"I never said yes." Her reply came out with a taunting edge and smoky inflection that should not have matched the unfurling scenario, yet it did. In that instant, Eve lost a sense of time. Moments stretched to eternity in a taffy string made from urgency, danger, and anticipation.

In her mind, she fell backward without a net. Into a place or irrationality and desire, into a chaotic chamber of debauchery. A place of forbiddens and taboos and delicious mysteries. Into the part of herself that chased curiosities and questioned assumptions of good or evil. Into dark delights.

Into the part of herself that would run away with a vampire and dare herself to discover what happened.

He stepped closer, intimidating in his presence though slight of build. His posture was perfect, his dark eyes keen. "Are you saying no?"

Eve wasn't sure if she heard the nascent spark of a threat in his voice, or if in her worked-up state she imagined it. In any event, the whole drama ignited her like a firework.

"Would it matter if I did?" Her chest swelled, every nerve ending of her body flush with awareness. She gazed up into his intense stare, lust between her legs, hunger in her throat.

An uncanny sensation adjacent to déjà vu swept through her. Something unfathomable had passed between them, and a watery psychic memory of it still clung to the edges of what she was able to perceive, tantalizing and menacing. Ephemeral, subliminal, whispered at a volume one note too low to hear. Made her crave the real thing, whatever that was.

"Of course it matters. I want you to want this, Eve." He brushed her cheek with cool, graceful fingers. They travelled a languid journey down her neck, ghosting her jugular vein. Her blood pounded like it pushed against her skin, magnetized to the man who they both knew longed to feed off it. Her clit swelled, stiffened. And she wasn't even positive what he was talking about. But it was enrapturing and wicked, as decadent as the first bite of a fine chocolate mousse. The essence of sin, distilled into syrup.

He licked his front teeth in a quick swipe. She swore she saw the fangs, those miniature tusks of ivory winking in the lamp's golden halo.

"I want to, yes. I want this."

His body heat tormented her skin with the promise of a touch.

"You have a passport?" With movements as crisp and efficient as his businesslike tone, Jonnie darted to the bedroom section of his spacious home. Drawers flew open. He dragged a suitcase out from under his bed and tossed clothes and other items into it.

Meg's frowning face flashed in Eve's mind, joining Jonnie's breaking of the mood to remind her of the irrationality inherent in all of this. The statement "what in the actual fuck are you doing" shouted a bewildered accusation in her brain.

She followed him to his sleeping space and watched him pack. Beyond another bohemian window with a couple of cracked panes, a neon sign, the silhouette of a naked woman shimmying, spread its pussy-pink glow across rain-streaked glass. The erotic light bathed Eve. She could strip for Jonnie, basking in saturated color while she stoked his desire.

But she snapped out of her fantasy once and for all. He was right, they had to act. "I left it in Louisville." Fortunately, at Meg's behest, she'd renewed the document. Eve chewed her lip. Did she keep thinking about Meg, her anchor of practicality, because she had doubts as to what she was doing?

"What's wrong?" Jonnie zipped up his bag, looking at her with a tilted head and concerned expression. He slashed a hand through messy hair, erotic pink glimmers from the sign dancing on his face. "Look, Eve, I hope you don't feel pressured here. If you aren't sure, or you don't want to do this, tell me. I don't want you to have regrets."

The pain in his voice steeled her resolve. He thought she'd bail on him, let him down when things got difficult. And if he thought that, he was wrong. Because Eve didn't fail people who turned to her for help. Not anymore. Never again. It was time to quit being a coward and take another fucking risk.

"No. I don't feel any of those things. I'm a little overwhelmed, but I want to do this. If a certain undead rodent is any indication, we're in this together. Meaning we need to pool our resources and collaborate." Eve congratulated herself for framing her statement in a way that sounded sane and businesslike.

Not like the dictionary definition of a harebrained scheme.

"Good. I'll have my driver ring a pilot, and we'll stop off in Louisville to pick up whatever you need. After, we'll catch a red-eye to South America." Jonnie swished by her, texting, causing another surge of excitement to swell. He'd switched into important mode, famous man mode. Witnessing it, to her surprise, got her motor running.

A first, but then again, Eve had a feeling that a string of firsts would soon be defining her life. "Sounds like a plan."

"Tickets are purchased." He pushed one more button with a

definitive poke, shoulders square and head high. A smirk snuck out. The big-shot, rock star persona suited him.

Eve peered over Jonnie's shoulder as he composed another text: *I'll be AWOL for awhile. I need some rest, but I'm okay. Don't worry about me.*

Instantly, it blooped a reply.

Brian: *Alright. Take care of yourself, mate. Sorry I was snappy in the dressing room. Call me any time.*

Jonnie texted back a thumbs up and a heart and stuck the phone in his back pocket.

Even given the grim circumstances, she tingled. This shouldn't be so exciting. Shouldn't sound so thrilling, like so much fun. "What if we can't find the community? Or if they tell us to leave or won't let us stay?"

"Well, then, it looks like we'll have to find a hotel and keep each other company until I pass my expiration date and go comatose, doesn't it?"

He threw in a sexy wink, but dull pain kicked into her ribs at his mention of dying. "I'm sorry. I didn't mean to be doubtful. I guess I felt like I should at least perform some nominal attempt to be practical."

A lopsided smile curved Jonnie's mouth before he reached for her hand. "I appreciate you taking this risk with me."

"I'd like to start taking risks again. With life in general. With people."

His charming smile deepened into a devilish grin. "You're certainly diving right in."

"Go big or go home."

"Size queen, eh?" A second wink made her clit pulse as her mind drifted away from concern and to a sense memory of his long, stiff erection pressing between her legs.

"You have a dirty mind."

"You don't know the half of it."

A heat wave licked over her skin. "Tease."

"You want me to tease you, Eve?"

Before she could answer, a text pinged his phone and killed the flirty vibe. "He's here. Let's go." He led the way, firing off a reply.

As Eve bounded down the musty entryway's creaky spiral staircase, imagined peeks into tempting unknowns buoyed her steps. She was the fool, skipping off the cliff. No point in denying an incontestable fact. But she wasn't doing so blithely, far from it. An apartment door on the first floor opened with a slow creak. In the doorway stood an ancient woman in a pink bathrobe, holding a calico cat in her liver-spotted arms.

The old lady smiled at Eve, revealing mossy stumps of teeth. The effect was auspicious, a positive omen, good tidings for a journey.

Eve smiled back as Jonnie pushed open heavy white double doors, introducing a warm, wet, and spicy blast of air. The surrounding energy elevated and encouraging, she walked on feet lightened with purpose and confidence. She wasn't skipping over the cliff blithely, not at all. She marched with direction, resolve. The calculated steps of commitment, of someone taking action to solve her problems.

The rain had tempered into residual drips. Humidity plastered her face like a stuffy mask. Jonnie slunk into the backseat of the white Lexus that he'd summoned. As he slid into the plush leather interior, his eyes lit up with a playful glimmer of youthful innocence that she hadn't seen on him.

She hadn't seen it that first night in the rain, when he'd shivered on her doorstep like a lost puppy. Not when they'd pored over research, not even when they'd kissed and touched.

But that gleam gave her strength. It shored up her surety. Her mission was to heal souls, to nurture the grandest light inside of people. And maybe not only after their deaths. Perhaps she could tend to that light like an attentive gardener while also caring for the warm, vital person it inhabited.

Perhaps she'd find her true self on this strange and terrifying journey, the way normal people found themselves on post-college backpacking trips through Europe.

But she and Jonnie weren't normal. She talked to the dead, and he was undead. They chased vaccines for vampirism and solutions for hauntings, not Eurorail trains.

Silent understanding passed between them, a current of communication. Jonnie extended a hand. Eve accepted his offer and settled into the luxury car's squishy seat, focused yet nervous as she courted the abyss.

EIGHT

The speed boat's grinding motor churned up froth while Amazon waters stretched to foliage-lined banks, yawning black beyond Jonnie's gaze.

"How did you figure out the exact location?" Eve raised her voice over the mechanical noise, leaning in close. Her leg brushed his, distracting him with the velvet feel of her skin. She wore short khaki shorts, showing off lean, toned calves and thighs. His pulse accelerated as he glanced down to their twin pairs of legs. His were beige and hers light brown, though in the dark their colors merged into one.

Hot air, muggy even in the dead of night, lashed their hair about. Droplets illuminated by the boat's headlights sparkled on her arms. Frogs and cicadas performed their serenade, a din punctuated now and then by more exotic animal sounds.

Curtains of lush rainforest framing the twisting river led his mind to wonder about other lush, damp places. Namely the one between her legs.

She waved a hand across his face. "Should I be worried about you? Have you lapsed into some kind of vampire death trance?"

Jonnie broke the sex spell he'd put himself under, forcing his focus onto something other than her edible, delicate scent. "I gathered enough details from the research to scare up a few names. From there, it's unsurprising how far money gets you." He gestured to the front of the boat, where the driver navigated the twisty body of water with a firm grip on the wheel.

It hadn't been all that challenging, really. Everyone knew a guy who knew a guy, and a few hundred dollars' worth of PayPal transactions made through an anonymous account later, he'd linked up with Carlos, the boatman. Originally from New Mexico, Carlos knew two American expatriates in the shifter clan who'd agreed to meet Jonnie and Eve.

A quick but careful vetting process assured Jonnie that Carlos wasn't a conman or kidnapper who would deliver them into the hands of drug cartel hostage takers, and here they were.

Besides, one false move against him or Eve, and the boatman would lose his life force to a quick, fanged strike. Jonnie's newfound speed astonished him, an enhancement he'd discovered when leaving Eve's house. He could probably take out an entire gang of armed men, which he would do in a second to protect Eve from any shenanigans he might inadvertently drag her into. And as awareness of his powers grew, so did his confidence. His bravery.

At times like these, he forgot his original request was for her to kill him. The old plea seemed outrageous now. A goal he'd outgrown. He didn't want to die. He wanted to thrive, to live his best vampire life. With the help of the jungle antidote he sought, perhaps he could subdue the wretched symptoms and enjoy himself for the first time in ages. Enjoy Eve's company and show her, in all sorts of ways, the extent of his gratitude. The extent to which he cherished her presence in his life, her generosity in offering to help him.

Eve toed her mid-sized hiking pack, a relic stuffed with a week's worth of clothes and capped by a tightly rolled blue sleeping bag. The expats had offered cabins but warned that arrangements would be rough, nonetheless. "I feel like I should be more scared than I actually am."

Before he could think, he wrapped an arm around her. She clicked into his hold in one natural motion, relaxing as she nestled into the crook under his arm. "I've got you. What, you don't like camping?"

"Nope. Glamping all the way for me. Hot tubs and electricity." She rested a hand just above his knee, stroking him with the intimate touches he'd forgotten he craved. "And I've got you, too."

Jonnie savored the impact of their statements, the increase in their comfort zone. Around them, monkeys whooped and foliage rustled. The speedboat motor groaned out its lone, clanking metal tune. The sickly sweet, shamefully enjoyable odor of gasoline wafted up from the bottom of the boat, the craft's sides framed by foamy black waters that glinted under the moon.

His heart swelled as he cherished the feel of Eve's warm figure. Lost in himself, in them, part of him longed to speak words of endearment to her. But of course it was too soon, or perhaps too late.

Carlos steered to the shoreline, killing the motor with a series of marble-in-a-barrel clatters. He docked into mud and sand, rocking the boat with a jolt that knocked Eve and Jonnie's bodies closer together. The driver jumped out. Water splashed, and a few feet away, something large and unidentifiable slithered into murky depths. As Carlos used thick nylon rope to secure the vessel to a tall wooden post, Jonnie held Eve tighter. For his assurance as well as hers.

The adventure began now—their journey into the unknown and, with it, their shared effort to cure a mutual psychic woe.

Carlos affixed his headlight lamp to his forehead and helped Eve out by the hand, stealing a peek at her breasts as he did. Not like Jonnie could blame the man. Eve had a great set, round and full and perky beneath her fitted tee shirt.

Jonnie jumped out on his own and swiped her fingers from the driver's hold, a needling pang of jealousy pinching near his breastbone.

Securing her own wearable light behind her head, she smiled knowingly at him. He quirked a brow at her while he clicked the elastic strap of his lamp, pretending not to understand that she had registered his flash of envy. The woman could read him so easily.

"Ready?" Carlos asked, pushing a button on his gear and sparking a bluish halogen cone of light into existence. It gave the jungle an eerie look, a cave of a forest cast in a punishing spotlight fit for exposing the secrets that the darkness masked.

Jonnie looked to Eve for confirmation, and she nodded and turned on her own light. He followed suit and took her hand.

Carlos led the way, marching the trio down a well-trodden path.

Sticks crackled under their boots, underbrush crunched, and bugs chirped all around.

As he traipsed behind the guide, Eve's silken, strong grip linked with his, an alien sensation stole over Jonnie. Part of his consciousness left his body and flew through the trees. He'd split, he still saw the path ahead of him, but at the same time he picked up more around the edges. Leaping monkeys, the canopy's huge rubbery leaves, and coils of vines snaking up fat tree trunks rushed through his visual field.

A sprinting jaguar with night-vision eyes like golden balls ran in his direction. As the passing big cat saw him, whatever aspect of him was visible, it nodded. The feline morphed into a woman with dark hair and kept on sprinting through the jungle.

Beside him, Eve gasped. Jonnie clicked back into himself, rejoining wholly with the part of his consciousness inside his body, the physical aspect hiking the trail. "You alright, love?"

She touched her neck. "Yeah, it was weird. I lost myself for a minute. I spaced out and felt like I was floating above myself. I saw the top of my head. Like an out-of-body experience."

First the dream, now this. Did their shared esoteric experiences mean they were psychically connected?

"Sounds rather fun," Jonnie said. Though he didn't distrust Carlos, had no reason to, he also didn't see a reason to go blathering about mystical powers and psychic connections and the like with a virtual stranger in their presence. The man knew Jonnie sought the shifters for what he'd called research purposes, and he figured the expat didn't need anymore information beyond what Jonnie'd already proffered.

Eve laughed, the sound clear and mirthful like wind chimes. He squeezed her fingers. Perhaps they could build in a diversion or two on this trip, visit a waterfall or some such thing. Good heavens, they both needed a holiday.

"It was random alright. Not bad though." She glanced up at him, headlamp illuminating her pretty face and kind eyes.

The path opened to a clearing, and Carlos stopped the trio. Brilliant starlight that put their lamps to shame spilled over flat grass and the greenery that flanked it. Above them stretched a starry network of overhead lights, bright enough to read by, like those that bathed the stages he played upon.

"It's a node," Carlos announced in a thoughtful manner as he walked to a landmark in the middle of the clearing. A circular wooden disc the size of a gong hung suspended from a post. Without explanation, Carlos picked up a baseball bat off of the ground and banged the circle.

Sure enough, the disc was some kind of homemade gong, and its low, foreboding booms vibrated through the air, echoing off of the trees. "What do you mean, a node?" Jonnie asked.

Carlos dropped the bat and held his arms high. "This place. It's sacred, a doorway. That's why the star children and otherkin, both born and made, flock to it. To thrive, to travel, to soar through the cosmos."

A shooting star zipped across the sparkling obsidian blanket, raining down a trail of glittery dust like magic powder. Jonnie had to concede that magical happenings were in play. More to the point, Carlos's comments about a special place for people who were different struck him with a case of the warm fuzzies. Followed by an ache of disappointment. He wished he could have brought his bandmates. Perhaps he'd take pictures, clue them in on what he was up to.

"And did you ring the star children and otherkin's doorbell just now?" Eve asked.

Carlos chortled, tapping his temple. "Smart woman. I'll wait with you two until your host arrives."

Damn straight she was a smart woman. Eve took off her backpack and set it on the ground, moaning slightly as she rubbed her shoulder.

Jonnie stepped behind her and massaged her shoulders until she sighed in contentment and melted into his touch. He looped his arms around her front, inhaling her fragrant hair. Jonnie admired the constellations domed above his head, trying to remember names and placements from science class. Brian had always been the brainy one. If he were here, he'd give them a rundown.

But Jonnie couldn't concentrate on the sky because suddenly Eve's heartbeat filled his ears. So loud. So strong and vital. And her tempting neck was inches from his lips.

He caught the unique sent of her blood, a rich and earthy animal fragrance complemented by notes of cherry, currant, and barrel-aged whisky. A delicacy far grander than the expensive wines they'd drunk at Brian and Helen's wedding at the Sonoma Valley vineyard. The beat pulsed in Eve's neck. Desire pulsed below his belt. His cock rose to half mast, pressing into his fly.

"Big Dipper," he said as he managed to stop thinking about his dick and finally identified Ursa Major, pointing upward.

"Yeah, it definitely feels big alright." The slightest wiggle of her bottom against his ever-stiffening knob let him know she wasn't thinking about stars either.

Carlos cleared his throat, and Jonnie released Eve and stepped back a couple of inches. Thank heaven they lacked privacy, or he might just throw her down on the ground and ravish her in the open air. She made a cute huffing noise and slung her pack over her shoulders. He couldn't help but smirk. She wanted him as well.

But acting on lust didn't suit their needs right now. They'd better stay on task and find a way to reduce carnal distractions.

A fourth headlamp beam glimmered in the trees. Clomping feet and a whinny caught his ears. Leaves parted, and a figure emerged from the jungle's black cauldron of a belly. A horse came into view. White as ivory and topped by a short-haired woman in cutoffs and cowboy boots, the well-behaved steed trotted over.

The rider pulled on reins, halting her mount a couple of feet away from Jonnie. Equestrian smells of hay, leather, and beast washed over Jonnie's senses while he wondered who this new person was. As Carlos helped the stranger dismount, the horse stomped a foot and snorted.

Jonnie's eyes widened when he saw that the woman was hugely pregnant. A baggy men's flannel engulfed her petite, swallowed-a-bowling-ball frame. She approached, her expression difficult to read, even in the harsh, bluish glare of the light strapped to her forehead. Neutral tending towards skeptical, perhaps, her wholesome and pretty face was unsmiling though not frowning either.

"Welcome." Her tone was polite but crisp. "Thanks, Carlos. I can take it from here."

"Yes, ma'am." Carlos left the way they'd came, and in an instant the jungle absorbed him.

A bit of worry needled Jonnie, though he supposed the guide was at home in this environment and could make his way back to the boat just fine. He and Eve, though, were neither at home nor at peace with the jungle wilds. And now, they were stranded. Though this woman greeting them looked harmless, a young blonde with child, he needed to remember that he and Eve were strangers here. On the turf of others. Meaning he ought to keep his protective instincts, instincts he'd never really had to use, keen.

"I'm Taylor." The pregnant horsewoman stuck out a hand.

"Jonnie Tollens. How do you do?" Jonnie shook, finding Taylor's handshake strong and confident. A good sign. He'd protect both women if he had to, but this one seemed set up here in the way that Carlos did.

"Eve. Nice to meet you." The women shook hands. Without another word, Taylor took hold of a rope attached to her horse's bridle and led everyone down another path. This one was colder, darker, less trampled. Its smell was rich with the mineral essence of fertile soil.

"Got some rain recently?" A shiver made gooseflesh burst on his arms, and for a second he considered rooting in his pack for a jacket but nixed the notion. He didn't want to look scatterbrained in front of their guest, in case she was sizing them up.

She hitched a shoulder. "It's always like this."

They walked for another ten or so minutes, the only sounds coming from the horse, the trees, and their three sets of feet. Taylor wasn't much of a conversationalist, and he got it. He was grateful to her for taking them in in the first place, and it was selfish to expect a warm welcome like one might get at a bed and breakfast. He and Eve hadn't yet earned these people's trust, not by a long shot.

"When are you due?" Eve asked.

"Any day now." Yet her breathing was steady and unlabored as they hiked, a marker of fantastic endurance and fitness. "My husband tried to insist on coming out to pick you guys up, but I need the exercise." She tossed a glance over her shoulder and winked. "Besides, he's way scarier than I am. Didn't want him running the two of you off."

"Scarier?" Normally, Jonnie would have been more than a little unnerved. He wasn't a huge or ripped man. Personality-wise, he was an artist and a friend, and not some hulking alpha male bruiser. Except now he had cool new moves and was more than a little curious about Mr. Scary.

In the distance, a wolf howled, followed by the wild whoops of several others. Taylor offered another smirk. Jonnie quirked a brow.

"Showoff." Taylor chuckled.

He and Eve exchanged looks. The slight upturn of her lips and glimmer in her eye let him know she wasn't afraid either. His brave woman. Well, not his exactly, but...

"Alright, welcome to your five-star hotel," Taylor said. A second clearing emerged, yet this one held three enclosures. Each structure, about the size of a modest den, consisted of a wooden foundation elevated several feet off the ground by four thick posts. On each flat surface sat two pairs of bunk beds, visible through sheer tents of mosquito netting.

"We do eco tours." Taylor tied her horse to a tree. She motioned with a hand, walking up a short set of lumber steps and parting a mesh curtain. "It's how we sustain ourselves, other than hunting and farming and selling our wares at the market. Oh. That reminds me." Taylor went to a dresser and pulled open a drawer with a soft wooden squeak. Rummaging sounds ensued.

"Ugh, where did he put it?" The pregnant woman opened and closed creaky drawers.

Jonnie set his pack down, heat rising from crotch to hairline as he realized that he and Eve would be sleeping in such close quarters.

"Top or bottom?" A naughty, self-aware lilt lifted Eve's speech as she shed her backpack and leaned against the bunk's ladder. In sensible shorts that wrapped around her curvy hips and a snug tee shirt, Eve had him wondering what color bra and panties she'd chosen. If the hair between her legs matched the dark curls topping her head. He'd sure like to slide into her.

"I can go either way." And boy, could he. He could pound Eve from behind, lie on his back while she fucked him senseless. Urge her to her knees and feed her his cock. Finger and lick her cunt.

"A switch, are you?" Her eyes gleamed, seductive even with that clunky piece of camping gear stuck to her face.

He gave her nothing more than a shrug in reply. He'd explored all sorts of things, with both men and women, in the pursuit of pleasure for his partners and himself. He supposed that made him bisexual, though he'd always just thought of himself as having an anything goes mentality. Jonnie was a trysexual. He'd try anything.

"I'm so intrigued, it's not even funny," she said.

Right now, more than anything, he longed to alleviate Eve's intrigue.

"Argh, here it is. No playing grab ass until you drink this, Lestat." Two hard pats to his arm broke the flirtatious mood. In her hand, Taylor held a plastic two-liter soda bottle with the label ripped off. Some thick substance the color of tomato soup filled it halfway.

"What is it?"

Taylor poked the bottle into his shoulder. "The stuff that'll keep you from dying of heatstroke when dawn breaks tomorrow."

His heart leapt. "How did you know...that I was a...what I was?"

The expat rolled her eyes. "You think we didn't vet the shit out of both of you before agreeing to take you in?"

He took the bottle from her and tilted it in her direction. "Touché. Well, cheers." Jonnie unscrewed the cap, paused for a breath, and chugged. The thick brew, pungent and bitter and tasting of all sorts of herbs and vegetation, made his mouth water and his gag reflex lurch. Nausea clamped down on his guts as the stuff hit his stomach, but he forced himself not to puke as he drank the shite until it was gone.

"Bloody hell," he gasped when he was through. "What the fuck did you feed me, love?"

"Ayahuasca. It's a sacred hallucinogen our shamans concoct using certain leaves and roots. Most people take it for the intense visions as part of a spiritual quest, but we found out that it also keeps vampires alive. So those of you who can't or choose not to use blood can take it for said purpose. Tomorrow I'll show you how to make it yourself and where to buy the ingredients when you fly back home. Until then, enjoy your ride through the cosmos, and I'll see you in the morning."

Taylor patted his stomach, took the empty and shoved it in her backpack, and rejoined her horse. She mounted up and rode off into the jungle.

Ride through the cosmos?

NINE

RESTLESS AND SWEATY IN HER TOP BUNK, EVE STARED AT THE triangular apex of the translucent cloth roof while its fabric flapped gently. A light, hot breeze trickled through netting walls. The cries of monkeys and other nocturnal jungle fauna supplied a soundtrack of life.

Though she could make out the movement of leaves dancing in the minimal wind, a cloud cover had rolled in and blotted out the stars and moon. She took in the sawdust scent of what had to be a new structure, a smell of homey, rustic freshness that should have comforted her.

Darkness pushed in from all sides, so heavy her bones felt like lead. Itchy sheets chafed her overheated, sticky skin. Jittery energy as restless as the leg she couldn't stop shaking filled her belly.

Taylor had made it sound like Jonnie would go on some wild and trippy ride, but instead of flying through a hallucinogenic cosmos, the lucky bastard slept peacefully in the bed below her.

Though she envied his tranquility, empathy for him underscored the petty emotion. From the sounds of things, they'd found a promising solution to his problem with this ayahuasca.

No promising info on the squirrel issue or Lacey conundrum lay on the foreseeable horizon. Eve had felt a little invisible in front of Taylor, like Jonnie's affliction was the only thing on her and her community's radar. A lump cemented in her chest. Had Jonnie even told these people that Eve had a stake in coming here? Did anyone involved care, or was it all about him?

If the latter was in fact the case, then what in the fuck was she doing down here, at the edge of civilization? Looking at mosquito netting, her hands tangled in her own hair as she begged some unknown sandman for the blessing of sleep. Frustration cinched her midsection, making it tough to breathe. She had a job, a life, and didn't make a point of chasing men around the world.

Perhaps a drink of water would clear her head. She hadn't packed her Ambien alongside the malaria pills Jonnie's assistant managed to scare up at the last minute, and of course her dumb ass regretted her dubious decision to seek natural sleep on the Peru trip.

How misguided, to think her fear of sleep wouldn't chase her down here. God, she'd been thinking like a naïve college kid with *Walden* shoved in her backpack, seduced by a facile fantasy that retreating into nature would cure her woes, salve her wound. At least the demon rat hadn't reared its skinned head. The absurdity of it all startled a barking laugh out of Eve as she adjusted her body and made her way down the bunk bed ladder.

Midway to the ground, a warm hand gripped her ankle.

"I care," Jonnie said in a calm, reassuring voice. "And I told them as much about you as I did about me. We're in this together, Eve. Don't forget it." He let go of her leg.

She hopped off the ladder, coming to stand on the unpainted lumber floor. He lay there in his bottom bunk, on top of the sheets, in blue silk boxers and nothing else. The ultimate distraction from her hamster wheel of angsty ruminations.

At the sight of so much of his exposed, taut flesh, her panties dampened. His legs were crossed at the ankle, a position showing off the flexed curve of his thigh muscle. Muggy humidity heightened her senses, steering her mind to thoughts of nakedness and sweat. Bodies banging together in primal abandon.

"Have you always been able to read my thoughts?" More curious than scared or offended, she sat next to him on the bed, fighting the urge to touch. He scooted a few inches closer to the wall to make room for her.

"No. It's what I drank. It's incredible, Eve. I feel things inside of me, speaking to me. Truths. I see my DNA changing, merging. There are snakes, everywhere, in this room. But they aren't bad. They are sacred, ancient, wise. It's this new me, and I'm merging into it completely. And it isn't bad. It's true and right and good."

Though amazed, she tensed in jealousy. Shame for her selfishness kicked in. What the hell was her problem? She'd come to Peru to help him, and now she resented him for finding closure simply because it hadn't come to her as quickly.

"That's amazing, Jonnie." An attempt to produce enthusiasm didn't make it into her tone, and her shoulders slumped. She felt about an inch tall, at once petty and petulant, inconsequential and unimportant.

He closed his eyes, shook his head, opened his lids. "I'm sorry for rambling. I'm just overwhelmed at the moment. But I meant it, Eve. Your—our—monster, the situation with the girl...I haven't forgotten. I won't leave here until you've found peace. Understand?" He cut a gaze to her, and its intensity made a tingle comprised of both hot and cold parts chase down her spine.

"I do. Thank you. I need to stop moping." She rubbed raw and tired eyes, her thoughts a soupy cloud. Dwelling on her problems wouldn't do her any good. She needed to start fresh in the morning, find someone in the shifter pack with whom she could discuss the haunting. With all his talk about star children and cosmic nodes, Carlos had intimated that this was the place to address such topics.

"Like what, love?" With gentle, callused fingers, he grazed the underside of her arm.

The stiff mattress squeaked as it adjusted beneath her. "I can't sort out my thoughts right now. Sometimes I feel like I'd give up a lot to have a normal mind."

He kept up his strokes, gaze drifting to her face. "Mustn't be easy, eh? Dealing with all those souls? Listening to them and their problems. And then I come along, all 'me, me, me.' More of the same, in a sense."

She shrugged. Helping others was what she did, and she did not resent her gift. But having someone to talk to about her own stuff was nice. Someone who understood and could relate. Therapist couldn't. Lord knows Eve had tried and failed to bond with enough of them.

"I consider it a blessing. But I wonder, too. If I'm more open than most people. If things slip through and get to me. If I'm more susceptible to curses." What else could explain the rodent, a menace that was, as far as she could tell, connected to Lacey and her disgruntled parents?

Jonnie rested a palm against the curve of her waist. "One thing I managed to learn was you can't obsess over this shite all of the time. It'll suck you dry. You have to try and take mental breaks when you can. Remember how to smile."

And she did manage a wan half-smile, resisting the temptation to crack a joke about his 'suck you dry' comment. She stole a shameless peek at those delectable flashes of tattoo ink above his waistband. "I smile sometimes."

"I know." His voice took on a husky, gravely timbre. Her pussy slicked again, and the musty smell of his excitement graced her nose. A rising column of arousal pressed into the thin material of his underwear.

Jonnie pressed his hand to the small of her back, urging her body to his. "It's more like a siren's smirk I'd say, but I'm going to wager you like what you see. That true?" His lips parted, eyes hooded with lust.

She rolled on top of him. Fuck it. She wanted him, he was hot, and the thought of focusing on anything other than horrifying supernatural things sounded like heaven. Like a vacation from her own mind, and they were on vacation after all. A place where they could escape, together.

"Yes." She peeled off her shirt and tossed it to the ground, situating her body on Jonnie's lap so she hovered an inch or so above his erection. The top bunk scraped against her head, boxing them into a forced proximity that made the position even sexier. "But why are you asking me questions if you can read my thoughts and all?"

He sent those deft fingers of his up her back, caressing a route to her bra. He unclasped the hook on the first try, moaning as he pulled the elastic straps down her arms. "It's more like a flow of energy, like I'm a radio transmitter picking up bits and pieces of your conscious thought."

"What about what's in my subconscious?" She freed herself of her undergarment and cast it aside, sending it to join the shirt in a pile. Eve's mental chatter quieted into a lull of bliss. She savored the moment, temporarily paroled from the prison of her thoughts. Time disappeared, rendering everything perfect. Divine. Nothing but the good vibes of fading into another person, of truly connecting, remained. Her stiff muscles softened, the surface of her skin newly sensitive.

"Harder to explain. Not sure I completely understand. It's like an energy flow, a wavelength. An emotional meld. What happened to us on the trail is an example."

He cupped her breasts, each mound spilling slightly out of his palms. With his thumb pads, he rubbed the hard buds of her nipples in little circles. She sucked in a sharp breath at the pleasurable ache.

In a way, they'd already shared a tremendous amount of intimacy through their previous mental and emotional unions. The dream, their conjoined out-of-body experiences on the trail. Hell, perhaps their impending act would amount to a kind of sex magic. A sacred pagan ritual that would raise the vibrational frequency and summon epiphanies. Perhaps they could lure solutions from their bodies, like spirits hailed through a séance.

She leaned down and pressed her lips to his, sick of worries and fears. The flavor of antiseptic mouthwash mingling with his personal taste chased those dark clouds away. Eve kissed harder, while Jonnie pinched her nipples. The warm cavern of his mouth welcomed her, swallowing her troubles. Their tongues played, eager as they danced, exploring.

He moaned against her lips, erection pressing stiff as a bar between her legs. She ground her hips. He matched her thrusts. They kissed like they wanted to steal each others breath. A floating sensation overcame Eve as she lost track of where she ended and her lover began. It was spiritual, perfect, physically intense yet so much more. She'd never wanted anything or anyone like this. Never felt anything like this. Her chest heaved against his stroking hands and his fast fingers.

Her tongue brushed a sharp point—she gasped and her clit jerked. Game on.

Catching quickened breath, she drew back and pressed a palm against the wood above her head, gaining enough space to sit up a bit straighter. He gripped her hips and moved her, slowly, back and forth against his erection. So clearly lost to sensation, he bowed his back and arched his neck sharply enough to bring the jut of his Adam's apple into relief, letting out a sharp grunt.

Smirking like some wicked, fecund sex goddess, Eve kept up her thrusts. She gyrated her hips in circles, wet beneath her thin cotton shorts, shameless and wanton in the night. Fucking in the dark forest like a witch performing a heathen ritual.

She swung a leg over his hip and dismounted him, coming to kneel on the rough, unvarnished floor. Wood splinters pricked her knees, the slight pain enhancing her arousal in kinky, unexpected ways.

Eve pushed her own shorts down her thighs, teasing herself with the feel of humidity on her exposed crotch. Still air tickled her pussy lips, so saturated it made her nether hairs curl.

Mouth watering, she pulled on Jonnie's elastic waistband. He propped on his elbows, head tilted at a slight angle as he regarded her while she prepared to get to work.

She urged his silky boxers over the cock tenting them, bringing the fabric to rest at his thighs. His length, long like she'd pictured and thicker than his frame would suggest, curved upward. Eve dragged a finger down one of his lines of tattoo ink, learning his body art.

"What do they represent?" The dual, vertical rows slashed down each half of his pelvis like cat scratches. The full picture resembled the ones she'd formed in her mind, in her fantasies.

"They're latitudinal lines." He spoke in a low voice rough with excitement. Still fingering the marks, Eve looked up into Jonnie's face. He'd changed, his features had sharpened and darkened to the mask of the dream. Through his parted lips, fang points peeked out.

She leaned forward and kissed his shaft, trailing her lips down to his high, tight balls. His intimate scent of soap and musk sent another jolt of desire into her sex. "Of where?"

"Um." A clipped laugh. "You're really going to force me to use my brain cells right now, aren't you?"

"Yes." She licked the rigid seam dividing his sac. Perhaps part of her wanted to gain the upper hand on him sexually as some sort of payback for snaring her in his twisted web of a life.

She'd flown in willingly, a curious little fly, but still. In the moment she held a measure of power, the ability to make him a servant to the pleasure she rationed out. To the leverage she wielded.

With a slow hand, he petted her hair. "If you look closely—but I doubt you can see them in this light—you'll see numbers. Coordinates. They're locations. Each one represents somewhere our tour stopped, a place that was important to me. Brian and I each got our own versions of a tattoo designed to turn our bodies into journals."

Jonnie's gentle touch, how he stroked her locks like they were made of the finest silks, stirred a new ingredient into the simmering stew of her feelings. A soft, yielding, gentle element.

They were just two lonely, strange people, moving together under cover of night. Somehow, his touch registered that. Acknowledged that. Perhaps she was merely projecting more tender feelings onto him, maybe they were just fucking. But in her heart, she knew that the crudest explanation wasn't true.

The brush of his fingertips against her scalp, the meticulous exploration of her corkscrew curls like they were strands of DNA holding secrets to the universe, were not the touches of a man who just wanted to get off, wanted his dick sucked.

Eve laid off her kisses and rose, kicking aside her shorts in the process. She stood before him naked. His face hadn't changed back. Features still bore the serpentine slope of a brow, the catlike eyes and cheekbones fiercer than any found on a normal human.

"Can you control it?" She crawled back into the cramped twin bed, her naked body pressed against his. She swept her index finger over his eyebrow, admiring the cut of his striking bones.

Jonnie shook his head. "Not really." His expression was neutral, hard to read. Resigned, or wistful.

Heart heavy and limbs fluid, Eve returned to straddle Jonnie. She pressed her palms into his chest, feeling the rigid spear of his cock beneath the dampness of her lust.

Hovering there, staring into his chilling, uncanny face, she appreciated him. The effect was like staring into some esoteric window, into a portal to an ancient forest, a place where all manner of druids and fairies and grumpkins ran wild.

But she stared into her own brain stem, too, into something buried and latent. For an instant, clouds parted, delivering a fast flash of moonlight through their bunk. It revealed a miniscule crisscross of lines networking the tops of his hands. Like faint scales. As the light stole across his angular face, a brief gleam flashed in his green irises. It drew attention to the vertical black slits of his pupils.

A chill raced down her spine at the same time molten heat melted her sex. He was a monster. And she should have been horrified or alarmed, but she was too damn busy being wildly aroused by the dangerous, novel impossibility.

"I've had my tubes tied." She'd steeled her commitment to remain childfree by choice awhile ago. Kids didn't belong in her world. Simple as that.

He licked his lips, chest rising and falling with accelerated breath. "Good. I'm clean."

"Same."

"So what are you waiting for?" A tantalizing smirk graced his stunning face.

She grabbed the base of his hard penis and slid down, impaling herself with his length. The fullness of penetration made her moan, tingle, thrust. He clamped his hands on her hips and urged her, repeating the back and forth motion he'd used earlier. She moved, undulating, in tune with some unseen force pulsing and chanting beyond the trees.

Jonnie dropped a hand between her legs, finding her bulging clit with his thumb. He rubbed, up and down, in a steady rhythm that soon had her writhing and gasping. She quickened her pace, rocking against him as the sweet pressure built, coiling tight and hot in her core until she could snap like a rubber band. But he just kept stroking, and she continued to soar as her pleasure built to bliss, to crazed and brutal need—

At the moment of truth, she lurched forward, feral and out of her mind, and pinned his earlobe between her teeth.

"Bite me," she hissed, twisting one of his nipple rings between her fingers. All she wanted was the pain, the abject abandon of fiendish, inhuman fangs sinking into her neck. Sweet explosions wracked her, a series of pulsing shocks.

Moaning as she came apart, she anticipated his bite, the thought enhancing her climax. Yes, yes, he would spill her blood, drink her blood, make her dizzy. Make her into a vampire. Make her into someone, something, different than who she was.

"Eve, I…" His protest came out a grunt as his body tensed beneath her, his hips bouncing as he plunged in and out. He flicked her clit faster, wringing out every drop of the orgasm from her body.

"Please, please," she whined as the shocks rolled through, unhinging her soul from her body, splintering her world. Why couldn't he give it to her? The one final piece to take her, make her, ruin her.

"Not now," he grunted out, muscles clenching. He sent his free hand to her butt and smacked twice, filling her ears with the obscene sound of wet skin slapping.

She screamed in frustration and relief, riding out the end of the hard, angry orgasm.

He squeezed her ass desperately as a long, tortured groan erupted from his throat. He bucked underneath her, pumping through his release as warm fluid soaked her insides.

She wound down with a gradual tapering of bursts into aftershocks. He stopped moaning and slackened against her chest.

Tears pricked her eyes, and a burning ache slammed her chest. She peeled her slick flesh from his with a wet suction pop.

"Eve, wait," Jonnie whispered, out of breath as he reached for her hand.

His face had returned to normal, but his appearance had nothing to do with why she couldn't look at him. She turned her face to the discarded clothes pile, picking them up and yanking them on with shaking hands.

Nausea twisted her insides. He'd held back from her. Deemed her unworthy of exploring total abandon together. Rejected her at her most vulnerable, pushed her aside when she'd yearned to venture to new depths together. Served her right, she supposed. She couldn't be trusted with souls, not always. Couldn't be trusted with a risk. Stupid of her, to offer herself up in the most exposed of ways. He probably thought turning her would unleash some new evil on the world or embolden the demon. And maybe it would. There was a good chance she was being irresponsible here, reckless. But she wanted what she wanted and was okay with being a disaster as long as she had someone to fall with. Which, apparently, she didn't.

"Leave me alone." Sticky perspiration coating her skin made tugging her clothes on a challenge. A seam on her shirt ripped, making her feel slovenly and gross. She saw red. Flames burst in her stomach. "Shit. Fuck."

"Eve. Let me explain. Let me talk to you. There are reasons." He sat up in bed, pleading in a stern yet gentle way that only made her more upset. Of course, he had to be the voice of reason, too.

"I said leave me alone, okay?" She strangled the small part of her that yearned to jump into his arms, seek comfort, and cry. Those things weren't for her. Nobody refilled *her* well. That wasn't how it worked.

"Please don't push me away like this. You don't have to."

She stormed up the ladder, curled into a ball, and pulled the sheets over her head. An hour or so of tense, hateful insomnia later, Eve was twisted up inside a blanket and staring into the nascent beginnings of dawn, a scabby hue discoloring the space above the trees.

A feminine shriek cut through dour, tepid stillness, stabbing a needle full of scuzzy adrenaline into Eve's hardened heart.

TEN

JONNIE UNDERSTOOD, HE DID. EVE HURT. SHE SUFFERED FROM emotional undernourishment, hunger for care and comfort that she wasn't sure how to ask for. Instead, she reached out then lashed out, in a cycle of advance and retreat.

He formed a hunch that the pattern repeated as she struggled to figure out how to lean on others, set boundaries, and prioritize her own needs.

His mum and sisters fought similar inner battles as Eve. They shouldered the guilt, the burden, the bone and soul-crushing physical and emotional labor that came with caring for Cara.

Boundless, formless, endless routines involved triage staff and appointments and an ever-expanding cast of professional characters spouting jargon-filled advice and opinions. Their husbands and brothers, himself and his pop included, helped, but it wasn't the same. Burdens of care fell upon women. And as soon as he had phone service again, he'd call and check on his family.

But right now, he needed to tend to Eve. Help her cope, find her balance, ease her toil. But what had he done instead? Gone and fucked her, a woman whose feelings he cared about, like some meaningless conquest. *You stupid, horny sod.*

He plastered a damp palm onto his warm forehead, guilt as sticky as the sweat on his brow. "I'm sorry, Evelyn."

Rustling sounds came from her top bunk. "You heard the scream." She stated the fact in a tone as flat as the wooden slats above his eyes.

He had, and he got it. Freaking out would accomplishing nothing. They needed to remain calm in the face of new madness.

"Yes. But that could have been due to anything. We can't worry about it until we know more. Can we please talk about what happened between us?" Jonnie cared more about Eve's feelings than the sharp yell from far away. If it became a problem, they'd deal with it.

Of course he'd wanted to bite her, but acting impulsively on his wants could backfire badly. What if he got hooked on her blood? Or couldn't stop drinking and killed her by mistake?

He'd been a vampire for a mere twenty years, and what he knew of his symptoms, his *powers*, continued to unfold in a disturbing rollout of surprise reveals. Why would he put her at risk for tragedy, accept her desire to put herself at said risk?

Creaks and groans issued from the wood as she shifted her weight. "What's there to talk about? I acted like some groupie with kitty litter for brains, and you screwed me like you'd screw any one of them. The end."

A distinct quiver of shame wobbled in her caustic tone, yet a vise clamped his chest. Anger flashed through him. She knew nothing about his sex life and had no right to judge anyone involved in said sex life. He sprung from bed and crawled up the ladder, finding her sulking on her mattress with her arms crossed. "You're being cruel and unfair, Eve."

"Go away." The lingering tremble in her voice neutralized an attempt at driving him off.

"Eve. We had sex. Perhaps it was a mistake. But you have no right to lash out at me like this. I know you're upset, but believe me when I tell you that by not biting you, I was trying to protect you."

She uncurled her arms and wiped an eye, back bowing and ribcage collapsing as her posture caved. "Ignore me. My head's a wreck, and I can't sleep."

What little remained of his aggravation tempered to concern. Of course he wouldn't ignore her. Who could reasonably be expected to stay cool and collected amidst this madness? Lesser people would have cracked long ago.

He touched her smooth upper arm. "I wasn't using you for quick sex. I got swept up in the moment, but I didn't bite you because I care about you. And because I care about you, I can't bear to see you like this. Try to get some rest, okay? For me?" He tossed optimism into the universe like a dart thrown in a dark room.

She blew a ragged exhale from her lungs. The beginnings of a smile twitched her lips. "Okay."

Jonnie smiled too, though his was bigger. He adored seeing signs of life animating her face.

"I apologize for snapping at you. I'm going to try for a nap before Taylor gets here." The word "try" fell from her mouth as a heavy stone of pessimism.

"You can do it, love." He leaned in and dropped a kiss to her shoulder, smelling himself on her and cherishing the trace remainder of their intimacy. Their supposed *mistake*.

Eve laid a squeeze on his forearm before she pulled the sheet to her neck and closed her eyes. "Thank you."

Jonnie climbed back down and rooted in his pack, excavating the mystery novel he'd brought. He struggled to concentrate for a few pages, admitting defeat after reading a paragraph three times. Fortunately, not too much time passed before a faint, horsey whinny broke through the jungle clutter of chirps and bird calls.

He threw the paperback on the bed and tugged clean shorts and a tee shirt from his bag. Took out his phone and checked—still no signal bars. Sighing, he stuck the thing in his back pocket in case they had service in the village, and changed clothes.

Taylor emerged on horseback, pregnant as ever in polyester athletic shorts and layered tank tops. He parted the mesh doorway and walked out to greet her, sweat beading on his forehead at the first direct lick of rainforest atmosphere.

She tied off her horse and turned to Jonnie, planting her hands on her slim hips as she did.

"Morning," Jonnie said, wincing on the inside as he registered Taylor's severe countenance. His grandma Priyanka used to claim that foul moods in the morning brought bad tidings for the rest of the day, and all signs so far pointed them in a negative direction.

"What does she know about poltergeists and exorcisms?" Taylor's stern, low tone and the scowl knitting her brow made it clear small talk would fall by the wayside.

"Hazarding a wild guess that whatever triggered that scream earlier relates to exorcisms and poltergeists."

With a single, tense nod, Taylor marched up the lumber steps and breached the tent's triangular doorway. "Wait until you see what poor Kathleen found on her morning walk."

"Eve's sleeping." Beside Jonnie, the horse vocalized, as if laughing at the idea that Taylor would back off her onslaught.

Taylor barked, "Hey. Wake up. You didn't say anything about a haunting or a familiar or whatever it is you've got tailing you." From inside the big tent, groans and movement came as Taylor tugged on Eve's covers.

A moaning yawn begged for more rest. "You said you vetted me. Can I please lie down for a minute? I haven't slept in—"

"Yeah, well, we clearly missed something. Talk. Spill. Now, or I send you both up the river before the sun rises the rest of the way."

Jonnie bounded up the steps, hastening to Eve's bedside. Taylor tapped a foot, her hands grafted to a spot below her bulging pregnancy.

Face drawn with exhaustion, Eve gave Taylor the gist. Lacey, the cult parents, her history with the zombie rodent. The gestalt of the story, in all its insanity, broke Jonnie's heart. From the bite of quiet shame and hurt in Eve's voice, Jonnie drew sad conclusions. The whole ordeal had ground her spirit into dust.

Taylor scoffed as she threw up her hands, bringing them to rest on the front of her belly. "How could you keep this from us? Do you have any idea what you inflicted upon our home? I don't know what you're mixed up in, but it's put us all at risk. Our babies. And if you knew what we suffered through last fall, you'd understand why I can't have evil near us. Never again."

Eve hung her head, mop of hair blocking her face from Taylor's gaze. "I understand."

"It isn't Eve's fault," Jonnie interjected. He turned to Taylor. "She needs help. We need help. All she does is give and give, trying to help people in this life and beyond. Something went awry, but she didn't mean for it to happen. Give her a break and help us figure out how to lift this bloody curse."

Taylor's jaw clenched. "Bloody curse is right, Mr. Brit. Get out." She pointed at the door.

"It wants me." Eve spoke in a tone pummeled into the flat affect of resigned defeat. "Bring me to it."

"Oh, no way in hell are you setting foot anywhere near our encampment."

Of course he could glamour Taylor, though Jonnie refused to use coercion or deceit to insist his way into their Peruvians' territory. Because as much as he hated to admit it, he couldn't argue with Taylor's logic.

Taylor narrowed her eyes at him. "I can see the gears in your head turning. I'm well acquainted with vampires. The part about needing to be invited in is real. And as a water divinatory, I'm immune to your tricks in the first place. Ditch any notions of mind control like you'd kick a smoking habit."

Eve sat up straighter and cocked her head. "What's a water divinatory?"

"None of your business, Morticia."

"What a fine hostess we have here." Though Eve spackled on the sarcasm, watery hurt liquefied her eyes. Her profession was a sore spot that Taylor, in her anger, couldn't help herself from striking.

With the Peru excursion circling the drain, Jonnie put up his hands in the universal gesture of surrender. But he didn't give up. "Taylor, love, you have grounds for being upset. Pissed off, in fact. And you have every right to protect your home and family. But we're here because we're desperate. My niece is dying, my condition's worsening, and I'm losing faith. Eve provides a valuable service to her community, and she is in desperate need of some spiritual and psychic peace right now. We're good people. We're trying our best. This is the last stop on the line for us."

His heart poured out of his chest alongside his confession. Hope hung in the air, one remaining pearl suspended by a flimsy thread.

Taylor clamped her unpainted lips shut. Worry scrunched her smooth young brow into a puckered knot. With an exhale, her face released tension, smoothing to communicate resigned acceptance. "My father built a teleportation machine in his basement and had agreed to have me programmed to lure supernatural creatures to Scarab. That's how forces outside of my control were screwing with me. You've heard of Scarab." The glance she chanced at Jonnie mirrored her droll statement, matching the bitter aftertaste of her voice.

"They did this to me." He took Eve's hand and squeezed. "To us."

Eve interlaced their fingers, a nonverbal gesture speaking volumes. The hand clasp symbolized a coalescence of their bond. Their flesh latticed together, stitching their two halves into a whole. A team.

For a few beats, Taylor stared at the joined hands. "Wait here."

And off she went, pausing as she parted the screen to afford him a dry, savvy look. "I love your band."

Accepting the twig of an olive branch her parting words offered, Jonnie waved the mother-to-be goodbye. She untethered her mount and set off, the horse's bottom vanishing into the trees as a tail the color of chalk flicked away bugs and foliage.

Jonnie crawled into the top bunk and held Eve. Held her in silence, caressing comforts into her hair and back. The feel of her sweat-damp skin, velvet-soft even for a woman, hatched within him a nest full of instincts. To care, to soothe. To defend and protect. His chest swelled, a balloon filled and buoyed with warm water.

"I'm sorry." He'd never heard anything more earnest than her apology. Or more vulnerable, or more encompassing of so much.

He'd sunk inside of her, though the shy flower of *them* waited until this moment after the physical closeness to unfold into beauty.

"I know, Eve, but you needn't be. Let it out. Let it go. I'm here. I've got you."

In his arms, she jerked. Made a soft sound, like a cross between a mew and a gasp. Twitches came faster.

"I'm here. I've got you. Let it go." He wrapped his arms tight around her feminine curves like his embrace could erase the tension in her body, soothe the sadness in her heart and soul. At the same time, he willed his hug to act as a barrier, preventing any more sorrow and unrest from storming the gates of her psyche. Eve had endured enough.

A tense and release of muscle, and she let her cries go. Big ones, sobs, poured. He swore he heard cracks breaking deep inside of her as she gave in. Tears soaked his shirt straight through, and he held on tight.

He'd comforted many a crying woman and gotten rather good at it. His mum and sisters, when devastated by the latest facet of the tragedy. Of less importance but with more shame, women who shared his bed and struggled to accept that the relationship would not extend past the tour stop.

He closed his eyes and hummed a favorite Fyre tune, brushing his nose and lips into Eve's scalp as he offered solace as best he could. Wails tapered to sniffs. A sigh, then silence. Her body slackened in limp abandon. Jonnie lowered her onto the pillow while she snored softly.

As she found respite in sleep, his head cleared with the onset of peace.

With steps taking care not to disturb her, he descended the bunk ladder and returned to his bed. Jonnie had gotten comfortable and finished half of the mystery novel before a stir of brush accompanied by gagging coughs and curses turned his head.

His hands stiffened to a rigor mortis of shock as a horrid sight emerged from the trail. The book fell, landing with a muted thump.

Four men trudged, working together to hoist a crucifix fashioned from rotted tree branches. It towered above the tallest man's head, bearing the body of a sacrifice.

But it wasn't a person nailed to the cross. No, the pale body was no bigger than a stuffed rabbit, itty bitty arms pulled into a T. Its head, as red as a cherry lollipop, glistened in the sun as the gang of four hauled it across the clearing separating the covered bunks from the jungle perimeter.

Jonnie ran out of the big tent and into the patchy grass. Two lads plunked the end of the cross onto the ground and stood in silence, faces stony with accusation as they held it in place.

The zombie rodent hung from the cross, death mask of a face a gruesome contrast against mangy white fur.

"Ms. Adyemi?" The high-pitched voice of a young woman shook with terror as it came from the squirrel's mouth. "Help me. Help. It hurts, it burns. It burns!" Following this gut-shredding plea came a metallic shriek so abject that Jonnie grimaced in horror. Glistening jaw hanging slack, the animal's skull lolled to the side, slippery muscles as pink as raw steaks. A trickle of blood crept down the scraggly branch.

Jonnie's edges went fuzzy. His tongue turned to cotton. The entirety of him sinking to hell, he shook his head.

A built man with a black ponytail walked out from behind the aberration, his dark eyes ablaze with disdain. A few decisive steps and he stood before Jonnie, neither fearful nor intimidating. The man was simply *being* in the awful moment, rendering his mere existence into a silent act of performance artistry.

"We can't have you bringing this shit around here." He delivered brusque words in an accent that was hard to place, facial muscles softening as if extending an apology. "My wife, you met her, she's about to have a baby."

"It's following Eve. And me. I...I don't want to be any trouble to you, but I've hit a wall. And you know what it's like, to care for someone. Did you find it nailed up like this?"

The big brown man nodded and pulled up his tee shirt collar to wipe his brow. "I can't take any risks, man. Not now."

"I realize that. But hear me out. The company that sold me this treatment is called Scarab. You've heard of them."

Taylor's husband scowled, clenching his teeth. "I was hoping never to hear that name again. Not after the trial."

"Appears they've just gone deeper underground. And look, man, I'll level with you. All I want is to make an arrangement to buy some of your organic blood substitute, stock up a supply to last me a good long while. But the woman in there is special." He bent his thumb in the direction of the hut to where Eve slept.

The big guy listened while the other three men looked on in silence, their skepticism palpable.

"I want to help her find the peace she needs. She performs a selfless, admirable service, and she's tortured. By this monster. By what happened with the girl. And I was hoping, well, by being here we'd find some answers. Taylor can divine the water, right?"

A proud smile from the husband. "Yeah."

"The two of them can work together. Combine their powers and look for mystical solutions. In return, I'll buy enough of that dreadful orange goop to keep your clan sustainable for the next five years. You won't have to host another obnoxious European businessman for an eco tour or perform a healing ritual on a spoiled American celebrity for a good long while if you don't want to."

"What if he's full of shit?" A man with a red Viking beard and ham hocks of biceps bulging under his leather vest piped up. "Trying to sic this thing on us to get it off him. Pass the buck."

"Makes no sense." Jonnie sliced a cutting glance to the doubter. "There's no reason to believe that would work, that this little demon would forget about Eve and randomly latch onto you. It has a motive to torment her. No offense, but you aren't even close to blipping on its radar."

"Man's got a point." Mr. Taylor told the Viking, who curled his lip but grunted an acknowledgement. "Back up. You said Scarab performed a procedure on you that made you into a vampire?"

"Yes." It released a weight to confess to someone who understood. For whom supernatural creatures were normalized.

Mr. Taylor nodded. "Yeah. We've got a couple down here like that. Synthetically engineered vamps."

"And they sustain themselves with the ayahuasca?"

"Oh, yeah." Mr. Taylor gazed off into the jungle, swallowing a gulp that made his Adam's apple bob.

"But?"

Mr. Taylor struck a guarded pose, drawing back and tilting his head. "What do you suppose they do with the blood? The blood they take from you and the others?"

Jonnie's insides did a flip. Deep in his subconscious, a door opened. Beyond it lay a wall of question marks. He circled his thumb over one fading bruise, a penny-sized yellow stain speckled blue. "I always assumed they disposed of it, being toxic and all."

Mr. Taylor's scowl deepened. "You never want to assume anything with these people. Unless you're assuming the worst."

"So you're saying the degraded blood might have answers?"

"Not sure. It's a nagging thought I have, I suppose. Like my intuition's dogging me. Look, man, I'll see if I can get my wife back on board, but she's pretty upset about...you know." He bent his head at the crucified remains of the squirrel.

"I appreciate it." Jonnie patted the other man's hard upper arm. The guy was doing him a favor when he didn't have to, sticking his neck out for him and Eve.

"Don't thank me yet. And find something to do with this. Taylor will rip my guts out if I haul it back to the camp." On cue, the remaining three men lugged the cross to the sleeping quarters and leaned it against the elevated platform. The heinous little thing's head swayed side to side with the movement, settling to bend at an unnatural angle.

At least Eve was still asleep. "What's the plan?" Jonnie scanned the area for a tarp or large blanket or something equivalent to cover the monstrosity.

"Wait. I'll go talk to my wife and see if I can convince her to give you two another chance. If she agrees, she'll come on the horse. If not, Carlos will stop by to escort you away. Either way, I'll make sure someone brings you guys some food and a couple bottles of ayahuasca."

Jonnie's stomach growled. He hadn't eaten since yesterday. But a knotty unpleasantness eclipsed hunger when he realized that a couple bottles of ayahuasca wouldn't go far. Walking away from a failed mission would mean a coma. His fate lay in the hands of others, in their generosity and the hope that they would take a leap of faith on behalf of a fellow supernatural's life. "Thanks, man. I appreciate it."

"Name's Julian. And don't thank me yet. We both know who the alpha wolf is around here, but I have some strategies to soften her up." A randy wink made Jonnie nod with amusement and a quickening of hope.

The crew of locals hiked into the jungle while Jonnie got to work scrounging for something to disguise the ghastly surprise they'd dropped at his doorstep.

Eve deserved a pleasant awakening from the first good sleep she'd had in ages. Gathering handfuls of big dead leaves, Jonnie decided that, from here on out, he'd do his best to give Eve whatever fleeting snatches of happiness and contentment he could.

ELEVEN

Eve's heavy lids fluttered, opening to welcome light as she roused from blissful rest. Afternoon rays glazed the cabin wood and greenery beyond it in a reflective sheen, rendering the jungle into a piece of shiny kiln-fired pottery, like the kind she used to make in her amateur ceramics class.

Nourishing warmth coated her inside and out. Dust flecks hovered in yellow light. She stretched, joints popping, content as a lounging cat. A gently flapping tree leaf, so sparkly it rivaled glass, captured her sleepy attention. Some therapist once suggested she take up throwing pots to relieve her stress, but in the moment the beauty of the shimmering globe of a rainforest melted the concept of stress into nothing. A massive yoga inhale drew scents of damp earth and crisp water into her lungs.

Light and airy, she descended her bunk, finding Jonnie reading in bed. Concentration showed on his face, in his parted lips and quick eyes. He flipped a page near the end of his paperback. She watched for a second, a flutter dancing in her stomach. Nothing charmed her quite like a man who devoured books, and he was so engrossed he hadn't heard her approach.

Instead of bugging him, she slipped out of the tent and sat on its steps, getting comfortable on pulpy and unfinished lumber, the sort that spears splinters into your butt if you aren't careful.

Sawdust scents brought back memories of shopping for planks with her folks at the hardware store, gathering materials for the secluded cabin in the woods they'd built long ago.

She'd been around six when the onset of her abilities manifested. No seizures or other fanfare marked her initiation on that unseasonably mild Kentucky August, when she'd bounced off into the ragged trees with her best friend Jenny Dartmouth to gather sticks for marshmallows.

After many years, the memory blazed as vivid as a scene from a horror movie watched again and again. Her first glimpse had been the remains of a shot doe, butchered and cleaned, a tan and red ruin of life crumpled on her final bed of trampled sticks and scruffy land.

The past flashed in the forefront of Eve's awareness.

See me on. The feminine, elfish voice manifested in Eve's head as a tender command.

Jenny had dropped her kindling and run back to home base crying, leaving Eve and the slaughtered animal alone together.

See me on.

Bumbling her way through her initiation into soul work, she'd laid a hand on the deer's pelt, the fur short and coarse over hard ribs. The warm golden orb flowed right out of the animal's body and into her palm. She'd nestled the circle of light into the crook of a tree branch dotted with red berries, figuring the doe had liked to graze there, hoping that spending eternity in the spot might bring her peace.

No animal had spoken to her since, and the first person had taken years to reach out. Many elements of Eve's abilities remained shrouded in mystery. It wasn't like she had a wise relative with knowledge of a secret lineage of mysticism. Her book and web searches leading to articles about clairsentience sufficed.

Wind shook the Amazonian trees in shuffling rustles, snapping Eve from her musings.

"Lacey." The whispered word, a caliber too audible to qualify for immediate dismissal as imagination, chased the breeze.

"I'm doing my best," Eve said to the jungle. The next tremble of air brought with it a rank tendril of decomposition.

"Lacey."

"See me on." A different voice, ethereal and childlike in the androgynous way the doe's had been, curled upward in the distance.

Where are you? Clouds blotted sun, bringing forth darkening shadows. Gooseflesh prickled Eve's arms as her neck hairs stood. She told herself it was merely the cooling effect of the sudden temperature change, though from her subconscious a threat advanced.

"Witch bitch." A voice she knew, uncanny in its throatiness. Disruption shook the leaves. Sweat leaked down her sides, though her body still registered a chill. She tensely assessed the perimeter for movement, tracking her gaze through dark green jungle, a vegetal wall demarcating what lay beyond the clear-cut, familiarized camp boundary.

Though she fought to ignore it, the odor of decay ripened to a stench that smothered her other senses. Breathing through her mouth, she did her best to focus her concentration. *Can you hear me, Lacey?*

Gibberish babbled in her subconscious, draining away like water through cupped hands. Still, something persisted. She could make contact but not sustain it. Heat simmered all around her. That smell—which yes, could be nothing more than a random carcass—soon drove Eve back into the tent.

Jonnie sat on the edge of his bunk bed, texting like someone had a gun to his head. "Signal cut in for a split second." His crisp English voice was breathy as he fired off communication.

Involuntary warmth laid Eve bare as she sat beside him in the force field of his personal-space aura. She hadn't felt the intrigue of new affection for another person in a long time. Not since her ex, a man whose patronizing concern about her "delusions" frayed her psyche, pulled at the coiled strands of her brain until it unraveled like an old sweater. Toward the end of the relationship, she'd accepted that she was crazy. Then she got wise, dumped his manipulative ass, and got back to work with the ghosts.

Blowback for opening up to someone, showing them the depths of her differences, left her marinating in bile. Until whatever power had blessed her with her first good sleep in ages, that rejuvenating boost to soothe a mind frayed by insomnia, Eve had lacked the clarity to see how bitter she'd become. How angry, how distancing, how defensive.

She'd hidden behind the obligating drive of her abilities, a furious martyr stewing in self-righteous poison. But without the ability to see past herself, her woes, she'd been unable to harness the insight and empathy needed to move past resentment. Transcending the souring, alienating refrain of "why me" eluded her.

Forcing the past from her mind, Eve rubbed her own legs so she didn't touch Jonnie. Crossing such a border would be inappropriate. On a couple of levels. They must not continue to give in to desire, to lust. He was right. Devastating repercussions, possibly exacerbated by mysteries and shaky control, could follow.

She chose compassion. "Is there an update with Cara?"

"Stable for now. She's had a good week." A few more blue and white bubble messages flew across his screen and stopped. Jonnie mumbled a British curse and pocketed the phone.

From the looks of things, the cellular signal gods had revoked their temporary gift.

"Do you ever feel like you're walking through life across a melting sheet of ice?" Except with water pushing up against the solid surface, insisting its way out of frigid depths, a cold hell of sinister things, sins and buried evils.

His profile cut a cameo in the lazy remnants of shadow-play sunlight, all carved edges and points and contemplation. A side tilt of his head in her direction was sexier than it should have been, as if he moved his body with supreme irony and awareness.

Jonnie vamped with subtlety: a swish of black hair, wine stain pout, graceful limbs. Eve caught flecks of red in his eyes, crystalline shards she couldn't say had always been there. His irises gleamed like bloodstone.

A hum of energy skated across the spot between her legs as she realized those slivers of blood were only visible at kissing distance. A slowdown seized her. All she wanted to do, all she could do, was stare at his face. The scariest part? He wasn't using his powers. The rapture came from within, the sense in which she'd agreed to her own bewitchment.

"You feel things on a deeper level than I do." His tongue swiped across teeth, pairing with the clouds chasing over his dark eyes. In a zip of inhumanly fast motion, he shot out his hand and grabbed her chin, then bent her head back with firmness not approaching brutish force, though it bared her neck to an invisible lance.

A maelstrom of energies thudded inside of her as she merged with her deepest, most forbidden desires. Perhaps she'd danced with the dark so long, she now craved the border-crossing thrill of taboo. And what captured that better than a vampire's teeth in one's throat? Her chest heaved with breath.

"Makes me want to devour you. Drink that current of thick, wet awareness pumping through your body. You're primordial, Eve, a fecund creature. A repository of energies. God, the things I could do to you. That I want to do to you." He spoke a dark dream.

He pressed his other hand against the crotch of her cargo shorts, fingers offering hardness and enticing pressure. Her clit swelled, aching against his still touch. The moisture of her excitement mingled with teeming humidity, slicking her head to toe with juice.

Fluid need ripened her, changing her into a fantasy version of herself. She was a peach for him to pluck, to eat, tender flesh in his mouth. She would dissolve into sweet liquid running down his lips and chin as she offered her life to his consumption, a selfhood surrendered to bleed as it dribbled off.

"Tell me." Her whisper was fast and lascivious, obscene in its sharpness. She widened her legs, feeling the spreading damp of excitement in her core, merging panties to skin.

A taunting brush of knuckle over cloth gave way to real strokes, his grip on her chin persistent. She gasped at the friction, the sweet ache at the juncture of her thighs gaining a modicum of satisfaction.

"Your throat hides the fountain of youth." Rubs intensified, fast enough to bring her close to release.

She humped his hand, hips rising and rolling, lungs panting the pitiful affirmation of a flesh prisoner blood-bound to him. "Take it already."

"I think of you submissive, giving it to me. My source to feed off of. My supplicant. I think of breaking your skin, tearing it. The flow of ambrosia. Red at first, bright trickles from my first cut, then a scarier color as your artery ruptures. Dark and thick, syrup, as primal as the magic in your soul." His posh voice had grown menacing, the snarling, fire and ice timbre of a villain in control.

God, he rubbed faster. Her motions quickened against his, her body begging him for relief. For abandon. For surrender and escape.

In her throat, a fast, hard beat thumped. She swallowed, snapping her head down to catch his reaction to the movement in her neck. He surely saw the pulsing throbs in there. Did he register the pattern with his musician's acumen?

Could her daydream of their blood-erotics make a symphony, melodies both sacred and profane? Could their taboo art smash all walls, fold heaven and hell into an undifferentiated flow of good and evil, chaos into order?

He hadn't morphed into vampire face, but the lust in his expression gave enough of an illicit thrill to tide her over for now. Eyelids at half-mast, ringed by thick lashes the color of soot. Lips he'd licked, the smell of musk and sweat. The long outline of his cock stood in sharp relief against the fabric of his shorts.

"Keep talking about what you'd do to me after you turned into a vampire." She dry fucked his hand, shameless as a happy whore.

"I'd lick your deepest secrets off your own skin and drink them down like warm red wine. I'd eat the essence of you, the enigmas encoded in your DNA. Take you. Make you. I'd open you up and consume you until you are mine and I own the extent of you."

From some pit crawled a boundless shadow demon. It mated with Jonnie and revealed a bit of itself through his crisp vocal inflection. Teetering at the edge of madness, Eve courted the imaginary fiend like a snake charmer.

A tangle of pressure built at the base of her spine. She smelled her own excitement, fleshy and tart in the relentless equatorial heat.

Deft, Jonnie popped the button of her shorts. Unzipped. She moaned as his middle finger breached her soaked underwear, parted her soft curls as he shot his touch to her clit. Desperate for him, she gazed into his eyes. Somehow they stimulated her too, rubbed a secret spot in her reptile brain, provoking her pleasure. "Please keep talking dirty. Please, please."

"I'd make you into nectar of the gods. Lap your port wine from those hard nipples, scoop it from your belly button. Make your hot, sweet

pussy a sacred chalice for your precious fucking blood. For *my* blood."
His warm breath kissed her neck, merging with jungle steam.

With one callused finger pad, he circled her clit in wide, fast motions.
Her mouth dropped as she pushed into his touch, pushed at him to
relieve her greed, her pressure, to take away the constant pushback of
her dull pain. So mystical, so sacred and strange.

"I'd turn you, Evelyn. Turn you into what you really want to be.
Someone who isn't frustrated or confused by those dark waters you skate
over as you teeter on the ice. You're a mermaid who swims in them. A
sorceress who commands them, controls them. They fill your veins and
you shoot them back out as magic."

She came in a violent, cracking jolt, erupting hard in erasing shocks.
He changed up his strokes as she did, doing it faster and faster, hard,
lubed flesh on hard, lubed flesh.

Eve bowed her back and shoved her belly forward, moans and pants
in her ears as she burst, taut and erect and slippery against his hand. Her
own ugly, uninhibited noises carried her through the upending wave of
destruction as he milked the climax from her.

When oversensitivity set in, she ripped his hand free, knelt, and went
for his shorts. His hands were in her thick hair. The world spun off its
axis.

"Yeah." Still humming with aftershocks, she gasped out the wicked
word as she opened his pants and grabbed the silken bar that she craved.

Eve looked up into his eyes as she freed him and lapped at his slit
with the wanton ways of a pagan sex goddess coaxing his fluids forth. He
grunted, hair in his face, and urged her head down. She licked up the first
dot of white cream like a dirty little cat girl, her tongue flicking and
darting over the opening. The crown of his tawny cock darkened to a
plum shade, jerking as it begged her for more sustained attention.

"You want to drink me, too, don't you Eve love? Feed on me." He
smirked a twist of a smirk, the nastiest and hottest thing she'd ever seen.

"Give me a taste of you. Please." Invested in her performance of
submission, she tugged at his waistband but didn't urge the shorts down.
Not without his permission.

Jonnie fisted his cock, hard enough to make the fat crown throb with
a fresh bloom of blood. Another milky bead of pre cum bubbled at the

tip, and she went for it with her mouth agape and tongue outstretched. Sweat taped streaks of hair to his face, making a peekaboo of his features that brought both the danger inherent in him and the abandon of their passion into relief.

"Beg for it." His voice came out a gravely grunt. He shook a finger at her and waved his straining dick, gripping the base.

"One taste. Please." Her fantasies danced a circus as she licked her lips, batted her eyelashes, stared up at his affected sadism.

They skirted the edges of something mean, played at the borders of doom. He could bite, attack, drink.

In the landscape of her imagination, he had. This would be the cure for her. His seed down her throat would make her sickness better as she knelt before him and wheedled, weak from blood loss and sticky with the residue of her own life painting the hot skin of her neck, chest, tits.

"Just a little bit, love." He swiped the tip across her parted lips, leaving a treat of bitter musk.

"More." She stuck out her bottom lip in a theatrical pout.

He lifted his ass, pushed pants and underwear to his knees, and sat back down. "Slow. Start with my balls."

His brown, heavy sac was drawn up close to his body, full and tense. She licked the rigid seam dividing his testes. When he sighed in pleasure, she sucked one heavy ball into her mouth, massaging with lips and tongue. He moved one hand from her head and pumped his length.

Eve drew his other ball into her mouth and nursed the entire bundle, teasing deep grooves in leathery ball skin with her naughty tongue.

He slid his hand up the shaft and stroked his cockhead with a curled fist. Snatched his bottom lip in his teeth and bit, increasing the speed of his pumps. Fangs came down.

Yes.

"Yeah, Eve. Suck my balls."

Emboldened on her knees, Eve surged with a dark charge. Whether it was his bossiness or the appearance of his vampire teeth, she couldn't say. But in the interests of stepping it up a notch, she secured a thick fold of his loose skin between her teeth and nipped.

A suck of air hissed between his pursed lips. The hand on his cock dove into her hair and pulled, close to the scalp, drawing her off his steely erection with a stinging pull. "Careful."

In that moment, Jonnie infiltrated Eve's head. Not literally, but through insidious seduction more potent than any drug. Jonnie used Eve's craving, her forbidden curiosity, against her, opening dark doors in some subbasement of her self. A dungeon where hunger and torture danced, a hidden chamber of horror-delights and whining, whispered pleas of *kill me*. But not to kill in the permanent or literal senses. Here, to kill was to break down to zero and remake, to sire a phoenix born of abjection, to produce glory from the ashes of misery. Here, killing meant alchemy.

"Or else what?" She fired off the taunt in a warning shot. She was utterly defenseless and far from unaware of the contrast inherent in her word combined with the supplicating posture. Wood slivers burrowed grit into her sensitive kneecaps, the sting of some emergent S&M ritual unveiled. She licked and kissed his stiff shaft, keeping him primed.

"Or else you might be in real danger. I changed." Unambiguously, he cautioned her, the voice he used firm in its concern. "Into something I haven't felt before. And it wasn't good."

Eve backed away from the edge. Not because Jonnie scared her, he didn't. But because she scared herself. The caves in her soul, full of monsters, scared her more than anything. She'd already unleashed enough. Harmed enough. Nothing good would come from skipping around the borders of the abyss.

Yet she kept its temptations in her periphery as she lowered her head and took him in her mouth. Kept it looming near the forefront of her conscious mind as she teased at first, caressing his hardness with her tongue, massaging the head with her lips. Her curls tangled in his fingers. She bobbed. He groaned and grunted, thrusting tip into tonsils.

Eve slowed her technique, delaying his climax as she delighted in the visual of her saliva running down his erection in clear rivulets that made his dusky, veined staff glisten in the sunset. Rolling his balls in her free hand, she sucked in a steady pace, working him over.

After a few minutes, he clamped his hands to the sides of her head. He punched up his hips, thrusting his dick down her throat. Her gag reflex seized, but she kept up her motions until he stiffened to fleshy steel against her tongue and moaned out her name, followed by a long groan of male pleasure and satisfaction.

His thick fluids coated her mouth, salty and rich. Grateful for his essence, she gulped him down. His handsome face melted into a mask of pleasure, reverent and boyish in its disbelief. She swallowed until he stopped spurting, thinking of the magic powers of blood as she drank cum.

Two fluids comprising the ancient, liquid life beneath and behind us all coiled a vortex in her mind.

The shift in Eve was subtle, a blink-and-miss level of nuance. But pieces inside of her broke off and reformed, sending currents into motion as they clicked into fresh alignment. And what emerged from those new relationships was power. From her gut, ancestors or God or something else, chanted. Though she didn't trust it, she moved in the groove carved by its authenticity.

Eve smiled at Jonnie as she pulled back from him, sending a signal of awareness as a slow morass of oil seeped coolly through her system, sealing holes and cracks as it did. It was macabre and morbid, primordial ooze, ancient tree roots stabbed into graves and drawing forth their energy. Skeletons and rot, the dark and heavy drag of what remains.

The things we bury, shove into the ground out of sight and mind, don't go away. They lie in wait. They remain.

They awaited her, and they'd found her.

Her heart beat faster as she knelt there smiling, feeling that obsidian magic course through her veins and penetrate the cells of her marrow. Her core temperature dropped a few degrees as some part of her psyche broke away and wormed deep, deep into the earth. Into the crevices the life force leaches into, the part of the world that absorbs and holds those elements of the dead not allowed to join the pretty golden spheres.

She could gather that darkness, take it in through a controlled osmosis. Two versions of her thrived now, the one on her knees before Jonnie in the bunk, and the one patrolling the bowels of the earth. Magic stepped in to replace the part of her that fled, or perhaps that part of her fed on necrotic magic from her station beneath, amidst opportunistic worms and decomposing flesh.

Jonnie was not smiling back, not by a long shot. He regarded her with two fingers pressed to his lips.

"I can bring it up." Dark death magic sealed her gaps, rendering her whole. "Death. I can marshal and manipulate the essence of death."

The force inside of her buzzed in a bass tune, a response of confirmation. Uncertainty dissipated into the ether as Evelyn actualized, became one with herself. Unified.

Jonnie opened his lips, though he made not a sound.

Eve rubbed his bare thighs in playful reassurance. He'd said that this development was bad, but it wasn't, not at all. It was glorious. It was crucial. It was key.

TWELVE

Jonnie had been distant ever since the pair had set off on the trek to the jungle camp. He walked beside Eve, silent, radiating an unapproachable aura with his hands shoved in his pockets. Working with people in a de facto caretaking role had groomed Eve to notice nonverbal gestures and the messages behind them.

Taylor, sensing the tension, had taken up the conversational mantle, which Eve admitted she appreciated. He needed space, fair enough. Whatever development she'd ridden after they'd fooled around was new and wild to her. She could only imagine how strange he must feel being implicated in it.

Their three-person and one-horse march concluded at a flat patch of land enclosed by trees. Four reddish log cabins ringed the area in a wide half-circle, and an extinguished pit fire flanked by benches sat in the middle of dirt ground. A large, fenced-in pen and three-stall equine stable rounded out the arrangement, a rustic setup which reminded Eve of the summer overnight camp she attended annually as a kid.

She drew in a lingering breath of cedar and burnt embers, looking up at Taylor on her steed. "Thank you for coming back."

Taylor dismounted and led her horse into the corral. She pulled a paper lunch sack from her backpack and fed the animal apple slices from it. "I want to apologize for freaking out earlier."

The white horse accepted the treats in its big humanoid teeth, huffing as its owner stroked its snout.

"It's fine. Extenuating circumstances. Do you think your work with the water might have some answers?"

A few feet away, someone whistled. "Hey, man, you're the one who needs the ayahuasca, yeah?" A hippie guy with beads woven into natty brown hair halfway down his back shouted the interruption, tanned arms full of firewood.

"Yeah, mate." Jonnie sounded relieved to have something else to do.

"Step into my pharmacy, brother." The hippie dropped his load by the ashy remnants of the fire, wiped dirty hands on tie-dyed sweatpants, and motioned for Jonnie to follow him to a cabin identical to the others. A cloth flag bearing the band name Phish hanging in one of the windows distinguished his pharmacy from the other structures.

Jonnie hustled on over, hazarding Eve not so much a single backwards glance.

She sighed, a screw of regret and frustration drilling into her heart.

"What's his problem?" Taylor sat on a bench and patted the seat next to her.

Eve picked up a long stick and drew random shapes in the dust. "We fooled around, and I felt changes in me. New magic. It's hard to explain." She etched swirls and clouds in the dirt, a halfhearted attempt to give form to the gooey morass teeming within her. A tsunami of sludge storming at her gates, a drooling tongue of molasses licking her veins.

"This place will do that. I leveled up when I first touched the river. It's a node down here, charged with mystical energies and forces. My theory is that if you have anything in you, no matter how latent, being here will bring it out."

A faint southern twang in Taylor's voice coaxed a smile from Eve, the little reminder of the south demystifying the other woman and imbuing her with the sound of an old friend. She traced a series of three cresting, crashing waves with her branch.

Taylor watched, pulling a piece of twig from her blonde hair. "Earth." She muttered the muted word with the certainty of a shouted eureka.

Eve got it. "Earth magic. I have some kind of earth magic. But it feels like more than that, like there's a connection to death in there. Which would make sense, given the other things I can do."

"Right. Earth and death are related, as you of course know. The body returns to the earth, the soul flies away. As above, so below." Taylor pointed up, then down.

Eve smirked at the other woman. "Uh oh. Don't go all basic witch on me now."

A good-natured chuckle from Taylor. "I'm serious. You're earth, I'm water. Two elemental witches, both activated as soon as we show up here." The pregnant blonde stamped a hiking-boot-clad foot into the ground, kicking up a puff of dust. It dissipated, catching the remaining sunlight as the bleeding orange orb dipped below the tree line.

The onset of twilight brought the distinctive cast of Taylor's features into relief. Keen blue eyes as sharp as thorns, large pointed ears like a hybrid creature from a highland fantasy tale. An uncanny exoticism shaped her face, too, a lupine and feral cast. Her beauty was unusual, untouchable, too rare to relegate to the usual accolades or comparison to pretty celebrities. Striking came to mind as an adjective, and one not spoken lightly. For Eve suspected that Taylor would strike, if provoked.

"That leaves fire and air," Eve said. They knew so little about what it all meant that there wasn't much to say beyond stating the obvious.

"And the fifth element. Spirit or soul or what have you." Taylor tipped her head to the heavens and their mysteries. Those first winks of starlight emerged as sky changed from blues to indigos. Bugs struck up a croaking serenade, a firefly or three greeting them in blips of electric yellow. A cool front slid through, prompting Eve to rub her bare forearms.

Eve drew a line in the dirt, allowing Taylor's comment to settle in her thoughts and knock around a bit. She had a feeling she'd only begun to scratch the surface of this magical place and what it had to offer. "What now?"

"Let's try the water." Taylor hopped to stand.

"Lead the way."

* * *

A SHORT, MUDDY WALK DOWN AN INCLINED TRAIL PAVED WITH A scattering of wood chips led the pair to a stream. The narrow tributary flowed in a steady pace, humming its lapping lullaby as it sparkled in the light of dusk. A fat tree branch served as a bridge over the stream. Eve smiled at a plastic pail, shovel, and toy dump truck abandoned on the bank, charmed by the suggestion of children. "Do you know what you're having?"

Taylor patted her bump as she sat on a large rock by the stream's edge. Wetness licked the toes of her boots, staining leather dark. "One boy, one girl."

Mud sucking at her soles, Eve took her place beside the expat. "Congratulations."

"Thanks." Without further ado, Taylor leaned to the side, avoiding her protruding stomach. When she stuck her hand in the water, her eyes rolled back in her head, turning completely white.

Eve watched the spectacle with surprised interest. "Alright then."

"There's a few things going on." Taylor swished her hand around, stirring faint splashes. A few tepid drops dampened Eve's calf. "We have your lost soul...Stacy...Lucy..." Taylor scrunched up her face, diving her hand wrist deep in the tributary.

"Lacey."

"Can you hear me, Lacey?" Brow knotted, Taylor chewed her lip as she waited.

"Are you picking up on anything?"

"It's like a ball of voices, all blurred together. I can't...I can't tease out distinct threads. God, they're screaming. Screaming." Taylor's pitch dropped to a trembling murmur and shook.

"Where are they?"

"There's your fucking squirrel." Taylor stabbed a free hand in the air. "But it's not the squirrel, it just grabbed onto the squirrel. It's like a hitchhiker, or hijacker. A tagalong. It wants to possess things....aargh. I just get these little bits. It's got Lacey, now it wants you. You and her, you fit somehow. Like pieces of a set."

"What else?" Eve croaked through a dry throat. She needed to get the drop on this squirrel-spirit thing and help Lacey. Information played a clarifying role, however scant.

"I have a theory. Hold my hand and stick your other in the mud."
We'll form a circuit. Eve took Taylor's warm, slender fingers in one hand and plunged her other into the brownish-black goo squishing underfoot. Moist and soft and cool, it molded around her submerged knuckles.

As glop burrowed under her nails and invaded her pores, every saturated dirt particle a soldier storming her skin's defenses, Eve spaced out. Her consciousness seeped into sticky wetness, a million tiny mouths sucking her fingertips and palm lines.

"Are you feeling this?" She directed her question to Taylor, though her bowling ball of a head wouldn't turn. The earth slurped and nibbled her flesh, massaging lips stealing her essence and claiming it for their food.

Eve blacked out. A second later, she awoke in total darkness. Spots flickered in front of her eyes.

A cool, fleshy mass slithered between her toes. Eve blinked, vision blotchy as details came into view. She lay in a coffin, surrounded by poufs of white satin. Confusion and claustrophobia jarring her brain, she pressed her hands into narrow walls, thumped the sealed lid above her. A bloated pink earthworm, mottled with dirt, squirmed. She swallowed a scream, but her labored breath might as well have been as loud as one. "Hello?"

Air whooshed from her lungs, leaving her gasping and dizzy. She couldn't draw a full breath. The walls collapsed, coffin lid bearing down. The worm, a shade lighter than her toenail polish, writhed over the top of her foot. Terror and panic seized her in discombobulating quakes. Her lips quivered. *Don't scream, don't freak.*

"You're right, conserve your air." Taylor sounded underwater, warbled and surreal. "I've got you. Lacey's dead. Connect with Lacey. If your powers can make a through-line to anyone or anything that can help, it's her."

Lungs hot, Eve took three conservative sips of oxygen. She squeezed her eyes shut. *Are you there, Lacey?*

"It burns." It came from a million miles away, but no mistaking the voice.

Three more sucks of breath, longer on the exhale to preserve the ration. In her stifling tomb, she could smell the carbon dioxide exiting her body. Funky, toxic, sour with bacteria. In the dank coolness, sweat slicked her palms. The worm lolled off of her foot and coiled by her ankle. *Where are you, Lacey.*

"I'm...I'm underground. I think. There's fire everywhere. So hot. Everything hurts. Please help."

White sparks danced in Eve's vision. Her head swam. One more baby breath into her cramping lungs didn't bring enough relief. Black spots spread over her eyes. On the verge of passing out, Eve focused what remained of her consciousness on the dark current within her. *Follow my power, Lacey. Follow it.*

The force gathered steam in the pit of her stomach, churning, pulling in more and more dead earth magic as it increased in density. Energetic ropes, knotty and braided umbilical cords the color of a deep bruise, shot from her hands and feet. The lines of power penetrated the coffin and stabbed into the dirt beyond it.

"I see it." Lacey squealed with naked joy, unchecked hope that made Eve happy even in her weakening state. "It's a rope with bumps in it. Like a ladder. And it leads up."

Eve was panting involuntarily now, sight blurry and fuzzy. Tight heat wrenched her insides. But she managed a smile. *Good. Climb it.*

"I'm halfway up."

Eve's hands shook. A series of little tremors wracked her body. She slurped up a stuck fish gulp of air with a pitiable squeak. *Keep going, Lacey. You got this.*

"I sure do." Something in Lacey's voice disturbed Eve. A sneer of victory. Smugness. *No.* She was just lightheaded and anxious, her mind playing tricks.

"You okay down there? Your energy changed." This from Taylor in her wobbling, bottom-of-the well voice.

Yeah. I've got ahold of my powers. I've got her. Heart palpitations followed her words. She was so close, renewed with confidence that she had a shot at rescuing Lacey's soul.

"You need to hurry. You don't look so good," Taylor said.

Come on, Lacey. Eve swallowed into a swollen throat, greasy nausea spreading through her stomach.

"Listen to me very carefully." Following Lacey's order, two fish-belly white hands, broken nails long and caked with dirt, erupted from the end of the casket.

Eve clamped a hand over her mouth, blinking a few times in case she was hallucinating.

She wasn't. Next came the matted nest of blonde hair, the graying face with its vacant, raccoon-rimmed eyes. Lacey wore her burial dress, a flirty, violet frock stained with blotches of decomposition.

"Eve," Taylor shouted. "You're having a seizure. I'm going to reach over and pull out your hand."

No. She had to do right by the innocent girl she'd wronged, the only way she knew how. *I've made contact. I need a few more seconds.*

The dead girl crawled up Eve's body with frigid hands, coming to hover on top of her. Decay thickened already oppressive grave air into a solid wall of stench. Spiders crawled in the ragged swatches of remaining hair hanging from Lacy's head, bald patches as large as saucers gaping on her scalp. The animated corpse stared Eve down with cloudy, death pits of eyes the color of old hamburger.

"You will go to my parents and atone for what you did." Gray teeth showed when the undead girl spoke. Her heavy, strong breath made Eve's eyes water until tears slipped down her cheeks. Tears triggered not only by the viscera of the encounter, but by guilt and horror.

Eve nodded.

"Bring your vampire's lover's blood. A drop will do." A green-spotted tongue flicked across purple lips as they twisted into a sneer. Eve shuddered, Lacey's expression of craven greed more horrifying than her dead face.

Her foggy head spun as she struggled to breathe, but she kept her wits about her. *No. Something else. I won't let you stir Jonnie into this. My book is full of spells. I'm sure there's one that can bring you back to life.*

Lacey snarled, grunting. "My familiar is getting stronger. You know that, right? My pet?"

"Eve. Hurry." Taylor's frustration kicked her voice up high.

"You have two choices. Listen to my instructions and bring my parents his toxic blood as your peace offering. Or my pet kills you both."

Eve lapsed to a hanging state of pre-unconsciousness, hyperventilating. *I don't believe you.*

"Now, right now." Taylor shouted. A force tugged Eve's wrist. Her awareness jumped between the grave and the riverbank.

The dead girl's eyes turned to screens and revealed an unspeakable picture. Eve's parents lay dead in their bed, faces masks of frozen shock as a zombie rodent perched on each of their chests slurped up red curls of smoke. Next flashed a picture of Jonnie, who, from the looks of things, had succumbed to a similar scenario in his New Orleans loft. "Which is it, witch bitch?"

Prove to me you aren't bluffing. Pulls jerked Eve. Lacey faded in and out as the scene above ground became more prominent in Eve's perception. Taylor couldn't break the spell yet, not before Eve figured out a solution.

Corpse eyeballs clicked to white and played a new image. Eve's father ambled through the living room, balanced on his cane. Relaxed in her favorite recliner, her mother read a newspaper, the current day's date visible at the top of the page. Behind her, atop the china cabinet, a zombie squirrel watched. It divided into two, then four. "If you return to earth not having made a choice, mommy and daddy die now."

No. No, no, no.

"A drop won't hurt your lover. Which is it, witch?"

"Fine," she gasped out, hacking a cough as toxic odors flooded her system.

"Fine what?" Lacey leaned in close, close enough for the tip of her frozen nose to touch Eve's. Sharp nails scratched her forearm.

"I'll visit your parents with an offering of Jonnie's blood." God, what an awful, deceitful thing to inflict upon a person she'd pledged to help. But she would not put his life or the lives of her beloved parents at risk. No more death on her watch. If she warned Jonnie, perhaps they could stay one step ahead of this unfolding nightmare.

"He must not know of your harvest."

What? Why does that matter?

Lacey laughed a sick laugh, lungs glugging like fluid filled them. "Vampire awareness of harvest changes the blood energy and compromises the Pollyannas."

"Eve, you're waking up in three, two..."

What the fuck are the Pollyannas?

"The embodiment of indefatigability. You'll all soon see."

"One."

Eve's consciousness ebbed in her cramped grave, but she clung to a remaining sliver of lucidity.

What are the Pollyannas? Nothing good, of course. But if she could pull but one clue from Lacey, she might have a heads-up on how to keep everyone as safe as possible.

Lacey's death mask of a face stretched into an obscene grin, highlighting a smattering of florid lesions pockmarking her right cheek. "Optimism made flesh. Tenacity. All vital skills in surviving the impending apocalypse. You have one week to turn over the blood, and after the Pollyannas feed you can tell your vampire whatever you wish."

"Come back."

A sensation akin to the ripping of fabric tore through Eve. Above her, Lacey erupted into a cloud of ashes. Eve hacked and spat, swatting soot from her mouth and nose as remnants of dust infiltrated her system in itchy invasions.

She awoke with a start, struggling for air. The familiar creek purred away. Night draped its ebony blanket across the sky. A painful stab of flashlight pierced Eve's eyes as Taylor leaned in, examining with her forehead bunched.

"Get that away, it hurts." Eve's throat burned as she croaked out her words through cotton-mouth. She rubbed a temple, head full of shit and broken glass.

As she reconnected with her conscious mind, Eve gained awareness of a third presence. Invisible, in front of her. Or beside her, or next to her. She moved her head back and forth, glancing over her shoulder. The unseen thing moved along with her.

"Eve." Taylor drew out the syllable in a protracted stretch of confounded dread.

No point in bullshit at this stage in the game. "I brought something back with me. Her. Lacey. Or whatever she is." Eve wiggled on her hard rock of a seat, acutely aware of the silent passenger mimicking her motions. Its energy was vexing, an irritant. The feeling of *off*, that presick malaise that sets in the day before the cold symptoms start.

"She's—it's been here. The squirrel. A few of us hauled it away and brought it to you. One of the villagers found it buried in a shallow grave back at your camp and disposed of it."

If the zombie had, in fact, tracked her and Jonnie here, the odds were that Lacey told the truth about its power. Within, in some preconscious nook, the invader lurked. Sort of sat in a basement corner of Eve's self like a slumped ragdoll, blinking in a stupefied daze. All around, the jungle chittered and sang its night symphony. The rock was a relentless hardness under her bottom, the truth oppressive in the air.

"I know what I need to do about it. Thank you for everything, but I need to leave. We need to leave." Eve jumped to her feet.

"Wait." Taylor stood, reaching out a hand. "Stay the night. You don't need to rush off or make any rash decisions tonight. We'll regroup in the morning."

A lump of shame growing in her throat, Eve shook her head. "Call Carlos. Jonnie can have a private plane in Iquitos in a few hours."

Taylor stepped closer. "My husband does spiritual work. He might be able to help. You don't need to go at it alone."

But that was the thing. She'd always been alone at the end of the day. And now, with some vindictive ghost-girl hitching a ride in her soul, demanding she beg forgiveness for her sins through a scheme involving vampire blood?

With ominous, cryptic knowledge of an impending apocalypse and something called the Pollyannas weighing on her? Fat chance she'd suck anyone else into her dark mess.

"Take me back to the camp, Taylor. Because I'm pretty sure the last thing you need anywhere near you and your loved ones is a necromancer with dubious control over her magic and an angry dead person on her heels."

THIRTEEN

JONNIE ALLOWED HIS GAZE TO REST ON THE CARDBOARD BOX BETWEEN
his black boots as the jet sailed across the Atlantic. He had enough
ayahuasca to last him three months, the hippie naturopath had
explained, as long as he rationed it carefully. After that he'd need a plan
B, but he wasn't there yet. A few months of symptom-free living awaited
him, months during which he could visit with family, make music with
his band, and all-around enjoy life.

Beside him, Eve stared out the window. All of her talk of marshaling
death disconcerted him, to say the least. To say nothing of the wild,
vacant look that had overtaken her eyes.

But that didn't excuse his putting his cock in her mouth and then
giving her the cold shoulder.

Jesus, he prided himself on being better than that with all women,
especially ones he cared about. Yet he'd reverted to the kind of man-
child he saw everywhere in his line of work, selfish and oversexed,
treating partners like objects instead of people with feelings.

Shame on you, mate. Perhaps one day, he'd stop bolloxing things up
with Eve so he could stop apologizing. Today would not be the day.

He squeezed her knee. "I apologize for how I acted."

She flinched, then relaxed as she turned to face him. Worry lines he hadn't noticed before creased her forehead. "Yeah, well, I was pretty off the rails there."

A twist in his chest hurt his heart. "What happened exactly? In the hut, and with Taylor?"

She tapped the toe of her muddy hiking boot into his box, nudging a loose curl of packing tape. "My powers. They're changing. It was—is—scary, but I have leads. On the girl, and what we, I mean *I* can do once we get back." Emptiness in her voice, that matter-of-fact tone that comes with scrubbing emotion from thought, prompted him to keep his hand on her leg in an offer of assuring touch. He made a silent promise that he wouldn't balk at her again.

Plus, her correction of "we" to "I" saddened him. He'd grown to appreciate the thought of them as a "we," however unusual their "we" was. "Tell me how I can help."

Several beats of silence followed. The plane dipped, making its initial descent. Jonnie's ear popped and he rubbed it, awkward as a schoolboy having uttered "may I kiss you" as he awaited her response.

A few more seconds of quiet dragged. She looked at her short red nails and finally asked, "You said you know a witch, right?"

"Yes." He sat up straighter in a goofy tell of relief. She smiled. He smiled back, not giving a fuck how silly he appeared.

"I was wondering if she might be able to help me. Point me toward some resources, help me figure out these powers."

Jonnie drew back as confusion set in. The confounded feeling curdled to suspicion as he realized she'd broken eye contact upon bringing up her magical abilities. Eve was hiding things.

"Taylor wasn't able to help you?" But something had gone down. Eve's insistence that they leave Peru immediately after her excursion into the jungle made that much evident.

"I didn't want to burden her, in her condition. I thought it would be best if I wasn't around." She picked at her nail, hair shielding her face.

"Eve, look at me." The sternness in his tone startled him. But he didn't do secrets or head games. "I want to help, but I can't if you're hiding important facts from me."

"I'm not." She said it too quickly, voice kicking up an octave. The mark of a lie.

Pressuring her to confess wouldn't do any good, might accomplish nothing more than driving her further away. Besides, whatever she was dealing with was none of his business. He could offer his support and empathy, though it was not his place to demand answers or go poking at the tender spots of her secrets. The magic was obviously rather personal to her, as was the debacle with the girl.

Eve needn't suffer alone, but she did deserve her privacy. "I'll put you in touch with Helen as soon as we get back in the States. What's going on with your work?"

Her wan smile was a thank you, a gesture of appreciation offered in exchange for his backing down. He'd rather have her trust, the full disclosure of her honesty, but Jonnie was mature enough to accept that they were not there yet. "My apprentice seems to be holding down the fort. No phone calls or emails. But yeah, I should get back to work. I'm sure Meg is worried about me."

A dull ache spread through Jonnie. The way she spoke bothered him. The spaces between her words were lagging dips of resignation, goodbye kisses. Outside, the maudlin effect of starless sky lit only by the plane's red taillights mirrored his regret-tinged sadness. At the moment they were in transition, in the air, though upon landing they would part company. He wasn't dumb. He saw it coming.

Jonnie rubbed his kneecap, massaging a tendon he'd tweaked jumping off an amp during some outrageous stage antic years ago. "Surely you could stay a little bit longer."

She laid her hand atop his, gesture straddling the border of reassurance and frank honesty. "I—"

"I understand." Though he really didn't. Despite their rough patches, he and she made sense. They were travelers of the same path. "At least spend the night in New Orleans before you fly back. You must be exhausted. We can just hang out, no pressure."

"I'd like that. To stay one more night." He swore her voice shook, like the goodbye hurt her too. She laid her head on his shoulder, treating him to her soft, feminine fragrance of fruit and flowers.

"One more night." Jonnie swallowed a lump in his throat and kissed the part dividing her locks. Another altitude drop tumbled his insides as the craft approached the small airport runway.

Time slugged along in a flow thicker than the humid atmosphere as they deplaned, teetering down narrow steps on the way to the waiting car. Even the palm trees waved goodbye, coy flicks of leaves animating the darkness.

* * *

A CALL ZAPPED JONNIE FROM HIS COMATOSE SLUMBER. HIS MOBILE buzzed on the end table beside his couch, shaking as it clattered against wood. In a second he processed the ringtone and Cara's picture on the glowing screen.

His heart plummeted to his feet as he snatched up the phone and answered. "Anya. What's happened?"

Though the line, his sister sniffled. "I'm not sure. The doctors haven't said much. She's refusing food...they admitted her to ICU...oh, God." Whimpers deteriorated to broken cries.

"I can get there by the morning." He ran to his room, where Eve slept alone in his bed.

Packing with one hand while awaiting Anya's reply, Jonnie threw essentials into his duffel. A few more hours in the plane would land him in Iowa. The nomadic life of a traveling musician had prepared him for all this running around, and he wasn't about to take a gamble when time with his niece was so precious. Queasiness rippled through him. Jonnie rubbed raw, tired eyes.

"I think that's a good idea." Fresh sobs, the animal sounds of a grieving mother's sorrow, wracked Anya's hoarse voice.

"Hang on. Both of you, hang on. I'll be there soon." He was halfway to the door when he remembered his medicine. "Shite."

Jonnie ran to the kitchen and flicked the light switch. Hands shaking, he pulled a plastic bottle of his organic antidote from the fridge. He fumbled with the dishwasher, tugging the door open and pawing at a short glass on the top rack.

The cup, wedged between two others, would not budge. Frustration scraping his already frayed nerves, he pulled at the stubborn thing. "Come on, stupid."

He freed it with a yank, but it slammed into something else on the way out and broke in his hands. A big triangular piece fell to the floor, its destruction filling silence as it shattered on the tile.

In a mind-erasing slash of hot pain, the jagged edge slashed Jonnie's palm from the crease of his fingers to his wrist. He dropped the rest of the glass, and it landed with a crash.

"Fuck." Agony throbbed in his hand. He clutched the damage. Warm, sticky blood oozed down his wrist and landed with pitter patter drips on the tile. He snatched a dish towel and pressed it to his cut, grinding his teeth and leaning over the sink. To add insult to injury, his blunder messed up his livelihood, his means to play guitar. If he couldn't play, he couldn't earn money.

Should have gotten your hands insured like Brian did. Brian, forever the smart one, was tirelessly pragmatic and replete with sensible decisions. Cranky, miserable thoughts sloshed around in Jonnie's brain as his body glimmered with pain.

His throat tight, he held the cloth against his injury. A sob broke from his mouth. His eyes dampened. He was spiraling out of control, running himself into the ground. He needed a break, a rest. But he couldn't take one.

"Hey, what happened?" Heavy with sleep and confusion, Eve spoke behind him.

"Cut myself is all," he gritted out, willing the bleeding to stop as his flow soaked the rag.

"Oh no, it's bad." She took his wounded hand and held it an inch from her face, wincing like the pain hurt her, too.

"I'll be fine. Look, Eve, I have to run out. Cara's taken a turn for the worse, and well, any time now could be the end. Stay here as long as you need to."

"You have a stocked medicine cabinet, right?" The tenderness in her voice walloped him, though it shouldn't have. Empathy was one of Eve's core traits.

In one swift motion, an inward shift in perspective, Jonnie saw into his own soul. The defective parts he tried to deny, gloss over, or ignore because they were too hard and painful to really look at faced him. "Yes."

He was so used to being the good friend, the support system, old reliable that he forgot sometimes how he deserved care in return.

Someone to nurture him for a change, make sure he was alright. And his bandmates did, of course, though now Jonnie realized how he kept them at arm's length. Afraid they'd reject him if they knew his secret, his truth, he'd unconsciously rejected their attempts to reach out, to deepen the bond.

But Eve knew the secret, the entire story. She was privy and still present. More than that, she cared. That marked her as special in his book. She'd shown her devotion. And he had to get better about honoring and acknowledging her steadfast loyalty. Because these qualities made Eve the most caring, precious woman he'd ever met—even though she was by far the riskiest.

But rather than running from the danger she posed, balking like he had in the jungle, he could fully embrace it. He really could accept her in all her magic and darkness and messy contradictions. Just like she'd embraced his messiness. And he'd better do so soon, because he couldn't expect the woman to bestow upon him an unlimited number of chances and mulligans.

She looked in his eyes like she could read his thoughts. Her somber yet solicitous expression hinted that she registered his moment of clarity, his lighting strike of awareness.

"Come on." With a tug on his wrist, she led him to the bathroom.

He sat on the toilet lid while she got down supplies: tape and bandages and hydrogen peroxide. Sutures would be best, but they both understood there wasn't time for that.

In a slow, tender pull, Eve peeled the towel away, revealing a deep crimson gash. She slung the cloth, light blue fabric dappled with red blotches, over the sink and poured peroxide on his wound. It tingled and stung, bubbling into white foam.

Comfortable silence passed as she performed her healing ritual, a series of steps undertaken with meticulous care. Several dabs with a cotton ball cleaned his marred flesh. A generous daub of clear, gooey ointment soothed the burn.

The gauze, unraveling as the wispy material unspooled from its coil and wrapped his injury, unfurled with precision. He was enchanted. Eve was so careful, covering the injury while allowing enough give in the layers so his skin could breathe.

He needed stitches, but in the moment Jonnie didn't care, for, along with patching his hand, Eve had sewn up a hole in his heart.

The first slices of morning sunlight peeped through his bathroom curtains, imbuing her with the glow of an angel as she taped the bandage. When she was through, she rubbed her fingertips in a little circle on his palm.

Jonnie smiled at her, drinking in the effect of her face in concentration. Her lips pursed, drawn in focus as she devoted the entirety of her attention to treating him.

He could only imagine the gratitude of her clients at the funeral home. Could only imagine the dedication and sensitivity with which she must have cared for the deceased, paying individualized attention to each and every one as she ensured their final appearance on earth was one of grace and dignity.

To *see* a person in this way, to comprehend and cherish and accept them as a bundle of traits comprising a whole greater than the sum of their parts, was a magic he'd only experienced with a few. His family. The band brothers to a lesser extent. And now, Eve. Such an awareness of the wholeness of another, and of locating unique beauty in that other, was one of the fundamental building blocks of love. Did he? Want to hold her in his arms and never let her go?

Could he say those words beginning to form in his heart?

"You're beautiful, Eve."

Her cheeks pinked. Her lips quirked into a half-smile he guessed she didn't want to let show. "I didn't know you had a Florence Nightingale fetish."

"I'm serious."

"Go. See to your family." She touched his arm above the elbow, an affectionate though undeniably platonic touch.

"I don't want this to be goodbye."

In a strange but disarming show of intimacy, she sat across from him on the bathroom floor and stretched out her legs in a V shape.

In some other context, he would have laughed. What a pair they made, two reluctantly magical people stumbling through an insane situation, flailing to get a handle on themselves so they could cope with their lives and do better by those who mattered to them.

Eve laid her hands on his knees. "I think we need to take a step back. It's been an intense few days, and you need to focus on being there for your family. Not on starting something up with me when. Let's be real, my shit is far from together."

He made a study of her delicate hands, her healing hands. Long fingers suited to a pianist, those cute painted nails of hers. He imagined there were practical reasons for keeping nails short in her line of work.

"I don't know how much time I have left." This was not a guilt trip, it was facts and figures. He had a couple of months worth of medicine and no subsequent plan.

Eve's eyes misted. She twisted her lips into a scowl. Incoming light morphed from stark gray-blue to sunny yellow, bringing into relief their sad, private moment. Her on the floor, processing his words. Him on the pot, bruised and bleeding. They were the walking wounded, he the walking dead and she who walked with the dead. But at least they had each other.

In his estimation, they were two people who belonged together.

"Please don't walk out of my life, Eve. I'm here for you." He wasn't begging, and he'd abide her wishes with dignity if severance was what she wanted. But he suspected it wasn't. In the moment of the reckoning, she spoke with hesitancy. The guarded parry of a person protecting the final vestiges of her secrets from exposure. And he wouldn't pry, but he'd damn sure offer her the safe haven of his loyalty and trust.

"There are things you don't know about me."

"But I want to." He leaned forward and spoke in a stage whisper, adding the dramatic emphasis he figured she needed. "I'm not afraid."

Déjà vu washed over him. She'd confessed a lack of fear to him a little while back, soon after he'd shown up on her doorstep and entangled their lives into this sloppy knot.

She shook her head, pulling her touch away in a retreat that copied the distant mask slipping over her features. "You need to go, Jonnie."

And she was right. The hourglass emptied his sand. He stood up. "I won't forget about you, even if you want me to."

She rose to join him. For a few perplexing seconds, her stare lingered on the bloodstained towel. "You probably should, though." A dark laugh.

"What is it, Eve? What are you hiding?"

"Go," she hissed, throwing the splattered cloth across the room. "Stay away from me. I'm poison."

"Don't you dare say that."

"It's true though."

"It isn't. It absolutely isn't. You think I don't have guilt and shame? Over what I am? You know I do. Goddamn, Eve, I've shared every corner of my darkness with you. Why can't you do the same?"

Miserable eyes met his. "There are things I can't tell you. Things I'm obligated to do. And if I tell, it could hurt you. And I don't want to do that. Sometimes I feel like I'm going crazy—like it's a prophecy. When you came to me and asked me to kill you. A prophecy coming true."

Cruddy, half-formed thoughts fogged his mind. Was she in cahoots with Scarab? Had they led him to her, somehow? No. But she was right about one thing.

"I do need to go now. But I won't forget about you, Eve. You and me, we're special. Meaningful. And I know it's frightening. And hard. But the most rewarding things in life are. They're scary. And strange. Not easy. But that's how you know it's the good stuff." He clasped his hands on her soft upper arms and gave a little shake for emphasis, not caring that the contact made his hurt palm throb with hot pain.

"One week. In one week, I'll reach out to you."

"Why one week?"

"I can't say."

"Yes, you can."

"I swear to you I can't."

He threw up his hands, exasperated, though more intrigued by this woman than ever. He'd never met a person with such depth before, never crossed paths with someone so capable of, at once, beguiling and frustrating him. Someone whose difficult parts, the contradictions in their nature, drew him in. Made him want to figure her out, take her apart and put her back together. Find the dark spots she hid and shine light on them. Claim them for his own in a way that no other man would or could. Because he found harmony in her discord.

Jonnie pulled Eve's body to his, cherishing the feel of her muscles relaxing in his hold, her special scent. He brushed a kiss to her forehead and mumbled, "If you think one week is all it'll take for me to grow bored and vanish from your life, you're wrong."

Breaking away, he caught a miniscule twitch on her lips. Not a smile, but perhaps the memory of one. She nodded once, the definitive yet demure gesture serving as a concession.

"One week. I'm holding you to it. Stay here as long as you like. Slide the key under the door after you lock up." With that, Jonnie sprinted from the bathroom. He took two bottles of the thick orange drink from his fridge, shoved them in the bag, and texted his driver.

FOURTEEN

AN ACRID BITE OF EMBALMING FLUID AND RUBBING ALCOHOL STUNG
Eve's nose. She swiped two streaks of coral lipstick across a dead
woman's mouth. The contrast was garish against heavy pancake
foundation, but oh well. The deceased's survivors wanted the woman to
look her Sunday best, and customers had the final say in aesthetic
matters.

Seven days had passed in a mundane drag. Eve worked, then returned
home to binge-watch Netflix and eat takeout for one. Meg and Eve's
folks had sensed she needed to be alone and let her be, considerate and
supportive people they were. So she had stewed in her loneliness and
regret, regret for what she'd agreed to do while tranced out and deep in
the bowels of Amazonian soil. Regret for failing to be there emotionally
for Jonnie, to offer support or an ear while he faced tumult and sorrow in
his personal life, plagued her.

But she'd made a pledge, and she had to quit stalling and fulfil it.

Eve fussed with the body's brittle hair, folding its cool hands in a
demure fig leaf over the midsection as she finished those final dignified
touches. The steady whir of the funeral home's central air conditioner,
the only sound in the basement, calmed her some.

She took a step back and appraised her work. Imperfect, but

perfection was an unobtainable platonic ideal in her line of work. Due to their very nature, corpses never looked quite right. They sagged with a peculiar deflation. Clothing refused to fit them properly. Heavy makeup and slack musculature gave their faces the appearance of uncanny rubber masks.

They looked as if they were missing something, incomplete, which of course they were.

The dead surrendered their souls, their spirits, that mysterious fifteen ounces that came to Eve as golden balls of light. The waste, the corruption of turning meat, remained.

But in a sense, imperfections defined what Eve loved about her work. She dealt in entropy and chaos, striving to bring a modicum of beauty, or at least integrity, to the physical evidence of something intrinsically ugly. The ugly truth of us all.

When facing what we will ultimately become, Eve theorized, we might as well allow ourselves to see the bit of ghastliness, wrongness, that without fail seeps through puritanical attempts to mask it.

Eve smiled at the prepared cadaver. The dead were stubborn, insistent upon showing their grotesque faces. She respected that about them.

And now magic bound her to both facets of the departed, shimmering souls and rotting bodies. Eve chuckled, her voice making an echo against shiny metal walls. She'd been promoted. Go her. She removed her blue rubber gloves with a snap, tossed them in the trash, and washed her hands.

But enough reflection. Duty called. She yanked her purse off its wall hook and slung it over her shoulder. The blue towel, saturated with Jonnie's blood, weighed about a million pounds in her bag. It was an albatross, her guilty remnant of him.

Her heart thudded as she raced up the stairs, checked the lights, and locked up. A perfect fall day, all robin's-egg sky, red-kissed trees, and fallen brown leaves blowing across sidewalk, dared her to feel like shit. But as she unlocked her car and threw her bag in the passenger seat, she for sure did.

Get it over with. She ground her teeth and accelerated down the ramp merging onto 65, south. Eve still had Lacey's parents' address in her email, and she bet they hadn't moved. Save for financial crisis, older folks ensconced in the familiarity of rural home life rarely found much reason to leave.

Dread chased through her as she exited onto the highway. Her guts twisted. A force squeezed her chest, impeding her breath. *You should have brought Meg.* Or someone. But Eve refused to implicate anyone else in her problem.

Besides, what did Lacey's parents have to gain by harming Eve? She had what they wanted, a solution to their daughter's suffering. Despite their bluster and bravado over the last few months, hurting her wasn't in their best interests.

Internal assurances failed to allay Eve's worry as she came up on their home, a one-story bungalow begging for a fresh coat of puce paint. Tucked an acre back from the road, it gave off furtive and shamefaced energies. Gravel clattered underneath Eve's tires as she maneuvered the length of the winding driveway. To her left, a ragged willow tree with a tire swing tied to a big branch wept its droopy branches onto a patch of land comprised of more dirt than grass.

A shudder licked up Eve's skin. The view of the yard evoked a memory of Lacey's patchy scalp, her pallid complexion and lesions of rot.

Remembering Lacey triggered an awareness of her presence inside of Eve. The girl loomed, unobtrusive and eerily patient, an ever-present passenger lying in wait. But this was Eve's problem to solve, her obligation, her duty. *You should have called Helen. To what end? How dare you burden others, good people, with your curse?*

Thoughts warring factions in her weary mind, Eve parked beside a red Ford Fiesta with rust plaques crawling up the sides. Someone had slapped a confederate flag decal onto the back window. A vanity plate read REBEL4LIFE.

Her mouth soured as she jumped out of her car and slammed the door, acutely conscious of her brown skin, her black hair, her Black heritage. Were they bigots? Violent ones?

"Quit being paranoid," she hissed at herself, balling a fist as she hoisted her purse high on her shoulder. For all their many foibles, Lacey and her family had never shown racist tendencies.

Besides, plenty of Southern yahoos, fattened on vague notions of regional pride but starved for historical facts, displayed the stars and bars because they thought it was edgy or cool. Marshalling her professional comportment, Eve walked onto the porch. Decaying wooden boards groaned beneath her feet. She stabbed a finger into the doorbell before she changed her mind.

"Somebody get the damned door." Lacey's mother's distinctive bellow, frayed from heavy smoking, carried from deep inside the house.

Atrocious feline howling stabbed Eve's eardrums. Coarse fur coiled around her calf, the animal's ribs pushing through. She glanced down to see a scrawny orange tabby encircling her leg. Three tiny bugs sprung from its mangy coat. Worse, a socket gaped where one eye should be.

Cringing, Eve trained her gaze back to the ripped screen door and the brown one behind it. Claw marks and mud marred the bottom half, evidence of some poor neglected pet shut outside.

Soft footfalls advanced, Eve deflating more and more as the steps approached. God, there was nowhere she wanted to be less than on the threshold of this fucking house.

The cat launched into a chainsaw purr as it twisted around and around her leg. Eve ground her teeth until her jaw hurt.

The door creaked open a sliver, revealing the skulking form of Susan Mudd. She looked roughly the same, skinny as a scarecrow, with bleached blond hair and a wrinkled smoker's face like a topographical map. In her younger years, the woman had probably been hot in a trashy way.

The cat purred, meowed. Out of nowhere it hissed. Sharp claws stabbed into the top of Eve's sandaled foot, four penetrations of stinging pain. Next came the lingering itch unique to a cat scratch. Sometimes Eve swore the little devils inflicted a bit of venom or poison when they lashed out.

"Nice to see you again, Mrs. Mudd." Eve spat out her lie, miserably failing an attempt at vocal authenticity as she fought an urge to kick the crazy cat.

"Harrumph." Lacey's mother swung the door wide. A bandage dress the color of a wino's vomit stretched across her saggy skin and bony figure, its color obscene against pallid flesh. Sunken eyes slathered in blue eye shadow slid over Eve's body as they sized her up. "You look chubbier."

You look like a whore who could charge five dollars. Tops.

"It's tough to find the time to work out. I have something you want."

Get this over with. Get this over with and call Jonnie.

Susan grunted, turning around and walking barefoot back into the house.

Eve wiggled her leg and shook the starving cat off her, sweaty palm clutching her purse strap. She entered the Mudd residence, the screen door banging shut in a tinny, ominous portend.

Abandon all hope, ye who enter here.

A mordant laugh morphed into a cough as stale cigarette fumes invaded Eve's lungs. Translucent smoke seemed to float in the air, a formless apparition permeating every cell of the home and fouling its energy.

Jolts of bovine snores issued from behind a door at the end of a short hallway. Lacey's father worked the night shift at a factory and slept during the day.

Susan ducked into a kitchen marked by cracked linoleum tile.

Eve shifted on her feet, posture stony and rigid with discomfort. She appraised her surroundings. Dusty bookcases stuffed with knickknacks and trinkets, those bug-eyed, ceramic religious figurines, ringed the walls.

Plastic sheeting covered a couch matching threadbare golden carpet. Blackout drapes, drawn tightly, imbued the smelly house with a morbid vibe that, in an impressive show of irony, was a hundred times more dim and dank than Eve's funeral home.

A boy, tall and developed enough to be seven or eight, yet clad only in a saggy diaper, wandered into the room. His mop of sandy blond hair had perhaps seen one home haircut before his caregivers had given up on the notion.

He held a revolver in one hand, his other absently spinning the chamber that hung loose. It made a faint click and whir noise. "Mama, I wanna play with the Pollyannas."

A sizzle and freeze chased over Eve's chest at the sound of that name. She wracked her brain, grasping for clarity as something important and familiar floated below the surface of her awareness. Stock still, she made eye contact with the kid.

He sneered at her, showing missing front teeth. "They're real fun to play with." The child pushed the chamber back into the gun, aimed it at nothing, and pulled the trigger. "Pew. Pew."

No bang sounded, nothing but a harmless snick. *Thank God*. She swallowed a gasp.

"Rustin, you git." Susan hustled back into the living room, two bottled beers in one hand. She smacked Rustin upside the head. Whining, he ran off. A backdoor slammed.

Eve looked at a candy wrapper on the floor. Heat crawled over her cheeks. Poor kid.

Pollyannas. The name stuck, sticky and thick as snot. She scanned her inventory of memories, hunting for where she'd heard it before.

Susan handed Eve a beer, locking her stare. Mrs. Mudd's pupils ate her irises, evidence of some habit that Eve didn't care to know about.

"You brung my blood, right?" Susan licked her lips, a flash of pink tongue drawing attention to her uneven lip-liner tattoo. It painted two mahogany peaks above the natural line of her top one, a poor attempt on the part of an aesthetician to create the illusion of a fuller pout.

"Yeah. I brung, I *brought*...the blood. I think I found a spell that will be effective in neutralizing the negativity attached to Lacey's spirit. So she can rest in peace." All she had to do was hand over her rag, convince Susan to give her something of Lacey's to focus on, and she could give it a shot. She wasn't positive the incantation from her spell book would work, nowhere near so, but she'd try. Do her best to heed her obligation and then get the fuck out of here.

Susan took a long pull of beer and snickered. She wiped her mouth with the back of her hand. "Girl, y'all sure speak in a lot of big words." A guffaw tore from Mudd's throat as the woman unleashed her mockery in full force.

Irritation bolted through Eve in a frying current. "I need something of hers. For the spell to work."

Susan shrugged, gulped the remainder of her drink, and released a belch so mighty, Eve swore the air trembled in its wake. "Come on out back, then."

Out back?

"Don't you have something in her old room? A piece of jewelry or an article of clothing—"

Susan got in Eve's face, close enough to trigger her gag reflex by way of a mingled stench of cigarettes, beer, and drug store cologne. The hatchet lines in her cheeks were deep enough to secret away loose change. "I *said*, come on out back, witch girl."

"Alright." Eve took a step backward, relief to her nostrils transcending offense at the derogatory coating slathered over the words "witch girl."

Susan laughed again and set her empty on a mantle. Full ashtrays and orange prescription pill bottles with other peoples' names on the labels crowded the shelf. "Damn uppity city folk."

Eve bit down on her tongue and put her bottle beside Susan's when the woman wasn't looking. No way would she consume anything offered here.

Susan led the way, walking the pair through a grungy kitchen. Mountains of crusty dishes erupted from both sides of a metal sink. Flies buzzed over them, landing on gobs of uneaten food. More bugs spotted strips of flypaper, asymmetrical black buttons down a yellow placket.

The women passed through a covered back porch stinking of ripe kitty litter and cluttered with piles of tin cans and glass bottles.

Some critter, wild or feral, had built a substantial nest in the corner. Shredded newspaper classified ads, and a pornographic magazine from the eighties, judging by the hairstyles, were stained light brown.

Empathy for Lacey pricked Eve's heart. *I would have run off and joined a cult, too. Anything but this, damn.* And now, she could help this girl find eternal solace.

As she traipsed behind Susan's emaciated form into a grassless slab of yard, Eve concentrated on the girl's presence, that silent specter within her. Lacey was there, though mute and uncommunicative. Eve wondered why her spirit was closed off, mum. She sighed.

"What?" Susan barked. They walked beneath a big tree blotting out the cheerful sun. A dead baby bird, featherless with bulging eyes, lay facedown in the dirt.

Like everything else in this hell hole, the victim of premature flight played the role of bad omen.

"Nothing. Just tired."

"Lazy fucking millennials." Susan spat onto the ground, rickety shoulders hunching to her earlobes.

The woman's sudden outburst of hostility threw Eve for a loop. As the absurdity of the situation caught up to her, she strangled a sardonic laugh in her throat. *Hope you step on a rusty tetanus nail, bitch.*

Inside her, Lacey giggled. *Whoa!* Energy crackled in Eve's veins. Lacey had come online.

"Ouch!" Susan hopped on one leg, leaning against the tree. Face contorted in pain, she cradled a dusty, unshod foot and brushed it off. Susan dug a tiny chunk from her dirt-caked sole, a blob of red appearing on the area as she flung the offending detritus aside.

Interesting. Mentally, Eve high-fived Lacey. The girl giggled again. Intriguing new development.

Susan growled, scowled, and resumed her walk.

Hidden behind the enormous tree was a rickety, pea-green shed the size of a two-car garage. The roof sagged, and a dusting of paint chips littered the perimeter of the structure like shed scales.

Thick chains secured two doors. Susan pulled a lone key from her bra and fumbled with a rusted-out padlock.

Oh, no. A realization hit. Lacey slept out here. Eve's heart broke for the poor, abused girl who had taken her own life. Out of despair, in a final desperate grab for freedom and independence from the nightmare she was trapped in, she'd killed herself. And perhaps an act of aggression, a final "fuck you" to the hag who kept her confined to this backyard prison in the middle of nowhere.

Eve pictured herself holding Lacey's hand. Quite possibly a return to this vile place could trigger the young woman. Spirts had feelings, too.

Though Eve expected a reply, Lacey offered nothing.

The lock clicked, and Susan muttered a triumph. Huffing and wheezing, Mrs. Mudd freed the chains with a big yank, sending them clamoring to the ground in heavy clinks. She sniffed and tugged on two wooden handles, bat wings of loose skin flapping beneath her triceps.

It's okay, Lacey. I'm here.

Lacey giggled. *You sure are.*

Eve's legs locked. Lacey sounded as nasty as her mother.

Pulse slamming in her skull, Eve spun around and prepared to run. But the diapered boy faced her. At some point, he'd slunk up on the women's heels and followed them. Now, instead of his unloaded revolver, he held a deer rifle. Pointed at Eve's face. He advanced, butting its hard end into her sternum. "Git on in now."

Eve swallowed her panic. She had something they wanted. She held the upper hand. Hands up, she turned and followed Susan into the shed. It smelled so bad that her eyes watered. She plugged her nose.

What the fuck was that smell? The distinct tang of bodily waste and a rotten assault of fishy water assailed her senses.

But something else, alien and scary, lurked in the atmosphere. A musk, animal, the effluvia of an animal you didn't want anything to do with.

Susan walked to the middle of the room, stood on her tiptoes, and pulled a string. From the ceiling, a single bulb flickered, casting the space in a menacing, shadow-filled light.

A sustained hiss tore through the air. The distinct, dull sound of flesh whacking against something hard followed. More hisses came.

Gun butting rudely into her back, Eve fixed her eyes on the poorly rendered dolphin tattoo staining Susan's left shoulder blade. Because she didn't want to see anything in this awful room.

Rattles buzzed. Ice water shot through her veins. Something alive squealed. Dust filled her mouth. Her knees went to jelly, knocking into each other as they shook.

"Herpetology," Susan announced, puffing out her chest as she stood tall and proud.

"We're gonna be rich." This from the boy, an ejaculation of venal greed.

"Shut up, Rustin," Susan snapped. She swiveled her head over her shoulder, her teased blonde crown immobile. Her hard and aggressive eyes betrayed a single, mercenary focus. "You brung my blood, witch girl?"

Eve surveyed the enclosure, nausea and terror blasting her as her surroundings came into revolting view. Her skin crawled. She shivered in the muggy air.

Stacked floor-to-ceiling in metal cabinets, aquariums lined the walls. Creatures of unknown taxonomy writhed inside them, the colors of their hairless, leathery skins ranging from slate gray to dark brown. Tan or olive splotches dappled the backs and blunt faces of some.

One, caged alone, stalked its empty home, back and forth in predatory frustration. It walked low to the ground, supported by an excess of tiny cricket legs. More so than its brethren, it moved with a self-aware gait. This thing was mad, pissed off.

Others pressed scaly, dishwater-pale bellies into cloudy glass. In one tank, several of the things lounged in a fleshy pile of light tans and muddy browns.

Eve blinked, clawing at the far corners of her comprehension. She struggled to determine what in the actual fuck squirmed and slithered and loafed in the cages before her.

Their bodies were long and sinuous, the tubular shape of a snake though notably fatter.

Each one had a zillion short, itty bitty legs and a broad back that looked tougher and hardier than their quivering underbellies.

Scales covered them head to toe. Stout feelers twitched on wedge-shaped skulls. Unlidded eyes the color of dehydrated urine were set deep in viper-like heads. A vertical, blood-red sliver bifurcated each yellow orb.

"You like my big boy, dontcha." Susan made a kissy face at the tank with the loner and ambled up to it, her baby talk a horrid, stunning incongruity.

The woman crouched and pressed her lips to the glass. The monster inside reared back, coiling as it hissed. Its entire body vibrated, emitting a distinct rattle-and-buzz. Susan tapped the glass in provocative bangs. The animal maintained its aggressive posture, mouth dropping to reveal two full rows of pointy, hooked fangs.

"What is this?" Eve whispered, the spectacle commanding her surrender to unholy terror.

"Come on, stupid." Susan stuck her tongue out at the angry beast. Growling in frustration, she leaned down, dragged out a Styrofoam cooler shoved underneath the shelving unit, and popped the lid. Stacked bags of red fluid filled the container, and Susan grabbed one.

Though many pieces remained missing, a handful landed in place. "This isn't right, Susan. Whatever you're doing is a horrible, terrible idea." After she spoke her feeble warning, Eve's focus returned to the gun shoved in her back.

"Don't you say bad things about the Pollyannas." The boy punctuated his inflamed, high pitched order with a mean poke of his rifle.

Idiotic grin splitting her face, Susan waved the blood in front of the Pollyanna's cage. Its face followed the motion. A wide ribbon of a black, forked tongue slid between knives of teeth.

In a swift thrust, it struck, slamming its face against the glass with a thump that made Eve jump back. Adrenaline cooked her extremities.

Viscous, milky liquid oozed down the glass in slow streaks.

Susan clapped and barked like a dumb seal. In that moment, Eve wanted to murder her. Could she act fast enough to pull it off in time? Swing around, grab the gun, and wrest it from the boy's scrawny hands? Bludgeon his menace of a moronic mother until she stopped twitching?

Blood bag in one hand, Susan used the other to free an empty water bottle attached to the tank. She filled the bottle with blood and reattached it.

The loner Pollyanna slurped at the metal tube, draining the bottle in under a minute. It grew before Eve's eyes, bloating like a fresh tampon dropped into a toilet. Satiated, the fiend tucked into a ball and shut its eyes. The animal slept, ponderous mass of flesh rising and falling with big breaths.

"My own mama said I was no good, good for nothing but turnin' tricks. But I knew she was wrong. I almost wish the mean old cunt was alive to see me, her worthless white trash daughter, working for a big old fancy corporation." Susan rooted under the front of her dress and excavated a cigarette and lighter. She lit up, closing her eyes as she sucked and released smoke, face puckering into an anal knot.

"You do this for Scarab." It didn't take a genius to guess the origin of the bloodthirsty monsters.

"I'm their best breeder and caretaker." She fluffed her lacquered hair.

"Get a shipment of eggs every month. Hatch 'em, feed 'em, breed 'em, and send 'em back plump and fat and ready to go."

Ready to go?

Susan stooped and peered into a cage, presenting the back of her head as an easy target.

"What are they?" Even if she could subdue mother and son, she'd need more information to plan the next steps. Determine how to manage Lacey, whose role in all of this remained a mystery.

"Equal parts cockroach, rattlesnake, tick, and piranha. Custom-made agents of biological warfare tailored to withstand the harshest conditions. Survive a nuclear apocalypse or extinction-level natural disaster. The real deal."

"The vampire blood makes them so hardy." Eve's heartbeat quickened. She had to keep the rag soaked with Jonnie's blood out of this psychopath's hands, because it was anyone's guess how exposing the Pollyannas to his life force could impact him.

"Buncha geniuses at Scarab, lemme tell ya. They reuse, recycle, upcycle all their byproducts. Great company. Real great people." Susan voice dropped to a hushed tone as she mused on the virtues of her employer.

Now. Eve whirled around, disarming the boy with a single confident tug. He yelped as she pulled his unwashed, wiggling body to hers and pressed the business end of the rifle into his chin. It gave her no pleasure to take a child hostage, but she needed Susan's cooperation to fix this fiasco.

And beating the bitch unconscious would not help her gather intel.

Susan charged, then stopped. Her bony chest rose and fell in deliberate breaths, mirroring the rhythm of the slumbering abomination behind her.

"What is Scarab doing with dead people, cults, and demons? Vampires. The squirrel. Lacey. How does it all connect? Speak."

"Don't hurt my baby, my only living baby." Susan doubled over, yowling hysterical wails.

Rustin sobbed infantile, womb-stabbing cries. The bitter stench of fear seeped from his dry skin. "I don't wanna die, don't wanna die."

Shame saturated Eve all the way to her bones. She had to get this over with ASAP. "Talk, Susan, and, nothing bad happens. Tell me what I want to know, and I release Rustin."

Lacey raged around Eve's subconscious, screeching and pounding walls.

Well, you aren't going to get whatever it is you want right now. Accept it.

The possession screamed, haggard tangle of hair flying every which way as she flailed her tantrum.

"Fine." Susan gathered her bearings with a choppy, audible inhale. Her nostrils flared, the frown on her face a stoic portrait of acceptance. "Guess I'll take it from the top."

FIFTEEN

Jonnie didn't break promises. That wasn't the man he was, plain and simple. For now, the medical team had Cara stabilized and back to her normal, following the latest scare. He looked at the picture of her, smiling and awake, that Anya had sent him right after he'd left. They'd borrowed a bit more precious time.

He hopped over to PayPal, sent his sister another five-figure deposit, and closed his phone with a sigh. Hi bank account was running low, but in a few days a royalty check from the summer mini-tour would drop and build it back up.

Enough worrying about money. He returned his thoughts to Eve. Because one week was up and she hadn't made contact. This was Eve, though, he thought as the Uber drove him from the airport to her funeral home. She was probably swept up in her work, her mission, and due for a reminder that she was cared for. Classic Eve.

The rangy driver grooved to the tune of Swedish orchestral heavy metal, leaving Jonnie plenty of quality time to sink into his thoughts.

Classic Eve. He smiled along with the intimacy, the familiarity such a moniker brought.

Beyond the hatchback's windows, overcast skies painted the day in blah, muted tones. But Jonnie glowed with pleasant warmth. Classic Eve. Honor-bound, dignified and serious, loyal to a fault. He supposed it was the loyalty, most of all, that got to him. Jonnie drummed fingers on the door handle.

He knew the deep things about Eve, how she lived with integrity and focus, did right by those who expected it. He knew her mysteries, the barbed gift of her magic. She kept a bit of distance from others, was guarded, lived in a snail shell of self-protection. And who could blame her?

Still, did she order her life in a way that favored loneliness and solitude as the default setting? Starting with her career, did she arrange the pieces of her world, of her, in a manner intended to scare off those who dared get close, who sought to breach her tight inner circle?

Perhaps. But as thorny as she could be, as spiny and defensive, her inner beauty was too grand to stifle. But beyond the big stuff, Jonnie yearned to grasp the little bits of Eve. The trivia that's as much a part of intimate knowledge of someone as their values and flaws. He longed to know her favorite things, her quirks and habits, her preferences and aversions.

He wanted all of Eve. He was greedy like that. There was the whole vampire issue to deal with, but he could cope. He could control his darker urges, of course he could.

The car pulled up to the curb, coming to idle underneath an awning supported by pillars. A classy, homey white building bragged a landscaped front yard and tasteful façade.

Miniature Halloween pumpkins, their cute faces drawn in black marker, peeked up from flower beds. No other decorations, certainly nothing ghoulish or skeleton-themed, adorned the place. Jonnie smiled. He imagined Halloween aesthetics could amount to a delicate subject for a funeral home to negotiate, and of course Eve navigated the maze with sensitivity and finesse.

Very much one of the Eve-details he craved, right there.

He scooped up the gift basket he'd bought for her, a collection of self-care items ranging from lotions and candles to wine and cheese and chocolate. A punch card for yoga classes and a gift certificate for a massage rounded out the presents.

Because if anyone needed a bit of pampering, it was Eve. Eve, living in service to others, could stand to be a bit selfish for a change.

"You lose someone?" The driver raised his voice over deep, melodious male vocals and soaring stringed harmonies blending violin and electric guitar.

"No. I've just now found her."

"Right on, man." With a chortle, the scruffy chauffeur cranked his music.

Jonnie got out of the car, the basket of crinkly cellophane and artfully displayed personal products bulky in his arms, and went to the front door.

A man in a black suit stood vigil, facial features youthful though male pattern baldness crawled over his shiny head. Beside him on an easel rested a glossy poster of a pretty middle-aged woman, her name printed in cursive beneath her photo.

The guy smiled dryly at Jonnie. "Of course she can't use any of that, but it's the thought that counts I suppose. You one of the cousins?"

"Oh, no. I stopped by to see Eve. My apologies, I wasn't aware services were going on at the moment." Now he felt like an arse. In his excitement, he'd forgotten to check and see if a funeral was taking place.

The gatekeeper cocked his head, confusion bunching his face. "Who's Eve?"

Vicarious offense made Jonnie draw back in surprise. His lips parted. The woman had put together an entire program for this lad's dead relative, and he didn't even know her name.

He no longer felt like the arse in this situation. "The director," he said curtly.

"Oh, right, right." The man shook his head. "Duh. The staff have this way of being invisible. Fading into the background. Come on in." After issuing the invitation, he stepped aside.

Jonnie bit off a smartass remark. An ache pulsed beneath his ribs. Eve deserved to be acknowledged, cherished for the important work that she did. Not deemed invisible, a non-person who best step aside when others were finished using her labor.

"Yes, well, I thought she could use a bit of recognition." He brushed past the man and walked into an open, airy room perfumed with floral aromas and decorated in classy hardwood accents and a dusky rose sofa, loveseat, and easy chair set.

Healthy plants and white wooden furniture imbued the space with the vibe of a grandmother's house. People in black sat around on the couches and other seats, sniffling and playing with their phones as they awaited the event.

An ajar door leading to a smaller room offered a coy peek at an open oak casket. Three women hovered in front of it. One whimpered softly, struggling to read a note. The other two rubbed her arm and back in support.

Stirred in with a generic empathy for the bereaved strangers was a mild curiosity as to the origins of the myths that vampires slept in coffins. But now wasn't the time to navel gaze or ponder folklore.

Jonnie swam through a growing crowd of attendees with the deft movements of a seasoned backstage shark, ignoring the smattering of oohs and ahs as people placed his identity.

A rhythm guitarist was blessed with a bit more anonymity than a solo star or singer, but it never took more than a short time in public before he started getting stares. No bother. On most occasions he was happy to mingle with fans, but not today.

Tucked in a nook near the exit was a door with a gold plaque in the middle. Jonnie sauntered over to it, read Eve's name, and knocked.

She answered, looking sexy as hell in a tailored pinstripe skirt suit and black heels. She'd straightened her hair, and it hung glossy at her shoulders.

But the pleasing sight of her attractiveness was subsumed by worry the moment he looked into her eyes. Her gaze was numb. A blank hollowness blotted pain, betraying something terrible.

"What's wrong, Eve? My God, what's wrong?" He stepped forward, hitting an invisible wall as he moved to breach the doorway. Right, silly vampire rules.

The rueful ghost of a smile drifted across her lips, and in a wink dissipated into the ether. "Right. Come in."

She stepped aside and beckoned warily, shutting the door and locking it. He walked into an organized, tastefully scented office.

An ancient fern in a woven basket hung from the ceiling, dripping ropy Medusa leaves halfway to the neutral-hued carpet. Poster prints of mindfulness-related sayings and modern art paintings decorated the walls.

He lowered to a plush loveseat bookended by two short tables displaying stacked pamphlets discussing grief. Jonnie held her hand, tugging until she sat beside him. "Talk to me. What's wrong? How can I help?"

"I went over to Lacey's old house yesterday." She spoke like each word threatened to level a hex.

"And, Eve?" Jonnie urged in nurturing tones, offering comfort as best he could while beset by the foreshadow of grim revelation.

"This, uh. This was yesterday."

Fuck. Was she in shock? She sounded like a trauma victim, deadening her emotions as a coping mechanism. He'd heard the distinct vocal inflection before, in the cadence of his sister's speech when she spoke of her daughter.

Jonnie tore open the gift basket and freed a chocolate bar. Eve likely hadn't eaten recently enough. People enduring acute emotional suffering rarely did. And if her nutrition faltered, her health could suffer.

"Here." He opened the candy and held it out. He'd cook her a proper meal later, but for now she needed an immediate influx of calories and sugar.

As she accepted his offering and fidgeted with the paper, Eve's eyes slid to the basket on the floor. "I'm sorry I spoiled your surprise with drama. I'm sorry I'm not a normal person."

"Stop. You're a beautiful person. What happened over there? Did someone hurt you?" Heat coursed through his veins. If someone did, they'd regret it.

"No. Not like that." She bit of some chocolate, chewed, and swallowed. "Ugh. I needed this. You're an angel. I was up all night, surprise surprise. But I found things."

Eyes that knew too much, that knew atrocities, moved wearily to lock in with his.

Eating, she rose, still holding his hand as she led him to her tidy desk. Jonnie refused to allow their imbroglio to ruin the simple pleasure of touching her warm skin. They deserved every bit of happiness they could steal. He stroked the inside of her palm with a single, slow caress.

She replied to his gesture by petting his index knuckle with her thumb pad.

Jonnie shoplifted a smile, a stolen ration of happiness proffered in a time of famine.

She broke the clasp, circled to the front of her desk, and got down to business, pawing in a drawer.

A few framed pictures decorated the top of the polished wooden surface. Eve riding with a pack of cyclists, black hair a parachute opening behind her helmet. Her and Meg posing by the Mona Lisa. A close up of a beagle.

While Eve rummaged, Jonnie studied the photos. One held his attention over the rest, and he picked it up.

It featured four people. The first impression of it gave Jonnie pause, and his world shrank to awareness of the photo in all its minute detail. Everyone gathered on majestic stone steps. Behind them, a gold-domed building towered.

In the middle of the group stood an older, interracial couple. A bespectacled man leaning on a cane beamed, and a woman with a shock of red hair and a huge, colorful tattoo peeking out from beneath her tee shirt collar grinned. Beside who was likely her mother, Eve wore a sundress printed with roses. On the opposite flank, a young man in a cap and gown held a diploma and showed off a big smile full of perfect teeth.

Three of the people glowed.

A photogenic gestalt of perfection blessed the parental couple and the graduate. Mellow afternoon light blew a flattering kiss, highlighting laugh lines and joy and overall comfort in the skin. Blue morning glories climbed up a brick wall in the background, bringing out cobalt tones in the mum's ink.

But Eve didn't enjoy the same camera love. Though her mum hugged her, Eve's posture gave off the effect of pulling back. She'd been adjusting her body when the lens clicked, a miniscule movement at the wrong moment that created an impression of off-ness. A shoulder hunched too high, an awkward bend of the knee, a squint.

An odd, blotchy shadow struck one side of her beautiful face, eating her left eye in a macabre erasure of natural light.

As Jonnie stared at the picture, his heart grew larger, expanding in a swell of maudlin awareness. The body has a way of keeping the score, of registering epiphanies through sensations impossible to ignore. And his was doing exactly that in the moment.

Eve didn't *fit*. She was the oddity, the abnormality, the rock in the shoe.

There was a second puzzle piece left over when the rest of the jigsaw came together in harmony.

The first hint of water trembled in the corners of his eyes. They were two pieces, he and she, that never fit.

But she did fit. She fit with him, in their own bizarre puzzle. The two of them together sculpted a new whole out of broken, damaged, and cast off parts. A Frankenstein's monster, sure, but one with a good soul.

A soft, affectionate laugh came from Eve. Soft and affectionate, but coming out corrupted with the tiniest clove of bitter astringent.

"You're looking at my brother's graduation from medical school. I love my family with all of my heart, but yeah. It was a weird day. My parents were overjoyed. I could tell they felt guilty, too, bad for me, and they kept trying to mask how giddy they were. And failing, because they're the sort of wonderful people who can't hide the truth of their happiness no matter how hard they try. My graduation from mortuary school was awkward at best. Vince's, well, it was the moment they'd been waiting for since they decided to have kids." A dry chuckle shot through with sadness pierced his skin and stabbed his heart.

Eve took a step closer, close enough for him to feel her body heat, smell her sweetness. "It was made official that day—they officially got one normal kid. Not just a normal kid, a great kid. One perfect kid on his way to becoming a hero, a gifted surgeon who saves lives. People have been comparing him to Obama since high school and...I'm happy for him, happy for Mama and Daddy, too. They really lucked out with my brother. He makes up for getting stuck with the freaky daughter who cuts up corpses and talks to ghosts. I was up late that night in the hotel, cause you know how I can never fucking sleep, and I heard them popping the champagne and crying tears of joy. I don't blame them—"

He set down the picture and swept Eve into his arms. "I love you, Eve."

The words poured from his center, truths that paused the moment in a paradox of brevity and eternity.

Time's passage ceased to exist as the world flowed in a stream of perfection.

She'd rested her head on his chest and nuzzled. Flow slowed to trickle as silence elapsed.

Jonnie came back to himself as his awareness of past and future returned. The magic of being in the eternal present drained away. Eve wasn't going to return the words.

She didn't share the sentiment. Jonnie stayed in this reality without resentment, though he'd be a liar if he failed to confess a smarting of humiliation. Being a vampire didn't render him immune to the machinations of the ego.

Eve's breathing was audible over the air conditioner, the pall of her emotions palpable amidst a mellow room tailored to calm angst and lift spirits.

"It's really, really, hard for me to be happy." She clutched the back of his tee shirt in two tight fists.

He stroked her hair and neck, nonverbal assurances communicating his intention to listen without taking up space for his voice.

"I want to say it back to you, I really do, because you're amazing. And I have feelings for you. But it's like..." She whimpered, her breath hitching.

"What's it like, darling? What's it like?"

"It's like my heart is buried in a crypt. A mausoleum. I can feel it down there, but it's covered with dirt. And it's not healthy. It's rotting." A tragic sound, mirthless laughter mixed with pain. "See? I'm morbid. Other people have all these great feelings, and I have ghosts and dead bodies and a fucked-up spirit possessing me."

As the delicate situation presented itself, Jonnie gathered his thoughts. Eve was opening up, which was good. And he should offer help without condescension. Center her needs while adding something of value that she could use. But never patronize, never explain her feelings to her. That was rude, the purview of arrogant men who thought they knew everything, knew what was best for a woman. "Have you ever talked to anyone about these feelings?"

"Like a therapist?"

Jonnie hadn't noticed the music until now, until the pauses stretching between their tender moment took command. Gentle classical music, soothing piano notes, drifted in through an unseen sound system. You didn't notice it unless you tried to, giving the soundtrack the nuanced effect of subliminal messaging. "Yeah," he whispered.

"Oh yes, many of them over many years. But the lessons and advice never resonated. I suppose I've been too ashamed to internalize the therapy, too ashamed to take the initiative to try and be better. Maybe that's one of the reasons I was drawn to Meg. Because of her career. Could be that on some subconscious level, I've always known I needed help but haven't been capable of doing the self-work necessary to help myself heal."

"How can I help?"

"Stay. Stay with me."

"You've got it." Of course he remained on permanent call for his family, but his career afforded flexibility. Fyre wasn't set to head back to the studio for a couple more weeks, meaning he had time. To hold Eve like he held her in her office, to hold her so that she understood he'd never let her go. Even if she couldn't return his feelings, he'd still hold her.

He'd love her while expecting nothing in return.

"You deserve so much better than me." Her tone flat and sad, she hung on to him.

"Stop it."

With a thousand-pound exhale, she broke their press of bodies and took a step back. Eve brought her hands to rest right above his belly button.

His dick thickened, and he bit his tongue in a failed effort to make it wilt. This wasn't the time for those thoughts. The woman needed consoling.

Three knocks pounded the door.

"I ordered one hundred mint chocolate chip cookies for the funeral party," a female voice shouted in a shrill tone. "There are basic ones mixed in there. Fix it."

The customer's outburst killed his hard-on right and proper.

Eve dashed toward the door shaking her head. She opened her mouth, but before she could speak Jonnie caught her wrist and put a finger to his lips.

He strode to the door in her stead and opened it. A slim woman wearing a turtleneck and a pinched countenance glowered at him.

Jonnie looked down at her, putting on his best rock star cool. "Is there a problem here?"

She cocked her head, brushing a strand of blonde bob out of her eyes. "Holy crap. My cousin said there was a famous musician here. Are you Jonnie Tollens?" Green eyes widened in recognition.

Jonnie nodded. He drew a nip of glamour magic up his spine and poured it into the woman's star-struck eyes. "Run along and go eat a cookie. You'll feel better."

"Yes, sir." After drawling the words in hushed reverence, the mourner sprinted off in the direction of the refreshments.

Jonnie closed the door with a nick of victory. Vampire powers came in handy when dealing with pesky people, he had to admit.

Leaned against her desk, Eve offered him a slow clap. "Mint-flavored sweets gross me out. It's like eating toothpaste. Why would you want an entire table of them, to boot? With none of the basic kind for balance? I was looking out for the other guests. But fuck me for being conscientious, right?"

He sauntered up to her, drinking in the sight of her beautiful face and figure as he slid his hands around her slim waist. "What other culinary acts of war gross Eve out? Or better yet, what makes her moan in delight?"

His cock swelled again as he stared at her sensuous mouth, remembering all of the things they'd already done. All the things they had yet to do. He hadn't even tasted her yet. Jonnie licked his lips.

"We, uh. We should." Her own hungry gaze swept over his body, palms returning to his torso. She slid her hands up and down in a languid, teasing stroke that left him aching for more.

He could smell the fleshy scent of her arousal. His nostrils flared, cock pulsing in the confines of his tight jeans. He fought temptation, fought the urge to quell this talk of "should" by slipping his fingers between her legs, where he'd wiggle them underneath her panties and slide them into her wet heat.

Eve sucked air. "We need to talk about what happened yesterday." The resignation behind her words shrank his rising desire. Because she was right. Now was not the time to play.

"We do. You were going through your desk."

"I was." She circled back to the desk in question and fired up a thin silver laptop sitting on the surface. Beside the computer lay a notebook, sticky notes, and three pens in an assortment of colors. "After yesterday, I have some information to add to your Scarab chart."

SIXTEEN

After Eve ducked out to quickly fulfil an obligation to mingle with the funeral party, Jonnie studied the web of pens and yellow stickers and notebook paper stretched across the top of her desk. It mirrored many of his own Scarab-related findings and added to others. Such a loopy, precise thing merged his and Eve's lives. If that didn't signal they were meant for each other, what would?

"Okay," she said breathlessly upon re-entering the room. "Everyone's gone." Chair legs scraped against carpet as she pulled up a seat next to Jonnie in front of the computer. "Let's do this."

Rearranging a grainy printout from a website so it sat beside a page of notes, Jonnie rubbed his chin. "So the endgame of this project, as I see it, was to create vampires using the treatment, then feed the toxic blood to these mutant creatures."

"Yeah." Chewing her lip, she leaned in an inch from her computer screen. "They're deep underground, rebranded. But its an offshoot of the same company on trial for war crimes. The one they mentioned in Peru."

"It's the cult and demons element that I can't quite place." Skimming text from a conspiracy theory website, Jonnie remembered something Eve had said a moment ago. "What did the girl's mother tell you?"

She collapsed backward in her chair and stared up at the ceiling. "She was babbling incoherently. Hysterical, word salad kind of stuff. But there were bits and pieces."

"Such as?"

"The mother intimated that Lacey didn't actually commit suicide."

"She was killed?"

"Voluntarily sacrificed." Eve ejected the words like rotten food. "Some kind of botched spell, using insight she supposedly gleaned from her time in the Hollywood cult. The idea was to kill her, then bring her back as a vampire. They have to pay this company for the blood to feed those mutant monsters. It's like a multilevel marketing pyramid scheme. So the idea was, if they have Lacey on deck as a vampire, they have a constant food source and can save a bundle on overhead."

"It all boils down to greed eventually." Brian's image popped into Jonnie's mind. His bandmate had said as much, after going through some rubbish with Fyre's former manager and his attempts to indoctrinate the man into a cult.

"True. So their attempt to turn Lacey failed, and she stayed dead. From what I could surmise, they reached out to me because they had this notion that they could merge whatever magic they were doing with my powers."

"So what's up with the squirrel? And you said that Lacey is haunting you?"

"They killed a squirrel as part of their ritual. If Susan is to be believed, the idea was to make a familiar for Lacey. To protect her, help her strengthen her powers. It's so nuts, Jonnie."

"So what, she and the familiar are stuck in some limbo land? Purgatory? And they want to get to you?"

She nodded in a resigned manner as if his words had really made landfall. "I think so. I think Susan still has designs on me. Like the idea all along has been to force me to use my powers to get Lacey to manifest in vampire form, which is impossible as I see it. So I can't say for sure what they're plotting, but I think they're plotting. And I don't think it's a sound bet that you're safe."

Jonnie's stomach fluttered. His thoughts gummed. The agitation in his stomach hardened into a knot. After voicing her odd statement, Eve turned her attention to the papers. "Why would I be on their radar?"

"They've stalked me in the past," she said quickly. "Stands to reason that they might have learned about you."

His brow tightened as he tried to get his head around logic that didn't add up. As usual, Eve held back. "Did she ask you about vampires, what you knew?" Perhaps the woman intimidated Eve into spilling some incriminating detail. He wouldn't be upset, but he needed to know in order to determine how to best keep them safe.

"No." Fast movements of her hands. Hair in her face.

"Eve."

She sighed, halting her busywork. "I feel so stupid. I thought Lacey needed my help, my council. But apparently not. I need to figure out how to get this spirit out of my head. Get rid of both of them and move on. If I knew what sort of magic they were messing with, what they supposedly picked up from this cult, that would help."

Jonnie shoved aside his lingering suspicions. This was a topsy-turvy state of affairs, was all, prompting him to doubt and question everything. Eve wasn't hiding anything, and she certainly wasn't up to something bad. She was a good person. He loved her. He trusted her. "We should talk to Brian and see what he knows. I have a strong hunch that we'll be able to trace the debacle with my manager back to Scarab, or whatever they're calling themselves now."

Eve picked up a sheet and read it. "Pentagroup Affiliates, Inc. God, talk about on nose." She snorted.

He scooted closer to get a look at what she held. The paper featured a graphic in the middle, a clean circle with five lines shooting from it. Each line had a bold-type heading accompanying it: private defense services, health care products and supports, entertainment and talent management, biotech and agriculture.

"Here's Scarab." Eve drew a blue squiggle next to a teeny graphic of a black beetle hovering beneath the "private defense services" line.

"I suppose creating vampires through shady drugs falls into the bucket of health care supports." He squinted at the categories. Under each heading, numerous subsidiary company logos, fonts and symbols, attention-grabbing yet cryptic, peppered white space in bursts of color.

"And the mutants I saw at the house must qualify as agriculture."

Eve tapped a pen in the middle of the blank circle. "Notice how this space is empty."

He circled a familiar name under the "entertainment and talent management" line. Aries, Inc., the conglomerate whose subsidiary had operated Fyre's record label before the band broke from them and went indie. "I definitely notice."

She looked up. He did too. A current of recognition flowed between their eyes.

"That's where the magic happens," Eve said.

"Perhaps literally. The glue that holds it all together."

"You know what's weird about this?" Eve held up the paper to the window, where waning daylight infiltrated the sheet with a translucent glow.

"Everything?" Jonnie quipped.

She proffered a whisper of a smile he now gathered was for his eyes only. "Touché. But no, seriously, look at how the lines are arranged. In a cross overlaying the circle. But the biotech line juts out from the top."

Eve was right. The graph consisted of the empty circle and its four-pointed arms arranged into clean ninety-degree angles, but the biotech line wrecked the symmetry. It sat between the health care and agriculture lines, sticking out like a vestigial limb. "Perhaps it was added last, after they'd settled on their original design. Like an afterthought."

"Could be." She tossed the scrap back onto the desk. "At least I know a little more now. What's happening. Can you get your plane here tonight? I want to get over to Minneapolis as soon as possible and meet with the witch you were telling me about. You could talk to Brian then, too. Two birds and a stone and all."

With a clipped moan, Eve slipped off her heels and rubbed her feet together. Sheer black stockings shrouded her painted toes. The glimpse of her skin under see-through fabric was as erotic as looking at someone else's breasts.

"Let's take a night off." He took one of her hands in his and kissed the top.

"What?" She blinked, face and voice registering so much confusion, he wondered for a moment if he'd spoken in tongues.

"I want to spend time with you. Just for the rest of today, tonight.

Relax." They could pretend to be a regular, happy pair getting to know each other. Laughing and flirting and, heaven forbid, having fun.

"I suppose it would help to recharge."

"Yes." And if he played this right, he could stretch their day of down time into two or three. Days where they could enjoy a break, where he could get to know Eve's city, her favorite things in it, her friends and family.

She toed a pair of running shoes out from under her desk, slid them on, and laced them up. Jonnie smiled at this, this Eve detail. Every tidbit he scooped up whetted his hunger for more. "You run?"

"I used to. But I ruined my left knee. So now I just walk as much as I can. It's a solid two miles each way to work. You up for it?" The question came out a bit pointed, as if she lobbed a dare. Eve crossed her legs while she waited, teasing him with a glimpse of her firm thighs.

He adored those legs of hers. Defined, with lean lines of muscle delineating calves, quadriceps. Plenty of feminine softness balanced out her tone. His balls tightened as he admired her sculpted stems under that prim outfit of hers.

"You bike, too." Jonnie glanced at the cycling picture, where her full bottom was pressed against the lucky seat.

"It's been a while, but yeah. There's something so freeing and empowering about becoming one with an instrument. The first time I bought those clip-in shoes—they actually snap your feet into the pedals —I was terrified. Of the loss of control. But then when I got used to it, it was like I was flying. Down the highway, nothing but the hum of the wheels in my mind. Pure bliss."

And there it was. What Eve needed. Escape. Liberation. Freedom, like she'd said. "Let's get out of here."

She rocked on her rubber heels, the effect adorable in its playful innocence. Finally, she let her guard down. "What do you want to do?"

"Lead the way. Show me your favorite places." He popped out an elbow in invitation for her to link his arm.

Her face relaxed into a visage of lightness. She looped her arm through his. "Let's do this."

Jonnie enjoyed the silence with Eve as they strolled through the dark parlor. She locked up, the click of key in door a comforting bit of closure to their research session. She led him on a short walk through her historic residential neighborhood. Three-story, narrow brick mansions towered on both sides of the street.

The turning of leaves had accelerated, a brush stroke of decay painting trees in palates of red, gold, yellow, and brown. Their perfume, earthen and crisp, imbued the air with the essence of fall. Carved pumpkins grinned at them from stoops.

When was the last time he'd stopped to smell the proverbial roses?

They came up on a quaint Italian eatery at the end of a city block. It wasn't quite six, though the place was decently populated. Eve giggled a little as they approached the entryway.

"What?" He stooped to murmur his question into her ear and tickle her side. These little gestures of happiness on her part amounted to priceless treasures.

"It's silly." She bit her bottom lip, a display almost girlish in its goofiness.

"Tell me." He opened the door with a tinkle of hanging metal chimes. A brief clench of worry set in as the invisible, energetic wall pushed him out. But a host behind a podium said "Come on in, guys," neutralizing the unseen barrier. Whew. Vampire problems.

Eve on his arm, Jonnie stepped into a charming nook of a boutique restaurant decorated with lots of dark wood and oil paintings in ornate frames. Scrumptious scents of garlic and basil made his mouth water. They walked to an intimate table for two set with sleek menus. A lit candle dripped red wax onto a wine bottle coated with layers of the hardened substance. The sum of it all made for a homey, accessible elegance.

"The night we met, I passed by this place. I was in one of my funks and looking in the window made me crabby. Because I wasn't allowed to have a nice date here like they were," Eve said.

"Ah. But you are. And you'll have a nice time tonight, Eve. I'll see to it."

A waiter with a handlebar moustache and a necktie made to look like piano keys sidled up to the table. "Whoa. I know you. Holy shit, you're Jonnie Tollens."

Jonnie forced a polite smile. He wasn't in the mood, but such was the nature of the fame beast. He was lucky, blessed, to have the admiration of fans.

"How do you do, mate?" He offered a hand, and the young man shook it with robust enthusiasm.

Other diners turned to gawk, whispering and tittering.

After several minutes of talking about his favorite Fyre albums and shows, the bands he'd played in over the years, and something having to do with a Hollywood audition Jonnie didn't quite catch the gist of, the waiter got to listing the specials.

Jonnie deferred to Eve with a tip of his hand.

She pursed her lips like she was fighting laughter. "I'll take the pork bucatini and a glass of pinot noir." Pressing two fingertips to her mouth, she looked to the side, her full chest rising and falling with stifled chuckles.

He licked his teeth, consumed by the sight of her amusement. He'd get to the bottom of this laughter in a second. "Spaghetti carbonara, please. And make it a bottle of pinot for the table."

"You got it...mate. Say, can I get a quick autograph?" The man fished a white rectangle from the pocket of his apron.

Jonnie signed his name on the back of a business card and handed it over with a smile.

Beaming and giddy as he admired his prize, the flushed waiter took off.

Eve threw her head back as a peal of laughter tore from her throat.

"What?" Jonnie leaned forward, chuckling in sympathy. Perhaps if he prodded her, he'd keep her smiling and laughing. What a treat.

"That was absurd. Dude was fanboying so hard I thought he'd fall to his knees and kiss your feet."

Heat crept up Jonnie's cheeks. He rubbed a lock of his hair between two fingers. "Yes, it's a bit ridiculous. But things like that happen all the time, believe it or not."

"Is it fun, being famous, or weird?" She took a sip of water, regaining her composure.

"Both. I'm honored and blessed for everything I have, everything we've built and sustained over the years. The music business is brutal, we're talking hundreds of thousands of top acts competing for a shot, and there is a ton of luck involved. That's not lost on me. So I don't let myself take the fans for granted. Same with roadies and staff and all the rest, you know? Because the same people you see on the way up? You'll see them all on the way down."

A glimmer dashed through her gentle eyes. "Where are you hiding the big rocker ego you're supposed to have?"

Jonnie considered the question, smiling a thanks at the waiter as he laid down bread and a complimentary appetizer plate of fried calamari rings. The man popped a wine cork and poured him a sample. Jonnie tasted the light, fruity sip, tendering his approval with a slight nod. Waiter filled their wine glasses and left.

"It always seemed too dangerous to get an outsized head." He dunked a calamari ring in a small dish of red sauce and munched, enjoying the texture contrast of chewy and crisp, the light sweetness of seafood cut by its tangy condiment.

"Elaborate." She raised her brows, buttering bread.

He settled a little deeper into his chair, melding with his surroundings. It had been ages since someone new had expressed such a genuine desire to get know him as a person, shown real interest in what went on inside of his head. Most of his interactions outside of those with his family, band, and music industry people mirrored the one with the waiter.

Though in his romantic life he was careful to screen out both star-chasing opportunists and groupies with hero worship in their eyes, he couldn't remember the last time he'd been out on a date with someone as down to earth as Eve.

He could exhale and be a person around her, let go of the celebrity construct. He loved this with a refreshing intensity. "The larger the ego gets, the more fragile. It's like a balloon that way. A bubble you must baby and protect. It's why so many famous people surround themselves with flunkies and hangers-on, you know? People who won't remind them they put on their pants one leg at a time."

Another good-natured laugh, wide enough he caught sight of a silver filling on one of her back molars. "As opposed to putting on pants how?" she asked in a dry, amused voice as she lifted her glass.

He watched her throat move as she swallowed wine, heat gathering below his navel. They might have to cut this dinner short and head back to her place sooner rather than later. "With rock star magic, I suppose."

"So that's not a thing?"

"Nah. At the end of the day, I'm just a gawky boy from East London with a knack for stringed instruments and the blessing of the gods."

Their entrees arrived, fragrant with spices. Steam clouds rose from artfully plated, tasteful portions of pasta. Jonnie thanked the waiter, and the lad bowed slightly before heading to another table.

"We both know you're a hell of a lot more than that." After her statement, candied with a glaze of suggestive temptation, she leaned her head back enough to reveal the pulse in her neck.

He stifled a moan as he stared at that sweet column of smooth skin and corded muscle. He could hear the throb, too, the fountain of life pumping under her supple flesh.

"You know you want it." Maintaining the arch of her upper spine, she speared a bite of meat and pasta and popped it in her mouth. Flicked her tongue over the pointed tines of the fork.

He pictured that hot little tongue of hers lingering on his fangs, tasting her own blood. In his pants, balls tightened and cock grew to near-fullness. "You're torturing me."

"Good."

"We don't know what would happen." Excitement kicked up his heartbeat, proximity of forbidden desire luring him. He wouldn't hurt Eve. He had self control. But who knew, though, what would happen if they released the demon in full force. Things could go awry if they offered Eve's delectable essence to the monster man within.

Her dark dare of a gaze pinned his as she drank. A red bead of wine touched the corner of her lip, and she captured it with a finger and sucked the tip.

His thoughts spun in a fuzzy haze of desire and anticipation. Somehow, God help him, he managed to kill his lust and tuck into his food.

"This subject is closed until after dinner." He threw a randy wink in the teasing little minx's direction. "Now tell me about Eve. Why did you choose the career you did? Have the dead people always sought you out?"

Between bites, Eve shared her story with him while he listened.

Driven by both an interest in biology and a desire to help others, she'd enrolled in mortuary school instead of traditional college. Plus, she noted with irreverent and savvy recognition, her chosen profession would never want for customers.

Smart, in this uncertain economy. Jonnie twirled the last bite of his dish and ate, savoring creamy sauce and perfectly cooked al dente noodles. Being famous had its perks. Restaurants *never* bolloxed up his order.

He learned of her preference for solitude and down time, her propensity for movie nights with close friends or family as opposed to big parties and such.

Eve dreamed of visiting Hawaii one day, adored wallpaper for its vintage aesthetic, and had an ambivalent relationship with the sunrise.

"Because of your insomnia?"

"Yeah. I have this visceral negative reaction to them, because they symbolize my not having gone to sleep. But I get how that's selfish. They also represent optimism, which I could use more of. A beginning, not an end. The promise that this day will be better than the last. After all, if the sun is still coming up, that's one more day where the world hasn't ended."

Eve's brand of optimism tickled him. It was a sort peculiar to her, sardonic without being cynical. And she needed to give herself more credit. The landscape of the woman's mind might might not be a field full of grinning daisies, but it was no graveyard either. There might be some weeds growing in her yard, but so what? A strategic blemish on a portrait made it interesting.

"What?" Shooting him a gotcha look, she swiped bread across her cleaned plate, scooping up the last of her russet sauce.

"I'm glad we're doing this."

"I guess if we keep hanging out I'll need to give up on sunrises altogether, huh?"

Nah. If anyone needed to adapt, it would be him. She was exactly right, just who she was. Eve was where she needed to be, and he would help her see that. "There's no if about it."

The waiter brought the bill in a long black sleeve. He set two truffles, wrapped in tinfoil so they looked like swans, on the burgundy tablecloth. Eve scooped her purse off the floor and unzipped it.

He laid a hand over hers. "Let me."

They play-bickered over the bill for a minute, but when Jonnie finally managed to swipe the narrow folder and open it, he discovered the house had comped the bill. Following a flirty round of back and forth, he and Eve each slid in a big bill as a tip for the waiter.

"Now let's get out of here." She picked up the chocolate birds, proffering him a coquettish glimpse into some dirty thought machinating in that mind of hers.

Jonnie took her hand and led her into the night. He couldn't move fast enough.

SEVENTEEN

EVE REFUSED TO THINK ABOUT THE BLOODY TOWEL. SHE FUCKING refused. Because she deserved this. A fun night out with a man she liked —a man she cared about. Her mind latched on to the memories of the last hour. Enjoying a sexy, intimate dinner at *the cute little couples' place*. His snuggling her close as they'd walked to her home, the closeness of their bodies offering a buffer against the wind. The autumn smell of wet leaves and glowing jack-o-lanterns, enjoyed together. His interest as she'd given him the tour of her place, told him of its history.

And now they lay on her bed, his hands buried in her hair as he kissed her jaw, his breathing growing excited as he moved on top of her.

But that ugly remainder persisted, marring contentment. The towel she'd left with Susan after the woman had spilled her guts but held back crucial details until she'd gotten what she wanted. A bit of vampire blood direct from the source, for which she would have sacrificed her only living child.

Stains on a towel, stains on Eve's soul. Damning, besmirching marks on her character. The mark of betrayal, out damn spot. There was blood on her hands.

"Are you into this, Eve?" Jonnie's fingers slipped under her shirt and stroked her ribs. Her skirt was bunched at her waist. His stiff excitement pressed into the hot juncture of her spread legs.

"I so am." She spoke a truth, begging her thoughts to still. Whatever Susan would do with the rag, feed it to her monsters or hand it over to her employers for money, Eve and Jonnie could manage. She hadn't let herself back down or hesitate at that house. No way would she put the life of her lover or parents at risk.

Senseless fear gnawed at her thoughts, but she stuffed it deep down in her mind. She was being paranoid, dark and morose, standing in the way of her own happiness like always.

"Are you sure? You feel a little tense, seem a bit distracted." He pulled his touch and body away, looking in her eyes for honesty.

Enough. He'd sensed some reluctance off her, and she wasn't going to let her downer worries take over and spoil the mood. She deserved this pleasure tonight, deserved his attention and company and caresses. And he deserved to feel good, too, deserved her participation as an enthusiastic partner.

"I am." She kissed the tip of his nose. "I promise."

"Good. I am, too. I love your sexy body on this elegant bed."

She sat up on her four-post queen. Diaphanous canopy trim the color of the sky hung above their entwined bodies. For the first time in her life she felt cherished upon her princess bed. Everything was fine. Susan got what she wanted. Like Jonnie had said, evil boils down to simple greed at the end of the day, and the Mudd family greed had been satiated. The end. Right?

Jonnie unclasped her bra, pulling it and her shirt off her torso with an upward tug. The garments joined her blazer on the floor. She went for the zipper on her skirt.

"Leave it, please." Arousal thickened his voice. He peeled off his own tee shirt in one swift motion and undid his jeans. Off they went, leaving him lithe and lean in dark boxer briefs speared with need. Those wild tattoos on his tawny skin made her even hotter.

He slid down her figure, trailing fingertips along her sensitive skin before circling each nipple. She moaned as tingles and aches obliterated her mind and turned her into a being of pure sensation. She spread wide, presenting as she propped herself on her elbows for a better view. So wanton and unabashed, to want to watch.

The last of her anxiety dissolved, and she refused to fight it.

Jonnie gripped her stockings on either side of her crotch and yanked. She gasped, wet and tender as fabric tearing filled her ears. Cool air greeted the hot spot between her legs, a tactile preview of sensation that stoked her craving for more. Next, he ripped holes in her stockings at the toes, his pulls erotic in their purpose, their methodical confidence.

He smirked as he tore one final gash in the thin nylon, a big one right above her knee. "Dirty you up a bit."

Breathing heaved her bare chest. Everything he'd said was nasty, perfect, a passport to paradise.

"Hand me one of those chocolates." He massaged the insides of her thighs with slow hands.

Her clit jerked. God, yes. She saw where this was going. Eve scrabbled a hand on her nightstand, knocking a pen and a coin to the hardwood floor as she scooped up a foil swan.

"Greedy." He licked his lips as he took the bird and unwrapped it in a slow torment, revealing the brown orb of a treat within. A chocolate vein dripped down its smooth surface. She stared at the ball of candy, overcome with a hunger having nothing to do with food.

Fortunately, Jonnie bypassed the teasing games. He pulled her panties to one side and rubbed the truffle into her pussy, melting it into liquid as it mingled with her juices, her heat.

Moaning from the rubbing pressure and the decadence of it all, Eve thrust her hips into his touch. Her ache spread to her lower belly, pleasure coiling and growing as she relished the contact with her most sensitive part.

"I want to eat you." He said it with a dark urge that shot fire through her veins. His face sharpened in the low light, taking on that uncanny, draconian cast that drove her wild.

"Do it." Jesus, she was already close to climax, tense as pleasure rose to need. "Bite me."

Instead he smeared more chocolate into her folds, around and around in big circles, bringing the truffle to rest right at her opening. He held her hips and dipped his head down, lower half of his face vanishing between her legs. His tongue hit her slick, swollen center and lapped, the first contact with his firm lick prompting Eve to suck air through her teeth.

"She likes that," Jonnie murmured, lapping melted chocolate from her, sweeping his exploration over the chunk dissolving at her entrance.

Her eyes watered. She held her breath. He delivered a few licks to her hidden lips, then to her outer ones, tasting the candy here and there. Everywhere but where she needed him to lick and suck. She panted with anticipation and frustration. Mindlessly watching him work, she studied his sharp brow line and dark eyebrows, his tousled black hair.

His tongue shot out in a flash, a long slide of red. He used the top, skated it over her rock of a bulged clit.

With an unladylike grunt of greed and relief, Eve sat up more, widening her legs as she sought her finish. She parted her lips and rolled her eyes to the ceiling as she lost herself to the warm, wet strokes of his mouth. Liquefied chocolate and her slickness flowed.

She was there in a minute, groaning with triumph as urgency cracked into ecstasy. She bucked her ass, the mattress squeaking underneath her motions. He flicked his eyes up to hers, surprising her with the sight of his monster eyes.

A mindless chorus of "oh yeahs" tumbled from her mouth in selfish screams as his tongue slid up and down and his gaze made her woozy with forbidden lust. Twin points of white, the little spears she wanted stabbed into her flesh so, so bad, taunted her. Two chiseled tips of bone, sharpened ivory pencils, flashed her from the edge of his top lip.

Eve howled as she came apart under his relentless ministrations. Fantasies of those fangs sinking into her tender thigh, her engorged pussy even, spurred her on as she rode it out. When it was over, she flopped back onto the mattress, panting and spent.

The fabric of her underwear strained against her body in a tight pull, then tore. It took her climax-clouded brain a second to process what had happened: he'd used a fang to rip the material from her body. A shiver of titillation stole over her.

Jonnie gave her nary a second to recover before he crawled up her body with the fixed determination of a predator.

"Hand me the second one." His order was dangerous and hard, a sword forged in darkness.

She lit up with recognition, catching the secret meaning in his low voice. It was time. It was on. In one quick swipe, Eve snagged the remaining truffle.

"Your cunt tastes like heaven." Flimsy foil came apart in his hands, shards of silver that rained specks onto her blue comforter.

The coarse word in his polished voice, the bluntness behind it all, threw lighter fluid on her raging fire. Rules and boundaries between them dissolved. No more decorum. No more holding back. *No more secrets*. But she wouldn't tell him right this minute and ruin their moment.

"What do you think the rest of me tastes like?" She drew out her whisper, egging him on.

It was obvious to her that the feminine cavern between her legs was only the beginning of the personal parts of her he hungered for, longed to taste and claim. She could see it in his eyes, all over his face. Pressing into his boxer-briefs.

Instead of commenting, he trailed the confectionary ball down her throat. She arched into it, eager as she surrendered to masochism. "Christ, Eve. Why do you do this to me?"

"You want it." She craned her head back so far the crown touched the pillow. "I want it. So let's do it." Muscle and skin stretched tight as she bared her throat.

"We don't know what happens next. I might lose control." He murmured a warning, clear concern for her intervening amidst lust encroaching the edges of taboo.

"So we find out. I trust you."

"When do you want it?" The truffle licked her skin, leaving a trail over the sensitive pulse point behind ear. "Now? When I'm inside you? When you're coming? When I am?"

Could she have the bite at all of those moments, again and again? "Whenever you want to most of all."

"Christ, Eve. Fuck." The piece of candy explored, painting as it slid its way back and forth. As it dissolved into liquid against the heated surface of her body, tantalizing scents of cocoa and sugar and sweet milk perfumed the air.

"All you need to do is feel." Her gaze fixed on the molding trim framing the tops of her walls, the white paint swirls decorating her vaulted ceiling. "Here. With me."

"Oh, Eve. Look at you." He rested his palms on her breasts, cupping and squeezing. He licked and sucked her peaked nipples, brushing the hard buds with his fangs. The littlest poke made her gasp in anticipation.

She was ready again, like the first climax hadn't happened. In invitation, she pushed up her hips, presenting the target he sought.

A quiet rustle of friction signaled his underwear sliding down as he answered her nonverbal communication. "Look at me, Eve."

Moved by the stern kindness in his voice, the conviction, she returned her head and neck to their natural positions. Jonnie was flush with her, strands of his hair tickling her cheeks. In that moment, his beauty wrapped all around her.

Those wild pupils and irises and monstrous fangs stood in profound juxtaposition to the love in his eyes. The soft slack of his face, relaxed in appreciation, regarded her.

Contrasting elements created a powerful effect more vulnerable than scary as he exposed his deepest truths to her. The poetic incongruity of frightening eyes betraying a gentle soul was not lost.

A man who cared deeply for her, her needs and feelings, lay with her. A man who worried about her nutrition and told rude customers where to shove it—who spoke up for her when she didn't have the strength to stand up for herself—was here. A man who loved his friends and family with ferocious devotion, empathy pouring from his heart in thick streams. A man of passion and integrity, principles and humble gratitude.

Someone she didn't deserve, but was lucky to have, was here with her, right now.

Nothing else existed but that face above her in all of its moving tides.

Eve put a hand up and touched Jonnie's cheek. He closed his eyes and sighed, and that was when she nearly wept. He was so sweet, so pure.

"It's okay," she whispered while touching his face, caressing supple skin arrested in a youthful state. It saddened her that she'd never see his face develop wrinkles and lines beyond the few subtle notes of one's early thirties. If they stayed together, she'd be the only one who grew old. But now wasn't the time for maudlin, philosophical musings. "I trust you not to hurt me."

"Eve." His hushed tone met hers, a parity bringing intimacy. "Are you sure you want to try this?"

He opened his eyes and held her hand, their shared gazes shifting her into a space of truth. The rotation inside of her was subtle, but at the same time acute in its impact. All of a sudden she floated, at one with herself in a supreme state of unity. Poignant energy rolled through her in a warm wave.

And Eve was grateful. So grateful, because she'd never felt anything this lovely in her heart. Her shitty, broken heart, the gangrenous organ marking her as flawed, outing her as some malfunctioning human prototype. No more. Now she felt like a true person inside, clean and good, right.

"I'm so sure." Eve swallowed as she prepared the next part. "Because I love you, Jonnie."

"Oh, Eve." Jonnie's mesmeric gaze scanned her face in a slow slide of pure appreciation. Nobody had *ever* looked at her like that, like she was priceless treasure. "I love you. Your beautiful, special self."

"You forgot broken." That was the word that Kyle used after she spilled her secrets to him. Then he'd left while she cried.

"We're all broken, love. But sometimes the broken parts fit together."

As she pressed her lips to his, initiating a kiss borne of gratitude and passion, it struck Eve how the mojo of the bedroom had changed. The lust between them softened as their declarations shaved off its sharpest edges.

What remained was mutual desire, muted compared to ripping panties and growled expletives, but more vast and encompassing in the range of emotions.

He slipped his tongue in her mouth, confident and frisky, nudging and sweeping as he explored. She felt everything in keen clarity. His belly, skin and muscle and a scrim of soft black chest hair, brushing hers.

Vocalizations and changing breathing patterns, every hint of a moan, delighted her ears.

Personal smells, the residual chocolate sticky on her neck, cocooned them in the closeness of a shared ritual.

Heat seeped through the white corner vent, its roasty dust aroma a harbinger of late autumn solace. The subtle clunk of the boiler as it traveled through the pipes from the depths of her basement played a calming bedtime song.

Right now, right here and now, Eve was exactly where she needed to be.

Jonnie moved down a bit, maneuvering so the bare flesh of his manhood settled in the crease of her thigh. While they kissed, he rubbed himself back to full, steely hardness. She encouraged him to thrust with squeezes and pulls on his slender hips.

He pulled his body back enough to get the right angle. The movement broke the lip-lock, and she gazed into his eyes as he nudged his crown into her opening. He slipped inside, filling her with pressure and fullness. A tingly promise appeared as he pushed in an out, slowly, his gaze trained on hers. Barriers fell as Eve surrendered herself to intimacy, her universe becoming the joined bodies and hearts of herself and her lover.

His breathing quickened as they moved together. Sweat beaded on his brow, and a muscle feathered in his jaw. Cords tensed in his neck. The visual proof of his climbing arousal heightened her own. A pleasure sound escaped her throat. Tension and awareness built deep in her core.

Moaning more frequently as he stroked faster, Jonnie grabbed one of Eve's legs and hooked it under his elbow. "You feel so good."

"You do, too." She clutched the carved bulges of his biceps, fading into the sights and sounds and smells of their bodies locked and thrusting as one.

Wet skin slapped as he picked up his pace, uttering muted curses and groans as he chased a payoff. Eve's arousal joined with Jonnie's, merging into a feedback loop. Damn, he was hot like this. Animal and greedy, a wild beast close to coming undone above her.

And she climbed, higher and higher and faster and faster, ratcheting as she hurdled to the edge. She became the edge, the edges of her collapsing into the dense point in her center.

He clamped one of her breasts in a frantic clench, palming and kneading as he grunted or swore on every stroke.

Eve's heart beat faster. Sparks crackled at the base of her spine, their vibrant bursts gathering. She caught Jonnie's gaze, asking for what she wanted with the weight of her stare. Her eyes slid to the spot where their bodies joined, where his glistening shaft plunged with animal fury.

A long, deep groan as he pushed in to the hilt and shuddered. She came right then, screaming as she splintered into a million pieces of bright, wonderful energy.

Two spears breached her neck, bringing a brilliant jolt of pain that stole her breath. But she kept right on coming, writhing and moaning and rolling her hips in shameless undulations designed to prolong the bliss.

Jonnie jerked in her arms, body smashed against hers. His tight ass clenched and released in time as he emptied.

Bright slivers sparked in her field of vision. She blinked, sliding into a fuzzy stupor as she lost track of where pleasure ended and pain began. The two sensations met in a swirl of transcendence.

Wet warmth slicked the side of her throat, pooling against her earlobe. Eve went far away right then, stopped being a person and became an eternity of pure, positive, heavenly energy. Planets aligned.

The moment outside of time vanished from the corner of her eye like a glimmering desert mirage. Regular time resumed, and she grasped at concepts while regaining lucidity. Two hung low enough in the space of her psyche for her to pluck. Religious experience. Sublime witnessing.

With a fierce grunt and a jerk, Jonnie threw his free arm around Eve's back, yanking her into a semi-upright position. He sat back on his heels, cock and teeth still buried in her, and hauled her to sit on his lap. He moaned muffled cries into her neck, lodged as he drank and drank. Her heart fluttered, and she faded to a second of black, woozy from blood loss and the sudden change of position.

Her thousand-pound head lolled on her spine. Liquid flowed down her sternum. Comforter stuffing filled her skull with furry thickness. The strangeness of it all, the danger and impurity, spun her around in a tornado of insanity as she played at the border of annihilation.

Despite the intensity of the moment, an undeniable brush with scariness, she wasn't afraid. He would stop when necessary.

"You need to stop. Drink it from my skin now," she said in a hoarse, slurred voice.

He broke away with a suction sound, leaving her neck damp and cool.

Dazed, she looked at her chest. Streams as bright as cherry juice streaked the skin between her breasts as they slipped to her navel, down her pelvis and into her crotch. A stain spread on the portion of the bedspread visible between their mating forms, a circle the hue of a fire engine that grew as it seeped.

Eyes faraway and wild and lip curled with wickedness, Jonnie balled a tight fistful of Eve's hair and pulled.

"You're mine," he snarled, licking fluid from the impact site. He lapped from her breasts, her sensitive nipples, the lower half of his face red and sticky. In a swift toss, he flipped her to her hands and knees.

"Oh, yeah." He spoke with unbridled obscenity before burying his face in her wet cunt.

His laps were harsh and methodical on her clit, an assault. Eve had her third orgasm a minute after he began, shrieking his name as she watched her own blood drip from the bite wound and cry crimson tears onto her pillow.

The exalted frenzy wound down, pulses tapering to aftershocks as Eve, on all fours, stared at her headboard. Their shared gasps filled the bedroom. Smells of sex tinged with the impossible tang of copper made a forbidden cloud.

She turned around with a head rush. Jonnie sat on the bed with a hand laid on his chest, looking around like he'd lost something. Maybe his mind. She wondered as much about herself.

The sheets were a literal bloodbath. So was his stained face, her coated body.

He laughed first, giddy bursts of disbelief and euphoria, and beckoned her with a hand. She scooted over, giggling at what they'd done. What she'd done. But as soon as she nestled into his hug and felt the comfort of his arms around her, doubt vanished and all became well.

"Are you alright, love? How do you feel?" He laid two kisses to her temple.

"I feel great. A little spacey." No worse than after she'd donated to the Red Cross, but she could use some refreshments. "There's brownies and ice cream in the fridge."

"Say no more." Jonnie leapt from bed, tugging on his underwear as he dashed from her room.

Eve stood, stretching as she sauntered to the master bath. She'd just turned on shower when her phone buzzed on her dresser. With a yawn, she checked the text.

From Meg: *I know you're home, why aren't you answering the door? I have something you want to see, let me in!*

EIGHTEEN

Seated across the polished dining room table, Meg ate her brownie a la mode as she studied Eve with a combination of suspicion and amusement. "What's with the scarf?"

Act normal. Eve petted the chunky yarn her mother had knitted. "I just showered. I'm cold."

"It's like seventy degrees in here." Meg snorted, scooping up another spoonful.

Jonnie held Eve's hand under the table. A satisfied smile and a gleam in his eye betrayed their secret, though Meg hadn't seemed to notice his tells.

"It's good to see you again, Meg." He took a bite of food. Eve couldn't help but admire his polite English table manners.

"Likewise, though I wasn't expecting to see you," Meg replied cautiously.

Eve didn't blame her oldest friend for her apprehension. The woman cared about her, and Eve hadn't been herself as of late. And now, she was lying. Guilt set in. Should she tell Meg the truth?

The silence seemed to further arouse Meg's suspicion. "What is it you two are doing, again?"

Jonnie looked at Eve, stretch of a grin and crinkling corners of his eyes making for a boyish portrait of pleasure.

He opened his mouth and spoke the beginnings of an utterance. She attempted something intended to be "we're figuring it out," but her words came out garbled. They spoke at the same time in a mishmash of stumbled phrases and laughter.

Jonnie chuckled and rubbed the top of her leg. He picked up the scarf and smelled it, prompting her to cover her face and chortle.

A sugar rush from the creamy, chocolate goodness she'd devoured blended with her happiness. Her stomach was satiated, her heart was full. But she wouldn't feel whole, not completely, as long as she went on deceiving Meg. The two friends had only ever been honest with each other, and Eve wasn't about to break that trust now. Steeling her decision, she looked at Jonnie as if to say, *tell her*.

"Jesus Christ," Meg groaned, spoon scraping bowl as she polished off the last bite of her snack. "You two are ridiculous. And I meant with your project or spiritual mission or whatever, not dating and sex. Because it's *obvious* what you're doing on those fronts."

Eve finalized the plan with a single, definitive nod at Jonnie. He returned the gesture, heeding her wish.

"I think I need to be brutally honest from here on out." Jonnie pushed his empty bowl away.

Eve scooted her chair closer to him with a scrape of wood on wood before looking to Meg. "We're all friends here. Accepting. So, Meg, there is a pretty big confession coming that I'm asking you to accept."

Meg froze with her spoon at mouth-level, her expression transforming to a startled mask. "Guys. What's going on?"

"I'm a vampire. In a shameful moment of celebrity vanity, I underwent a procedure that was pitched to me as a radical youth treatment. In return for halting the aging process, it gave me a blood condition and sunlight allergy."

Meg gaped. Melted white goo dripped from her spoon.

"I thought at first that I wanted to die, and that your friend could help me pass on to the afterlife, with the work she does with dead people and all. I was desperate when I reached out to her, desperate for help. It was misguided, deeply so, but the upside was we found each other." He squeezed Eve's hand, his face calm with contentment as he stared into her eyes.

His healthy complexion complimented the reassuring words he spoke. A vibrant flush graced Jonnie's skin, like he'd been upholding an extended commitment to healthy eating and exercise. She felt pride that her blood could give him such vitality.

"Exactly." Eve kissed his cheek.

"What. The. Actual. Fuck."

"Come on, Megs. It's not a huge leap of logic. You know I talk to dead people, and you can accept that."

Meg threw her hands in the air. "As a matter of fact, it is a big leap to go from comforting lost souls to freaking dating a vampire. You let him bite you, didn't you?" With an angry point at Eve's wound-covering scarf, Meg finalized her accusation.

"I did. And I enjoyed it." Eve fingered the yarn above her puncture marks, tickles flittering over her neck as memories of the unforgettable sensation resurfaced.

"Oh, my God. I can't with you right now." Scowling, Meg shook her head. "You let a fucking vampire bite you, and you are sitting before me defending that choice. Listen to yourself."

"It's like BDSM. Don't kink-shame me. Besides, I love you, but my sex life is none of your business."

With a harrumph of defeat, Meg turned her narrow-eyed gaze to Jonnie. "And what do you gain from noshing on my best friend's neck, Mr. Rock Star Vampire Dude?"

"You know his name, Megs."

"It's okay, Eve love. I understand why you're upset, Meg. Any reasonable person would be. But please trust that I care about your friend. So much. And this was something we talked about for a long time before we decided together to try it. I'd never do anything to harm Eve."

Meg puffed out her cheeks and blew a loud exhale. "So ripping into her jugular vein isn't harming her? Please."

"Meg. He already told you this was something we decided to do together."

She proffered Eve a glance of reluctant acquiescence. "Your body, your choice I guess."

"Thank you." Eve popped the final nugget of chewy, vanilla ice cream-covered brownie into her mouth. Rich chocolate lathered in sweet cream coated her taste buds and filled her with bliss anew. Maybe she'd put some logs on the fireplace later. Cuddle up with Jonnie under the old afghan, where they'd fool around. She knocked her knee into his in a random gesture of endearment.

"Stooooop with the excessive canoodling, I beg of you." The beginnings of a smile on Meg's lips hinted that she'd softened a tad. Eve didn't hold Meg's initial reaction against her. This was all a hell of a ride.

Meg played with her empty bowl. "So is it just a sex thing for you?" she asked Jonnie.

"No. Part of this condition is that my blood goes toxic. I was getting transfusions for a while, and then I got this plant-based remedy in South America that works to manage my problem. But after Eve and I did what we did, I could tell. That it's the best way to stay viable, to do this."

"You two realize that you're in the ultimate codependent relationship."

"Megs, please take off your therapist hat for a second." Eve mimed removing the hat in question and tipped her invisible cap to Meg.

Meg sighed and rolled her eyes.

"What was the big news, anyway?" Eve rose, gathered spoons, and stacked bowls.

"I don't even remember. I am utterly bereft."

"I'm serious, what is it?" A ripple of anxiety heightened Eve as she sauntered to the kitchen, rinsed tableware, and stuck dishes in dishwasher. Meg, pragmatist extraordinaire, didn't blow up drama over meaningless nonsense. She'd come by with legitimate news, albeit something that Jonnie's reveal overshadowed.

"I don't know if it's still a thing for you, but that dead girl's mom crawled out from under her rock again." Meg's voice from the dining room, pitched with disengaged boredom, made it sound like the Lacey matter had faded into non-issue status.

Eve's hands shook as she wiped them on a towel. Her skin crawled. Déjà vu gave her the weirds. How creepily apropos that a reference to Susan cropped up the moment she dried her hands on a dish towel, the moment she stood in a space recreating the incident where Jonnie cut his hand. Fate would not allow her to forget what she'd done nor erase the secret she kept.

Lacey's presence, a silent specter, rose from its dormant, temporarily forgotten state to loom in her mind. *Think of the haunting, and she appears.*

"Still a thing." Eve injected fake casualness into her voice, relieved it came out sounding normal enough.

She gathered her bearings and returned to the dining room, where Meg was showing Jonnie something on her phone as she cranked the volume.

Susan's unmistakable, wrecked voice ranted, "I got proof. Of some truly abominable actions on the part of these people. They're doing experimentation, Rick. Making mutants in labs. Splicing genes. I've seen 'em with my own two eyes." A subtle whine of electronic feedback came through the phone as Lacey's mother's salacious statements tapered into a dramatic pause. "Makin' mutant people, too. Monsters, Rick. These goons are doing experiments to make people into monsters. The ultimate genetically modified organism."

Horror sizzled under Eve's breastbone. Heavy with dread, she watched Jonnie and Meg watch the screen.

"So what you're saying, what you're telling me here today, Susan, is that you've seen this madness with your own two eyes?" Rick Smith, an infamous household name of a conspiracy theorist, affected shock in his gravely, lower-than-baritone southern drawl.

Stunned, Eve returned to her seat beside Jonnie. On the screen was Susan, proud as a peacock in a tacky red dress as she sat across the desk of a bloated Rick Smith. Behind the Internet sensation host, a wall of flat screen computer monitors flashed inflammatory web pages accusing various politicians of sordid dealings.

Smirking like a punk kid who'd gotten away with shoplifting, Susan drummed hot pink talons on the shiny black surface in front of her. "Exactly. And I'm honored to be here today, blowing the whistle on these criminals. They're gonna pay. For what they did to my girl, my baby."

Eve rubbed her face in a futile effort to calm her spinning thoughts. Did Susan think she had the drop on Scarab, with her shed full of Pollyannas? No way was the woman smart enough to double-cross the powerful mega-conglomerate and emerge victorious. Worse,

Eve had enabled the bitch's harebrained scheme with that godforsaken towel.

"And what do you want out of this, Mrs. Mudd? What would justice for Lacey look like to you?" Smith's mammoth gut pushed into the edge of the desk as the podcast agitator bent into a deep forward lean.

Susan sniffed, fluffing her tangerine crown of box-dyed hair as she milked a second pause.

Jonnie arched a brow at the images on Meg's phone. "Even in the eighties I never teased it that high." His quip brought out dry chuckles from Meg and Eve, loosening some of the tension in the room.

Lacey's mother turned to a camera, meeting the lens head on. She yelped and wiped an eye, though no actual tears cut tributaries into the heavy foundation slathered on her cheeks. "They damn well better bring me the witch and vampire they got working for them. You heard me right. These people are making vampires, and I have me the proof. And I know they can use their freaks to bring my baby girl back to life. I know it in my bones. That's my justice, right there."

"These are wild accusations, Mrs. Mudd. Big demands." Smith growled the rejoinder in his famous, menacing voice.

Susan replied, mostly repeating things she'd already said.

When the video ended, Meg set her phone on the table. She'd paled to a sickly yellow hue. "I didn't watch the entire thing before coming here. Eve, what's happening?"

"She's working with them. It's a long story, but the overview is I went over there to talk about Lacey and found out that Susan is breeding these mutant creatures in her backyard. For Scarab. And I guess she's cooking up some scheme on how to blackmail them."

"Do you figure the witch and the vampire refers to you and me?" Jonnie spoke in a curt, crisp tone. His eyes narrowed. He obviously knew the answer to his own question but wanted to get her side of the story.

Eve's stomach clenched around her food. Thick with guilt, she fidgeted with a ceramic coaster on the table. "Highly likely."

Shit. All she'd wanted to do was set things right with Lacey and protect her loved ones from harm, but the situation continued to deteriorate.

"Is there something you aren't telling me here?" Notes of pain in

Jonnie's voice struck her right in the heart. She'd hurt the man she cared about.

"Hold up," Meg interjected before Eve could hazard a reply. "What happened, exactly, when you went over there?"

Eve screwed her eyes shut and opened them. "I went with Jonnie to Peru to pick up a plant-based blood substitute for him and look for answers on how I could use my magic to fix my mistake. There are people living down there, magical people. My powers started changing while we were there. I met a woman and she took me to the river. We did some sort of ritual."

"And what?" Jonnie pressed. "You never told me the whole story on what happened with Taylor. What happened down by the water that had you so scared and wanting to run?"

"Lacey happened." Eve's mouth soured. "I communicated with her, and she made threats. About her familiar, the little squirrel, coming to kill us and my family. She's attached to me now. I can feel her spirit in my mind. I looked up a spell that I thought I could use to help, and I drove to her parents' house to see if I could elicit Susan's participation. But then she showed me these creatures she farms, and I knew it was a lost cause."

"I'm worried about you, hon." Meg chewed a nail. "Is there anything I can do?"

Eve scrabbled for a kernel of reason. People here cared about her. And she cared about them. Together, they could work through this. "I hate to say it, but I think I need to know what scheme she's concocting here. How she sees us fitting in."

Jonnie murmured a pensive sound as he twiddled with a tiny silver cross hanging from his earlobe. "I didn't buy from the clip that it's justice she's after."

He was correct. "Yeah. I see now that she and Lacey are very much a team. It's like Lacey's lying in wait. Biding her time. I can't tell."

"What if you could get the ghost talking?" Meg offered. "What if there isn't much she can do while she's hitching a ride in your head or whatever, but maybe there is something you could do to get information from her."

"I don't think she's on our side."

"Where did you find the spell you intended to use while you were over there?"

Eve squirmed in her seat. It wasn't the wisest move to go over to Susan's armed with nothing but some random incantation she had a spotty at best grasp on. But she'd been saddled with guilt and driven by a misguided desire to fight her battle alone. Driven by fear that Jonnie would leave her if he knew the truth.

"It's an old book my mom gave me after I told her what I could do with the spirits. She found it at a yard sale a few years ago. I feel so stupid. I didn't want to drag you into this." She looked at Jonnie apologetically.

"How have I never seen this book?" Meg quirked a brow.

"It's not exactly something you break out at parties or in casual conversation."

"Considering we have so few resources at our disposal, perhaps we should give it another go. Can we see it?" Jonnie touched her elbow in support.

"Sure. Hold on a sec." Eve ran up the staircase and to the room where the ghosts lived. She tugged open the bottom drawer of her bureau and swept the tome into her arms. The heady, earthen scent of its engraved leather cover and old pages brought grounding as she hauled the fat encyclopedia downstairs.

She plopped it on the table with a thump. Jonnie and Meg's presences were an unsettling trespass in the presence of the private volume, spectators bearing witness to the most personal of her truths. Her strangest secrets. And she made herself grow accustomed to that feeling, the air-clearing confessional aspect of it all, in preparation for bringing up the towel.

"Unbelievable." Recognition and surprise rang in Jonnie's voice as he ran a finger through the maze of swirls etched into the reddish-brown cover. "Where did you say you found this?"

"My mom and I picked it up at a yard sale somewhere here in town a while back. Why?"

Eyes wide with a startled awe, Jonnie cracked the book and flipped thin, translucent, pages. Familiar sketches and text flew past in a flurry of papery flutters. "Unreal. I've seen one of these. One exactly like it."

"What are the odds?" Meg craned her neck, leaning forward on her elbows to get a better look at the text in Jonnie's hand.

"Low, I imagine." He ran a finger down a page.

"Where did you see a similar book?" Eve asked.

"Brian's wife Helen has one. It's nearly identical from what I saw of it. She was studying it during the tour, working on something for her yoga and meditation workshops. Wild stuff."

"The witch." Gears in Eve's head turned.

"Yep."

"So the books must find their way to us somehow. Check this out." Eve slid the book away from Jonnie and flipped open the front cover. She tapped her finger to the symbol nestled in the lower-left hand corner of the inside flap. An upside-down black triangle with a smaller, also upside-down triangle comprising its tip made for a discreet brand.

"Does Helen's have one of these markings?" Eve's heart rate accelerated. If there were other women with these books, these powers, out there, they might have answers. And no small part of her liked the idea of finding other women like her.

"I can't remember." He squinted at the drawing.

Shoring up her resolve, Eve patted the spell book. "I want to meet her."

"You never showed us the spell you were going to try for Lacey." Meg rose from the table and took a seat next to Eve. Her brows lifted as she thumbed through pages of magical text.

Eve divided the paper a third of the way through and flipped until she'd found the spell in question. The black and white drawing showed a woman on her back, levitating. A cloud of dark smoke flowed from her mouth and drifted into the plastic eyes of a teddy bear held by an assistant.

Jonnie read the description at the top of the page, his eyes darting back and forth over small typed words. "Necromancy, level fifty. Banish Intruders." He slid Eve a concerned look.

"Necromancy," Meg repeated, blinking. "So, like, you have this dead person's essence in you, this element that isn't at peace and wants to get up to something. And basically you need to exorcize it before it and its batshit crazy garbage person of a mom stir up some new, worse toxicity."

"Yeah. I think that's what's going on here, and this power came into its own in Peru. Lacey contacted me, she came up from the earth, and now she's stuck to me. I was hoping this would help, that Susan would cooperate, but as soon as I stepped foot on that porch, I sensed the energy was all wrong. It's like Lacey doesn't want peace. And I'm worried that she's doing something while she's stowed away inside of me. Plotting. Gathering her reserves or strength. And now Susan's changed the game. I don't know what they're doing, but I know it isn't good. I'm so sorry to subject you guys to my bullshit."

Eve sagged into her chair, her posture crumpling. Fatigue and regret weighed on her shoulders. She'd dragged innocent people, her dearest friend and the man she loved, into her latest supernatural catastrophe. But it wouldn't do any good to wallow or flagellate herself. She needed to act.

"It's okay, Eve. We've got your back on this. You hear?" Jonnie dipped his head down to her eye level and cupped her chin in one hand, capturing her fallen eye contact.

"He's right. Ride or die." Meg pumped a fist in the air.

Jonnie swiped his phone from back pocket and keyed in a number. After a couple of rings, someone must have answered, because he said, "Helen? Yeah, I'm fine. Sorry I've been off the grid. I hope you guys weren't too worried. Listen. I need your help."

NINETEEN

A DELICATE CRUST OF FRESH SNOW GAVE WAY UNDER JONNIE'S BOOTS as he and Eve climbed the front steps of Brian and Helen's Spanish-style home and came to stand on its wraparound terrace. Low-wattage security lights blinked on, imbuing the darkness with a pleasant yellow glow.

A few snowflakes drifted through the air, those first sparkling night kisses of a winter coming early to the upper Midwest.

He popped the collar of his black pea coat and took Eve's cold hand in both of his, rubbing them together to give her some warmth.

She blew out a cloud of white vapor. Tucked under her arm, the spell book was as visible and prominent as a third guest.

"Don't be nervous." He rang the doorbell, confident that his friends could help.

Inside, dogs yapped high-pitched barks while footsteps approached.

"Thank you. I suppose I've never felt comfortable asking people for help. Or bringing new people into my circle."

"Why's that?" He kissed the cool top of Eve's palm. Though he'd figured as much about her, he'd rather hear her explanation than make assumptions or put words into her mouth. As her comfort with him grew, he enjoyed getting to know her as she showed him her layers.

"I have these abilities, these strange powers that make me unlike others. Maybe on some level I've worried that if I try to bond with people or get close or reach out, they'll see what's different about me and run away. Easier to hide those potentially stigmatizing parts than risk being vulnerable."

Jonnie considered her thoughtful point, but before he could elicit a supportive response, the door opened to reveal Brian. Two vocal Chihuahuas, barely larger than rats and outfitted in glittery rhinestone collars, bounced at the ankles of his faded jeans. "Come in."

Guiding Eve by the small of her back, Jonnie led the pair into his bandmate and wife's Minneapolis home, allowing himself a moment to take in a space he hadn't seen before. A spiced-apple fragrance added to the atmosphere's hominess. From a den, a shiny baby grand piano captured the eye. Books stocked built-in bookshelves, and sleek modern furniture was arranged in a half-circle. Several acoustic guitars resting in floor stands peppered the living room. A bit crisp for Jonnie's taste, but elegant nonetheless. "Great place."

"Good to see you, mate." The singer drew Jonnie into a bear hug, deep voice coming out in a rush of relief as he slapped his back. His familiar warmth and scent offered brotherly assurance. "Are you alright? Feeling better?"

"I am. And I have a lot to tell you." Jonnie broke out of the hug. "But first, Brian, this is Eve. Eve, Brian."

Brian offered his hand in greeting. "Welcome. How do you do?" His voice was polite though not exactly personable. Jonnie hoped the man would relax. Brian didn't open up or trust easily and was initially aloof toward new people. He hadn't told Brian about Eve, so the front man no doubt wondered why Jonnie was bringing a new person into the inner circle without warning. Fair enough, but Eve was here to stay, and Brian would have to adapt.

"I'm good. Thanks for having me. My best friend is a huge fan of yours." Eve shook Brian's hand.

A startled look crossed Brian's face, disappearing a second after it arrived. His brow arched as the two broke the handshake. "Not you, I take it?"

Jonnie battled a snicker. Eve hadn't meant to take the piss out of

Brian, but nonetheless, seeing him stumble atop his pedestal was a rare treat.

"Our singer is an egomaniac," he said to Eve in a stage whisper. "He can't fathom that there is anyone on the planet who isn't a card-carrying member of our fan club."

Eve laughed a sporting chuckle. "No, you guys are great from what I've heard. It's on me. I'm the boring person who only listens to classical music."

"I am not an egomaniac." Brian's cheeks pinked, and he furrowed his forehead in the way he did when someone called him out.

Jonnie allowed himself a chortle and patted the other man on the arm. "It's okay, mate. We love you anyway. What's with the dogs?"

Brian glanced at the hyper pups circling his bare feet. "The lighter one's Dolce and the other's Gabbana. They're Tilly's. A gift for acing her midterms. Speaking of, she's supposed to be taking them for a walk. We've got cider on the stove, so grab some and make yourselves at home. I'll take your jacket, Eve love."

Brian collected the coats and strode through the living room, soles padding across gleaming hardwood floors. He disappeared down a hallway while calling for his daughter.

Eve walked up to a wall covered in mounted gold and platinum records, and Jonnie admired her reflection in a shining silver disc.

"You need to bring Brian up to speed." She spoke curtly, right to the point.

Embarrassed, Jonnie studied Eve's profile instead of looking at his own reflection. She cut a regal portrait with her high cheekbones and corkscrew curls piled in a bun atop her head, stately as a Victorian cameo.

"You're right." He kissed the shell of her ear, brushed his lips against a warm spot on her neck right above her scarf. "I'd struggled for years trying to figure out how to choose my words, how to frame it. But after talking to Meg, I see the value in pulling the trigger once and for all. Launching right into it."

She stared into that record like the thing was an oracle. "Well, there are those things we can't say or don't quite know how to say yet, even to those closest to us."

Jonnie played with his tee shirt collar as he processed her words. He caught strange notes in her voice, the sound of things unsaid creeping to the surface. She spoke of something other than the matter at hand, but it wasn't his place to pry. "I thought that for a while, but now I'm a firm believer in honesty and bluntness. It worked out earlier, more or less."

Tilly breezed by, lissome in a velour track suit whiter than the virgin snow settling outside, her excitable dogs in tow. A matching stocking cap covered her cropped hair. She waved, hustling to the front door and pulling on a pair of brown sheepskin boots. The girl and her barking pets exited the house.

Eve hugged the massive volume to her chest. "I guess he's no stranger to the weird and outlandish, but we should play it carefully all the same."

Jonnie laid his hands on Eve's upper arms. "It'll be fine. These are our friends, we don't have to worry about getting stories straight. We've got support."

Wood flooring creaked as someone approached. Jonnie turned to see Helen, dressed in dark jeans and a black hoodie that had seen many washings. A faded graphic of a kitten riding through the cosmos atop a slice of pizza graced the front.

"The witch has arrived," Brian's wife said in her thick Minnesota accent.

"Make that witches." Eve held up her book, a sly hint of humor drying her voice.

"I am so here for this. Excuse us for a minute." Helen grabbed Eve by the wrist and led her off.

"We need to talk." This from Brian, who sidled up to Jonnie as he watched the women duck into a room.

"Uh oh. The worst words. If we were in a relationship, I'd be wincing."

Brian stepped an inch closer, his gaze heavy. The lines cornering his eyes and grooving his forehead deepened with concern. "I'm serious, mate. This—whatever this is—has gone on far too long."

In the grand home, Jonnie turned inward as the gravity of it all hit him. He'd been keeping a monumental secret from his best friend for decades, hiding a life-changing facet of his identity from the people he considered nearest and dearest.

He'd acted on fear. Fear of rejection, alienation, being marked as different and strange. How wrong of him, to assume the worst of his best mates. Because that's what he'd been doing. Using lies and secrecy to protect himself from exposure and rejection. But reckoning time had arrived.

"You're right." Jonnie met Brian's eyes, settling into his truth. "You're absolutely right."

* * *

Awash in night, Jonnie leaned over the second-story deck railing and appreciated his view. At least the move outside to the deck, where he and Brian could talk in private, provided a serene setting to offset his impending, bombshell confession.

The Lake of the Isles lay beyond the yard and quiet street, placid black waters dotted with frost patches shining beneath the moon. Robust breezes zipped across his arms and face, carrying scents of burning wood. A carved pumpkin decorated a glass patio table, its interior candle peeking through triangular eyes and dancing in the wind.

Jonnie silently thanked the autumnal evening energy for providing the backdrop of his confession. Inner warmth compensated for his lack of coat.

Brian's hand came to rest on his shoulder. "What is it?"

He mentally bumbled through a few attempts at opening lines, then spit out, "You've felt it. The pressure. To stay young forever." Jonnie's breath came out in white clouds, corporeal traces of his speech giving the words heightened impact through their tangible presence.

"Well sure, but it's about reinvention at the end of the day. Negotiation and growth, the growth that happens when we acknowledge that we aren't the same people, the same band, that we were twenty years ago. I don't have to tell you this, mate. You know this. We've talked about it."

"I suppose I haven't internalized it before now."

Brian bent into a deep lean, resting elbows on the wrought iron railing. "Is this what's bothering you so much that it's making you sick? A personal crisis over the industry, the trajectory of our career, and your role in it? Because believe me, I've been there. And if that's it, I'm your ear. I'm here for you."

Brian's face came into and out of relief in the pumpkin candle's jerking glow, bringing Jonnie's attention to the wrinkle splitting his cheek. Awareness of the line, the character mark of a life fully lived, filled Jonnie with an odd mixture of envy, resentment, and discomfort.

The context of the conversation, its subtext about aging and death and all the rest, penetrated every small and inconsequential detail Jonnie would have otherwise taken for granted.

Regardless of how the next few minutes transpired, Brian would get to go on as a regular person. Instead of someone's blood or rancid vegetable juice from the Amazon, he would drink apple cider with his family.

He would lovingly nag his child about taking proper care of her silly little dogs without worry of when he'd need to manage his vampirism again. Brian was normal. Uncorrupted and clean, at peace with the lines on his face and the linear shape of his life cycle.

Brian was united with his humanity, at one with himself.

Heat balled in Jonnie's stomach, followed by a guilty, draining sensation and desire to apologize to Brian.

"Jon." Brian shook his head. His distinctive, classically handsome face went blank. He tilted his head and touched his lips. Even in the low light, Jonnie could make out the clouds in his distant gaze. He detected palpable confusion setting in as Brian tried to figure out where they stood, what was happening, how to acquire sufficient detail without acting insensitive.

Jonnie clenched the railing, his stare falling to the tendons straining beneath his knuckles. "I bought the pitch. That the greatest asset is youth, the most valuable commodity. And I accepted a treatment, and it had side effects. Then they got worse and worse. I've been managing it, sneaking around as long as I have. Until I couldn't anymore. Then I sought out Eve because of her work with dead people. Thought perhaps she could help undead, too." He muttered the last sentence.

A gust whistled, bringing with it a flurry of dead leaves that skittered across Brian and Helen's frosted lawn. Quiet followed, as deep as the abyss of a lake stretching beyond the two mute men. The flow of time calcified, everything locking up.

"What are you saying?" Brian whispered.

"I'm a sodding vampire. An actual, real, vampire." In a sort of perverse humor, his declaration echoed off the trees, raised voice splintering into a chorus of accusatory ghosts.

"Bollocks. Vampires aren't real. Everyone knows that."

"A year ago, you would have said the same about witches. But you've witnessed the symptoms of my transformation firsthand."

Several more awful seconds of mummified silence lurched forward.

"The episode on stage."

"Yes."

"The disappearances."

"Yes."

"How long?" Brian's voice trembled.

"It's been twenty years now."

Far off, a dog barked. A ripple of water glimmered in wobbling concentric circles as a fish surfaced, splashed, and vanished. The waves smoothed before they hit the shore. Jonnie swallowed a lump, his heart aching. He sought numbness, but the crunch in his chest wouldn't abate. He'd betrayed his dearest friend. For decades, he'd lied to the person he considered a brother.

"What the fuck, man?"

"I know. I know." Jonnie swallowed tears and pain, along with the more articulate words and eloquent explanations in his vocabulary.

"This is a lot." Though shock flattened his voice, Brian laid an arm around Jonnie's shoulders, his touch bringing relief. At least the man didn't storm off in rage or contempt.

Jonnie squeezed Brian's hand. "I guess this was the only group I've ever fit into, and I wasn't about to jeopardize that. At some point the secret took on a life of its own and became a project that I protected, kept safe. As twisted as that sounds, perhaps on some level I got invested in it. I had a thing that was just for me. Because let's be real, you have Fyre. You're the leader, the one on magazine covers, the face people picture. And the lead guitarist, to boot. I'm second fiddle. Literally. But with this, I had something no one else had. I was peerless. Alone at some imagined pinnacle of my own making. And the cliché is true, in case you were wondering. It's lonely at the top."

Brian hugged him tighter, a wholesome assurance. His healthy smell of fall spices and cooking smoke promised the permanence of home. "What do you go through?"

Jonnie spilled his guts. The treatments, Connors, the symptoms, and fears of coma. His wrongheaded plan to die for Cara. All of it. When done, tears streaked his face. But a hundred-pound millstone dropped from him at last.

Shedding the weight of the ages left him so unburdened he could fly. Chase the gossamer strips of clouds racing through the October sky and run with them to the edge of the world.

A hard hug from Brian yanked Jonnie close. Brian cradled the side of Jonnie's head with one hand. His breath was hot on Jonnie's jawline, his hand dove in his hair.

"I love you. And don't you forget it. Never ever, no matter what." The private words, an intense and hoarse whisper in Jonnie's ear, stoked within him a grand fire, a marked elevation.

With it, a mysterious cousin to sexual arousal lit him up, expanded him, merging with the magic of night. The pair, closer than twins as it was, now shared a bond of fierce and surprising intensity. Together, they identified and embraced the limits of loyalty.

As if joined by a psychic wire bringing them into attunement, the bandmates broke away at the same time. Two sentinels looked out over still waters and fast skies. Streetlights like giants offered muted illumination. A pedestrian passed on the sidewalk, two leashed Saint Bernards walking him as he stumbled behind.

"So how do Eve and the book fit in?" Brian asked, his tone returning to its conversational cadence.

Metal burned icy hot against Jonnie's palms, dampening as sweat melted snow crystals. "She does spiritual work. She's trying to do right by a family she made a mistake with, and in the course of doing so ended up at their home with the intention of casting a spell. She showed me the book where she found it."

"I can tell there's more." Brian waved at his daughter as she hiked up the stone steps inlaid in the steep front lawn, Dolce and Gabbana buoyant at her feet.

Jonnie hung his head and lifted it before relaying more information. "The company I got my treatments through is part of some conglomerate dealing in all kinds of shadowy business. This family Eve's trying to help is mixed up in it, too. She went to their home and found some kind of exotic species of bloodthirsty animal penned up in the mum's shed."

When conversations veer in a certain direction, into the realm of the esoteric, the conspiratorial, the outlandish, one expects the other person to balk. To laugh a derisive snort and dismiss certain suggestions as barking mad lunacy. But Brian didn't do that. He simply stood, gazing out over his front lawn, posture rigid and exhalations translucent clouds. "There are things I never told you, either."

In the film of snow covering the deck, Jonnie made a fan with the bottom of his shoe. When you tell your best friend you're a vampire and he replies with such a remark, there isn't much to do except wait.

"Last summer I found myself deep in an unspeakable nightmare with Joe Clyde."

"Haven't heard that name in ages." Fyre's former manager committed suicide. Before he'd taken his own life, Brian had fired him over irreconcilable creative differences and inability to reach a consensus on Brian's vision for Fyre's artistic future. Shortly thereafter, the band had survived a stage disaster, but Jonnie hadn't seen a reason to connect the dots until now.

During that tumultuous period, Jonnie had been happy to focus on making music and playing onstage while Brian handled the uglier aspects of band leadership.

"I suppose I can relate to you. About being unsure. How to tell anyone, even those in the core of your inner circle, about a secret you yourself can't fully believe." Brian's shoulders relaxed, and he tilted his head as if to invite a response.

Jonnie scratched the side of his neck, a vise in his midsection creating discomfort. Anything having to do with secretive involvement couldn't be good. "Sounds like you need to get whatever it is off of your chest."

"The cult that Joe was mixed up with was deeply into demonology. Thought it was rubbish at first, but then he led me to a party with masks and ritualistic overtones. I got the hell out of there and cut him off Fyre like a melanoma. But the cult didn't give up. They used the stage accident as a ruse and kidnapped me. They'd summoned some fiend."

In the cold evening, warmth crawled over Jonnie's scalp. He bit a hangnail. "A demonology cult."

Brian's jerked his neck, his face swiveling in Jonnie's direction as he slashed him a scalpel-eyed stare. "Sounds like it's not a closed subject after all."

"No. The girl who died, whom Eve couldn't help pass over, was supposedly in a Hollywood cult before her family brought her back to her hometown. At first her death was listed as a suicide, but after visiting with the mother, Eve came to believe it was something else altogether. More akin to a voluntary sacrifice."

A low growl from Brian. "That's how Joe died. It wasn't really suicide. He was sacrificed."

Jonnie almost asked Brian if he thought the two deaths might be connected, then with a somber awareness realized that he knew the answer. He'd known at the time that the circumstances surrounding Joe's death were strange but had chosen, for his own well-being, not to involve himself to closely in the matter. "Why did Joe want to bring you into the fold of his cult? What was the endgame?"

Brian hissed out a ragged breath. "They wanted me to consent to my own murder at the hands of this entity they had in their thrall. Then, as best I could surmise, they'd have a better shot of guiding their demon into my body, to possess me. So I'm easier to control, a more profitable singing, dancing monkey. And, ideally, immortal."

Light flashed in Jonnie's brain. His thoughts raced. "That's the agenda."

"What's the agenda?"

"To make a race of immortals. To synthetically engineer beings who will live forever. First, they gain control of the body through procedures like mine. Then they claim the mind. That's where the possession element comes into play. So we're pliable drones they can pilot, control. Living, breathing ATM machines that they can bend to their will."

Jonnie's speech sped to a rapid spray of bullets as it struggled to keep up with his sparking mind. "How did you break free?"

"Helen. She used her magic. Saved my life."

Ideas unspooled at a breakneck pace. "It's Eve, too. The women and their books. They're some kind of counterbalancing force to whatever this cult is doing, to how they're using the conglomerate to execute their deeds. Susan, the girl's mom, she's a wild card right now. But she's significant. Important. She wants to get her hands on Eve because her magic matters to their scheme." He paced back and forth, treading a track in the snowfall.

"Helen blamed herself for what was happening to me. She claimed the demon came into being when she got in touch with her powers, when she activated them. She thought she cursed me."

"Mmm. I don't think that's quite it. It's more like some cosmic machinery, seeking equilibrium." Still pacing, Jonnie raised a palm. "When one side takes an action, the other responds." He flipped his other hand.

Brian tapped his chin with two fingers. "Think it's about time to see what the ladies found in those books?"

Jonnie could only nod.

TWENTY

INSIDE THE FRONT FLAP OF HELEN'S BOOK SAT A SIMPLE BLACK CIRCLE. Eve lay on the floor of the other woman and her husband's bedroom while the duo silently perused each other's spell texts. Heady jasmine incense filled the cozy space, a sanctuary decorated in sea foam and cream tones. Two decrepit old cats, one black and one white, napped on a king-sized bed.

"It makes sense that you have the earth one." Helen brought Eve's book close to her face. "Checks out with the necromancy. Your ability to pull their spirits from their bodies and reach the parts of them stuck on the material plane after death."

"And if you're spirit." Eve touched the inked hoop marking the other woman's volume. "It makes me think there are three others." One doesn't go through life with magic without knowing the symbols of the five elements, the fifth being spirit, or ether.

"Didn't you say the lady you met in Peru was using water as part of the ritual you two did?" Squinting at something as she read, Helen flipped pages.

"Yeah. But she didn't have a book. At least not that I saw or she told me about." Eve closed Helen's tome. Their Minneapolis host's abilities, she'd learned from their chat, involved things like remote viewing and astral travel. Helen could also move and direct unseen energetic forces and enter trance states. Such things both made sense, as aspects of spirit powers that aided her in her profession of teaching yoga and meditation.

"What are you smiling about?" The tone of her voice melodious with good-natured teasing, Helen nudged Eve with the clawed toe of her Godzilla-foot slipper. She set her book on the lush throw rug cushioning their bodies against a wooden floor.

"I like how both of us leverage our magic as an asset to our careers."

"Witches are smart. The ultimate businesswomen. We always have been." Helen narrowed her eyes and rubbed her hands together in a comic mime of entrepreneurial shrewdness.

"Ha. Fair. So what do you suppose happens when we find our fire, air, and water sisters?"

"Beats me. Form a coven and be witchy and awesome I guess. You have any way to get in touch with Peruvian water lady?"

Eve pulled her phone out of her purse. "Yeah. She's on social media. They're secretive about the exact location of their camp and make a big show out of being covert, but other than that, it's not exactly a blackout of info."

Helen scooted close, leaning in as Eve pulled up Taylor's page. Her profile picture showed her reclined in a big bed, red cedar log walls behind her. Glowing, Taylor cradled two swaddled newborns. Pink faces gazed upon their mother, tiny mouths open and eyes wide in awe.

Her panorama cover photo displayed the majestic, foliage-flanked river bathed in a bleeding magenta sunset. The networking site listed her location as the city of Iquitos, Peru.

Eve typed out a congratulations accompanied by a couple of emojis, adding to the dozens already plastering Taylor's wall. She typed a short private message asking Taylor if she knew anything about the elemental spell books or owned one herself. Before sending, Eve wrote that the matter was one of some urgency.

A wave of moving dots popped up in a reply box, indicating that Taylor was typing. But she replied with a dismissal: can't discuss.

"That's that I guess." Eve closed the message window.

"It's fine. At least we put something on her radar."

Eve liked how Helen had referred to them as "we." All her life she'd felt unlike other girls in the worst of ways, weird and skewed and hopelessly flawed, looking in from the outside as cliques formed and broke and formed again without her. In high school, she would have cut out a tooth to get invited to parties, to jump into a car with the popular crowd and go for tacos after the final bell rang.

To be part of the chummy, feminine "we" that forever eluded her.

But now, in the course of a week, she'd met two women with whom she had some pretty significant things in common. Helen's offhand mention of the coven idea continued to swirl through her mind in an amorphous pink sparkle of unspecific crystal fantasies and childhood impressions.

"I agree. We wait." Of course, Eve added nothing to the conversation and she knew it. She'd repeated the "we" to say it, to feel it. She pretended to read the book in front of her, sneaking a glance at Helen and hoping the woman didn't judge her as a complete and total moron.

Helen smiled knowingly, the whole-face grin of a sister, a friend. "Exactly."

"Knock knock." Brian spoke from the doorway, knocking on the open door as he talked.

"Hey, babe. We're talking witchy things. Turns out sister books came to each of us separately. Talk about a synchronicity, right?"

Unbidden, the smallest of happy dances animated Eve's shoulders. Must have been the "sister" comment.

"Absolutely." Helen's husband leaned against the jamb. "And I think it's time we debrief. I've got a nice whiskey to pour into that cider."

* * *

STANDING IN A NOOK OF A ROOM OVERFLOWING WITH PLANTS AND decorated with pewter statues of Hindu gods, Eve petted a weeping fern overflowing from its painted clay pot. The silent home grooved with understated energy.

She supposed the presence she sensed came from some trace of spirit, the imprints left behind by those who passed through. This element of her gift appeared when she was around ten and started hearing faint, indecipherable babble emanating from the box air conditioner in her room.

She was lucky to have spiritually inclined parents who believed her.

Eve allowed the subtle wave of blurred gibberish, the whispers that ran together, to wash over her as she sat in a firm chair and enjoyed the feel of its linen upholstery. Spell book open to the page she'd memorized, she closed her eyes and concentrated on teasing apart the threads. Her breath became oceanic, an elemental rise and fall powerful enough to pull the moon.

Staying with the yogic breathing pattern Helen had taught her, Eve catalogued the whispers. First, she did away with the inconsequential ones, people of little import who'd passed through Helen and Brian's home. His musician friends, her yoga friends, Tilly's study buddies.

The superficial layer shed, she dug deeper. Her heart hammered. Warmth rose from her feet to her face, making her sweat in the mild air.

"Good," Eve assured herself as vibrations hummed through her body and buzzed in her head. She'd put herself under hypnosis. An ideal state for contacting the spirits of the turbulent dead, those who'd died without peace.

Reach the Unpeaceful, not Banish Intruders, was *the* spell she needed to make and sustain meaningful contact with the malcontent spirit who'd taken up residence in her head.

As directed by her book, Eve visualized herself walking down a staircase. Into a basement, into her subconscious. She pictured the staircase carpeted in evergreen, its steps soft beneath her bare feet.

She held an ornate banister carved in dark wood as she descended the staircase into the recesses of her mind, where Lacey dwelled. Where she'd demand answers—answers she'd use as ammunition to defeat the skulking dead girl and her scheming, reckless family. Answers she'd use to protect Jonnie from any harmful effects of her secret.

If she was going to have a spirit knocking around in her head, she'd meet it on her own terms.

The staircase ended in Brian and Helen's kitchen. She wandered the chic space, stroking cool white marble kissed in moonlight. Their chrome stove gleamed, shiny even in darkness. A pleasant humming filled her head. Her movements were slow and thick, languid.

"Are you without peace, love?" Jonnie's distinctive, smooth voice emerged behind her.

Pulses of energy massaging her, she turned around to see him standing in the doorway, long and lean in the black silk pajama pants he'd worn to bed. A slight downward tilt made his hair shield his face. Both hands rested on the top of the door frame, like he wanted to do a pull-up.

The gestalt of his pose was sexy-dangerous, the brooding bad boy. His shadow self, his alter ego was out to romp.

"Yes. I'm possessed." She walked to him, affecting a roll of her hips, a swing of her arms. Heat gathered in her center.

He stalked to her and backed her into a wall, caging her with planted hands. Spears of erect fangs showed behind parted lips.

"What is this place?" Jonnie growled his whisper, head cocked as he studied her neck.

"The other place." She matched his tone. "Of possibility. Where our kind roam." For much of her adult life, Eve held her insomnia in impotent, rage-filled disdain. It was a burden, an ailment to be medicated, a plight to be cursed with pre-dawn tears of exhausted frustration.

She laughed, free at last. How wrong she'd been. All those years, she hadn't gotten it. Eve hadn't needed some pill or relaxation technique to help her lie in bed and fall into typical dreamland.

She'd needed a spell to give her a passport to travel.

He moved with unnatural speed, ripping at her clothes. Shocking sounds of shredding fabric filled her ears as her chest heaved up and down, breasts swelling beneath his touch.

Good God, he acted with efficiency, his movements shot through with brutal precision. How he hoisted her leg, her back warming cold tile, thrilled her with the vibe of repressed brutishness unleashed. Jonnie wasn't *like this*, except when he was.

Locking his devilish eyes, lost in the rapture of emerald irises and vertical pupils, she curled a hand into his elastic and yanked the smooth material of his pants down just past his groin. His sac was tight, a gathered ball dense with need. His dick, rigid as a poker and bracketed by the inked lines raking down his front, jutted from his body in an upward arc.

In a swift and fluid motion, he lifted her off the ground, impaled her on his cock, and started thrusting. The first stab of penetration, exquisite, annihilated her with pleasure.

He groaned into her neck. She moaned into his ear. Soon, Eve lost herself to sensation. The smell of their excited bodies, his punching hips plunging glorious length inside of her, took over.

When they came at the same time, voices a blur of hoarse cries and panted moans, Jonnie stabbed his fangs deep into her neck and sucked. She wailed, coming apart in those perfect, mind-erasing quakes of release made complex by exquisite invasions of pain.

He pulled away as they finished, gasping for air. She stumbled, woozy, stars littering her vision. Jonnie's warm hand gripped her above the elbow, catching her before she fell to the floor. He bit his own wrist and held it high.

A warm ruby trickle splashed her chin and nose. The first drops hit her parted lips and outstretched tongue, their flavor as addictively sweet as a raspberry snow cone at a hot summer carnival. Eve caught every bit of the ambrosia as she could as blood splattered her mouth.

"My blood is your mask," Jonnie murmured as he lowered his arm and pressed the heel of his hand into the wound. With his free fingers, he pulled up his pants.

In a daze of bliss, she connected, albeit in the vaguest and most amorphous way, with his words. Eve smeared his thick offering over her cheeks and forehead and nose, covering herself with a protective film of sticky residue.

Jonnie nodded once and walked away in the direction from which he'd come, a hint of a post-coital swagger in the sway of his hips, the square of his shoulders. A rock star gait if there ever was one.

The perfume of him heavy in her nostrils, Eve resumed her now-nude walk. She ducked through a doorway and entered a room full of doors. Helen floated in the corner, arms outstretched like a statue of Christ as she hovered near the ceiling.

White cue balls of eyes regarded Eve. Helen grinned, the effect uncanny when set against her blank orbs. "Where our kind roam."

"Fire." The voice of an invisible feminine stranger drawled.

"Air." A different mystery woman's whisper.

"Chaos," hissed another. "Squares the circle."

"They're here." Helen's words shot out in breath of hushed excitement. "They're here, they're here, they're here."

Evie's bite wound buzzed, throbbing without pain. The coating on her face, combined with her nakedness, intoxicated her with a foreign, erotic feeling. Heightened, fleshy, alive with pungent realness.

She chose a red door whose hue matched the blood on her face, ducking to clear the doorway as the dimensions shrank. A cast iron staircase twisted into a claustrophobic coil as Eve wove down, down, down. It morphed into industrial metal, rusted and urban, as she wound her way into an unfurnished basement with a cavernous quality.

Naked except for the dried vampire blood painting her face, Eve stood on a hard-packed dirt floor.

"Stuck in death, appear to me. Rise from your grave so you may be free."

After Eve spoke the opening words of Reach the Unpeaceful, the crown of a head, its blonde hair thinning and mussed, rose from the dirt. Lacey came up, decomposing beneath her burial dress. She was a little more worse for wear than she'd been in Peru, more sunken and blotched, her decayed face twice as angry.

Beside her, the squirrel-thing wrested gray flesh from one of her toes. Eve tried not to look, locking the spirit's dead eyes instead as she opened conversation. "So what you want is to come back to life as a blood-slave for your mom's fucked up pets? For real?"

Lacey sneered. "Yeah, right. You bring me back and your boyfriend makes me into a vamp. You think I'm going to sit back and relax while my dumbass mom uses me as a blood bank? Puh-lease?"

The corpse girl stepped closer, stretching the gaping pit of her mouth into a blackened maw. "Bring me back now, witch. Raise me from the bowels of the earth. I command you." Lacey's mouth, frozen in its terrible death gape, didn't move as she spoke.

Eve stood her ground as she faced down Lacey's encroachment. The smell of Jonnie's blood ensconced her in positivity. Protected her, she bet, from Lacey's attempt to block her incantation with some type of counter spell.

"I command you, witch. You are my necromancer. You are my sage, my guide along the path to return to my earthly station. Bring me forth, necromancer."

"Sorry sweetie, but I'm going to have to pass. I'm sure another necromancer will feel differently and snap you right up." Eve recited more lines of her Reach the Unpeaceful spell.

Lacey doubled over and screamed, pulling what was left of her hair out in clumps as she freaked out. The squirrel started and leapt in the air. "Give me my life back, or in one night my pet kills everyone you love. Take my soul forever. I don't even care."

Eve shook her head. The nights from Lacey's initial threat had come and gone, triggering in Eve skepticism about the range of the squirrel's ability. And right now the messed-up rodent was focused on freeing Lacey's toenail from her big toe, not stealing anyone's life.

"I'm not buying this. I don't think your familiar is nearly as strong as you claim it is. You're bluffing. And I don't accept souls as payment for magic. So let's get down to business and take stock. Your mom is an insane idiot who is so far out of her depth, she's lost at sea. You're sick of being dead and buried and want to come back to life as a vampire. I want you and the thing chewing on your foot to leave me and the people I love alone for good. I also want your mom to not end the world with her asinine scheming. So instead of pretending you can defeat me with the roadkill currently snacking on you, I propose we look for a compromise."

Lacey crossed her arms and scoffed, shaking the opportunistic eater off her with a jerk of her leg. It chittered and ran back to its place at her heel. She pursed her pallid lips and scratched a sore above her eyebrow with a broken yellow nail. "Fine. You win."

"If not out of loyalty to your mom, why do you want to be a vampire?"

"Uh, duh. Power, immortality, eternal life. They were supposed to bring me back right away. I wanted to be an actress, and they said this way I'd stay young and beautiful and loved forever." Lacey stuck out her lower lip, girly pout garish against the gruesome appearance of her rotted face and body.

Empathy for the frustrated zombie overcame Eve. The world was a rough place for a young woman as it was, and she couldn't imagine how trying to make it in the entertainment industry compounded those natural feelings of insecurity and self-consciousness. And desperate, insecure girls agreed to lots of exploitative things.

Lacey had reached for some shiny bauble Hollywood types dangled before her with all the starry-eyed optimism natural for a beautiful, ambitious woman at the height of her physical prime. Instead of reaping the spoils of her Faustian bargain, she'd gotten screwed. No fame, adoration, or ticket to eternal youth for Lacey. She'd ended up an agitated member of the walking dead, stalking a necromancer and vampire while a gross squirrel-thing pecked at her flesh. Poor dear.

"Who are they?" Eve asked. "Who did this to you?"

Lacey unfurled her arms, undead face transitioning from fury to sagging defeat. "Secret society people. They called themselves the Gatekeepers of Sirius. I didn't take it seriously at first, assumed it was more ridiculous Hollywood occult nonsense. I mean, I saw posers everywhere out there, you know? Starlets who blathered about worshipping Satan and wore pyramids with eyes in them on their shirts. Movie directors who said they could summon demons to brainwash celebrities and do CIA mind-control tricks to give people multiple personalities they could activate through programming. I assumed it was bullshit for attention, you know? Stupid conspiracy theory crap they threw around in LA to look edgy." Lacey put air quotes around edgy.

Eve smiled, nodding. They were making solid progress.

"So when some producer said the Gatekeepers needed to initiate me before I could get A-list roles, I was okay with it. At least I didn't have to suck any old-man dick or pose for sleazy pictures, you know?"

Eve nodded. "Right." She teemed with anticipation. The meat of the issue was about to emerge.

"I get an invitation to a party called Silver Phase. Long story short, this dude comes to my condo and leads me to an SUV. There were like ten other girls in there. The car drives us to this mansion. They made us put plastic baggies over our high heels, so we didn't scratch up the big shot's marble flooring. Weird, the details you remember." Lacey tilted her head to the side, prompting acknowledgement.

"In strange situations our awareness has a way of shrinking. Maybe it's a survival mechanism." The beat-up rodent wrested a scrap of Lacey's mottled skin free, holding it in its little paws and eating while Eve forced down the urge to puke. She pointed at the scavenger. "Can I, uh, do anything to help you with that?"

Lacey rolled her cloudy eyes. "I'm used to it. So anywho, some other guy leads all of us girls into this basement with a black and white checkerboard floor. There were mirrors all over the walls and pentagrams and this chair." The girl shuddered.

"What happened with the chair?"

"It had restraints, and these robed dudes strapped me in. They were dancing and bowing and chanting 'Sirius.' That's when a giant ball of light appeared in the middle of the room. It was so bright, like a star. Four points stuck out of it, like one vertical line and one horizontal going all of the way through. Next thing I know my chair is hurling into it. I wake up in the woods, my hands and feet tied with rope and secured to posts stuck in the ground. No idea how much time has passed. Everyone had on robes and masks, but I heard my mom's voice underneath one of the costumes. This fucker was lying next to me, dead and nailed to the ground." Chin trembling, Lacey pointed to the jittery animal beside her.

"Then they killed you."

Lacey lifted her soiled dress above her chest, revealing a red gash running from sternum to crotch. Black sutures held her incision closed. "It hurt like hell. They took out my organs. I screamed, but it didn't matter. They kept on cutting and pulling out parts of me. Then the pain ended, and so did I."

Why remove Lacey's vital organs? If these guardians took things out of her, did that mean they wanted to make room for something they wanted to put in? "I'm sorry they did that to you. I'll find you some peace. I promise."

"Thanks. I'm sorry, too. That I was hassling you and sending this freak show to disturb you. I thought being a vampire would solve my problems, and I didn't want to let go of the idea. But mostly I'm just tired."

Eve shrugged a shoulder. "Hazard of the trade. Why do you suppose your mom has flipped on her bosses?"

"She's dumber than shit and twice as foul. And unpredictable. I can only see what you see up there in the world, so I'm guessing she thinks she can extort them for money to pay for her opioid addiction. Hold their Pollyannas hostage, threaten to burn them up unless she gets more and more cash."

Made sense. Addiction was a powerful motivator. "Why does she want vampire blood so badly when she already has an entire case of it under those tanks?"

"She has this theory that the stuff they send her is diluted. No idea if it's true or not, but she thinks if she can get the real thing, directly from the source, the Pollyannas will grow faster and get bigger. And as a result, be more valuable as hostages."

Awareness of the blood-soaked towel hovered like a specter over Eve's head. But she consoled herself with the assurance that she would do whatever it took to keep Jonnie safe from Susan's nonsense. "Thanks for talking to me, Lacey."

"No prob." A hint of a smile curled the zombie's mouth. "Give these Guardian assholes hell for me."

Eve finished reciting Reach the Unpeaceful, and the dead girl and her familiar sank back into the ground. Perhaps Lacey gave up as a result of Eve nailing the spell. Perhaps the girl needed to speak her truth and have her story heard before she could rest, like the other souls Eve assisted. She chose to attribute the success to both factors.

Walking up the steps, Eve thought about the teleportation portal Lacey had described. It hit her, the reference to Sirius. These shadowy, unseen people at the top used star power to harness, teleport, and move energies. To possess celebrities and make them into the ultimate commodity fetishes.

Breaking into a run, she willed herself to exit the hypnotized state. She needed to have another look at her printout of the conglomerate's various subsidiaries and their holdings.

Each of the four arms aligned with one of Sirius's four points, but what about the fifth? And who or what inhabited the middle sphere, the magic sphere, and how much did Susan know?

Eve shook herself awake in the firm linen chair, dashed to the bedroom, and plucked the printout from her purse. Time to take this research to the next level.

TWENTY-ONE

Facedown on his pillow, Jonnie stirred from a dead sleep. He turned his head, eyes adjusting to morning brightness. The day's yellow slivers sliced through fluffy shrubs beyond his guest room window.

Brewing coffee filled his nose with perky, mouth-watering aromas that stirred memories of lazy weekends with scones and records. The faint hiss and gurgle of the pot chimed in with its unmistakable contribution to the universal signal of morning. In his dreamlike state, he imagined one of those perfect mornings with Eve. Happy, sweet, and slow.

Blinking, he groaned as the fantasy drained away and reality poured in. He sat up, groggy mind marinating in confusion as he worked to process his surroundings.

Computer paper lay strewn everywhere. Sheets of it, lined with black lettering, covered the floor and hung on the walls. Was he still asleep and dreaming after all? His thoughts scrabbled to make sense of things as he looked around. Christ, it was like he was living inside of a papier-mâché mask.

Pen notes marked several of the papers on the floor, stars and underlines others, while yellow highlighter stained the text of still others.

And he didn't have to wrack his brain too hard to determine the mastermind of the great paper deluge. "Eve, love?"

She whisked through the doorway a moment after he spoke her name, more pages in one hand and a coffee cup in the other. Dark circles ringed her eyes, though they shone with a fierce sparkle. A few black fingerprints smudged her pajamas with traces of printer ink.

Blowing clouds away from the top of her mug, she sat on an open patch of carpet and looked out over a fan of sheets. "Any arm can be the fifth, depending on the project they're focusing on at the time."

Jonnie slid off the bed, coming to join her on the ground. The point emerged as he surveyed the parachute of documents before his feet. Several showed graphs like the one they'd looked at in her office. On each, the fifth arm was streaked with yellow marker.

He scooted closer to Eve and urged a crinkled sheet from her fingers. Cupping her face, he looked into weary yet blazing eyes. "You haven't slept, have you?"

Hazy dream recollections returned in fits and starts. He and Eve had met in the third place, a brief encounter, before going their separate ways. And from the looks of things, Eve's journey had been productive, if exhausting.

She rested her head on his shoulder, a welcome gesture of intimacy amidst unexpected morning chaos. "No. But I'm okay. I found Lacey and learned some new things. I read up on our favorite shadow organization a bit more."

Jonnie's conversation with Brian floated back into his half-awake mind. He picked up a printout of a web page for an organization devoted to banning drinking straws. His gaze flicked from the thin white slip in his hand to the marked files on the floor. Mental lights flashed as he looked among the paper and the circle and line graphs with highlighted fifth arms. "They've manifested a kind of siphon. The fifth arm is a straw that sucks up magic."

"Bingo." Eve flopped onto her back. "Cosmic magic, and they've figured out how to channel, take, and redistribute it for their corporate holdings. Lacey told me about some ritual. Robed people made starlight appear in a basement, and it teleported her. All their projects involve dipping into an interstellar power and using it for the advancement of their various companies. The graph represents the star Sirius, and as best I can tell that's their source. When they want to use celestial energy for ritualistic purposes, they do their incantations to draw its cosmic magic into their hands and imbue their companies with it."

Elsewhere in the house, Tilly's dogs barked. "Morning, babies." The teen spoke in her faint flutter of an English accent, voice thick with sleep. A door opened and closed, taking the yaps out with it.

"I don't quite see how knowing any of this helps us. What you need is a spell that will put this girl to rest so you can move on, yes?" But as Jonnie scanned the papered room, a new possibility took shape within him. The documents talked about medical interventions. Radical treatments. Cures for cancer. Cara's face, plump with health from before she'd gotten sick, flashed in his mind.

"I took care of that in the third place, but remember how her mom is mixed up with one of these companies. I'm worried about her involvement."

Jonnie slid an article in his direction and read. Eve had circled the name of the subsidiary involved in conducting some cutting-edge clinical trial involving DNA modification to cure certain kinds of cancer.

His breath sped as he read the article, the rate ratcheting more as he glanced to a highlighted page showing the graph. Sure enough, the company names matched.

"What's your stake in what her family is doing now that you've helped Lacey?"

"Like I said before, I might need to do one more thing to finish the job." Eve's vocal timbre pitched high and tense when she spoke, and she pushed out her words in a forced effort.

He tried to snatch eye contact, but she was looking at a piece of her hair.

Jonnie slid her a quizzical glance. She wasn't being forthright about her investment in the girl's family. He'd fine-tuned his bullshit detector over the years, and it was time to admit that Eve was shoveling some rubbish his way. "Did she threaten you with something, the time you dropped by?"

"No." Tone crisp, Eve turned away and locked her jaw.

He took her hand. "If you're afraid, if something's going on, you can tell me. I'm here to help."

"I...yes...um. It's overwhelming is all, being possessed by a spirit of someone I was responsible for and failed. But I can handle it." He voice cracked, chin dipping as her posture slumped. She rubbed her earlobe.

A shiver of adrenaline rippled through him. His heart jumped. The first words she uttered—the I, yes, and um—contained more truth than the others. They were spoken in her natural tone, while the rest of them jolted out in quick stammers. She'd pinched off a confession before delivering it, stopping short of the truth.

"We shouldn't have secrets right now."

She lifted the mug to her mouth and looked into it before taking a drink. Her eyes popped, like she'd drunk while the liquid was too hot to give herself distraction, a means to avoid engaging with him.

A pattern emerged in Jonnie's mind, a pattern to Eve's evasive behavior. Though rare enough to allow him to forget, it was consistent. She'd gotten weird one other time they did research on Pentagroup, the time in her office. But not so much at his New Orleans flat. What had changed?

Jonnie swallowed a noise of frustration along with his suspicion. The last thing he wanted to do was accuse her of something and push her away. Besides, he had no concrete basis for calling her out. She could be acting odd due to stress or lack of sleep. He routed his thoughts onto a different track. "In theory these people could help Cara."

"Really? How?" She sat up straighter, brightening as her words flowed out in a gush of relief.

He forced himself not to overanalyze her reaction or indulge paranoid or cynical musings. Living a life of fame, having lived so much of his life under the eye of fame, played tricks on Jonnie's mind now and again. Made him hypervigilant, attuned to catch instances where others were lying to him or seeking to gain an advantage. These defense mechanisms served as assets for protecting himself from predatory entertainment industry types but became detriments when he sought closeness and authentic companionship outside of his tight inner circle.

With a deep breath, he stilled his mental chatter. Most people, normal people, didn't have hidden agendas, didn't plot or scheme or approach others as prey. And certainly not Eve. Not sweet Eve, not his Eve. And it wasn't fair to her to map his aversion to Hollywood ghouls and their tricks onto her motivations.

She inched closer and rubbed his back, kissed his cheek. "Don't leave me hanging. What's the good news?"

Dogged by a stubborn, sinking feeling, he shrank away from her as he gathered his evidence from the heaps strewn about the carpet. "I need to read more, but from the looks of things, they're in cancer treatments. Wondering if I could have my manager make a few phone calls."

He bit the inside of his cheek. The thought of doing more business with these sketchy Pentagroup types than he already had gave him no pleasure, but it was his only lead at the moment. Perhaps he could track down Connors. Or maybe Brian knew something by way of his involvement with Joe Clyde. Endless moving parts twirled by in a kaleidoscope, but for Cara he'd exhaust any and all possibilities.

"Holy shit," Eve said.

Jonnie turned to see her reading something, her lips parted and her eyes zipping back and forth over text.

"You were right." She snatched up a second sheet, mouth moving as she read it to herself.

A rush of energy lifted him. He scooped up the paper she'd dropped. In his excitement, the words of the fringe article ran together, but his crackling mind retained enough to get the gist. He made himself slow down and digest the information.

Our source, who wishes to remain anonymous, met with us to discuss the myriad ways in which the projects of various Pentagroup holdings and affiliates cross-pollinate.

"It's a hydra whose many heads feed each other," he explained. "So their far-out scientists mutate animals in labs, then their sorcerers and mages conjure demons to implant dark forces, sinister energies into those creatures. They harvest the blood for their Vampivax eternal youth treatment, and the injections modify human DNA as well as inflict upon the patient a kind of watered-down demonic possession. That's all a vampire is. A human-demon hybrid. They need fresh blood to live because Pentagroup hasn't yet found an innovation to get their bodies to fully accept the Vampivax treatment."

Once the vampirism process is initiated, our source tells us, associates of Pentagroup corporations stay close to manage the patient and control the process. Because toxic vampire blood—a certain amount of blood must be removed before a fresh injection will take—has a multitude of other uses. They feed it back to their monsters to prolong their life span and increase the amount of damage they can inflict.

Our source went on to elaborate how this interconnected system touches other branches of the Pentagroup tree.

"Vampire blood has medicinal properties. They involve it in their biotech, inject small amounts into their anti-carcinogenic chips. Which kills the host's cancer cells and modifies their DNA in the process. So we get people mutating into shifters and vampires. Bonus for Pentagroup when their defense contractor subsidiary needs a fresh supply of supernaturals to scoop up and ship overseas for the latest pointless, for-profit war."

Meaning poured into Jonnie like the voice of God.

"I need to get to Cara." He jumped to his feet. "Get her my blood."

"Hold on." Eve sprang up and joined him, laying a hand on his forearm. "None of this is substantiated. It's an anonymous source from a conspiracy theory paper. We should cross-reference."

Indigestion curdled in his stomach. Heat sizzled under his sternum. Was Eve trying to stop him from reaching Cara? What was her problem, anyway? "So why did you print it out in the first place?"

"You don't trust me. You think I'm on their side or something. I can see it in your eyes and hear it in your voice." Her chin trembled, fists balling as her shoulders bunched. She brought one clenched hand to her lips and held it there.

He exhaled some tension. "It's not that. But I'm going to be perfectly honest when I say that something doesn't feel right here. The last couple of times we've done this research, you've clammed up. And it's hard to work together and, well, be together as a couple without a climate of full honesty. Especially now. Especially with all of this."

They faced off in silence, a sheen in her eyes stark in the sunlit room. A tense pause zeroed in on the crux of a moment of truth more than any words could. Chills seeped through Jonnie's veins, followed by an acute, instantaneous sense of loss akin to the string of a balloon slipping through one's fingers.

As a light fled from her eyes, a sting under his ribs transformed into a dull ache. An invisible wall of barbed wire flew up between them.

She moved her hand and let out a whimper. "So being with me is hard. Some great burden. I see. Tell me how you really feel." Her vocal inflection was hard and caustic, though it wobbled.

He swallowed a lump in his throat. "No. All I mean is that we need to be forthright with each other right now. Transparent. And if *I'm* being totally honest, I can tell something is off. Up. I tell myself I'm imagining things, but to be quite honest, I'm hideous at denial. You get cagey when we do this research, or you have the last couple of times. And if you keep secrets from me, I can't help you. I can't help us."

"So you are accusing me of something."

"It's an observation, not an accusation. I know you, Eve, and I can tell when you aren't being yourself."

"You claim to know me, but at the end of the day I don't think you do."

"Why are you pushing back like this? Of course I know you. I know how the tone of your voice changes when you talk about Meg versus your job. I know you like to cycle for the escape. I know you're adventurous, yet cautious and so empathetic that setting boundaries poses a challenge. I know you're sensual and affectionate, but you struggle like the devil to trust. You love your family despite deep ambivalence."

She shook her head, her teeth clamped in a vise.

"I know you're your own worst enemy, Eve. You get in your own way and sabotage yourself, your happiness. Why? Because it's familiar? Because it justifies that nasty little voice inside your head that says 'I told you so?' That tells you you'll never be good enough?"

Pleading her to listen, drawing from everything he had, Jonnie reached for Eve's hand.

She took a step back.

A sinkhole of defeat swallowed his energy, leaving him scuzzy and drained. He laid both hands on top of his head. Time was a vat of quicksand. They drowned in it together, immobilized, no escape in sight. "Go ahead and put your wall up if you must. But tell me the truth. Once and for all."

"Fine. You want to know the truth?" She barked a bitter laugh, looking at her hands as she wrung them. Her spine bowed as her ribcage collapsed.

Exhaustion and dread waged a sickening war in his abdomen. Shoring up what remained of his emotional fortitude, Jonnie lifted Eve's chin with two fingers. "Yes. More than anything I want to know the truth."

"I'm toxic. Through and through. Misery follows me like a lost soul. I tried to tell you that in New Orleans, and you wouldn't listen. And now your life is in danger because I betrayed you. I sold you out."

He dropped his arm to his side. "You sold me out?" The words were broken glass in his throat, deep cuts inflicted on unhealed wounds.

"I sold you out," she said, voice as flat and dull as the computer paper surrounding them. "I'm a Judas. Thirty pieces of silver. As cliché as it gets."

His past spun by, a circus of memories both faded and vivid, bitter and sweet and everything in between. The school bullies who picked on him for being different, the solace he sought in his happy home, those garages where his band first played.

The loss of home when Fyre left for their first stateside tour, Jonnie eighteen and impressionable, an eager puppy hungry for all the love he could beg, borrow, or steal. Lots of facsimiles of love had gravitated to him, their forms tending more false than true.

Misguided attempts to get love led him to the first slew of girls and boys he'd been with, the ones who collected rock stars like friendship bracelets. Maladaptive yearning for family and mentorship steered him in the direction of managers and promoters and executives, all wanting a piece, who'd exploited his youthful naivete and enthusiasm for their greed.

He'd bought lie after lie. And finally, in the absence of sustained human connection over the years, he'd turned to his looks and youth as a primary source of validation. As long as he kept his thick hair and dewy skin and didn't get fat, the fans would cheer for him and with him, never laugh at him like the bullies did. Their adoration was never to wane, never leave the horrible threat of barren fallout in its wake.

His first real partner, a woman named Bebe, had slipped away as she sought to disentangle herself from his guitar strap and trade the vicarious perks of a rocker girlfriend's fame and chase stardom of her own.

Connors and those he answered to had smelled that hole in Jonnie's heart, that rotten pit no number of adoring fans or groupies, no amount of money or awards, could fill. Connors had stepped in with his eternal solution, eager to fill the gap.

Perhaps all of this was why Jonnie latched onto Cara after she got sick, doubled down on his obsession with keeping her alive. Because despite his supposed hold on youth, his radical move to clutch his greatest treasure forever, he was dead in his grave on the inside. A dusty cavern yawned beneath his ribs. His unnaturally pretty veneer masked an ugly disease. The disease wasn't vampirism, either. Vampirism was a symptom of his true malady: chronic loneliness.

"Eve, no." Water wobbled in his eyes, making his vision waver like a heat waves on concrete. His throat swelled while he fidgeted with his face. "Say it isn't so. Lie to me. I promise, I'll believe."

"I sold you out," she whispered.

A bomb of silence dropped.

"How?" Feelings drained from him. He remained still as a statue, his insides slowly turning to stone.

"Remember the towel I used to clean blood off your cut? I gave it to Susan, who works for these monsters. There is no telling what they'll do with it, but in light of this, in light of all that we've learned about their projects with magic and demons? It's anyone's guess. And it's not safe for you to be near me. I mean it this time, Jonnie."

Logic and reason left him. He could only hurt, a raw and gaping wound from head to toe. Eve had double-crossed him, like a long line of duplicitous people before her. A sweet baking smell drifted through Helen and Brian's house, the incongruity of its pleasantness adding to the discomfort of having an awful talk in someone else's home. "How could you?"

She stooped, gathered papers from the floor, and rose. Turning her back to him, Eve pulled sheets from the wall, stacking her findings into a neat pile. "I regret what I did. I love you. And because I love you, I'm telling you to turn and run in the opposite direction from me."

There were pieces of her story missing, gaps. But none howled as loudly as the abyss in his heart. Its presence drowned out everything else. "I loved you, Eve."

Two streams slipped down her cheeks. They fell to the page atop her messy stack of printouts. "Goodbye, Jonnie."

"Let me fetch you the plane at least. Will you at least give me details? Maybe we can still work this out together." Incoherent ramblings. His mouth was dry, his limbs lead. His thoughts fled. An anesthetizing thickness permeated his abdominal cavity.

"No. I can take care of it. I just need to go. Now."

He stood and watched, numb, as she threw clothes in her suitcase and the printouts in her purse. She yanked on her windbreaker and boots and, with a backwards glance shot through with sorrow, rushed out of the bedroom and down the hall.

"Eve?" Helen's confused voice. "We just made waffles, where are you going?"

The front door slammed.

Brian muttered something indecipherable.

"I don't know, she didn't tell me anything. I thought I heard them arguing, but I didn't want to butt in. Jonnie?" Helen spoke again, a bit closer now.

He would explain the hurtful new twist to his friends in a moment, but not now. His eyes burned, tender with the threat of tears. His hands shook. An invisible sword flayed his skin from bone. His heart was an open sore. He couldn't think.

Before he freaked out and broke something or screamed, Jonnie fished a receipt from his pocket and scribbled "will explain later, don't follow me" on the back. He dropped it on the bed.

With trembling hands, he tugged on jeans and tee and his canvas high tops, yanking his pea coat over arms.

He pushed open a window. Fall air prickled the tip of his nose as he crawled out of the space he'd made and hopped into the side of the yard. Jonnie pulled the storm window down behind him in case the dogs liked to escape, shoved hands in his coat pockets, and slipped across the front lawn. He scanned for Eve as he walked, squinting into the morning sun. Glittery beams glistened across the lake, cheerful atmosphere making a mockery of his hopelessness.

Frosted grass crunched beneath rubber soles as he descended the slope of the hill, unlatched the gate, and set off down a sidewalk circling the perimeter of the lake. No sign of Eve, only a couple of joggers and a chatty couple pedaling a tandem bike. She'd probably brought up the app on her phone and summoned a car in under a minute. No doubt drivers relentlessly cruised this hip, upscale neighborhood, facilitating her speedy getaway.

A tinny bell on the bicycle handlebar clanked, and the woman waved. Jonnie averted his eyes from the strangers, popping the collar of his coat in absurd homage to caricatures of cartoon burglars. Along with his identity, he hid his anguish, his confusion, his utter lack of interest in chatting with people or playing the rock star part. Not now. Maybe not ever again.

Though he couldn't deny that Eve's so-called admission left him with more questions than answers, he also couldn't deny that she'd pushed him away. With a puff of vaporized breath, he halfheartedly released thoughts of her.

Strides quick and purposeful, Jonnie routed his focus back to the epiphany he'd had in the bedroom. He might be chewed up and spit out, dejected in the nuclear aftermath of Eve's rejection, but that didn't mean he'd write off his goal of helping Cara in some callous tallying of collateral heartbreak damage.

Jonnie fished his mobile from his pocket and rang Anya.

"Morning, Jonnie. What's up?" His sister let out a clipped moan. No doubt was she ragged as ever, run into the ground. He made a mental note to send her more money.

"How are we doing?" Nervous energy jittered through him. There was an urgent quality to speaking with Anya, a palpable sense of the other shoe dangling from a frayed string as it threatened to drop. But at least he had something else in his life to focus on, and an area where he might be able to help.

"Same." She yawned. "But I have positive news. We got approved for a new clinical trial. I loathe to bring this up now, since you're already doing so much, but it's a stretch financially and we hit our lifetime insurance maximum a long—"

He put up his palm to no one but the chilly lake breeze blowing in his face, a nascent sense of triumph replacing hollow hurt inside. "I have a better solution for us."

A fried, confounded grunt from Anya. "Wait, what?"

A woman with a stroller passed, and he bowed his head so his hair masked his distinctive features. "I can't explain over the phone, but I can be at the hospital today. I'll text you when I arrive. Meet me in Cara's room and I'll explain in person."

The nerves of his exposed bits of skin picked up every sensation in a magnetic hyperawareness. Damp coldness, like a burst of air from the freezer, swirled around him. One tree to his right had shed all of its foliage, leaving it a bare brown network of capillaries.

The sight of dead branches lanced a new spike of pain into him. It dulled to a bittersweet bite as the precise nature of his emotion came into relief. Nostalgia. The sweet memory of him and Eve walking through those autumnal streets of her neighborhood, admiring the turning leaves while they nurtured their relationship. A budding relationship that had died on the vine, smothered by deceit.

"What are you talking about?"

"Be at the hospital in a few hours. This has to be face-to-face. I'm about to propose something outlandish, but I think I can save Cara. Please, trust me."

"Okay." He heard her suck in a massive gust of air. "Okay, okay."

"I'll see you soon." He hung up the phone, stuffed it in his pocket, and kept walking, putting the stupid bloody symbolic tree behind him.

He'd thought he'd had a great love with Eve, a pure and unusual bond reserved for two people custom made for each other. She'd turned away from him, but the more he thought about it, Jonnie didn't buy her story of selling out and betrayal. He'd been too blindsided at the time to see through it, but he did now.

She'd rejected him with a firing squad of half-truths designed to strike at his deepest wounds. And her strategy, for whatever reason she'd deployed it, had worked.

There wasn't time to mourn or brood. For now, Eve was gone. But he still had his family. And armed with the information Eve had brought to him before she'd walked out of his life, he could at long last do right by them.

TWENTY-TWO

CURLED AT THE END OF HER COUCH, EVE DUNKED ANOTHER TORTILLA chip into the pan of seven-layer dip resting on her knees. She scooped up a generous dollop. As she filled her mouth with bean and cheese and sour cream solace, she told herself she had done the right thing. Jonnie didn't need her. He needed to stay as far away from her and a certain conniving bitch with a bloody towel as humanly possible. If Eve couldn't protect him, by default she endangered him.

If she couldn't solve the problem, she *was* the problem.

Eyes swollen and puffy from the tears she'd cried, Eve tried to convince herself that pushing Jonnie away was best for him. But was she lying to herself, rejecting him out of cowardice in lieu of standing in her shameful truth and risking incurring his rejection? Yep. Pretty much. Instead of standing brave and tall in the face of judgment before someone she loved, she'd retreated into fear.

The bag crinkled as she fished out more chips and buried them in the dwindling goop of salt and fat comfort. When the food failed to suffocate her feelings, she turned on the television and brought up Netflix. She tried to watch some show about drug dealers and corrupt cops but couldn't pay attention.

Eve set the baking dish on the coffee table and hauled her leaden body off of the couch before she ate any more. Calories would not fill the hole inside, but they would make her pants tight in the morning.

Sighing, she picked up the rotary phone's receiver and spun the dial for her mom's cell.

"Hey sweetie!" Eve's mom sounded perky and a bit out of breath. Voices chattered in the background. "I just got done with my synchronized swimming class. Your dad found a Groupon. It's so fun. You should come with me next time."

A tentative smile crept over Eve's lips, along with a pleasant sensation of lightness and warmth. Maybe she should go to water aerobics with her mom. Exercise would boost her endorphins, and the company of her loved ones would feed her soul.

"Good idea. I could use a little fun and positivity in my life." She threaded the phone cord through her fingers and shifted on her feet. Mom was so upbeat and cheery all of the time that reaching out to her in times of sadness brought a measure of guilt. Eve tried not to be a Debbie Downer, often to no avail.

"Oh, hon." A sigh that bordered on theatrical. "What's wrong now, my poor sad baby blue?"

Eve winced as she perched on the arm rest. Mom didn't *mean* to be passive-aggressive, but she loved being happy so much that she struggled when anyone or anything compromised her good feels. The woman perpetually danced through a field of wildflowers like the hippie she'd been.

Where Eve was concerned, the apple had fallen pretty far from the family tree. "I was seeing a man, but we broke up."

"Why?"

"I couldn't be honest with him about me." True enough. Mom didn't need to know every grisly detail.

"Oh, Evelyn. One day you'll realize how precious you are. You're a goddess, my magical, special witch-daughter. Do you know how cool that is? When I was younger, I would have given up a hell of a lot to have your gifts. I still would. And if some guy isn't man enough to cherish the beauty inside of you, he isn't worth it."

This was all very sweet, but Mom didn't quite get it. "I broke up with him."

"Oh. Why?" The two little words came with so much surprise that Eve stifled a laugh. Of course Mom figured Eve to be the dumpee. All she needed was a "born to lose" jailhouse tat on her arm to solidify her role in Mom's eyes.

"I was scared I'd hurt him."

"Well, he's a big boy, sweet pea. And if he's well-adjusted, he should know how and when to put up boundaries. And if he's being hurt or something is happening that he doesn't like, then it's his responsibility to assert himself or take action by standing up for himself. Do you care about this person?"

"Yes. A lot."

"Does he have feelings for you?"

"Yeah." Fresh tears threatened as an army of memories tried to storm Eve's thoughts.

"Then I think you should try to work it out. And be honest with him, Evelyn Grace. Tell him how you fled because you were afraid of yourself, but you won't do so again. Tell him how you will open up to him wholly, put your heart on the line once and for all. He needs to know that you are learning as you go, figuring out how to succeed in a relationship and make peace with these tremendous gifts you have. And tell him how you need his help. For him to be strong and honest and patient with you."

Eve exhaled, releasing a burden of negativity. She drew in cleansing energy with a big yoga breath. Her arm twitched, and in her mind she reached through the line and hugged her mom. "Thanks, Mama."

"Just doing my job. You're coming to the Halloween party, right? I haven't gotten an email notice with your reply."

In all the nuttiness, she'd forgotten about the annual bash her parents hosted for the neighborhood. "Of course."

"Yay! What are you wearing?"

"It's a surprise." Like Eve had given her Halloween costume a single passing thought.

"Mine, too. Can't wait."

"Same. And thank you, Mama. For the talk. I needed it."

"Any time. Take care, sweetie. Bye."

"Bye." Eve replaced the receiver in its cradle, the soft click erasing what remained of her distress with its sound of closure. A Saturday with family, old friends, and childhood neighbors would be therapeutic, enjoyable, and above all an excuse to forget her Jonnie-related angst and misery.

On Sunday, after she'd cleared her head with festivity, she'd call him. Apologize and come clean about why she'd flipped out. Why she'd lied, or catastrophized the truth. Explain to him how, in a moment of panic and weakness and shame, she'd pushed him away before she could stand before him in accountability for the part of herself she hated most. The side of her that hurt people instead of helping people. The Eve who had failed Lacey. The Eve who had handed over the bloody towel and failed Jonnie. The Eve who worried her dark magic was a dark stain on her soul.

How she'd even begin to think about how to bare her soul, she wasn't sure. But for Jonnie, for the sake of salvaging whatever she could with the gentlest, kindest, and most thoughtful man she'd ever met, she'd sure as hell try. But first, she'd better to go shopping for a Halloween costume.

Eve turned around. At the first glimpse of the orange-blonde hair helmet, her heart froze like a cadaver organ on ice.

Before Eve could react, Susan swung the antique urn she held above her head. With a red and gold streak through the air, it connected to Eve's temple in a cracking jolt of agony. Fire alarms erupted in her ears. Her vision blacked, nausea shredding her insides. She staggered backward, grasping for purchase as her hands flailed in darkness and her knees wobbled.

Her butt and back hit the soft couch cushions as she fell. The world spun. A hacking cough triggered her gag reflex and sent poisonous vomit into her throat. She swatted at nothing, mumbling slurred nonsense as her consciousness ebbed. The last thing she heard was Susan's victory snort.

* * *

"Ow." Eve awoke to a world of pain. Her mouth and throat, sandpaper-scraped, throbbed. Stressed arms pulled angrily at their sockets. Her wrists were bound. A million icepicks stabbed her head.

She jerked to no avail, friction burning against her skin as she battled her restraints. She was tied to a wooden chair. Her vision returned in apprehensive bursts and flutters. The room was dim, stuffy. It stank of a barnyard. She faced a double set of wooden doors. The only light came from a fluorescent bug zapper, blue tube glowing like radioactive Listerine in a black cage dangling from the ceiling.

No light but for that iridescent chemical tube, the lone sound its electronic hum, but Eve's guts twisted as she recognized her surroundings.

The Pollyanna shed.

"No." She struggled in vain against her bindings. A quick glance over her shoulder revealed several loops of white plastic handcuffs securing her wrists and ankles in stacked rows of bracelets and anklets. A horrid cord of synthetic rope attached her arms to her legs.

Stay calm. Think. Heart thumping in her ears, Eve glanced around, cringing when a tweaked muscle in her neck smarted. Empty and undamaged tanks filled their shelves. Fuck. Was that good or bad? No time to ponder. There had to be tools in this shed, scissors or a knife or *something* that would cut.

She saw it beside a vacated tank—a rusty green box on a low shelf that she could reach. The sight made her surge as if the junky thing contained a ticket to heaven. Hope propelling her, she scooted her chair across the hard-pack dirt with a series of scrapes. Eve backed up, coming flush with the shelf.

Her fingers made contact with the hard metal latch, and she pulled it. It popped open. "Yes."

Her pulse a drum, she flipped the lid and felt the box's contents. Metal tools rattled and clanked. Tremors wracked her hands, but she groped at pointy hard things until a sharp edge poked the fleshy mound below her thumb. Quickly, she felt the rest of it, stuffing a victory screech as she identified the item in hand.

Scissors.

"Thank you, thank you."

Eve was hard at work sawing at her plastic binds when she heard a familiar rattle. The calling card of the mutants who'd once lived in this shed, much louder than before, sounded a buzzing rattle. She shook her head in clawing denial, slicing blades back and forth. Some of the tension in her arms eased as the restraints gave way under her assault.

The distinct hiss, a demonic fart from the bowels of hell, tore through the air beyond the shed. *No, no no*.

Chains clickety-clanked. A click signaled a padlock opening. Eve froze, scissors a lottery ticket for salvation in her palms, and watched her chest rise and fall. The ties securing her hands snapped and fell slack, taking the connecting rope with them. The cord flopped to the ground like a slippery piece of spinal column falling from the embalming table.

"Come on now, big boy, come on." Susan spoke with a mixture of aggravation and fear. Strained grunts punctuated her coaxed encouragement.

"Aieeee!" The yowl, inhuman and enraged, pierced Eve to the bone marrow. Her insides quaked as the abject sound branded its mark on her. Two solid thumps struck the door, followed by crunches as wood splintered. "Aieeee!"

"Come on, now." After Susan barked her order, the doors flung wide.

＊ ＊ ＊

Anya blew into Cara's hospital room with a massive cup of coffee clenched in one hand, her wrinkled tee shirt stained by brown and red spills, and her eyes bloodshot. She'd wadded her long, black hair in a halfhearted knot atop her head, several loose strands glued to her face by sweat.

Jonnie's heart broke for his saintly sister. She'd suffered enough, endured enough. Finally, he could do something to alleviate her burden and save the child they both loved, but only if she bought what he was selling. He put both hands on his sister's shoulders and gazed deeply into her eyes, eschewing glamor magic in favor of old-fashioned honesty. "I need you to remain calm and listen. What I'm about to propose is going to sound completely psychotic, but I swear to you, I'm telling the truth. If you listen to me very carefully and agree to this, we can save Cara's life. She won't be the same, but she won't die. You with me so far?"

"Yes," Anya said in a small, hopeful voice. "But I don't follow. Do you mean that you know about a method to prolong her life, some kind of fancy elite celebrity heath treatment? If so, how much more time will this give her?"

Before he could answer, a sharp headache stabbed his temple. He swore that he heard voices in his head speaking frantically. One thing at a time, though, and this moment was annexed for Anya. He swallowed to gather his bearings and brushed a damp piece of hair away from one of Anya's big brown eyes. "She won't ever die, Anya. If we go this route, she'll live forever."

Anya stammered, her face twisting into a rictus of confusion. "What the hell are you talking about? Is this some weird crackpot transhumanism thing about uploading her consciousness into a computer? Because I refuse to turn my daughter into a science experiment."

"No. Lower tech. And the experimental trials have already been completed. I was one of the experiments."

She grimaced as if losing faith, her chin trembling. "What sort of experiment?"

With that, Jonnie launched into the saga. Vampivax. Connors. The treatments, what he and Eve had learned about Scarab. The ayahuasca solution, and how he'd share as much as possible with Cara initially before he learned to make his own to sustain both of them.

Initially, Anya gaped. Shook her head while biting a nail and looking at the floor. "You're right. That's the most outlandish, improbable, far-out story that I have ever heard in my entire life." But as she finished her thought, her tone lifted. He caught no judgment, no dismissal, no rejection. Curiosity buoyed her vowels. Finally, after mouthing some unspoken words and chewing on her finger some more, she steeled her spine and met his eyes again. "Fuck it," she spat out with an undercurrent of triumph. "Do it. Save my little girl. Save my baby."

Jonnie pressed his hands together as relief and joy crashed through him. Anya was so damn open-minded, an adventurous spirit and a fierce mama bear. He should have known that she'd be amenable to rescuing Cara from the grips of death by any means necessary. "What about her dad?" Mark listened to his wife on almost everything, deference that went double for Cara's health care. But the respectful thing to do was ask.

"It'll be fine," Anya said confidently. "I'll tell him myself, and he'll cope."

"I'm here for all of you any time, if anyone has any questions or needs support. Seriously, anything."

Garbled nonsense words rang out in his head, faint and distant. In his head, or his imagination? Or was he fried from lack of blood and poor sleep? Suddenly dizzy, he braced one of his hands on the wall until the odd spell passed.

"Hurry up before I change my mind and have you committed to a psych ward."

Jonnie moved deftly to remove Cara's IV line and empty the saline drip bag in a basin. Next, he performed a hasty bloodletting with a pilfered scalpel and hovered over the sink while transferring his blood to her bag via syringe and a cut to the plastic. Luckily, he'd prepared in advance by swiping the proper tools before Anya arrived, and he expressed silent gratitude that his nimble fingers and dexterous hands delivered in the moment of truth.

While his sister looked on from the corner of the dark room lit only with the moving line of Cara's heart monitor, Jonnie cleaned up all traces of spilt blood. As he replaced the drip bag, he sighed in relief. Mission accomplished. Nothing to do but wait. Jonnie snagged a handful of chocolate candies from a goody basket at Cara's bed table, shoved them into his mouth, and flopped into a chair with a ripped vinyl cushion. Sugar would sustain him for another day or so, until he could get back to New Orleans and reunite with his ayahuasca.

Anya fell to her knees beside him and clung to his throbbing arm, praying.

Waves of misery washed over him as he faced a return to reality, a return to life without Eve. Too spent to wallow, he zoned out in his uncomfortable seat.

"Uncle Jon?" Cara's voice snapped him from a stupor.

"I'm here, Care Bear. Are you alright?"

"I'm not sick anymore." Her bald head shone in the bit of moonlight coming through the barred, fifth-story window.

He bolted to stand and rushed to her, grabbing her hands in his. The changes struck him immediately. No more sallowness ruined her peachy complexion. The sunken look had lifted. But he couldn't get his hopes up yet, couldn't succumb to wishful thinking. "How do you feel? Tell me exactly how you are feeling."

His hope intensified the longer he looked into her sweet brown eyes. They were shiny and clear, without a trace of that watery, vacant haze. Her stare was free of the lurk of death, as he'd come to think of that sickening cast.

"My stomach doesn't hurt. I feel strong, like I could play basketball again. I'm hungry. Can I have a grilled cheese sandwich and birthday cake and milk and cereal with marshmallows in it?"

"Oh baby, oh baby." Sobbing, Anya rushed to her her only child's bedside and swept the girl into her arms. "We did it, we did it."

Tears streamed down Jonnie's face. His heart exploded. People liked to say fuck cancer. Jonnie was a humble man and hated to brag, but he congratulated his vampire self for telling cancer to fuck off and making it listen. He kissed Cara's smooth forehead. She smelled better too, fresh. No more pungent funk of illness. "You can have whatever you want."

Jonnie pushed the button for the night nurse. A matronly woman with a kind, freckled face rushed in, rubber shoes squeaky against linoleum. While the nice lady looked on in awe and Anya cradled her daughter, Cara babbled with pure joy about how good she felt.

"Can I have some food?"

Jonnie chimed in, "She'd like a grilled cheese sandwich and milk—"

"No." Cara's smile split her face, showing a mouthful of teeth. "I changed my mind. I want a steak. Rare. Super bloody. Mooing."

The nurse laughed. "She's craving protein."

Jonnie locked eyes with his niece as a sobering realization gelled. The mutation was underway, and fast.

"And blood pudding." She clapped. "Like we had in England that one time."

Nurse Lady had it wrong. Cara wasn't craving protein. She was hungry for blood already.

"I'll see what I can do." Chortling, the night nurse whisked away.

"I feel like a princess with magical powers. I can fly. I can do anything." Cara jumped to stand on her bed, the tubes in her arms stretching from her emaciated body like the bones of bat wings.

Cara's skin caught the night's rays in a certain illustrious way. Or maybe that was just her, the new her. A faint fluorescence made her sparkle. A chill raced up Jonnie's back as the presence of this newly minted night angel struck him with her macabre poetry. With her bald head, the name Nosferatu came to mind.

Before he could reply to Cara, the nurse returned with a plastic tray of food, two doctors, and Anya's husband Mark in tow.

"Baby girl, what's happening?" In a voice shot through with shock and tears, Mark rushed to his daughter.

"She's cured," Anya wailed, rocking Cara. "She's cured."

"I'm cured."

A doctor with a red French braid put her hand on Anya's shoulder as she took in the scene with a somber expression. "Sometimes cancer patients experience a rush of euphoria in the final—"

"Fuck cancer, right Uncle Jon?" Gemstones of amber eyes cut to Jonnie, alive with recognition and a sly wink of humor. She'd heard those words in his head, read his mind. It was official. Cara was a bona fide vampire, a bloodsucking fiend.

Everyone laughed at the rough cuss in the pretty teen's voice.

Welcome to the club. I'll explain how it all works soon, but for now don't bite anyone without their consent, you hear?

Cara saluted him with two fingers.

"I can call in a few favors at the Mayo Clinic and order some rushed tests. I've never witnessed a medical miracle firsthand, but I won't rule it out yet." The other physician, a man with a thick accent who reminded Jonnie of his cousin Pranav, dashed out of the room. With a nod and a point, the doctor communicated a message to the nurse.

The nurse returned his nod and got to work drawing Cara's blood. The girl stared, rapt, as red fluid shot through a clear tube and filled a vial. Nurse collected her sample and ran after the doctor.

A flurry of activity ensued. Tests results confirmed the good news: Cara was cancer free. Screams, cheers, and sobs filled the hospital room as the patient devoured everything the nurse brought.

Still on her knees at Cara's bedside, Anya folded her hands in prayer and bent her head skyward. "Thank you thank you for saving my baby. I believe in you. I believe in miracles. I'm sorry I doubted, and I'll never doubt again."

Well, the god or gods upstairs didn't deserve *all* of the credit, but Jonnie wasn't about to spoil the celebration or make this moment about him. He listened politely as the thoughtful Indian doctor talked at him using a bunch of medical jargon, an attempt at scientific reasoning to make sense of the miraculous healing.

Someone brought in a music player, and an impromptu dance party sprang to life. A cake full of candles came in next, teardrops of yellow flames alight. A new dizzy spell struck Jonnie, worse than before, so intense that he had to sit. The speech in his mind intensified and sped up, static fading as crisp words emerged. Words spoken in a feminine voice.

"Jonnie...I...don't..." Eve's voice. Miserable with despair and distress, she spoke in his head.

"Where are you? What's happening?" He used telepathy.

"Susan...let me...untie." More slurred gobbledygook. "No!"

Fuck. If Susan was involved, Eve was in trouble. And likely in Louisville. He jumped to his feet and bolted to Anya. "I have to go. It's an emergency. Call me if you need anything, okay? I'll be in touch soon."

"What's wrong? Something with the band?"

"I'll explain soon." He had no idea if that were true, but he needed to go. Because Eve was in danger, and despite what had gone down between them, he would protect her. She'd reached out to him, and he wasn't about to let her down.

Muffled screams banged in his head as he grabbed another handful of candies and shoved them in his mouth. Sprinting down the hallway as he fled the hospital, Jonnie used his mind to tell Eve to hold on a little longer. Because he loved her, he was coming for her, and he'd never let her slip away ever again.

TWENTY-THREE

It was all Eve could do to maintain control of her bladder and colon. The monster, secured with plastic-coated chain leashes by a straining Susan, her husband Dale, and Rustin, rivaled a wolf in size.

Her skin was ice. Horror gripped her stomach in painful contractions. Eve sized up the nightmare fuel before her and categorized the various assets its lineage bestowed. The snake DNA gave it muscle, the ability to jerk its captors to and fro as it struggled against its confines, lashing a rattle-tipped tail in the air. From the roach and tick it got hardiness and a tough exoskeleton she bet the sharpest cleaver couldn't breach. Thanks to the piranha element of its ancestry, the Pollyanna gnashed tightly packed swords of teeth built to rip flesh from body.

The thing's one weakness had to be its short legs. She could tell from its oafish, lurching movements that its low center of gravity and the poor support its stems offered impeded movement. No way could the Pollyanna move with anything more than a tipsy waddle, let alone give chase or climb trees.

It unleashed a barrage of its abject noises, belt of a forked tongue stabbing from a cavern of dagger teeth. A part of her hurt for this aberration. It was just an animal after all, and one that was suffering and ought to be put out of its misery.

"What have you done, Susan?" The dregs of Eve's hope drained into the ground. When she'd detected Jonnie's presence moving through the wavelength of her consciousness, she'd warned him to stay far away. She hadn't been able to make out his garbled reply, but she begged him to listen. Meaning she was all alone with two psychos and a killer mutant.

"Call up your fucking vampire." Huffing and groaning, Susan pulled back at the leash until it was taut. The Pollyanna thrashed and wailed, rearing an inch off the ground before crashing back down.

Eve cringed as its wee stumps absorbed the impact of its ponderous bulk.

"Or else what, you feed me to Fido? But if I die you'll never get to Jonnie, now will you?"

"Where's Lacey?" Dale wheezed his words out, jowls on his red face flopping.

"Resting in peace, you assholes."

"Goddamn motherfucker!" Susan stamped a foot.

The Pollyanna hissed, whipping its head from side to side in fast lashes.

"What's your agenda, Susan?" Eve clutched her scissors. If the Pollyanna broke free, she'd go for the eyes first.

Susan snickered amidst the struggle, red lips curling into a sneer. "They pay up or I keep right on talkin'. Tellin' anyone who will listen about their messin' with vampires and evil magic and all the rest. And with my big boy here? I got proof. The real deal."

The real deal screamed again, its rattle shaking so fast it streaked a blur in the air.

"Where are the others?"

"In his belly!" Rustin exclaimed, a sheen of sweat glistening on his naked chest.

Since Pollyanna bodies contained vampire blood, by cannibalizing others, the top beast would benefit from the growth serum in their sacrificed guts. A certain coveted item would likely also turbocharge the Pollyanna. "You fed it the towel soaked in Jonnie's blood to accelerate its growth."

"You bet your ass." Dale, hunched comically low with his clothed gut pressed into the beast's thorax, spoke like Eve was an idiot for questioning why anyone would make such a choice.

Yet somehow, Eve didn't feel like the idiot here. "What do you gain by growing it so huge?"

"Duh, they pay by the pound." Rustin stuck out his tongue.

"Well, now they'll be payin' to keep me quiet and shit." Susan corrected her son. "But I'll find somebody to pay a nice adoption fee for my big boy."

The mother did her gross, audible kissy-face thing and tugged the neon yellow chain.

All Eve could do was watch the spectacle of two dumb fucks and their spawn locked in an absurd tug-of-war with an awful, yet undeniably pathetic, mutant monster. Sobering clarity cleared her head. Sometimes nefarious motivations boiled down to greed, just like Jonnie had said.

And lust for money combined with stupidity? Now that's the stuff of evil.

Dale's chain snapped, the force making the father sprawl backward. The disruption startled a shout from Rustin, who dropped his leash as he staggered to the side. The Pollyanna bucked, sending Susan flying through the air. She flopped against a wall of empty tanks, moaning, limbs akimbo.

Rustin, in an unexpected flash of intelligence, darted from the shed like a slick minnow.

Metal clattered against metal as he locked the Pollyanna and three unfortunates in the building together. His choice rendered Eve screwed, but she didn't blame the abused boy for looking out for himself. Calmer than she should be, she held her scissors tight.

As predicted, the Pollyanna moved in an awkward gait, its bulk falling from side to side as it lurched to Dale first.

The man screamed while the beast made mercifully quick work of him. It used its teeth, landing a couple of strategically placed bites. Next it came for Susan, dispatching her with equal efficiency.

In tandem, Dale and Susan's souls rose from their corpses. Golden light spheres—all troubled souls got the same thing regardless of morality or character—floated to Eve and came to rest in her lap. They instantly launched into their life stories.

The Pollyanna turned its broad head in Eve's direction and slogged on over. Gritting her teeth, she focused on its left eye, the vertical streak of red pupil. The scissors were steel blades of hope in her hands, the closest she'd come to a magic sword.

Her heart slammed as she aimed her scissors and aligned her best shot, the extent of her world fixed on vulnerable spots amid hard, scaly flesh.

Rearing back, muscles taut, the creature opened its mouth and screamed, giving Eve a glimpse of its pink, massive, toothy maw.

Now. She pointed the tip of her blade at the eye and slammed it down, being the proverbial ball as she focused all she had at piercing that jelly-soft orb of tissue.

But the Pollyanna evaded her strike with startling agility, scurrying into a corner on those awful bug legs. The retreat didn't last long, as the monster recalibrated with a shake and grunt and stalked back to Eve with its back arched.

Shit. She'd missed, and now it looked madder than ever and intent on a new kill. Yet it crept to her slowly and with intention, taking its time in a way that it hadn't with Susan and Dale.

Sentient and intelligent enough to enjoy the hunt, Eve bet.

But she had a few seconds to think while the Pollyanna savored its foreplay. She wiggled her ankles, finding the binds looser than they'd been originally. The struggle must've given her some slack. So she jerked and bent, settling on a twist and turn motion with her feet that seemed to promise results. Sure enough, she created enough wiggle room to step out of her restraints slowly and discreetly, being careful in case the monster was smart enough to catch on to her impending escape and hasten its plan.

The Pollyanna closed two more feet of space between them, buzzing and rattling as it huffed big, aggressive breaths. Eve waited, teeth clenched and scissors clutched as hard as her grip would allow. *Closer, closer.*

And the fiend came closer, close enough for Eve to smell its fishy, reptilian musk. Once in striking distance, the Pollyanna reared up on its cricket legs, those teeny stubs writhing and wriggling all along the underbelly, and bared its mouthful of fangs. The black tongue shot out, tasting the air in front of Eve's face while she sized up the underside of her adversary.

Those cricket legs were, by far, its biggest weakness. Before she had time to overthink of miss her chance, Eve vaulted to stand and kicked the Pollyanna's stomach as hard as she could, her heel connecting to hard flesh with a nasty crunch. She'd broken something inside of it.

The creature screeched, flopping backwards, and connected with a thud on the dirt ground. Belly up, it howled and wheezed, its chest caved in, those feeler-feet squirming in every direction.

Eve knew what she had to do. She took no joy in the completion of her grim mission but, in a sense, her career had prepared her for grim and gory missions. She slit the Pollyanna's throat with a single, clean swipe to cleave soft skin. Black-red blood bloomed in the gash, spilling over the neck wound in dark swells that pooled crimson on the floor. The creature jerked one last time before going still.

No golden light emerged, which negated any guilt or shame that Eve was tempted to suffer for her dirty deed. This creature lacked a soul. It was never supposed to exist, and thus never truly existed in a spiritual sense. She dropped her scissors and backed away, covering her nose once the rancid smell hit.

Metallic bashing at the door prompted her to whip her head in the direction of the banging and clanging. Wood bulged and crunched as an unseen person attacked the lock. Three more slams, and it blew open wide. Jonnie stood in the threshold, holding a pair of bolt cutters.

"Come in," Eve yelled, her invitation so much more than a necessary formality.

In that moment, she invited him to see the worst of her, the awful wages of her mistake. Two dead bodies, their desperate souls clinging to her. A thing that should not be, slain at her feet. Whether or not the lunacy in the shed would have happened if Eve had properly processed Lacey way back when couldn't be decided with certainty. But beyond a shadow of a doubt, the scene mirrored her. Her powers and abilities, who she was at her deepest core.

And Eve had lied to herself when she'd reasoned that the essence of her shame was the mistake with Lacey, the incompetence. The powers themselves, her death magic, was the true source of her wound. Eve lived with the fear that she had been born with a fault. That she was wrong. No more secrets. No more lies.

Jonnie ran to her, wrapping his arms around her shoulders and back, and hummed a soothing tune. "I'm too late. I'm so, so sorry. Are you hurt, Eve darling?"

"No. I'm more or less okay, given the circumstances. And you're right on time." She'd needed to fight her own battle at the very end, she figured.

"I'm so sorry I didn't get here until now. I'm so sorry you went through this. I should have fought harder to keep you by my side. I should have never let you go." His murmured words were relief and regret and love, all spun together into a poem and a promise.

"No, I'm sorry. For lying and leaving and freaking out. I guess the worst part of me thought that if you knew me, really knew me, you'd never be able to love me. So I hid and I lied. I rejected you before you'd have the chance to reject me. But here I am. This is me, Jonnie. Right here."

"I know. And I'm here, Eve. I'm here to stay." Jonnie pointed at Susan and Dale. "I say we call in an anonymous tip about them. Claim to be door-to-door missionaries who smelled a bad smell."

"What about that?" She gestured to the monstrous remains.

Jonnie sighed. "Let someone else figure it out. Maybe the authorities will haul it onto a lab and trace it back to Scarab. Truth be told, I don't really care. This isn't our problem."

"You're right." Stench of the bodies overpowering now that her adrenaline rush had faded, Eve took Jonnie's hand and led the pair out of the shed.

They walked through the dirt back yard, wiggling through a gap in the chain-link fence that he'd used to bypass the problem of having to enter and pass through the house.

She allowed herself a moment to appreciate the perfect autumn day. The crisp air, blue sky, the late-afternoon sun brushing sidewalks with a buttery glaze. All of the beauty cleansed her of what she'd gone through, scrubbed away the ugliness of her ordeal.

A dart punctured her happiness with memories of an important fact. "There's a kid, too, somewhere. Rustin. He ran off."

"We can say we saw him in the house or backyard. They'll get Child Services involved."

"Rustin knows about all of this. What if he talks?" They curved around the side of the home and reached the driveway, where the black rental sedan Jonnie had driven sat parked.

Jonnie shook his head, mouth bending into a resigned half-smile. "Then he talks. And if they ring us for a statement, we give a statement. We're innocent and have nothing to hide."

With Lacey safe and at peace, Eve relished the truth of his claim. "I've never felt innocent."

"It's not the right word exactly." He stopped walking and cupped her face in both hands. "But you're pure. And principled, and gifted. You bring people comfort and peace when they need it most of all. And you're the proof, Eve, that's there's more to life than this. That there are mysteries and dimensions and aspects of spirit beyond our wildest dreams. Being with you taught me that. Being with you taught me that belonging doesn't mean conforming or even fitting in. It means embracing our true selves in all of their wild contradictions and eccentricities. Because we are worthy, Eve. Of happiness. Of love. Not despite what makes us different, either. Because of it."

A holy force went to work on her, rearranging everything inside to create symmetry where it hadn't existed before. Because there hadn't been completion or wholeness. Eve had lacked a crucial element to give to herself and to others, and to accept from others. Sure, she'd experienced it in muted consistency, and also in flashes and peeks. A perfect birthday party, cuddles with a happy dog, the cozy blankets of family traditions, and the medicine of good-natured laughter.

But she'd never before sat with the feeling in such totality, such awareness of sheer expanse. Of abundance and goodness for all. But ever since that rainy night on her stoop, that first walk along the river, a certain someone had been trying to show her the beauty in her heart.

It was there, locked in a tomb, but he'd patiently stuck with her, picking at the lock, until she'd come around and helped him open it.

Because he'd seen what she was capable of, he'd seen her potential, long before she had and in ways she'd never thought possible.

"I love you, Jonnie. I love you."

"I love you." He stroked her cheeks like she was something to be savored while appraising her face in gentle rapture.

A silence fell as they entered a private, perfect cocoon of unspoken cherishes. But right below the surface, at the water's edge of her conscious mind, Dale and Susan kept right on talking. Predictably sad life stories, tales of abuse and neglect and the deadening cynicism of lives born into poverty and rooted there until their extinctions. "I need to get home and transition them."

Jonnie's grin split his face. "You know why I love you even more, you having said that?'

She chuckled. "Why?"

"Because you would be justified in telling these two rubbish people to piss right off. Letting them fade away or putting them on a one-way express to hell is what they deserve. But I know you never would. You give people more than what they deserve."

She shrugged, sheepish. "I suppose I have scruples, yes."

"It's leaps and bounds beyond scruples. You live up here, my spirit goddess." He waved a hand above his head.

"My self-esteem is dangerously high right now."

"This is only the beginning."

He dropped a kiss to her temple, got in the car, and started the engine.

On the highway drive back into town, Jonnie told Eve about Cara. About how he'd saved her with his blood and turned her into a vampire in the process, and how he planned to be a more involved presence in her life as he walked her through the particulars of her new reality. His sister and brother-in-law were accepting, but if a time came when Jonnie struggled with his family, Eve would stand by his side in support.

A stop at a convenience store ended with a burner phone and an anonymous call to the police about a suspicious smell and an unsupervised boy at the Mudd property. Jonnie nodded at her once as they threw the phone away, his gesture an acknowledgement of their consensus. The tribulation was over. If the police got ambitious, they might attempt to track the burner phone, but this possibility was an unknown they'd deal with in the future. For the sake of their sanity and happiness, they'd best forget about it.

They resumed the drive. He parallel parked on the street, squeezing between two other cars. They strolled to her home holding hands, the two souls orbiting her waist like she was a titan of a planet, they two moons in her thrall.

Long shadows stretched from Eve and Jonnie's bodies, stilt-legged apparitions coasting along the walkway. She laughed and unlocked the door.

"Your gorgeous laugh is poetry to my heart. And what's so funny?" Jonnie nuzzled her hair, making an hourglass study of her curves with his touch.

"We've come full circle. You, me, and a lost soul or two standing at my doorstep."

"And yet everything has changed."

The lock opened with a click, and she led him in. So much meaning, dense as dark chocolate, filled his simple statement. Before was dark and wet, agitated and shot through with angst. Before was uncertain and flailing, two broken people advancing and retreating, reaching out and pushing away on an anonymous and lonely night.

After was comfort. Security. Healing. The sense that if they stepped over the edge, they wouldn't plummet off a cliff to certain doom. They would fly. Soar, together.

Sure, logistics remained. His recording and touring schedule kept him on the move, while her career rooted her in Louisville. But for now, they were together and happy. And Eve was confident they could navigate the ins and outs of maintaining a relationship in the face of life's mundane stressors and hurdles. They'd already defeated some mammoth obstacles as a couple.

"Be right back, okay? Make yourself at home." In the vestibule, Eve stood on her tiptoes and kissed Jonnie's cheek.

She raced up the stairs and took care of Susan and Dale, sending them somewhere where they would be content at last. Freed from their hate, from the fear that underpins hate, perhaps these two could learn love in the next life. Hell, if she could find true love, anything was possible.

The ritual went well, and Eve rode a lilt of euphoria as she came back down and breezed through her living room and into the kitchen.

Jonnie leaned against the island, reading the label on a bottle of wine he'd pulled from her countertop rack. "Notes of cherry, licorice, chocolate, and oak with a smooth finish and robust tannins."

She got down two wine glasses. "I have a confession to make."

"Hm?" The wine cork popped.

Eve set the stemware on the island. "I know it's classy to claim to be able to detect all of these different elements in wine, but mostly I just taste the alcohol."

He poured red liquid into glasses, a gleam shining in his dark eyes. "This is the starter course, love. Because I know something that tastes a thousand times sweeter and spicier and more complex than the finest wine."

"Your fangs are popping." She hopped up on the marble slab and wrapped her legs around his waist, pulling him close.

"That's not the only thing." He nibbled the shell of her ear as a full erection pressed between her legs.

She tilted her head back. A moan escaped him as he brushed warm lips against her neck.

"I hope I'm like wine and get better with age."

"I guess I'll find out, because I plan to enjoy you for a long, long time. Again."

He sucked the pulse point below her jaw, making her gasp with pleasure.

"And again." Sharp points dragged her skin as his lips traveled the length of a vein. Her center aching and wet, she ground against his hardness.

"And again." His whisper tickled her flesh with hot breath, peep of a tongue moistening the target area.

"Shut up and bite me."

"Patience, love. We have all the time in the world."

With that, Jonnie turned his face from Eve's neck and kissed her on the lips. She lost herself in the sealing of their union, a kiss so extraordinary she lost sight of where she ended, and he began. Bodies joined in licks and brushes and the crash of tongues.

Eve became one with herself, in perfect alignment with her man. Because together, more so than apart, each of them could do more than exist. In the face of so much death and darkness, together they would thrive.

Hot blood ran through Eve's veins, the offering which gave her lover life. And he returned that lifeblood to her, through the power of his love.

There was nothing sweeter.

***

Did you enjoy? Please add your review because nothing helps an author more and encourages readers to take a chance on a book than a review.

Then, sign up for the City Owl Press newsletter to receive notice of all book releases!

And don't miss more paranormal romance like EDGE OF THE WOODS by City Owl Author, Jules Kelley. Turn the page for a sneak peek!

SNEAK PEEK OF EDGE OF THE WOODS

JULES KELLEY

The sun crested the horizon, lighting the inside of the truck with an orange glow, and Leland stretched, trying to work eighteen hours of road stiffness out of his shoulders. In the distance, mountains rose above the scraggly pines like towering angels against the brightening sky, welcoming him to paradise instead of throwing him out. He spared one hand off the steering wheel to knuckle the dust and sleepless itch out of his eyes and wished for another cup of coffee.

Taking the job in Pine Grove had been a risk, but as far as he was concerned, it was already paying off. He'd washed off the last of the dust from the Arizona desert at a gas station somewhere north of Salt Lake City, and now, watching the foothills of western Montana fill his view, he barely remembered what Tucson looked like.

When he'd interviewed with the Upham County Sheriff's Department, Sheriff Rylan had told him that Pine Grove was the basement office of deputy assignments.

"'Bout once a month, you'll have to go out on the nature preserve to find some birdbrain out-of-towner who got lost on the full moon. The town trades on old folktales 'bout werewolves in the woods, and some people are dumb enough to go lookin'. Other than that, hope you like sittin' around with your thumb up your ass waitin' for somebody to lock themselves out of their house."

That sounded just fine to Leland. Hell, he might even have time to go fishing every now and then. The fancy fly rod he'd bought himself a couple of years ago hadn't been doing anything except collecting dust in his closet, and the Tucson PD staff therapist had brought it up in his final session.

"When's the last time you took some time off to just enjoy a hobby?"

Well, no time like the present.

A flash of movement on the side of the road caught his attention—an animal stumbling up out of the ditch right in front of him—and he swore as he stomped on the brakes, pulling hard on the steering wheel. His heartbeat thudded in his ears as the vehicle skidded sideways, tires squawking as they jumped and bounced over the asphalt. The SUV finally came to a stop with one tire in the ditch, and he pried his shaking hands off the steering wheel to scrape them over his face.

He turned to look at the animal he'd almost hit and sucked in a sharp breath when he realized it wasn't a bear or a deer, but a human, naked and filthy, hunched over as he lurched unsteadily across the pavement.

Leland was out of the driver's seat in an instant, automatically reaching for his handset to radio Guerrera, and then swore when he remembered. He wasn't in uniform. He wasn't in Arizona. Guerrera was twelve hundred miles away. He wasn't even a police officer anymore. He patted his pockets instead, looking for his phone and digging it out as he cautiously approached the man.

Boy, he corrected himself as he got closer. It was hard to tell what his face looked like under streaks of dirt—*And is that dried blood?*—but he was small, slender, his dark eyes large in his ashy brown face. Late teens, Leland guessed, forcing down the itch of memory at the back of his mind: another young face, another pair of haunted eyes. He didn't have time for that right now.

"Hey," Leland called, one hand out to him, moving slowly. "Are you all right, kid?"

The boy didn't answer him, but he watched Leland warily. He drew in several quick breaths through his nose, and after a moment, Leland realized he was sniffing the air. His mannerisms were more animal than human, but his hair was shaved close on the sides, a stylish—and recent —haircut, and a diamond earring glinted from the dirt caking his right ear, so he hadn't been out of civilization that long.

"It's all right. I'm here to help you," Leland tried again, keeping his voice calm and quiet. He thought of the legends of werewolves in Pine Grove that Rylan had told him about and just as quickly shook off the idea. The boy, naked and bloody, had clearly been through *something*, but Leland knew intimately that run-of-the-mill humans were more than capable of incredible cruelty without any supernatural assistance.

"Can you tell me your name?" Leland said, trying to keep the boy's attention as he inched back toward his SUV. Somewhere in the meager life's belongings in the back seat of the vehicle were clothes that might fit the kid, at least enough to cover him up and keep him from freezing. The day was rapidly warming as the sun rose, but spring nights in Montana were still chilly, and he'd obviously been out for at least a few hours.

Leland checked his phone as he sifted through one of his duffel bags. One bar of signal. Maybe it would be enough to call somebody, see if he could get an ambulance on the way. He only had two local numbers—the Upham County sheriff's office and the Pine Grove Wildlife Preserve. The sheriff's office was in Red Horse River, another hour and a half up the road, and Rylan *had* said that the preserve director would be his point of contact for problems with wayward tourists, lost hikers, and animal attacks.

Well, here goes nothin'.

He tucked the phone between his ear and shoulder, listening to it ring as he finally found a pair of sweat pants that looked like they might fit the kid if he pulled the drawstring tight.

There was a click, then silence, and Leland waited to hear someone on the other end. "Hello?" Nothing. "Hello, can you hear me?"

The beep of a dropped call mocked him, and he huffed out a frustrated breath. "Dammit."

The young man twitched, seeming to focus on him for the first time, his gaze confused and curious—but finally human, not glassy and alien.

"Who're you?"

"Hey, kid," Leland said, immediately pocketing his phone again. "My name's Leland Sommers. I found you out here on the road. You remember how you got here?"

The kid looked around, frowning, and Leland guessed the answer before he shook his head. "Where the fuck is *here*?"

He shivered, and Leland held out the sweat pants in offering. The kid's nose wrinkled, but he took them.

"You're on Route 23, right outside Pine Grove, Montana." He cleared his throat. "What's your name?" He focused on keeping his voice steady and warm. The boy didn't seem especially volatile, but neither had that one girl he'd found stoned out of her mind on the floor of her boyfriend's meth lab—until she'd damn near taken a chunk out of his arm.

This guy looked more like something had already taken a bite out of *him*, Leland thought, eyeing a fresh-looking wound on the kid's left shoulder.

"My name's Diego." Diego wet his lips, pulling the drawstring on the pants as tight as they would go. They still sagged on his narrow hips, the *Arizona Coyotes* logo down the leg looking bigger than his entire body.

Leland's phone rang in his pocket, and Diego flinched and immediately looked around as if he'd lost something, swearing under his breath. Leland guessed he'd had a phone with him before whatever had happened. But he'd have to ask questions later; the call was coming from a local number.

"This is Leland Sommers."

"You call this number a minute ago?" The woman's voice on the other end of the line was brusque, no-nonsense. "This is the Pine Grove Nature Preserve's ranger station."

"I did." Well, at least something was going right. "I'm the new sheriff's deputy, coming to fill the position in town. I'm stopped on Route 23 out here east of town with a young man who was in the road with no clothes on. Is there an emergency response service that I should call?"

The woman on the other end made a noise that might have been a snort. "Closest hospital's at least an hour away. Can you get him into your car and drive him in, or do you need a backboard and a neck brace?"

Leland darted a glance over at Diego, evaluating him. He was trying to pick the leaves and twigs out of his hair now; it didn't seem at all like he was nursing a spinal injury.

"No, he's ambulatory." Diego gave him an odd look, frowning, and Leland had a sudden flash of another kid—younger, smaller, but with the same mix of wariness and cautious hope on his face. He looked away. "Where should I take him?"

"There's a clinic. When you're coming in to town, turn left at the stoplight, and you'll see it in about half a mile. I'll call Haley and Doc Fenton, let 'em know you're comin' in."

"Which stoplight?" Leland asked, and the woman laughed.

"The only one in the whole town. Anything you want me to tell the doc when I call her? Injuries, things like that?"

"Just some contusions, abrasions. It does look like he got attacked by an animal, maybe. Large wound on his shoulder might be a bite mark."

The woman went so quiet that Leland pulled the phone away from his ear to see if the call had dropped.

"Hello?"

"I'll let them know," she said and hung up without a good-bye.

* * *

The clinic had a single lightbulb above the door, glowing brightly in the misty morning, and one lonely car parked in the parking lot.

Diego was shivering by the time Leland helped him down from the passenger's seat, teeth chattering, little muscle spasms shooting through him.

"You're gonna be all right," Leland murmured, supporting him carefully, noting the feverish heat in his skin. A peek at Diego's face confirmed that his eyes had gone glassy again, little beads of sweat at his hairline. "We're here at the clinic. We're gonna get you taken care of."

The door was locked, and Leland pressed the button labeled FOR SERVICE AFTER HOURS. Within seconds, a woman in jeans and flannel with short-cropped gray hair unlocked the door and pushed it open with an urgency that Leland appreciated.

"You're the one that called in to the preserve?" the woman said, already reaching for Diego, gloved hand brushing his hair out of his face to look at his eyes.

"Yeah." Leland lifted Diego over the threshold when the kid couldn't seem to pick his feet up enough to get past the doorstep. "You the doctor?"

"I'm Dr. Fenton." She locked the door behind them and led them through the empty lobby, the fluorescent lights flickering and buzzing to life when she flicked the switch. "Can you help me get him to the exam room?"

"Nice to meet you, Doc." Leland grunted at the unexpected weight as Diego went almost limp against him, and he hitched his arm more securely around Diego's middle. "I'm Leland." As an afterthought, he added, "His name's Diego."

She swept ahead of them into an exam room and helped Leland get Diego up onto the patient table, the white paper crinkling loudly.

A buzzer sounded, and Diego groaned, covering his ears.

"That'll be Haley," Dr. Fenton said, changing out her gloves for fresh ones. "The preserve director. Do you mind letting her in for me?"

"Yeah, I got it." Leland steadied Diego before finding his way back through the clinic toward the front door. When he first saw the girl standing on the other side of the glass, he wondered if maybe it was someone's daughter instead of Haley Fern, Director of the Pine Grove Nature Preserve. Nothing about her, from her blond ponytail to the soft roundness of her face and generous curves of her figure, matched the gruff, no-nonsense voice he'd heard on the phone that morning. Then again, she was clutching a travel mug with LUANN'S DINER emblazoned on the side like it was the only thing keeping her standing, so maybe that was just how she sounded when she got dragged out of bed at the crack of dawn on a Saturday morning.

When he approached the door, she lifted the huge sunglasses that had been covering half her face, and wow, those big, brown eyes could stop a full-grown man in his tracks. They almost did.

He fumbled the door open a crack and leaned out a bit, staying cautious in case he was wrong. He'd been wrong before. "Can I help you?"

She squinted up at him, her nose wrinkling under a dusting of dark freckles. Christ, she was so cute it was almost illegal.

"I'm Haley Fern, the preserve director," she said, and he knew immediately it wasn't the same person he'd talked to that morning. Her voice was too sweet for that. "And you are?"

He had the oddest impulse to take his cap off, but he just held the door open wider for her instead. "Leland Sommers, the new dedicated deputy. I called the preserve this morning about a kid I found on the way in. That wasn't you I talked to, was it?"

"Oh, no, that was my ranger, Michele." She ducked in under his arm as he held open the door, still eyeing him like she was sizing him up. "You're the one they hired to take George's place? We weren't expecting you until tomorrow night."

She was half his height, but he felt almost scolded. It was all he could do not to feel like he was telling his teacher why he didn't have his homework. "My lease was already up at my old place, so I figured I'd come up a couple days early, start getting settled in."

He locked the door behind her, and when he turned around, she was rubbing one eye and biting back a yawn. No one had a right to be that cute and that intimidating at the same time.

She caught him watching her and waved one hand apologetically. "Sorry. Not a morning person. Michele said the boy you found was injured?"

He nodded, shortening his stride so he could walk beside her down the hall. "Bite marks. Looked like maybe a dog or coyote from glancing at it. 'Bout the right size and depth, compared to other likely things." At her sideways glance, he shrugged, guessing at her unasked question. "Saw a few animal attacks on the force in Arizona."

He shut his mouth, clenching his jaw against the echo of snarls and growls that were even louder than the screams...

Haley pushed the door to the exam room open, and Leland was grateful for the opportunity to focus on something else. Diego sat on the bench, his knuckles almost white where his fingers were curled around the edge, his jaw clenched so hard the tendons were standing out in his neck.

"Diego, this is my friend Haley," Dr. Fenton said. "She'd like to talk to you about what happened last night, if that's okay."

Leland was several feet away, but he could still hear Diego's breathing go ragged, the whites of his eyes visible as he started shivering.

"You don't have to," Haley said quickly as Diego swayed, and Leland stepped forward, bracing Diego gingerly by his upper arms. The boy twitched at his touch, but his skin was clammy and cold underneath a thin layer of sweat. "Karen, I think he's..."

Dr. Fenton nodded, opening a drawer and pulling out a plastic-wrapped syringe.

"Can you breathe for me, Diego?" she said calmly as she pulled the wrapper apart. "Your heart is beating very quickly, so I'm going to give you something to relax you, but can you help me by focusing on your breathing? Breathe in...and out. In...and out." She kept up the soothing breath count while she plunged the needle into a bottle, pulling the clear liquid up into the syringe. "That's it. You're doing great."

Diego flinched when he saw the needle, but when he pressed backward, Leland was there, blocking his route. Dr. Fenton kept talking to him in a calm, soothing voice as she slid the needle into his arm, and within seconds, Leland felt Diego relaxing, starting to slump over.

He lowered the boy to the padded bench, moving out of the way when Haley appeared with a soft blanket that she wrapped around Diego's torso, tucking it under him gently. She didn't seem to notice Leland watching her as she leaned forward to look at the bite mark on Diego's shoulder, and...was she...sniffing him? Maybe to see if he smelled like alcohol, but Leland hadn't noticed any indication that the kid might have been drinking.

"I appreciate your help, Deputy Sommers," Dr. Fenton said, drawing his attention. "He's lucky you found him when you did."

Seems like it would've been luckier if someone had found him earlier, Leland thought, but he just nodded. "Glad to help," he said instead. "Sorry to ask, but do you have a restroom I could use?"

"Of course. Down the hall on the right."

He thanked her and headed toward the door she'd indicated, trying not to hurry too obviously. Now that the immediate crisis was over, his body was reminding him that he was only human, and he'd had approximately a gallon of coffee since he'd left Arizona.

As he washed his hands afterward, he caught sight of his reflection in the mirror and grimaced. It was a damn wonder not one of the three people he'd seen that morning had run screaming, what with the bloodshot eyes, two days' worth of stubble, and messy hair curling up from under his baseball cap. Then again, all three of them had bigger things to worry about. But so much for first impressions as the new deputy, he thought, scrubbing a hand over his whiskery jaw. Maybe Haley and the doc wouldn't hold it against him.

And maybe one of them could point him toward the best place to get another round of coffee to keep him on his feet until he could at least get his meager belongings out of the truck and into the new place. Maybe some breakfast too. He thought of the sticker on Haley's thermos and headed back down the hallway, intent on asking her for directions.

The door to the exam room was cracked open, and he could see the two women talking with their heads bent close together, though they stopped and looked up as soon as they heard his footsteps. It made him feel a little put on the spot, especially the way Dr. Fenton pressed her fingertips to her mouth like she was hoping he hadn't heard what she'd been saying.

"Sorry to interrupt," he said, trying for his best friendly smile now that he knew what a mess they were looking at. He wouldn't blame them if they'd been discussing him; he'd think twice about trusting the man he'd seen in the mirror too. "I was wonderin' if you could point me toward someplace to get some coffee and a bite to eat."

Haley's expression shifted from cautious to cheerful in the space it took her to blink. "I'll do you one better," she said. "I can't ask Diego any questions until he wakes up, and Karen says he needs to rest for a while, so why don't I just take you?"

* * *

The parking lot at Luann's was about half full, probably peak breakfast crowd, and Haley wrinkled her nose. A good half her pack was here, and if there was one thing she knew about small-town werewolves, it was that they stuck their noses into everyone else's business, especially hers. All part of being the alpha, her mother used to say.

But Haley couldn't imagine anyone sticking their nose in her mother's business and living to tell about it, so maybe it was just all part of her whole pack having known her since she was knee-high. Either way, they were all going to be extremely interested in the new deputy and in why Haley was out and about before ten a.m. on a Saturday, and she'd rather keep both things to herself for now.

Especially the new deputy, she thought as she watched him ease his Chevy Blazer into the gravel spot next to hers, his dusty Arizona plates catching the sunlight. Maybe it was because she'd broken up with her boyfriend before she left Seattle and hadn't been seeing anyone else in the nine months she'd been back in town, or maybe it was because the full moon was only three days away and making her antsy, but she was a little ticked off about how good-looking he was, especially when she knew she couldn't do anything about it.

"Welcome to Pine Grove, Deputy," she called as he opened his door and stepped out, moving stiffly. She guessed the long drive was starting to catch up with him. God knew that after the last time she'd driven back from Seattle, she'd shifted into a wolf and gone for a run just to stretch her legs as soon as she'd gotten home.

"Just Leland is fine," he said, removing his cap long enough to rake his hair away from his face before he settled it back on his head. "Hell of a welcome wagon you rolled out there." His smile was the barest quirk of his lips, and it did awful, terrible things to her pulse. *Dang.*

"Oh, we throw wounded kids at every new deputy that comes to town," she joked with a grimace. "He didn't tell you where he was from or anything like that, did he?"

He shook his head, and she wondered if it was bad to feel such a wash of relief. Notifying family members would have to wait until they could confirm whether that bite on Diego's shoulder had done what she thought it had, so she was glad she didn't have to make excuses for why she was putting it off.

"Nah, he didn't talk much. Barely got his name out of him. Figure it was the shock."

The bell over the door jangled as she pulled it open, and the smell of sizzling bacon hit her straight in the nose, drawing an audible growl from her stomach. She sensed the ripple of movement through the dining room as they came in, the curiosity of twenty werewolves and their family members at the sight of a new person in town.

"Haley Fern, what are you doin' out so early on your day off?" Sally called from where she was pulling down orders from the kitchen window. "And—oh, who's your friend?"

Well, whoever hadn't noticed them before sure as heck had now.

"Sally, this is Leland Sommers. He's the new deputy, just got in this morning. Leland, this is Sally Newcrow. She and her sister, Luann, own the diner."

"Nice to meet you." Leland nodded politely. "Sure does smell good in here."

"Tastes good too." Sally grinned at him as she loaded her arms up with plates of food to take out to the tables. "Well, sit your butts down, and I'll get to you in a second."

Haley led him over to the last empty booth, hoping the high benches would give them some semblance of privacy, and pulled the laminated, handwritten menus out of the holder, handing one to him as he got settled.

"You can't go wrong with anything here," she promised, looking at the menu to keep from staring at him, even though the offerings hadn't changed in twenty years and Haley always got the exact same thing.

Behind Leland, Sally caught her eye and mouthed, *He is so hot!* It took all Haley's self-control not to roll her eyes. Sally pulled her pencil out of her ponytail and flipped to a new page on her notepad as she sidled up to their table.

"It sure is exciting to get to meet the new deputy," she said brightly. "We ain't had anyone new in town since Jo Pham managed to convince Brooks Carmody to move in with her back when Haley's momma was still—"

"Sally," Haley interrupted before Sally could get off track and blurt out incriminating details. "I'm sure he'd rather order his food."

Sally giggled, waving her hand. "Oh, don't mind me, Deputy. What're you havin' to eat?"

He flipped the menu over, still scanning the list of items. "Uh, Miss Fern says I can't go wrong with anything here..."

Sally mouthed *Miss Fern!* at her over his head, and this time Haley did roll her eyes.

"So how about the pancakes and bacon?"

"You got it, sugar. And Haley's right—everything here's the best you ever had, includin' your momma's cookin'."

Leland snorted, tucking his menu back into the holder. "Well, that wouldn't be a hard standard to beat." There was a faint tension at the corners of his mouth when he said it that made Haley think there might be a story there, and she didn't realize where Sally was headed with her train of thought until it was too late.

"Well, at least that means your future wife won't be intimidated in the kitchen," Sally said cheerfully, and Haley gave her a horrified look that she didn't bother hiding from Leland. "Or are you already married, Deputy?"

"Give me the steak and eggs, Sally," Haley blurted, talking over her, desperate to stop the impending disaster of a conversation. "And coffee."

"Uh, no, I'm not married." Amusement sparkled in his eyes as he folded his hands on the table, glancing at Haley, and she wanted to slide right off the bench. "And I'll have a coffee too, please. Black."

"Comin' right up, sugar. Y'all just hang tight."

Haley shook her head as Sally walked off to put their orders in, embarrassed laughter bubbling up in her throat. "Sorry about that. It's a small town, and like she said, we don't get new residents often. People get nosy. You can tell 'em to buzz off, I promise."

Leland chuckled, leaning back in the booth. "It's all right. Small towns are like that. At least so far everybody's been friendly, not like where I grew up."

"Arizona?" Haley guessed, but he shook his head.

"Nah, Idaho."

She waited, but he didn't expand on that. "That's not too far away from here."

Sally dropped off their cups of coffee, black for Leland and with a pitcher of cream for Haley, and he hummed, noncommittal, as he picked his up and took a sip. Haley poured the whole little pitcher into hers until it turned light tan and added two packs of sugar. He didn't seem interested in talking about Idaho, and despite her rampant curiosity, she decided it would be rude to pry.

"Are you staying here in town?" she asked instead. There wasn't much in the way of lodging for visitors, just the twenty-two rooms at the Sundown Motel, the seven empty RV spots at the Timber Trails Trailer Park, and the three suites at the Carmody Bed & Breakfast. "Or did you get a place in Red Horse River?"

The county seat was where most of the rest of the sheriff department employees lived, although it wasn't a metropolis itself, by any means.

"I'm renting an apartment here, but I don't know if it's ready yet." He smiled, rolling his coffee cup between his palms. It was already half empty, Haley noticed. "I wasn't supposed to be here until tomorrow night, so I might have to get a room somewhere."

Haley blinked. "An apartment?" In Pine Grove? She couldn't think of a single place. Maybe someone was renting him a room in their house, in which case she was a little peeved that no one had told her that option was on the table. She had an empty room at her place—not that having him underfoot all the time would be a great idea. She kept catching a whiff of him on her inhales, underneath the coffee and breakfast scents of the diner. The full moon being so close meant that the wolf was right at the surface of her consciousness, harder to ignore than usual, and the wolf thought Leland smelled *delicious*.

Down, girl.

"Yeah, it's a room over the newspaper office, I think she said? The woman I talked to said it hadn't been lived in for a while." He took a sip of his coffee, watching her over the edge of the cup like he was hoping she'd have a clue what he was talking about.

"Oh!" She'd forgotten Jo used to put out a community newsletter before she'd gotten too busy with the bed-and-breakfast and then having a baby. There was a one-bedroom apartment above the old printing office that they used for storage now, and Jo must have decided to clean it up and rent it out. "Yeah, Jo used to live there when she put out the *Howler*. I forgot about that."

"The *Howler*." Leland smirked. "Sheriff Rylan said you guys have some kind of werewolf thing going on for tourists. What's that about?"

Haley laughed nervously, clutching her coffee cup. Her mother had always said she was a *terrible* liar, but when your regional alpha said that the new deputy couldn't know anything about the pack of werewolves that made up most of the town's population...well, she'd give it her best shot.

"Yeah, the original town charter has all these provisions for werewolves and werewolf-human cooperation. Nobody's sure what the founders were thinking, but it gives us a nice little draw for tourist traffic. Gotta pay for the nature preserve somehow."

"It's not a federal or state preserve, then?" Leland looked mildly interested at that, fiddling with his coffee cup—empty already, Haley noticed.

"No, it's private land. One of the town founders owned it and designated it as a preserve about the same time they drew up the charter. It's officially owned by the town these days. There's a small American gray wolf family that lives there, so at least there actually *is* something for the tourists to look at, if they're lucky enough to get a glimpse."

Sally's sudden appearance with the coffeepot as soon as Leland drained his cup meant she was hovering close enough to eavesdrop, but Haley couldn't really fault her for that. The whole diner was probably listening, putting that wolf hearing to good use. The pack already knew that the new deputy wasn't being let in on the secret, but it didn't hurt for them to know what he'd been told. The last time an outsider had accidentally found out about the town's unusual demographics was still a cautionary tale passed down through generations, and nobody wanted a repeat of that mess.

"Do you think that might have been what attacked Diego?" Leland asked, and Sally almost dropped the coffeepot. So that news hadn't spread yet, then.

"I hope not," Haley said, ignoring Sally for the moment. "They've never shown aggression toward humans before. We get campers and hikers who try to break the rules and stay overnight in the preserve, but we don't see many animal attacks. A couple of boys got scared up a tree by a bear last year, but she just ate their food and trashed their campsite before she moved on."

Leland snorted. "Guess people are the same everywhere. Can't tell you how many of my calls in Tucson were to rescue people from something that never would have happened if they'd just paid attention to the safety regulations."

Haley relaxed a little, grateful that he hadn't pushed her on it. "Yeah, some people are convinced the rules are only there to spoil their fun. In our case, a lot of people think they're also there to keep the werewolves a secret." Which was true, but that didn't mean it wasn't also for safety purposes.

"So how long have you been the preserve director?" He held eye contact with her as he took a sip of his fresh coffee, and she was struck by how *blue* his eyes were, even bloodshot and tired.

"Almost a year." Her smile felt tight and tense even to her, and she tried to relax. "My mom was the preserve director before me. I always expected to take over from her—went to college in Seattle to get a master's in wildlife conservation, even—but I just didn't expect it to be *yet*." She laughed ruefully, rubbing at her forehead. "It's been...a lot."

"What happened?" There was a gentleness to his voice that caught her attention, made her notice the way he leaned in, his face open. "Is she...did she...?"

"Got married," Haley said flatly, amused by the flash of surprise in his expression. "She met a guy while I was in college, brought him to my graduation with her, and that's when she told me she was moving to Columbus, Ohio, with him."

"Damn. That must have been a surprise."

"You're tellin' me." She shrugged. "Nobody else in town wanted to take over, and everybody figured I was going to do it anyway, so here I am."

"Funny." Leland chuckled, but Sally appeared at the table with plates of food, cutting off whatever he'd been about to say.

They got the plates arranged, silverware rolled out, and after Leland had spread butter on his pancakes and started cutting them into pieces, she prompted him.

"Funny?"

"Oh, just..." He popped a giant pancake triangle into his mouth, no syrup, and chewed it thoughtfully. "Sheriff told me nobody wanted the deputy job. You got yours because nobody else wanted it." He shrugged. "Funny coincidence is all."

Haley laughed, cutting into her steak, her mouth watering at the deep-red color inside. *Perfect.* "Well, when you go into town to do your paper work and orientation, you'll find out why nobody wanted the deputy position. This place has a *reputation.*"

"Oh yeah?" Leland grinned at her, seeming more relaxed by the moment, and she felt some of the stark loneliness of the past nine months ease away, like a weight lifting. "What, because of the werewolf thing?"

Haley nodded. "That, and by extension, the tourists. You really will have more work to do around the full moon."

"That's all right. Just promise me there's no Bigfoot to contend with, and I'll cope with the werewolves." The glint of mischief in his eyes belied his dry tone, and Haley's heart skipped a beat. *Dang it, he's cute.*

"No Bigfoot that *I* know of," she promised, holding up three fingers like a Girl Scout.

He laughed, breaking off a piece of bacon and stuffing it into his mouth. "Well, you're the first person I'm calling if I find him."

Was he flirting? *Don't I wish.*

"That's fair." She shoved a bite of steak into her mouth and immediately lost her train of thought, salt and blood flooding across her tongue and soothing the constant itch of hunger at the back of her mind. She groaned, her eyes slipping closed, and let herself get lost in the taste for a moment. When she opened her eyes again, it was to see Leland watching her, one corner of his mouth pulled up in a crooked smile, and she blushed.

"Sorry," she muttered, laughing, and covered her mouth as she swallowed. "I'm really hungry."

"No apology necessary," Leland assured her, and she wondered if she was imagining the extra rasp to his voice. She didn't have much time to think about it, though, as her phone vibrated in her back pocket, buzzing loudly against the booth seat, the sound nearly making her jump out of her skin.

A glance at the screen showed that the call was coming from the clinic, and she put her fork down and sat back from the table a bit.

"Sorry," she told Leland. "I need to take this." She didn't wait for his nod to accept the call. "Hey, what's up?"

There was a clatter in the background, and then Karen said, "Haley, I'm so sorry. I know you just left, but I need you to stop back by. The sooner the better."

Haley's heart dropped into her stomach. "Of course. I'll be there in just a minute." She hung up and gave Leland an apologetic smile. "Sorry to run out on you. Do you need directions to your apartment, or do you know where you're going?"

"I can figure it out," he said, polite, giving her an easy smile. "Thanks, though."

Sally appeared with a to-go box, confirming Haley's suspicion that she was still eavesdropping, but Haley couldn't bring herself to care. She packed up the steak and bacon, pushing the plate with the eggs on it over toward Leland.

"Here, as my apology for ditching you. Plus, they won't reheat very well."

"I won't let 'em go to waste," he promised, and she grabbed her box, headed to the register to pay.

"Put his bill with mine," she told Sally quietly. "Welcome-to-town breakfast and all."

"Uh-huh." Sally grinned at her as she rang up both meals and waited for Haley to count out the cash for the total. "I'd like to eat *him* for breakfast."

"*Shh!*" Haley hissed, glancing toward the booth. She could barely see the back of Leland's head over the high back of the bench, his blue baseball cap. There was no way to tell if he'd heard, but maybe she'd gotten lucky and he hadn't. "Just let me pay and leave in peace, for heaven's sake."

"If that's what you want." Sally took the cash, counted it, and glanced up at Haley. "You need your change?"

"No, of course not." She tucked her wallet back in her jeans pocket and picked up her box. "Although I should keep the tip as compensation for all the trouble you're causing, flirting with the deputy."

Sally snorted. "Please. He's too young for me."

"Plus, you're married," Haley noted wryly.

Sally waved her off. "Emmett wouldn't care. He knows I know what side my bread's buttered on. But, girl, your toast is dry as a bone." At Haley's sharp look, Sally held up her hands, the ancient register dinging as she pushed the drawer shut with her hip. "I'm just sayin', is all."

"Have a nice day, Sally," Haley said pointedly, loudly, and then turned toward Leland. "Have a good one, Deputy."

Leland lifted his hand in a wave, throwing her a nod over his shoulder, and she felt twenty pairs of eyes on her as she waved back and headed for the doors, her cheeks warm and a tingle in her stomach that she couldn't entirely blame on her breakfast being interrupted.

The Styrofoam box squeaked loudly as she set it on the passenger's seat of her Range Rover, and her thoughts shifted to the boy at the clinic and the bite on his shoulder, the clatter she'd heard on the phone, and the restrained urgency in Karen's voice.

The chance that someone *hadn't* illegally turned a human into a werewolf on her preserve was shrinking so rapidly it wasn't even much of a question anymore. But who the heck would have done such a thing?

She thought—hoped—that none of her pack would, but if it wasn't one of hers, that meant that there were trespassers in her territory, and that came with its own set of questions. But making sure Diego was all right was her first priority, and the Range Rover kicked up gravel as she gunned it out of the parking lot.

* * *

Don't stop now. Keep reading with your copy of EDGE OF THE WOODS available now, and find more from Kat Turner at katturnerauthor.com

Don't miss more of the Coven Daughters series coming soon, and find more from Kat Turner at katturnerauthor.com

Until then, find more paranormal romance with EDGE OF THE WOODS by City Owl Author, Jules Kelley.

* * *

There's something lurking in Pine Grove, Montana, and its bite is vicious.

Haley Fern has been the alpha of her local werewolf pack for less than a year, when their law enforcement liaison retires, and Leland Sommers, a man who knows nothing about werewolves or their world, is hired in his place.

What could be an awkward situation turns complicated when the man shows up his first day on the job with an injured teenage boy he found on the road—a boy Haley knows has just been bitten.

But discovering who bit the kid isn't as easy as it seems, especially with Leland asking questions and looking at Haley the way he does.

Can the alpha figure out who is attacking innocent people on her wildlife preserve and protect her pack? Or will the new sheriff and her growing attraction to him put her entire world in danger?

* * *

For books in the world of romance and speculative fiction that embody Innovation, Creativity, and Affordability, check out City Owl Press at www.cityowlpress.com.

ACKNOWLEDGMENTS

I am infinitely grateful to have enjoyed steadfast, broad support while writing Blood Sugar. Writing is truly a collaborative effort, and my community means the world to me. To my superhero editor, Tee Tate, thank you for believing in me, and thank you for your brilliant work to make Jonnie and Eve's story shine. I always look forward to receiving your edits, as you see to the soul of my stories and identify precise strategies for bringing out the best in them.

A huge thanks to the entire City Owl Press staff. Tina Moss and Yelena Casale, you are both rock stars. I dearly appreciate your ongoing work on behalf of my books. Heather McCorkle, thank you for the book love and for all you have done to bring our community together. Marianne Hull, thank you for your keen, incisive copy edits on *Blood Sugar* and *Hex, Love, and R&R* before it. You saved me from numerous embarrassments in the form of stubborn typos, small yet significant plot holes, and syntax weirdness. You're a lifesaver! Massive shout out to the MiblArt team for designing another stunning cover. Y'all are creative geniuses, and thank you for taking my input into account. You captured Eve and Jonnie perfectly.

My awesome agent, Jana Hanson, has backed every phase of my

author career through her championing. Jana, you're a superstar, and I'm lucky to have you.

Speaking of awesome, City Owl Press boasts a truly remarkable flock of talented, phenomenal authors who look out for each other. Janet Walden-West, Luna Joya, Lisa Edmonds, Gabrielle Ash, Jaqueline Snow, J.E. McDonald, Melissa Sercia, E. J. Wenstrom, Poppy Minnix, Kristin Jacques, Adrienne Blake, Linda Parisi, Debra Jess, Jen Karner, Megan Clark Van Dyke, Negeen Paphen, Rachel Sullivan, Lauren Connolly, Courtney Maguire, Lisa Gail Green, Charissa Weaks, Jess K. Hardy, E.E. Hornburg, Desirée M. Niccoli, Ashley R. King—I adore each and every one of you. You have all filled my heart immensely, in various, far-reaching ways. So much love to the owls! Oh, and buy their books. You won't regret it.

The 2020 Debuts continue to be a pillar of my writing community. Thank you all for the boosts, beta and ARC reads, reviews, and encouragement. A big virtual hug is reserved for fellow 2020 Debut Barbara Conrey. Your advocacy for our debut author community is legendary, and you consistently go above and beyond. Sending love to the Kentuckiana Romance Writers, in particular Krissie, Marilyn, and Mysti. Thank you for always being on deck to read my words and share your exquisite writing with me. Sending love to all members of my writing clan, especially Nathalie H., Katrina A., Barb Curtis, Reina, and Jaqueline Snowe (yes, this is a double shout out! Love ya, Jaqueline, my ray of sunshine!). This business can be tough, but the kinship of trusted author friends like you makes it so much sweeter.

I'm blessed to have a bevy of exceptional people on my technology and promotional teams. Jade Webb, I can't thank you enough for your stellar work on my website. Echo Shea and the folks at Psst Promotions, you are amazing. You've been indispensable in getting my book in front of readers, including into top-tier romance bookstores such as The Ripped Bodice. Thank you to all of the bloggers, podcasters (Kelly R., you are an absolute HOOT! Lemme know if you want to get witchy and bitchy this Halloween), influencers (esp. SBTB, Carly Rae, and Sil—love ya), booksellers, and stores (shout-out to Freethinker's Corner and The Ripped Bodice) who have shown love to my book babies.

Thank you to my husband and son for your unflagging patience and understanding when it comes to my sometimes-erratic writing schedules and need to go into writing cave-mode to meet deadlines. I'm lucky to have such a kind, flexible family in my corner. Finally, last but certainly not least, thank you to my readers, and to everyone who has bought, read, reviewed, checked out, boosted, promoted, stocked, and/or recommended my book. You all are the backbone of my career and the force that allows me to keep writing. I love you all.

ABOUT THE AUTHOR

Kat Turner writes urban fantasy, paranormal and contemporary romance, and domestic suspense. When not reading or writing, Kat works for a university, teaches yoga, and lives the mom life. She has two pet rats and too many plants, guards her gym time with her life, and is quite adept at picking up objects with her toes.

katturnerauthor.com

 facebook.com/katturnerauthor

twitter.com/Kat_A_Turner

 instagram.com/katturnerwrites

ABOUT THE PUBLISHER

City Owl Press is a cutting edge indie publishing company, bringing the world of romance and speculative fiction to discerning readers.

Escape Your World. Get Lost in Ours!

www.cityowlpress.com

facebook.com/YourCityOwlPress
twitter.com/cityowlpress
instagram.com/cityowlbooks
pinterest.com/cityowlpress